CONTEMPORARY AMERICAN FICTION

FOOLS CROW

James Welch is an American Indian—Blackfeet and Gros Ven-
tre. He attended schools on the Blackfeet and Fort Belknap res-
ervations in Montana; he graduated from the University of
Montana, where he studied writing with the late Richard Hugo.
He is the author of two other highly acclaimed novels, *Winter in
the Blood* (1974) and *The Death of Jim Loney* (1979), both of which
are available in the Penguin Contemporary American Fiction
series. Welch lives in Missoula, Montana, with his wife, Lois.

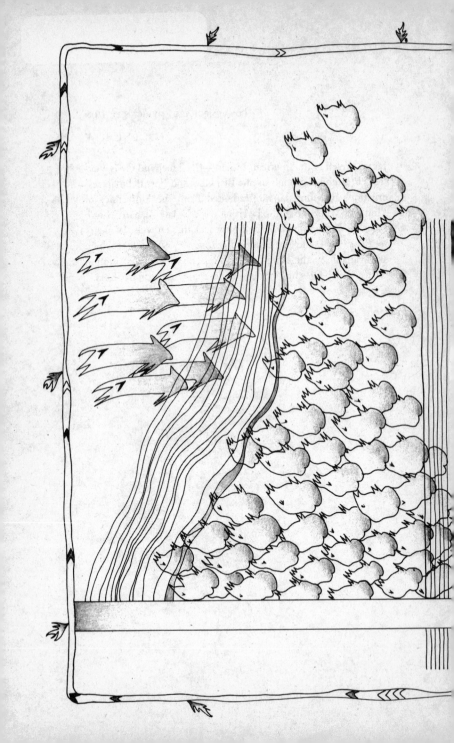

JAMES WELCH

FOOLS CROW

PENGUIN BOOKS

PENGUIN BOOKS
Published by the Penguin Group
Viking Penguin, a division of Penguin Books USA Inc.,
375 Hudson Street, New York, New York 10014, U.S.A.
Penguin Books Ltd, 27 Wrights Lane, London W8 5TZ, England
Penguin Books Australia Ltd, Ringwood, Victoria, Australia
Penguin Books Canada Ltd, 10 Alcorn Avenue, Suite 300,
Toronto, Ontario, Canada M4V 3B2
Penguin Books (N.Z.) Ltd, 182–190 Wairau Road, Auckland 10, New Zealand

Penguin Books Ltd, Registered Offices:
Harmondsworth, Middlesex, England

First published in the United States of America by
Viking Penguin Inc. 1986
Published in Penguin Books 1987

5   6   7   8   9   10

LIBRARY OF CONGRESS CATALOGING IN PUBLICATION DATA
Welch, James, 1940–
Fools crow.
(Contemporary American fiction)
1. Siksika Indians—Fiction.   2. Indians of
North America—Montana—Fiction.   I. Title.   II. Series.
PS3573.E44F66   1987   813'.54   87-6968
ISBN 0 14 00.8937 3

Printed in the United States of America
Set in Janson Alternate
Illustrations by Dana Boussard
Map by Paul Pugliese

For Dick and Matt,
For Melissa,
And especially for Ripley,
With love

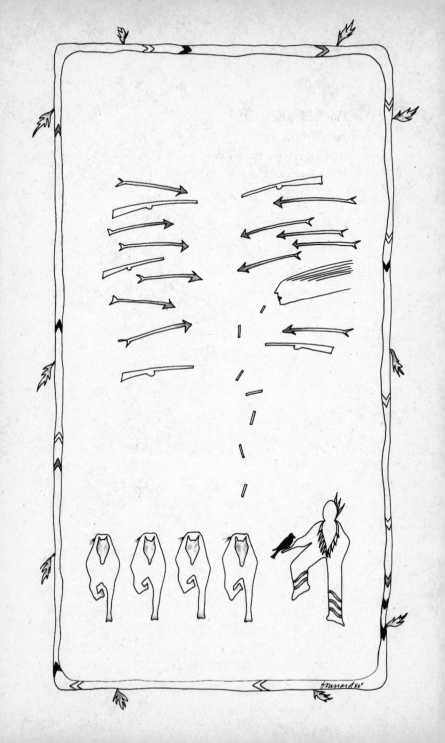

PART
ONE

1

Now that the weather had changed, the moon of the falling leaves turned white in the blackening sky and White Man's Dog was restless. He chewed the stick of dry meat and watched Cold Maker gather his forces. The black clouds moved in the north in circles, their dance a slow deliberate fury. It was almost night, and he looked back down into the flats along the Two Medicine River. The lodges of the Lone Eaters were illuminated by cooking fires within. It was that time of evening when even the dogs rest and the horses graze undisturbed along the grassy banks.

White Man's Dog raised his eyes to the west and followed the Backbone of the World from south to north until he could pick out Chief Mountain. It stood a little apart from the other mountains, not as tall as some but strong, its square granite face a landmark to all who passed. But it was more than a landmark to the Pikunis, Kainahs and Siksikas, the three tribes of the Blackfeet, for it was on top of Chief Mountain that the blackhorn skull pillows of the great warriors still lay. On those skulls Eagle Head and Iron Breast had dreamed their visions in the long-ago, and the animal helpers had made them strong in spirit and fortunate in war.

Not so lucky was White Man's Dog. He had little to show for his eighteen winters. His father, Rides-at-the-door, had many horses and three wives. He himself had three horses and no wives. His animals were puny, not a blackhorn runner among them. He owned a musket and no powder and his animal helper was weak.

Many times he had prayed to the Above Ones for stronger medicine but he knew that wasn't the way. It was up to him, perhaps with the help of a many-faces man, to find his own power.

Again he looked to the north. Beneath the boiling clouds, beyond the Medicine Line, lay the country of the whiskey traders. He had not been there but he had heard of their skinned-tree houses, full of all those things a young man would need to make himself rich. There was talk that they possessed the many-shots guns which could bring down five blackhorns with five shots, which could kill an enemy from far off. Such a gun would cost many head-and-tail robes, but White Man's Dog was determined to have one. Then he could bring about his own luck. He would have plenty of wives, children, horses, meat. He would have his own lodge, and his wives would cook boss ribs and blackhorn tongues while he smoked, told stories, recounted his war honors. The other men would be silent and respectful as he told of the day he had finished off the Parted Hairs and made their women cry. He would boast of the many horses he drove away from the Cutthroats' camp while they slept like old women.

White Man's Dog smiled to himself as though he had done these things. He smiled to think of his wives as he went from robe to robe, planting the seeds of his own family. And then he thought of his father's youngest wife, Kills-close-to-the-lake, and the way she sometimes looked at him. That morning he had helped her stretch a blackhorn robe so she could flesh it, and he felt her eyes on him and he left in haste. He had never touched the body of a woman. His friends teased him and called him dog-lover. His friends often took girls into the bushes, especially if they had plenty of the white man's water. Under Bull had humped two girls of the Entrails People as they were camped outside Many Houses fort on the Big River. He said they were the best because they whispered to you. He offered White Man's Dog some of his Liars' Medicine to make himself attractive but it did no good. Even the bad girls who hung around the forts wanted nothing to do with him. Because he did not own a fine gun and a strong horse they ignored him.

White Man's Dog watched Seven Persons rise into the night

sky above Chief Mountain. Above, the Star-that-stands-still waited for the others to gather around him. White Man's Dog felt Cold Maker's breath in his face, but it looked as though he would keep the clouds in Always Winter Land tonight. He was only warning the Pikunis that his season was near. White Man's Dog turned in the direction of the Lone Eaters' camp. It was time to go down to his father's lodge and listen to the stories, the scorn and laughter of the men as they ate roasted meat and smoked while the women listened and teased each other. Perhaps Kills-close-to-the-lake would look at him again. Perhaps she would save him a piece of back fat or hump meat. But even as his heart quickened, the cold thought struck him: She was his father's wife, his own near-mother! He pulled his blanket tighter around his shoulders and hurried toward camp. He glanced up and asked Seven Persons and all the Above Ones to take pity on him, to forgive him his bad thoughts, to light his way. But the stars were distant and pitiless and gathered their light within themselves. From somewhere far off he heard the hoot of an ears-far-apart.

2

"HAIYA! Dog-lover! Have you seen a ghost?"

White Man's Dog stopped. In the dark he saw a tall figure approach. It was Fast Horse.

"Here, near-woman! I have some white man's water to warm you up." Fast Horse had his arm away from his body under his robe. As he neared, his arm snaked out and hit White Man's Dog in the belly. "I joke!" He laughed. "I thought you needed some cheer since you don't have a woman."

"I wouldn't need you for anything—even if you were a woman."

"Ah, you will think twice about that. I have some news that will warm you up better than a woman." Fast Horse showed his teeth and walked on by.

"You have found a way to make love to skunks."

"Ha!"

"What news?" White Man's Dog called after him.

"Come, catch up. I can't talk so close to camp."

Near a thicket of silver willows Fast Horse stopped and squatted on his heels. The grass was beginning to shine from the dew. "It is this. Yellow Kidney leads a party tomorrow night against the Crow horses. He says the Crows are fat and lazy. They have meat and horses but no many-shots guns. He says they tremble like women because the Napikwans threaten to beat them up."

"What do I care about this?"

"Yellow Kidney knows I bring strong medicine, the same medicine my father has attained from the wood-biter. Soon I will be a very important man. Many women already find me attractive but their fathers know I am without wealth. I shall acquire this wealth from the fat Crows."

"You brag yourself up," said White Man's Dog. "Is that why you talk to me?"

"I told Yellow Kidney I would bring along my poor relative. I told him White Man's Dog is good for holding horses. After a couple of smokes he agreed. He agreed that you have much heart but are unlucky. So you shall be our cook. You will run errands and wait on Yellow Kidney because he is an experienced horse-taker and has made war on our enemies many times, often against the Crows. He has made the Snakes cry, and the Cutthroats too. He leads us only because he is bored with his wives."

"How many horses will I get?"

"As many as you can drive. The Crows are thick with horses. Of course, the good buffalo-runners will belong to those who sneak into camp and cut them loose. I will get one of the best."

White Man's Dog grew excited, but at the same time he didn't like the way Fast Horse talked. He had one winter on Fast Horse and in the past had beaten him up. But now Fast Horse seemed chosen beyond his accomplishments. It was because of his father's Beaver Medicine bundle, one of the most powerful bundles among the Pikunis. Soon Fast Horse would learn the ways of this bundle and someday inherit it. He would be powerful and, like him or not, the people would come to respect this power. White Man's Dog sighed and squatted back against a big-leaf tree. His words were not much louder than the distant mumble of the Two Medicine River. "I have been without luck for many moons, Fast Horse. More than two winters ago I went to seek my animal helper. I sweated, I prayed, I fasted, I smoked to him. And on the fourth night he did come—but he only came to look at me. He came close and I smelled his sour breath, I saw his yellow eyes, but he didn't speak to me. He gave me no song, no vision. He just looked and then he went away before I could offer him a smoke."

Fast Horse sat back and folded his legs. He had heard this story before and knew there was no end to it. The story would remain incomplete. He also knew that many had failed in their first fasting and had returned successful from their second or third. "You place too much importance on this one animal. As you can see, he offers you no help. You would do well to seek another—one with real power, like mine."

"Yes, you speak true, Fast Horse. But I feel that one day he will come to me and offer up his strength. Perhaps he is testing me to see if I am worthy."

Fast Horse laughed. "I will give you strength, dog-lover. I will make you wealthy in horses, Crow horses. We will make those Crows cry. Perhaps we will make their women cry too."

"You do not hear me. Without my good medicine I am afraid of the Crows. They will surely kill me, and our relatives in the Sand Hills will say, Here comes the coward, he was afraid of the Crows. I am not fit for such a party."

Fast Horse smiled as he looked toward the dark clouds in the Always Winter Land. Night Red Light had risen above the bluffs downriver. She showed only a sliver of her face. "I have already thought of a way to make your medicine good again, my friend. Before I came out here I spoke with Mik-api, and he asks us to build a sweat lodge first thing when Sun Chief lightens the sky. He will perform a ceremony, and he says he has some strong medicine to make you brave. He wishes us to bring our weapons."

White Man's Dog felt his blood move faster in his heart. Mik-api was a great and powerful many-faces man. He had often made men of puny heart strong again. For the first time in many moons White Man's Dog felt a surge of hope quicken his blood.

"Fast Horse, I don't know how you did this, but you have lifted my spirit. Surely Mik-api will work his magic on us and make us successful."

"I promised him we would each bring him four of the Crow horses. It will go hard on us if we don't." Fast Horse stood quickly and pushed White Man's Dog over. "Now go to your father's lodge and dream of all those women you desire. With the Crow horses they will be yours and you won't have to mount the dogs."

The wind had picked up and suddenly gusted around them, rattling the bare limbs of the big-leaf trees. White Man's Dog looked up and the stars were brighter.

"One more thing. No words to anyone about tomorrow night. Our women will try to talk us out of it. They will say we are needed to hunt. Youngsters will try to join us to gain glory for themselves. Old ones will say we are foolish, with Cold Maker putting on his hunting clothes." Fast Horse looked off to the north, considering the churning clouds. Then he grinned and shouted above a wind gust, "Yellow Kidney says we can reach Crow country in fifteen sleeps. Haiya, we shall make them cry!"

That night Rides-at-the-door sat in his accustomed place opposite the lodge entrance. Amid the confusion of the feasting, the story-telling and banter, he had been silently watching his elder son. He had not seen him so lively in a long time. White Man's Dog engaged in the teasing and mocking and gave as good as he got. At first, Rides-at-the-door thought his son had gotten into some white man's water, the Napikwans' whiskey that made men foolish. But he knew that none among the Lone Eaters band of the Pikunis had traded recently with the Napikwans. And, too, White Man's Dog did not act foolish, just different. Rides-at-the-door knocked the ashes from his short-pipe. For so many sleeps, moons, his elder son had been morose, even timid, and there was talk around that he might choose the coward's way, that he would never strike the enemies. No one said this directly to Rides-at-the-door, but he knew; one always knows these things. As he refilled his pipe, he glanced over at his younger son, Running Fisher. He was the one they talked about. At sixteen winters he had already taken two horses from the Cutthroats, including one heavy spotted horse that he was training to be a buffalo-runner. He was tall and wiry and the girls pointed him out. Men teased him but not too far, while the women made sure their daughters crossed his path as often as possible. Only the young men were wary of him.

Rides-at-the-door pulled a burning stick from the fire and lit his pipe, his eyes shifting back to White Man's Dog, who was telling a story about Napi, Old Man. As he watched his son act out the story, he felt a small seed of optimism grow in his chest. Kills-close-to-the-lake was bending over White Man's Dog now, placing a bowl of meat before him. As he leaned back against the willow backrest, Rides-at-the-door allowed himself to hope that the change he was seeing tonight was a real beginning.

3

YELLOW KIDNEY SQUATTED beneath a cutbank out of the wind and watched Seven Persons turn in the northern sky. He smoked his short-pipe and listened to the mutterings of the four other men. They waited a short distance from camp for Fast Horse and White Man's Dog. Of them all, only Eagle Ribs was an experienced horse-taker. He was a young man of twenty-four winters and had accompanied Yellow Kidney on a raid against the Parted Hairs two summers ago. He was shorter than most Pikuni men but he was thick in the legs and waist. His strength and balance made him the best wrestler in camp. As a youth he had thrown twelve young men, one after another, on their backs during a Sun Dance contest. He had won many possessions, including the long brass-handled knife he now wore in his belt. But Yellow Kidney had chosen him not for his strength but for his scouting ability. He could see without being seen and he knew what he saw. He would give an accurate accounting of the enemy.

Yellow Kidney ran his fingers over the butt stock of his many-shots gun. It would be the only gun among the horse-takers. Although a couple of the young men had muskets and Eagle Ribs had a single-shot, they were too cumbersome and inefficient for a quick strike against the Crows. So the rest of the men carried bows and knives. They also carried several pairs of extra moccasins, awl and rawhide, and enough pemmican to last them a few days should game be scarce or they need to eat on the run. Yellow Kidney opened his parfleche. The skin pouch inside contained forty greased shooters. He liked its heavy feel. He had not had the many-shots gun long enough to see what it would do to an enemy, but it shot true and it had brought down many black-horns. He dropped the cartridge pouch back into the parfleche and one last time felt for his paints and small medicine bundle. They were there.

He heard a call and in the quarter-moon light he saw the two young men approach. He stood and slung his robe pack over his shoulder. It was only now that he admitted to himself his two concerns. He did not like to have an unlucky man on this trip. Bad luck, like the white-scabs disease, can infect others. He had only agreed to take White Man's Dog along because he respected his father; Yellow Kidney would have to be alert for signs of bad medicine and turn the party around if the signs mounted up. But his real concern focused on Fast Horse. He was boastful and reckless and he wanted too much. Such a man in a small party like this could bring disaster down on all of them. Yellow Kidney did not like to begin such a long journey with these feelings.

The small group of men walked steadily all night and all the next day. The high, rolling plains offered easy going, and Yellow Kidney wanted to make time while they were fresh. He knew of a war lodge just below Red Old Man's Butte. It was in a stand of small pines and would give them enough cover and comfort for a good rest. They would come upon it before Sun Chief hid behind the Backbone, time enough perhaps to kill an animal for food.

The four-leggeds were many that day. They saw four large herds of blackhorns and several smaller herds of prairie-runners and wags-his-tails and once, on a bluff to the west, bighorns. In a draw that drained toward the Bear River they scared up a kit fox and Yellow Kidney took this as a good sign, for the fox was known to give men cunning. It was said that those to whom the fox came in dreams would become strong leaders.

Later that day a pair of golden eagles followed the party for a way, and again Yellow Kidney felt good, for they would give him eyes to see far off. Part of his war medicine was in the two eagle feathers he wore in his hair. But he was glad when the eagles turned away to their home in the Backbone. Any nearby raiding party would also be watching the large birds and wondering what they found so interesting to follow.

Finally, with Sun Chief still high in the western sky, they came within view of Red Old Man's Butte. From their angle it looked like a small sloping mountain with the top knifed off. Eagle Ribs ran ahead to scout, to make sure no enemies occupied the war lodge, for it was well-known to the Snakes and the Flatheads. The rest of the men found shelter in a cutbank below a wind that had turned chilly. As they sat and smoked, they looked to the north and saw the clouds had begun to move down. But they were high thin clouds that did not contain moisture. Fast Horse stood and walked a short way down the draw; then he turned and walked back.

"I had a dream two sleeps ago," he said. He addressed them all but he looked at Yellow Kidney. "In this dream Cold Maker came down from Always Winter Land. He came with the wind. He was all dressed up in white furs and he was riding a white horse. He carried a lance made of ice and a shield of hoarfrost that one could see through. At first I was frightened, for I was certain that he had come to kill me. I asked him to take pity on me, to allow me to live a full life. He laughed, and his laughter sounded like ice breaking up on the river. As you know, I am not afraid of anything in this world—I would make the Crows cry all by myself—but that laugh so filled me with fear that I fell down and trembled, waiting for him to stab me with that ice spear."

Fast Horse looked from face to face, challenging them to scorn him. But the men looked up at him with wide eyes, as though they shared his fear.

Fast Horse smiled then. "You understand my fear in the presence of one so powerful. But this story ends happily, for you as well as me. Cold Maker said, 'Rise up and look at me, young man. I know you go in two sleeps to raid the Crow horses. I have chosen to help you, and now I will tell you how to be successful. Give me a pipeful of your tobacco.' My fingers were numb with the cold he had brought with him but I managed to fill my pipe and light it for him. 'I have no tobacco in my home,' he said. After he smoked awhile, he told me this: 'There is an ice spring I keep hidden in the rocks on the side of Woman Don't Walk Butte. I like to drink there once in a while. It gives me strength. But now a big rock has fallen over it, and blow as hard as I can, I cannot dislodge it. I know you two-leggeds, puny as you might be, possess the cunning to move that rock.' He handed me back my pipe and it was so cold it burned my fingers. Then he said, 'If you do this for me, I will make your raid successful. As you drive the Crow horses home, I will cause snow to fall behind you, covering your tracks. But you must find my spring and remove the rock. If you don't, you must not go on, for I will punish you and your party. Either way, because I offer my help, you must bring me two prime bull robes for my daughters during the helping-to-eat moon. It will go hard on you if you do not do this.' "

The young men looked at each other with both fear and excitement. White Man's Dog stood. "Fast Horse, there are many springs around Woman Don't Walk. How will we know which is the right one?"

"There is only one that is covered with ice. So said Cold Maker." Fast Horse looked around the group with pride. "I will lead you to it. Even dog-lover here will drink from it and maybe steal himself a Crow woman. Next to the Liars they make the best lovers."

The young men laughed but Yellow Kidney did not. This dream was a complication he did not like. He had always been confident in his own medicine, and he was confident in his ability to lead these youths. Still, such a power dream could not be ignored. What if they could not find the ice spring? What if they could not move the rock?

He heard a whistle and looked up. Eagle Ribs had returned and was motioning them forward. Yellow Kidney climbed up out of the cutbank. "Any sign?"

"There was a party in the lodge not long ago. The ashes were high and I found this." Eagle Ribs handed him a brass powder horn. It was filled with stinking-fire.

Yellow Kidney replaced the cap. "Napikwan. I have never known the white men to use a war lodge."

"More likely one of the Snakes took it from a Napikwan. There were many moccasin tracks but no white-man shoes."

Yellow Kidney handed back the brass container. "You have taken the first spoils, Eagle Ribs. It goes good for you."

Eagle Ribs smiled, something he didn't do very often. "There are also many wags-his-tails on the other side of Red Old Man. They are fat and do not look around."

"Good. You and I will kill one while the others fix up the war lodge."

The lodge was a frame of long poles tied together at the top. It was set in a stand of pines overlooking the eastern plains. The young men gathered brush and cut boughs, building from the bottom up until the poles were covered and only the dark mass separated it from the surrounding trees. By the time they got the fire started, Yellow Kidney and Eagle Ribs were back with a female wags-his-tail. They brought only the hindquarters and heart and liver. That night they feasted and told stories. One of the men had brought cold roasted turnips. Fast Horse said that White Man's Dog should save his because the Crow women liked to sit on them. Maybe one would sit on White Man's Dog's turnip.

On the fifth day out they came to the head of the Little Prickly Pear where it empties into the Big River. A short distance to the southwest lay the holdings of Malcolm Clark. Yellow Kidney had told how, before turning to ranching, Clark had been a trader among the Pikunis and had married Cutting-off-head Woman. The Indians called him Four Bears and the chiefs respected him, but he was also known for his ruthless ways and bad temper. Now he raised whitehorns and had a big say with the Napikwan chiefs.

Yellow Kidney decided to ford the Big River downstream from Clark's holdings, not because he was afraid of Clark but because he wanted to stay far north of the Napikwan town at Many-sharp-points-ground. There the big chiefs hated and feared the Pikunis and wished to exterminate them. They wanted the Pikuni lands. They wanted the blue-coated seizers to ride up and shoot all the Pikunis so that they could graze their whitehorns. The Pikuni chiefs had already signed away much of their territory. Yellow Kidney had been at the treaty place at the mouth of the Big River and had watched everything. He remembered how the people were happy because the Napikwans promised them many goods in exchange for their land. When the wagons came filled with crates, the people gathered around and the Indian agent began to hand out small things. Cut beads, iron kettles, knives, bells, the ice-that-looks-back, carrot and twist tobacco, a few blankets. All the chiefs got Napikwan saddles to go with their medallions. Then the Napikwans gave the people some of their strange food: the white sand that makes things sweet, the white powder, the bitter black drink. The people were happy, for they knew these white men would come often to hand out their goods. Even Yellow Kidney had been happy. Along with the others, he agreed with the white big chief that the Pikunis should raise the puny whitehorns and dig and plant seeds in the breast of Mother Earth. Along with the others, he knew that the Pikunis would go away and hunt the blackhorns as they always had. But their agreement had made the white chiefs happy, for now the Napikwans could move onto the Pikuni lands. Everyone was happy.

Yellow Kidney watched the young men as they chopped down some small spear-leaf trees. These are good human beings, he thought, not like Owl Child and his bunch. His face grew dark as he thought this. He had been hearing around the camps of the Pikunis that Owl Child and his gang had been causing trouble with the Napikwans, driving away horses and cattle, and had recently killed a party of woodcutters near Many Houses fort. It would be only a matter of time before the Napikwans sent their seizers to make war on the Pikunis. The people would suffer greatly.

At last the young men had enough logs to make a small raft. They lashed the logs together with rawhide and dragged the raft into the water. The men yelped and hooted when the flimsy logs began to float. Then they stripped and piled their clothes, weapons and packs on the raft. They pushed off and swam with the raft, kicking and pushing to the opposite shore. The current carried them downstream, but soon they beached the raft in an eddy behind a sandbar. That night they built a fire in a stand of willows and roasted the rest of the deer meat. There was little talk.

The ninth day they didn't move. They were in the land of many enemies, and so they would travel only at night. They spent the day in a grove of alders by the Sweet Grass River. A short distance to the west, the Unfaithful Mountains loomed black against the blue sky. While some of the men dozed, others did the small chores that had been neglected during their journey. Eagle Ribs cut some rawhide soles and sewed them with awl and sinew to his two pairs of walked-through moccasins. Medicine Stab, the silent one, had noticed a small tear in his bowstring and sat twisting a piece of wet rawhide into a new string. He watched Yellow Kidney run a greasy rag over the working parts of his repeating rifle. He studied the designs of the brass studs in the stock of the gun. He would have to hunt hard this winter. The many-shots cost ten head-and-tail cow robes. He was determined to get them but first he needed a strong buffalo-runner. He looked over at White Man's Dog, who lay back against a downed alder. The day was warm and White Man's Dog was stripped down to his breechcloth. His eyes were closed but he was not asleep. He was thinking about a dream that had come to him three nights running: He was in the middle of an enemy camp and it was a bright winter night and the snow creaked beneath his moccasins. A black dog approached him and then walked away. Again it came up to him and turned to go. This time it looked back to him as though it wanted him to follow. The dog led the way through the camp until they came to a lodge on the far side. It was simply decorated with a star cluster on either side of the ear flaps. He pulled back the entrance skin and saw several dark shapes around the perimeter of the lodge. As his eyes adjusted, he saw that the shapes weren't breathing. Then, opposite him, one of the shapes lifted its sleeping robe and he saw that it was a young white-faced girl. She beckoned to him, and in fright he turned to leave. But as he turned away he looked back and saw that the girl's eyes desired him. Then all the dark shapes began to move and he saw that they were all young girls, naked and with the same look in their eyes. The white-faced girl stood and held out her arms and

White Man's Dog moved toward her. It was at this point that he would wake up.

He opened his eyes and watched Medicine Stab work on his bowstring. He had the string threaded through the eye sockets of an old blackhorn skull and was vigorously pulling the string back and forth to make it pliable and smooth. The others were all resting now, and the day was warm and quiet. The thin clouds that had been following them from the north had disappeared and Sun Chief rode high in the early afternoon sky. It was a good time and White Man's Dog should have been content to drowse with the others, but he was troubled by the dream. He had had many dreams of desire, he welcomed them, but this one was different. This one was a sign, and he didn't know how to interpret it. He wanted to go to the white-faced girl but knew that there was danger in that direction.

4

THE NEXT DAY they camped at the foot of Woman Don't Walk Butte. Yellow Kidney sent Eagle Ribs to the top to look around. Sometimes war parties camped at the top of the butte to offer prayers and plan strategies. Yellow Kidney himself had been a member of Big Lake's war party the summer they took revenge on a group of Snakes for killing three Pikunis and stealing thirty horses. They had offered their prayers at the top of Woman Don't Walk, and four days later they killed off forty of the Snakes and got their horses back and more.

Yellow Kidney sat on a rock in the morning chill and smoked his pipe. The others had scattered in all directions to look for Fast Horse's ice spring. Their young energy made Yellow Kidney realize that he was getting old too soon. His legs ached and the cold air was beginning to make them stiff. He had been shot in the left leg by a Cutthroat several summers back and it had given him trouble since. Although it was hardly noticeable around camp, it bothered him to walk a great distance. It hurt him most to squeeze his buffalo horse when he was running the blackhorns. His thirty-eight winters sat heavily on his shoulders and he knew he didn't have many journeys left.

Sun Chief had cleared the hills to the east, lighting the frosty yellow grasses on the side of Woman Don't Walk. Yellow Kidney offered up a prayer of thanks for so many days of smiling. This time of year, each day was a blessing. And Night Red Light, three quarters full, had allowed their eyes to look around each night. But she would be full by the time they reached the Crow camp, and this worried him. Her light could prove dangerous to those sneaking among the lodges for buffalo-runners. Yellow Kidney himself had two of the big fast horses and didn't need any more; nevertheless, he would be obliged to lead the way into camp. He almost laughed out loud at himself. He knew that once they were near the Crow camp, he would be as eager as any of the others to capture a prize horse. He knocked the ashes out of his pipe and stood, the frozen grass crunching under his feet. He spotted Fast Horse and White Man's Dog about halfway up the butte, where the yellow grass met the towering granite face. They were bent over and intent. Below them, Sun Chief hit the silvery brush with a glare that made Yellow Kidney shield the bottom part of his eyes. He felt his heart quicken until he saw them stand up and move away to the south face.

He knew it was wrong to question another man's dreams, but he couldn't help being skeptical because the ice spring dream had come to Fast Horse. The young man was ambitious and perhaps foolish, but his father, Boss Ribs, was a powerful heavy-singer-for-the-sick. He kept one of only three Beaver Medicine bundles among the Blackfeet tribes. The Kainahs and Siksikas possessed the other two. Beaver Medicine was even stronger than Sacred Pipe Medicine, so Yellow Kidney had great respect for the father of Fast Horse. For that reason he had agreed to take Fast Horse on the raid.

As he watched the two young men pick their way among the rocks, he found himself studying the contrast in their appearance. Fast Horse was half a head taller than White Man's Dog, and in his buckskin shirt and leggings he looked like a big man, an impression furthered by his erect stance that told of pride not yet earned. His long black hair was piled in a knot on the front of his head. Unlike the others, he had painted his face before each night's trek—three ocher streaks on either side of his face and a vermilion smudge on his chin. White Man's Dog, a year older, was broader in the body, unusually broad, although he was flatter in the belly and chest than Fast Horse. He wore his hair simply, his braids unadorned. He is like the wolverine, thought Yellow Kidney, low and powerful. If he has the heart to match, we will make these Crows pay.

Fast Horse pouted that day in camp because they did not find the ice spring. He had stayed out looking until Sun Chief was high in the southern sky. When he returned he ate a chunk of cold deer meat and stared at the butte. Yellow Kidney saw in his face that he was questioning his dream. Yellow Kidney questioned not the dream but the dreamer. He went off a way and prayed. He asked the Above Ones to tell him what to do. Asked Cold Maker to take pity on them. To turn back now would lead to ridicule when they got home. Yellow Kidney would lose face. But to go on, to risk the wrath of Cold Maker—wouldn't that lead to far more disastrous consequences? Why did he feel that he couldn't trust Fast Horse? He looked about him in the failing light. He looked at Woman Don't Walk Butte. He thought of the night Big Lake had prayed for guidance and the ensuing success. But Big Lake had proven warriors with him. Yellow Kidney had youths, except for Eagle Ribs. Anything could go wrong, even if the signs seemed right.

Yellow Kidney had one option and he decided to take it. They would go on, they would continue into Crow country, but at the first sign that things were not right they would turn back. Meanwhile, he would keep an eye on Fast Horse. As he picked his way down the rocky slope toward camp, he thought of White Man's Dog and felt his spirits rise. In spite of his unlucky reputation, there was a steadiness, a calmness in White Man's Dog that Yellow Kidney liked. These were rare qualities in a young man on his first adventure. He can be trusted, thought Yellow Kidney. He will do well.

After four more days making cold camps and traveling by night, they rested in a small deep draw that emptied out into the valley of the Elk River. Not far downstream stood a Napikwan trading fort. Eagle Ribs had scouted it from a nearby bluff. Many Crows were trading there, along with Spotted Horse people and Parted Hairs. Yellow Kidney was surprised because the Crows and Parted Hairs had never gotten along, but he also knew that the white traders made the tribes behave before they would trade.

"We are less than two sleeps from the Crow camps on the Bighorn," said Eagle Ribs.

"We will have to travel far tonight. We will strike them when Seven Persons reaches its highest point the next night." Yellow Kidney knew where most of the winter camps would be. He wanted the camp of Bull Shield because the Crow chief had made the Pikunis cry many times. He also had many horses. But mostly, Yellow Kidney wanted to take Bull Shield's buffalo-runner. He had thought many times on the journey of doing this. It would be a great coup and would be talked about among the Pikunis. But it had been merely a thought. Now he would do it. He took Eagle Ribs aside. "You must find the camp of Bull Shield," he said quietly. "He has many horses. If you leave soon, you can find his camp and double back to meet us at Black Face Butte by the time Morning Star comes up."

"I will eat something first."

"It will be dangerous to travel by day. There will be many Crow hunters out. But you are cunning, Eagle Ribs, and your medicine is good. You must remember to give the Underwater People some tobacco before you cross the Elk River. They will help you to stay unseen."

Eagle Ribs smiled. He liked the challenge of traveling in Crow country by day. Only the best of the wolves could do it.

After Eagle Ribs left, the young men sat back in a hollow surrounded by rosebushes. They checked their weapons and war paints; they prayed and thought of the night two sleeps hence when they would prove they were men of heart. The long march had sharpened their senses, the nights of seeing and feeling their way across the plains, the cold water of the fords, the almost constant hunger in spite of the meat they had killed and eaten. Each of them had watched the stars closely and had become attuned with the night and the four directions. Now they had to test their courage.

White Man's Dog held the small pouch of yellow pigment that Mik-api had given him. It was a strange powdery earth that Mik-api had obtained from the Siksikas in the far northland. Just to hold it made White Man's Dog tremble with expectation. He remembered the sweat he and Fast Horse had taken with the many-faces man. Mik-api had dabbed water on the hot stones with his blackhorn-tail swab and the steam took their breath away. Mik-api sang and prayed as the purifying sweat rolled from their naked bodies. White Man's Dog had felt then that the bad spirit that caused his misfortune had left his body. He had felt empty and content as the infant who just enters this world. After they had bathed in the Two Medicine River, Mik-api led them to his lodge. There they smoked to the four directions and to the Above Ones, the Below Ones, the Underwater People. Then Mik-api had given White Man's Dog the yellow paint and the instructions for its use. If he painted himself exactly as Mik-api had told him, he would gain the strength and cunning necessary to be successful. Now he packed the pouch away carefully in his war bag.

The dream of the white-faced girls had not come to him in several sleeps. During the long silent night walks he had tried to interpret the dream. He had memorized all the details and called them up, one by one, but the meaning was as far from his grasp as the stars. So he put the dream away and thought instead of his good fortune.

That evening the men got together and ate the last of a small deer that they had killed three sleeps back. The wind had picked up, forcing its way through the rosebushes the men huddled behind. The night would be clear but cold, colder than any of the previous nights. Yellow Kidney thought once again of Fast Horse's dream of Cold Maker. He looked over at Fast Horse and thought the young man seemed less confident, a little more drawn into himself, than he had before the search for the ice spring. Even now he squatted a distance apart, looking back toward the country they had come from. Yellow Kidney swallowed the last of his meat.

"We will walk long tonight," he said. "We must cross the Elk River and make it all the way to Black Face Butte this night. There we will meet up with Eagle Ribs and he will tell us about the Crows. I have it in my mind to strike the camp of Bull Shield."

The five young men looked at him with wide eyes. They had heard many stories of this hateful Crow chief from their fathers, their older brothers, the men who sat around the fires at night. Many Pikuni parties had gone after him only to sneak back into camp, their bellies low to the ground.

Yellow Kidney laughed at their startled faces and laughed at himself. He too had been surprised to hear himself speak Bull Shield's name out loud. But now it was in the open, and if Eagle Ribs could find it, Bull Shield's camp would be struck.

"Come now. You wish to be warriors? You wish to follow the war trail? Then let us count coup on this enemy who has made our relatives cry! When you get home you can tell your families you have done something. The way will be hard from now on. You will get little rest, less sleep. We have had a sign that does not offer us much encouragement." He glanced at Fast Horse. "But we have come this far undiscovered. Our power is strong and we are Pikunis, so we shall continue." Now he looked hard into each youth's eyes. He was no longer the tired, lame man who envied these young men's spirits; to them he had become the warrior who had returned to camp many times with horses and war honors. He turned and began to walk quickly down the draw. The young men scrambled for their weapons and packs.

Night Red Light cast her full face on Eagle Ribs as he came to the series of low hills above the Bighorn. He kept as best he could to the swales and washes, to the clumps of greasewood and sage. He had his short-robe over his head and back, but he knew he would appear as large and distinct as a real-bear in the bright light. The wind was in his face and he was grateful because it would blow his sound and smell back away from the camp dogs. The same wind carried the sound of drumming up the hills from the valley floor. He stopped and listened and heard the shrill voices of the singers. Near the top of the last hill he dropped to all fours and crawled around the sage clumps, sniffing the sharp sweet odor into his nostrils. He crawled until he reached the brow and then he looked down at the encampment.

The lodges loomed white and ghostly in the full moonlight, and he had to look hard to see the yellow glow of cooking fires. He lay and let his eyes adjust and then he saw figures walking among the lodges, women with kettles of water from the river or loads of firewood, a group of men in robes sitting around a fire by one of the main tipis. They would be young men. Then he heard dogs barking and children yelling. On a plain north of the camp he saw a large band of children kicking up dust as they played horses. The dogs milled around them, barking and feinting into the group. Three men on horseback left the south perimeter of the camp, and he followed them with his eyes. Then he saw the great herds of horses, hundreds of them, strung out on both sides of the river, the nearest bunch a good distance from camp. These would be easy. The young men would be able to sneak down and drive away many of them. Once again, he focused on the camp and began to pick out the buffalo-runners staked to the lodges. Because of the distance, Eagle Ribs could not make out the blue buffalo tipi of Bull Shield. But he would surely be there. And it struck Eagle Ribs that he had not seen such a large encampment outside the Sun Dance encampment of his own people. It was bundled up like a winter camp but it was too large. That many people would hunt out the game in a matter of days.

Then he heard talking and laughing almost beside him. He shrank back away from the crest and flattened himself against the cold earth. Not a hundred paces to the left, six men led a string of horses down a draw to the river bottom. Two of the horses had green blackhorn robes on them; the other five were packed with meat. The men were so close Eagle Ribs could see their bodies sway from side to side as their horses descended. He hugged the earth until he no longer heard the clatter of stones. When he looked again, the hunters had reached the valley floor and had broken into a trot, waving their arms and hallooing the camp. The children who had been playing now ran to greet them, followed by the barking dogs.

Just as he turned to leave, something across the valley floor caught Eagle Ribs' eye. At first he thought it was patches of old snow, but as he squinted his eyes, he made out the straight sides and sloping roofs of the Napikwan tents. Not far to one side he saw the hulking traders' wagons, their oxen teams grazing nearby.

That the white men came to the Crows to trade in such numbers was something new. Usually the Indians went to the trading houses. From the boisterous nature of the camp, Eagle Ribs knew there was much of the white man's water being passed around. That would be good. The bad part was there would be many new rifles in camp.

Yellow Kidney had been right. The young men did not get much rest the next day. They huddled beneath a rocky outcropping on the south side of Black Face Butte. They strung their bows, unstrung them, shaped the feathers on their arrows, checked the soles on their several pairs of moccasins to make sure they had on the best ones, felt in their war bags to make sure their medicine and paints were accounted for. They thought many fearsome thoughts: that they would be discovered, that they would choose the wrong horse to mount, too slow or not yet broken to ride, that they would be killed. Yellow Kidney himself had been affected by the young men's nerves. He caught himself thinking that he might not be able to lead them, that they would panic in the middle of the Crow camp. They had conducted themselves so well on the long trek—had he been lulled into thinking that the horse-taking would be smooth and easy? One thing he was grateful for. A long slide of thin clouds had come down from the north. While they wouldn't block Night Red Light completely, they would make a raider's movements less distinct. Experienced horse-takers could take advantage of these clouds, but what about these young men?

Just before the light went out of the day he called to Eagle Ribs to once again give an account of the Crow encampment. He listened carefully as Eagle Ribs detailed the locations of the lodges, the white men's camp, the horse herds. When he was satisfied, Yellow Kidney told the young men to eat a little of their pemmican and then make ready for the raid.

White Man's Dog squatted near a small spring and mixed the yellow pigment into a paste. Then he stood and stripped off his skin shirt. He dipped his finger into the paint and traced two lightning streaks from his clavicles to his waist, just as Mik-api had instructed. Then he drew two yellow sun dogs on each side of his face, from temple to chin. He said the prayers that Mik-api had given him. He prayed to Thunder Chief, whose long rumbling voice foretold the beginning of life and abundance on the ground of many gifts.

He prayed to Sun Chief, who watched over the Pikunis and all the things of this world. Then he dropped his head and made a vow. He vowed that if he was successful and returned home unharmed, he would sacrifice before the medicine pole at the next Sun Dance. Finally, he sang his war song, his voice low and indistinct. When he lifted his head he saw that the other men had painted their faces. Yellow Kidney had painted the left half of his face white with a series of small blue dots in a familiar pattern. Seven Persons, thought White Man's Dog. As he pulled his shirt back on, he glanced over at Fast Horse, who was tying a quill roach to the back of his head. He had three eagle feathers dangling from his topknot. With his face painted vermilion, he looked almost comically fierce.

But it was Fast Horse's shirt that made the others stop what they were doing. They watched as he pulled the cloth shirt over his buckskin top. They knew from the ragged holes and crude designs that it was an old war shirt. Yellow Kidney recognized it instantly. It had once belonged to Head Carrier and had deflected many arrows and greased shooters aimed directly at the warrior's heart. Because he was old and had no desire for the war trail anymore, he had sold it to Boss Ribs, Fast Horse's father. The shirt had great power and many of the men in the Lone Eater camp thought Boss Ribs, being a heavy-singer-for-the-sick, didn't need it. He never warred against the enemies. Now Yellow Kidney knew why Boss Ribs had acquired the shirt. Perhaps it will bring its protection to us all, he thought as he fastened his owl feather medicine to his left braid.

❑   ❑   ❑

Night Red Light showed her face through the thin clouds as the three men lay on their bellies on the crest of the hill overlooking the Crow encampment. Seven Persons was at its highest point and the camp was darker and less active than it was on the previous night. But there was enough light for Eagle Ribs to point out the lodges, the white traders' camp and, downstream, the horse herds. Yellow Kidney grunted as his eyes followed Eagle Ribs' hand. He was silent for a moment as he considered all that he saw. Then he leaned closer to White Man's Dog. "Now you see where the horses are," he whispered. "They are many and strung out. Take Medicine Stab and the other young men. Circle around—stay high on the bluffs—until you come to the end of the herds. Then look around, look around good before you decide which horses to take. Make sure you know where the night-riders are. There shouldn't be many of them. These Crows feel secure here. Take only as many horses as you can drive away safely. Do not run them. Let them move easily. Pick out strong horses to ride, strong and gentle so they will work the herd smoothly." Yellow Kidney looked up at Night Red Light. Her edges were hazy behind the clouds. "It is not as dark as I would wish."

"Where shall we take the horses?"

Yellow Kidney had watched White Man's Dog closely the past few days, so he wasn't surprised by the calmness of the young man's question. "When you get far clear of the village, drive the horses as fast as you can to Black Face, then on to Woman Don't Walk. Do not stop until you get there. Do not think about Eagle Ribs, Fast Horse or myself. We will not go into camp for the buffalo-runners until Seven Persons is well on its journey down. That will give you a good head start. We will catch up or meet you at Woman Don't Walk."

The four young men stood listening in the grove of big-leaf trees near the edge of the water. The river flowed slowly, silently, and they heard a distant drumming from the direction of the camp. They were between two horse herds, and they had not seen or heard any night-riders since entering the grove. Rattler, the youngest at fifteen winters, whispered, "They are ours, White Man's Dog! We can take both herds. These Crows sleep like old women."

"We will have many horses, as many as we want," said another.

From the ridge, they had seen three night-riders to the south and two to the north. They were in groups, talking among themselves. They were not alert, but White Man's Dog could not see them now and it made him nervous.

"I will walk first among the horses to the north. If it looks safe, we will take them." For the first time, White Man's Dog felt the responsibility of his charge. Suddenly it was not a game. They were in the country of the enemies, and it was up to him to see that the young men did not become foolish. He squatted and motioned the others to do the same. He looked from face to face, pale in the filtered moonlight. "I will decide which horses to take," he whispered. "You will do as I say. If we are to be successful, we must act as wisely as our fathers. We must be as brave and strong as our long-ago people. We have traveled long to reach this place and now we will take horses—but we must not be greedy. We will take as many as we can safely drive. If we create a commotion now, it will go hard on us and on Yellow Kidney and the others."

Medicine Stab, the quiet one who had spoken little on the journey, now surprised White Man's Dog. "We will wait for you. We are of the Lone Eaters band of Pikunis. We will do as you say."

White Man's Dog moved quietly among the horses. Some shied away but most stood still, regarding him with little interest. By the time he reached the north edge of the herd, he had counted well over a hundred horses. He looked off toward the encampment. From where he stood, he could barely make out the bulk of the lodges. He waited and listened, but he heard only a faroff barking. The night riders were not visible. As he passed back through the herd, White Man's Dog felt his heart beating hard in his chest. He couldn't understand the way he felt, the combination of fear and almost hysterical glee. It had come suddenly upon him and now he felt weak, light-headed. He was glad the others weren't there to see him tremble. He stood still and watched the horses around him, afraid his state would cause panic among them. But the horses continued to graze or doze and White Man's Dog became ashamed of himself. He had heard his father, Rides-at-the-door, and the other men talk of fear, their own fear in dangerous spots, but he had not really believed them. They were warriors, men who had proven themselves. They would laugh to see him tremble so. They would mock him, scorn him, and for good reason. He was not fit to be on such a raid, much less lead young men. Sun Chief, take pity on me. Thunder Chief, give me your strength. I will honor you all my days, I will live according to your guidance. White Man's Dog sang his war song in a low voice and felt his strength returning. His chest had quit heaving and he felt he could die with honor.

After White Man's Dog told them his plan, the young men walked among the horses until they found big gentle ones. They made bridles out of their lariats, then mounted the horses. They began to move back and forth behind the herd, clucking, swatting gently with the ends of their lariats. The herd bunched up, looking around, grunting, shuddering, uncertain what it was these disturbers wanted. Then they moved, away from the river, toward the west, across the wide valley floor. White Man's Dog rode at the north end, urging the horses forward and keeping his eye on the encampment. At the south end, Medicine Stab did the same, looking beyond the big-leaf grove to the herds below. The valley floor opened up before them, wide and long, but the clouds had thickened and the animals cast no shadows. The herd was moving slowly and steadily away from the river, stringing out as they moved. Once they veered south, but Medicine Stab was able to turn them without losing any. The hundreds of plodding hooves echoed in White Man's Dog's ears, and when the horses broke into a trot it sounded like all the drums of the Crow Nation were beating in his heart. He expected at any moment to see a ghostly stream of horsemen racing down from the camp, but so far—nothing.

The lead horses began to climb up a wide draw that led to the top of the plains. They were still in no hurry and the young men began to get excited. They cut back and forth and swatted at the rumps with more urgency. White Man's Dog was about to ride over to caution them when he saw a painted horse step out to one side and look back toward the valley. He began to trot to the outside of the horse when she let out a long sharp whinny. He turned her back, but again she stopped and whinnied. Then she began to run, stiff-legged, back down the draw. White Man's Dog looked beyond her and saw a colt running across the valley toward them. Somehow the colt had been cut out of the herd and had just noticed that its mother was gone. It whinnied in a high, sharper voice as it ran. White Man's Dog was about to let the mother go when he saw a rider galloping up from the south in an effort to head off the colt. He looked back. The horses were about halfway up the draw. Soon the rider would be able to see them. White Man's Dog looked around but there was no cover. The rider was so intent on heading off the colt he hadn't seen them yet, but soon he would see the mother and then he would see the horse-takers. The chances were too good that he would gallop off to camp shouting out the enemy. White Man's Dog bent low over his horse's neck and began to trot down to the valley floor, his knife drawn and ready to strike. He saw the mother and colt stop to greet each other and the rider circling behind them. Then the rider stopped and sat erect. He had just noticed the tall dark horse coming toward him at a trot. He seemed puzzled but still he sat, looking. At twenty paces White Man's Dog sat up and kicked his horse hard in the ribs. At ten paces he saw the look of recognition in the young eyes. Then the youth whirled his horse and the horse lunged away. But White Man's Dog was on top of the rider. He plunged his knife into the youth's back and heard him scream. But the knife hit bone; White Man's Dog felt the jolt all the way up his arm. Again he struck and the knife slipped in up to the hilt. He struck twice more before the youth fell from the horse. White Man's Dog reined up and looked down at the sprawled body. He heard the pounding of the riderless horse as it raced away to the north, toward the camp.

Just beyond the top of the draw White Man's Dog caught up

with the others. They watched warily as he caught his breath. He leaned off to one side and spit, then blew his nose.

"What was it?" said Rattler. His eyes were round and his voice high.

"Night-rider. He could have seen us."

"Then we had better go." Rattler looked quickly around the circle.

"He is dead," said White Man's Dog. "But his horse got away —in the direction of the Crow camp. Unless he slows down before he gets there, I am afraid the Crows will notice him and become alarmed."

Medicine Stab looked up. "It is snowing," he said quietly.

The others looked up as one at the heavy flakes drifting down. Cold Maker, thought White Man's Dog. He has come to cover our tracks. He looks upon us with favor. Perhaps the ice spring flows only in Fast Horse's dreaming mind. White Man's Dog felt suddenly drained. Although they weren't out of danger, the excitement of his first kill was beginning to wear off. He had killed a youth, not a man. The youth was an enemy and would surely have warned the other Crows, but he was not a man.

"Medicine Stab, we will drive these horses to Black Face. We have taken the Crow horses, but now we must move them as fast as we can. We must pray to the Above Ones to protect us and our comrades and lead us safely back to our home."

Yellow Kidney, Fast Horse and Eagle Ribs squatted in a spearleaf grove. They were well hidden by the wild rose that grew up around the trunks. It had begun to snow, and Yellow Kidney felt his heart rise up at this promising sign. They had scouted the camp for a long time, watching the fires burn down, listening to the various activities gradually ceasing. Once they had been nearly surprised by a pair of lovers who had decided to use the grove to declare their need for each other. After much giggling, rustling and panting, the pair had left, but not before Eagle Ribs had taken two eagle feathers from a roach the young man had put aside. Now, except for a drum group somewhere in the center of camp, things were quiet. It is time, thought Yellow Kidney. He tapped Fast Horse, then pointed to a small group of lodges on the perimeter of the camp. Then he touched Eagle Ribs and pointed to an area of darkened lodges. They had discussed their strategy beforehand, so there was no need for words. Each would go his separate way, steal a buffalo-runner, then meet at Woman Don't Walk Butte. Yellow Kidney had no more doubts about their success. The signs were right and Fast Horse seemed settled down. And now the snow.

As he watched the others move away from him, skirting the camp right and left, he prayed for the safety of the young horse-takers. There had been no disturbance in the camp, no scurrying, no yelling, no drumming hoofbeats. If White Man's Dog did as instructed, the young men would have gotten the horses and left by now. Those four would be safe.

Yellow Kidney stood and stepped from the grove. A hundred paces of open field lay between him and the edge of camp. He pulled his robe up close around his face. As he walked toward the tipis, he felt the power of fear sharpen his eye, quicken his blood, make him bold. He had burned the braided sweet grass and passed the smoke over his body; he had called to the Above Ones to give him strength, to take pity on him, to make him successful. He had rubbed his body all over with sagebrush to make the horses calm. And now, deep within the folds of the robe, he sang his death song.

5

THE YOUNG MEN HUDDLED around the small fire inside the makeshift war lodge beneath Woman Don't Walk Butte. They laughed and told stories of the raid, each one recounting his part, his acts of boldness, until the others mocked him and called him a near-woman. As they escalated their stories and responses, they all felt the thrill of their new wealth and the beginnings of their manhood.

Outside, over one hundred and fifty horses grazed under the watchful eye of White Man's Dog. They pawed easily through the flaky snow to reach the thick grass at the base of the butte. It seemed odd to White Man's Dog that two sleeps ago these horses were content to belong to the Crows. Now they were Pikuni horses and seemed equally content. There was something about this easy changing of allegiance that made him almost envy the horses. As long as they weren't harmed, as long as the grass was long on both sides, they would live in peace. As he sat wrapped in his robe astride the big buckskin he had selected, he thought again of his dream, which had come back last night. Again he saw the white-faced girl raise her robe to him and again he started forward, only to awaken listening to the wind drive the snow against the lodge. This morning he had sat in the lodge and thought about this dream, scarcely listening to the others, who were by turns joyous and somber. They had stolen the largest herd of horses any of them had seen or heard about, but Yellow Kidney and Fast Horse had not yet appeared. Eagle Ribs had caught up with them as they forded the Elk River, but he had no news of the other two. He had last seen them enter the quiet camp, but he had gotten his horse quickly and had gotten out quickly. Now, White Man's Dog looked at the big spotted-rump horse Eagle Ribs had captured. It grazed apart from the others but just as contentedly. Never had White Man's Dog seen such a fine horse. In spite of his dream, in spite of the absence of Yellow Kidney and Fast Horse, he felt a tingle of joy as he wondered how Yellow Kidney would divide up the horses when he came.

Inside the lodge the young men were roasting chunks of real-meat from a blackhorn yearling that White Man's Dog had killed. It was the first real-meat that they'd had since starting their journey over twenty sleeps ago. Already they were slicing pieces off the big chunks.

Eagle Ribs sat back against the backrest he had made of sticks and pine boughs. One of the young men handed him some meat. It was hot and juicy, and the odor quickened his appetite. But when he chewed the meat he felt his throat tighten. The hollow spot in his stomach seemed already to contain a lump. He laid the rest of the meat on a bough beside him and sat up. The time had come to tell them what troubled him.

"Haiya! Young men, listen to me. We have been in this place for a night and a day waiting for Yellow Kidney and Fast Horse. The snow and wind that Cold Maker sends is our friend and also our enemy. We have made a clean escape, the snow covers our tracks, the cold keeps the Crows in their camp. For this we must thank Cold Maker. But it is possible he keeps Yellow Kidney and Fast Horse from us. The weather is good to us now, but you saw last night how the wind howled and piled up the snow. I think we will have to endure another storm this night. Already the wind is picking up. I will tell you this: It is likely that Yellow Kidney and Fast Horse are holed up as we are, waiting out the storm."

The men had quit chewing. They had turned their backs to the fire to listen to Eagle Ribs.

"I have had a bad dream and it troubles me. It came and went so fast, I could make little of it. In my dream I saw a small white horse wandering in the snow. Its hooves were split and it had sores all over. It was wearing a bridle and the reins trailed after it. But it was the eyes. I looked into the eyes and they were white and unseeing. As I drew closer I saw across its back fingers of blood."

Rattler drew in his breath. He had heard of such a horse from his grandfather.

"Yes, it was a death horse, but that is not all. I saw in the sky behind it a face, but I could not see clearly because the face turned away. That's when I saw the hair and the two owl feathers."

"Yellow Kidney!" cried Rattler. "He has been murdered by the Crows! Oh, my uncle! Even now his shadow wanders, begging for pity in that strange country. We must go kill all those murderous Crows!"

The younger men covered their faces and began to cry, rocking back and forth in their robes.

"Why is it you cry, near-women? If Yellow Kidney is dead, he went to the Sand Hills covered with glory, for he has made the Crows to suffer. His shadow, if it be that now, will join his long-ago people there and they will welcome him as the brave man he was."

"Then let us go back and torture the Crows," said Talks Different. He was the older brother of Rattler. "We will make them pay."

"There will be time for that."

"What about Fast Horse?" Medicine Stab still had a chunk of meat on his knife point.

"I don't know. Perhaps I have not seen my dream in the right way. Perhaps Yellow Kidney will join us yet. And Fast Horse."

There was something in the way Eagle Ribs said Fast Horse's name, disdain or scorn, that startled Medicine Stab and the others. Eagle Ribs had never spoken before in that tone.

"Talks Different, go relieve White Man's Dog. I must talk with him."

That night as the fire died down, White Man's Dog listened to the wail of a coyote. He could barely make it out, and he thought that it had crept close to the war lodge in search of food. It cried again and the wind carried its voice away. He snuggled down in his robe and listened but he did not hear the little bigmouth again, only the wind blowing through the lodge. He closed his eyes and tried to sleep, but there was something about the voice that disturbed him. He sat up and pulled the robe over his shoulders. Then he crept to the entrance. As he pushed the brush aside, he saw first a knee-high drift of sculpted snow. He waited for his eyes to see in the dark and then he saw the horse and the figure wrapped in a white robe.

"Who are you? Speak!" he shouted. And he heard the thin voice without words. The robe shifted and fell away from the figure's bent head, and White Man's Dog saw, in the snowy light, the topknot, the quill roach and eagle feathers. "It is Fast Horse!" he cried, and rushed out to help the figure off the dark horse.

Soon they had the fire built up and Fast Horse covered with their own robes. They rubbed his hands and feet and fed him bits of roasted meat and hot broth from snow melted in a bladder sack.

When Fast Horse had recovered enough to sit up, White Man's Dog asked him if he had seen Yellow Kidney.

Fast Horse did not answer right away. He studied his fingers as though they would give him the words these men wanted.

"Where is Yellow Kidney?" The sharpness of the voice made the others look at Eagle Ribs. He had hung back but now he moved forward.

Fast Horse did not look at him. "The last time I saw him, Yellow Kidney was walking through the middle of the Crow camp sizing up the buffalo horses. He walked boldly as though they could not see him. I myself saw him disappear. I had already cut loose that horse out there and so I thought to catch up with you, but he slipped fording the Elk River and I lost my weapons and my sack of pemmican. I retrieved my robe, but as you saw, it became white with ice. I traveled all night and half the next day until I spied a little bigmouth den along the trail. I thought I would warm myself, so I crawled inside to wait for Yellow Kidney, and for you, Eagle Ribs, for I thought you were behind me."

Fast Horse closed his eyes. The young men glanced at Eagle

Ribs but his face had become impassive. There was no warmth, no anger in it.

Fast Horse rubbed his eyes. When he opened them, there was an intensity that belied his lack of strength. "It was then that Cold Maker joined me in that den. He said, 'You foolish one, you mean to forget the vow you made to Cold Maker. For this, I punish not only the Crows but you as well.' I begged him to have pity for I was nearly frozen to death. I told him that we had tried to find the sacred ice spring, but he said we should not have gone on, that we offended him by continuing our journey without moving the rock that covered his favorite drinking hole. Oh, he was angry! He took my hand in his fingers made of icicles and we flew north for many sleeps; we flew over the lodges of the Lone Eaters, over the Medicine Line and the Backbone of the World, until we came to his home in Always Winter Land. He took me inside his ice house and said, 'See my daughters there before you.'

"At first I was blinded by all the dancing ice and I couldn't open my eyes. But soon I was able to see a little and I looked upon his daughters and they were blue, as blue as the stone treasured by the Many Bracelets People. They were dressed in white grouse skins and they shivered and their eyes"—Fast Horse shuddered violently—"they had no eyes, only holes like small ice caves where their eyes should have been. 'Now you see my daughters and how they suffer because you and your people do not keep their vows to Cold Maker.' I could not look at his pitiful daughters any longer. I fell to my knees and cried, for I was sure he had taken me to that land forever. Then he said, 'I will give you one more chance. I will let you rejoin your friends, but you must promise me this: When the helping-to-eat moon is full in the sky, you must not only bring my daughters two prime robes but red coals for their eyes. As you see, they are sightless and they beg me to give them eyes but I have no fire here.' I vowed to bring him these things, and so I say it to you so that you may bear witness."

"He said nothing about Yellow Kidney?"

Fast Horse looked sharply at White Man's Dog. "He said nothing."

□ □ □

Eight sleeps later the men dismounted in a coulee not far from the camp of the Lone Eaters on the Two Medicine River. They put on their paints, their war medicine; then they painted the horses they chose to ride. White Man's Dog drew yellow jagged stripes down his gray horse's forelegs and yellow circles on each side of the horse's rump. He had been thinking about these signs; from now on they would be part of his medicine.

Eagle Ribs had divided the horses up earlier that day. Yellow Kidney or his widow would get the most, Eagle Ribs a few less. White Man's Dog and Fast Horse got twenty each; the rest were divided equally among the younger men.

White Man's Dog had painted a white slash across the left shoulder of his horses. Now as he watched them mingle with the other animals he felt that his change of fortune was complete. Mik-api's prayers in the sweat lodge for him had been answered. The yellow painted signs were strong, and he had been strong enough in his endeavor. He had not taken a buffalo-runner but he was satisfied. He would give Mik-api five of his horses.

At a signal from Eagle Ribs, the men started the herd.

"Oh, you are a no-good one! You run off with these other bad ones, you sneak off at night, you don't tell your own mother, you would let her die with grief—" Double Strike Woman could not go on. She had been scolding her son for so long she had run out of words. "Oh!" she said, and sat down with a thud on a folded-up robe.

White Man's Dog took a chance and lifted his head enough to look at his father. Rides-at-the-door had said very little since his son had returned. He leaned forward and pushed a stick into the fire. Without looking at White Man's Dog he said, "Tell me about Yellow Kidney."

And so White Man's Dog told him what he knew about Yellow Kidney, that he had gone into the main camp and hadn't been seen since.

"Was he a good leader?"

White Man's Dog told him about the march south, the night walking, the signs, and finally the raid. He told his father how Yellow Kidney had instructed him in the horse-taking.

"You were successful. He must have instructed you well."

"Everything worked out as he planned it."

"And you led the horse-taking."

"I was the oldest. I wanted to go into camp for a buffalo-runner but Yellow Kidney wanted me to lead the horse-taking."

Rides-at-the-door sat back and looked at his son. "Tell me, is Yellow Kidney dead?"

White Man's Dog was surprised at the directness of the question. He frowned. "Eagle Ribs saw him in his dream. He was on his way to the Sand Hills to join our long-ago people. I do not question this dream."

Double Strike Woman leaned forward to push a kettle of water closer to the flame. "Oh, his poor wife," she said. Her eyes filled with tears. "Poor, poor Heavy Shield Woman."

White Man's Dog felt the weight of that dreadful moment at the welcoming scene. Amid the confusion, the· hugging and scolding, he had watched Eagle Ribs walk to the lodge of Heavy Shield Woman, who stood expectantly by the entrance with her two sons and daughter. She was Yellow Kidney's only wife. As Eagle Ribs talked, she began to wail and cry, and then she fell to the earth and wouldn't let her sons pick her up. He had watched his mother and three other women hurry over and finally manage to carry her into her lodge. Any feeling of triumph he might have had left him in that moment.

He looked at his father. "I do not question Eagle Rib's dream —but I do not believe Yellow Kidney is dead."

This time it was Rides-at-the-door who was surprised. He smiled. "I think you are right, my son. Although Yellow Kidney is younger, he and I have done much together. He is cunning and his medicine is powerful. I think he will return someday." Rides-at-the-door pulled a twig from the fire and held it before him. He was considering what kind of man would return.

White Man's Dog was remembering the young Crow he had killed and wondering if this was the time to tell his father. But he was not really thinking about his father. He looked at his hands and listened to his sobbing mother and decided the time was not right.

That night there was a feast in the lodge of Rides-at-the-door honoring the return of his son. The people sang and told stories —some even mocked White Man's Dog—but the mood was not one of celebration. Striped Face and Kills-close-to-the-lake, the younger wives of Rides-at-the-door, served up the boss ribs, hump meat and back fat. Double Strike Woman, who usually oversaw such a feast, sat beside her son and periodically hugged him to her. White Man's Dog, his face flushed, accepted the hugs and mocking praise. Several times he glanced at Kills-close-to-the-lake, but she avoided his eyes, serving the food with delicate determination. Later, during an honoring song, she slipped out of the lodge to get a kettle of water and White Man's Dog felt his heart grow heavy. Then he felt the guilt that always accompanied this desire to have some small contact with his father's wife. Double Strike Woman squeezed the back of his neck and he flinched and she hit him on the head. The people around them laughed and White Man's Dog laughed too. But as he hugged his mother back he grew excited at the prospect, now that he had some wealth, of having his own lodge and his own woman. He would be his own man.

Heavy Shield Woman emerged from her lodge the third day after the return of the horse-takers and her cropped hair was ragged. She had slashed her arms and legs and painted her face with white ash. But she held herself erect as she carried the brass kettle to the river. The few people she met on the path stepped aside to let her pass. They did not speak but they looked at her expectantly. She passed as though they were not there but they did not take offense. They had seen grieving women often—many men did not return from the hunt, the horse-taking, the war trail. Even in camp there was the danger of being surprised by the enemy. So the people let her alone. They knew she would decide when to end her grief, when she would speak, when she would allow the people back into her life.

That night Heavy Shield Woman made a soup of dried sarvisberries and chunks of meat. She used some of the Napikwans' white powder to thicken it. Red Paint, her daughter of sixteen winters, was both heartened and puzzled. Her mother hadn't eaten for three days. She had ignored all the food the other women had brought to their lodge. Now she would have some of this soup. But it puzzled Red Paint that her mother would choose this time to make this soup. It was a special-occasion feast, one that Yellow Kidney loved above all else. And he wasn't here to eat it.

Heavy Shield Woman dished up five bowls of the sarvisberry soup, one for her daughter, one each for her two sons and one for herself. She placed the other bowl beside her, where her husband usually sat. Then she ate and the children ate, Red Paint watching her mother's ghostly face all the while. The soup was sweet and heavy and the boys ate three bowls apiece. Good Young Man was twelve, One Spot ten. They had mourned the loss of their father, sometimes loudly, sometimes silently, but now they were beginning to look on life again. One Spot slurped his soup down and belched. Heavy Shield Woman called to him, and he ran around the fire and sat down next to her. He pressed his knee into her lower leg, touching one of the swollen slash marks, and she winced. But she pulled him close and said, "Do you see that bowl of soup there?" All of the children looked. "That is for your father." One Spot looked up into her eyes, but she pulled him close against her breast. Then she told them that their father was still alive; he had come to her in a dream, covered with old skins and rags. He had told her that he was wandering in the land of the Crows, that he could not return yet, that he could not return until Heavy Shield Woman agreed to perform a task which only the most virtuous of women could accomplish. He said he would be home in time to see her do this thing but he could not say exactly when. But she must set his food out for him each night so that he could keep up his strength.

"What is the task, Mother?" said Good Young Man.

"I cannot tell you but you will learn soon. It is up to all the people to grant me the right to accomplish it. They will have to decide if I am fit."

One Spot threw his arms around her neck. She felt his small body shake as he sobbed into her ear. "Bring him back, Mother, bring back our father," he cried. "He is cold and alone out there. He needs to come and eat his soup."

Red Paint and Good Young Man cried too. They cried because they were happy, and they cried for their own loneliness.

Heavy Shield Woman did not cry. She smiled at her children and thought of her husband and how it would be good again.

Around that time when Sun takes himself to the farthest point from the Pikuni land, Heavy Shield Woman called on Three Bears, chief of the Lone Eaters. He smoked and listened to her request. He was a big rangy man with many war honors, but his sixty hard years had taken their toll. His knuckles were always swollen and painful when he moved his fingers. His back was stiff, and many times he had to be helped up. But his face, with its deep creases around the eyes and mouth, was strong and his eyes were bright. He listened and, when she was through talking, he questioned her keenly, asking her if she knew the seriousness and difficulty of her desire.

"I wish my man back. My children need their father. I have assisted twice as a coming-forward-to-the-tongues woman. With the help of my sisters and the older ones, I will carry out my duties correctly."

"You are a brave woman, Heavy Shield Woman. It will be an arduous task. If you fail, you know what the others will say about you: that you are not a virtuous woman, that you bring dishonor not only to yourself but to the memory of Yellow Kidney and his people. But I see you wish to do this and so I will speak for you."

Heavy Shield Woman had spoken strongly, but as she watched Three Bears burn a braid of sweet grass to purify them with its smoke, she couldn't control the small shiver of apprehension that rippled up and down her spine. It was out in the open now and she wondered if she had the courage for it.

That night Three Bears gathered the older and middle-age

warriors of the All Friends society—the Braves, the All Crazy Dogs, the Raven Carriers, the Dogs and Tails. He pointed the pipe in the four directions and to the Above Ones and Below Ones, then lit it and passed it around the circle to the right. It was returned to him from that direction because it could not be passed across the lodge entrance. He refilled it and passed it to his left. Then the old chief burned some sweet grass and watched the others smoke. At last, he spoke. "As you know, our Heavy Shield Woman carries with her a heavy burden of grief. Many in our camp think Yellow Kidney is dead and has gone to the Sand Hills to be with our long-ago people. If that is so, it is good. Yellow Kidney would have died a good death." The pipe was handed back to Three Bears, and he laid it on an otter skin. "Others of us think he might be alive, that he is too hard for the Crows to kill. Some signs point to this. But if he is alive, he is wandering out there and is likely to die a miserable death—unless we do something." Three Bears listened to the men murmur their assent. "Now our sister, Heavy Shield Woman, comes to me with a request to pass on to you. She appeals to your generosity and wisdom and to your loyalty to her husband, who is, as you know, a member of the All Crazy Dogs. You leave a space for him. That is good." Several of the men looked to the folded robe between Young Bear Chief and Double Runner.

"We think he will return," said Young Bear Chief.

"And so thinks Heavy Shield Woman. She has requested that should her man return safely to her, she be the Medicine Woman at the Sun Dance ceremony this summer." Three Bears had expected an uproar over this revelation—most of the bands did not like to have a woman declare herself for this role; if she failed, it would bring dishonor on them and disfavor from Sun Chief himself—but he was not prepared for the silence which followed. Even Rides-at-the-door, the man Three Bears depended on most, sat quietly filling his short-pipe.

This reaction annoyed Three Bears. "I myself am for it, for I know that Heavy Shield Woman has led a virtuous life. I am satisfied with her request."

"Has she the wealth for such an undertaking?" said one of the Raven Carriers.

"The raiders returned with thirty-five of the Crow horses for Yellow Kidney. She will have those, as well as the rest of his herd."

"The Medicine Woman bundle comes high. The transfer will cost her many possessions. And too, she will have to acquire many blackhorn tongues. Since she can't hunt, she will have to pay for them. She will be a poor woman when this is done."

"We talk as though it is a sure thing that Yellow Kidney will return. Only a woman whose prayers are answered can sponsor the Sun Dance. If Yellow Kidney is dead, all this talk is without meaning."

"It is as you say, Dull Knife. This is all up-in-the-air talk, but it would please and comfort this woman to know that we are behind her. If Yellow Kidney does not return by the first-thunder moon, we will know he is in the Sand Hills and will never come back. But we know he possessed strong war medicine and his success cannot be questioned. If anyone can escape from the Crows, it would be brave Yellow Kidney."

"If Heavy Shield Woman takes this vow I am with her," said Double Runner, Yellow Kidney's best friend. "And if our brother returns safely I will contribute twenty blackhorn tongues. I say this to you."

One by one the men voiced their support and help. Rides-at-the-door too signaled his agreement, but he did not speak as Three Bears and the others expected and wished. He was a wise man and his opinions were listened to with respect, but he simply smoked and thought of the man Yellow Kidney had been and the man who would return.

The men were silent for a time as they considered all that had gone on. Then Double Runner, filled with hope and joy, stood and acted out the time he and Yellow Kidney had made the three Liars smear blackhorn dung all over their bodies before they let them go. The men smoked and laughed, and then their women brought food.

6

WHITE MAN'S DOG had settled down into the routine of the winter camp but there were days when he longed to travel, to experience the excitement of entering enemy country. Sometimes he even thought of looking for Yellow Kidney. In some ways he felt responsible, at least partially so, for the horse-taker's disappearance. When he slept he tried to will himself to dream about Yellow Kidney. Once he dreamed about Red Old Man's Butte and the war lodge there, but Yellow Kidney was not in it. The country between the Two Medicine River and the Crow camp on the Bighorn was as vast as the sky, and to try to find one man, without a sign, would be impossible. And so he waited for a sign.

In the meantime, he hunted. Most of the blackhorn herds had gone south, but enough remained to keep the hunters busy. It was during this season that the hides were prime, and the big cows brought particularly high prices. Very few of the men possessed the many-shots gun, so they hunted with bows and arrows. Their muskets were unwieldy, sometimes they misfired, and always they had to stop the chase to reload. Every man was determined to pile up as many robes as he could in order to buy a many-shots gun the following spring. It was rumored that the traders were bringing wagonloads of the new guns.

Most of the time White Man's Dog hunted with Rides-at-the-door and Running Fisher and a couple of his father's friends. Because the many-shots gun was so scarce, not even Rides-at-the-door possessed one, but the hunting group had grown adept at surprising the blackhorns, riding down on them and among them and getting off their killing shots. They kept Double Strike Woman, Striped Face and Kills-close-to-the-lake busy tanning the hides. Once in a while, White Man's Dog would go off by himself to hunt nearer the Backbone. On those occasions he spent much of his time staring off at the mountains. He longed to cross over them to see what he might encounter, but the high jagged peaks and deep snow frightened him. There were no blackhorns in that country, but there were many bighorns and long-legs. Once he came upon two long-legs who had locked antlers during a fight and were starving to death. Both animals were on their knees, their tongues hanging out of their mouths. Although they were large animals, their haunches had grown bony and their ribs stuck out. White Man's Dog felt great pity for the once-proud bulls. He got down from his horse and walked up to them. They were too weak to lift their heads. He drove an arrow into each bull's heart and soon their heads dropped and their eyes lost depth. He did not even think to dig out their canine teeth, which were much valued as decorations for dresses. As he climbed on his gray horse, he thought of next summer when these bulls would be just bones, their antlers still locked together. He went home without killing anything more that day.

But he killed many animals on his solitary hunts and he left many of them outside the lodge of Heavy Shield Woman. Sometimes he left a whole blackhorn there, for only the blackhorn could provide for all the needs of a family. Although the women possessed kettles and steel knives, they still preferred to make spoons and dippers out of the horns of the blackhorn. They used the hair of the head and beard to make braided halters and bridles and soft-padded saddles. They used the hoofs to make rattles or glue, and the tails to swat flies. And they dressed the dehaired skins to make lodge covers and linings and clothes and winding cloths. Without the blackhorn, the Pikunis would be as sad as the little bigmouths who howled all night.

Because there were always dogs lurking about, White Man's Dog would halloo the lodge and then turn and ride off. Once, Red Paint emerged before he could get away, and he stammered something about meat and galloped his horse clear out of camp. But he had looked on her, and afterward her vision came frequently. Sometimes when he imagined himself in his own lodge, her face would float across the fire from him. She was almost a woman and he didn't know when this had happened. It seemed less than a moon ago she had been a skinny child helping her mother gather firewood or dig turnips; now, her eyes and mouth had begun to soften into those of a young woman and her dress seemed to ride more comfortably on her shoulders and hips. Except for that one time she had surprised him, White Man's Dog observed her only from a distance. He had acted foolish and he knew she would scorn him.

One day while he stood on the edge of camp watching the children slide down a long hill on their blackhorn-rib sleds, he had the uncomfortable feeling that he too was being watched. For an instant he thought it might be Red Paint, but when he looked up the hill behind him he saw Fast Horse, arms folded, near the brow. They had not talked much since returning from the raid, had rarely sought each other out. On the few occasions they did get together, Fast Horse seemed sullen. He no longer made jokes at White Man's Dog's expense; he no longer joked with anybody. He didn't brag about his buffalo-runner or flirt with the girls. He didn't hunt with the others and he tended his horses poorly, allowing them to wander a good distance from camp. Most of the time the day-riders would bring them back, but once seven of them disappeared and Fast Horse accepted the loss with a shrug. If the weather was good, he would go off to hunt by himself, seldom returning with meat. When the storms came down from the north, from Cold Maker's house, he would go inside his father's lodge and sulk. His father, Boss Ribs, keeper of the Beaver Medicine, often asked White Man's Dog to talk to Fast Horse, to try to learn the nature of this mysterious illness. Boss Ribs was sure that a bad spirit had entered his son's body. But Fast Horse would have little to do with his friend. Once White Man's Dog almost told Boss Ribs of his son's dream of Cold Maker, but to tell another's dream could make one's own medicine go bad, so he held his tongue. But it troubled him that Fast Horse had not made good on his vow to Cold Maker. The helping-to-eat moon was nearly over and Fast Horse had not yet acquired the prime blackhorn hides for Cold Maker's daughters. To break this vow was unthinkable; it could make things hard for all the Pikunis. But White Man's Dog had another reason for wanting the vow honored. It had come to him one night while lying in bed listening to the wind blow snow against the lodge. Perhaps Cold Maker, not the Crows, held Yellow Kidney prisoner. Perhaps he was waiting for the vow to be fulfilled before he would set the warrior free.

The next day White Man's Dog caught up with Fast Horse just as the young man was starting out on a hunt.

"Fast Horse, I would like to talk."

Fast Horse glanced at him. A fog had come down during the night and the air was gray between them. "Hurry, then. You see I am off to hunt."

"That night you caught up with us at Woman Don't Walk— you told us about a vow you made to Cold Maker."

Fast Horse looked away toward the Backbone.

"You vowed two hides. And you vowed the red coals for the eyes of his daughters. Because of these vows you said he spared your life."

"You stop me to tell me what I already know?"

"I have come to tell you to fulfill your vows. The helping-to-eat moon is passing and soon it will be too late. If a vow—"

Fast Horse laughed. "So you think I am incapable of keeping my word. You think Fast Horse has become a weakling, without honor."

"No, no! But I wish to hunt with you. I would like to help you acquire the hides." White Man's Dog hesitated, but he knew he would have to go on. "You see, I have it in my mind that Cold Maker holds Yellow Kidney prisoner and will not let him go until this vow is fulfilled. It is your failure that keeps Yellow Kidney from his people."

The look on Fast Horse's face almost frightened White Man's Dog. It was a look of hatred, cold and complete. For an instant White Man's Dog thought of taking back his words. But then he saw another look come into the eyes, a combination of fear and hopelessness, and he knew he had been right to confront his friend.

"I will get the blackhorns. I do not need you—or anybody. I am a man and have done no wrong." Fast Horse kicked the buffalo-runner he had acquired from the Crows in the ribs and led the two packhorses away from camp.

As White Man's Dog watched him ride away, he knew there was something going on inside of Fast Horse that he didn't understand. But it had to do with something other than his vow to Cold Maker. It had to do with Yellow Kidney.

White Man's Dog had given five of his best horses to Mik-api upon returning from the Crow raid. They had sweated together and prayed together, thanking the Above Ones for the young man's return. White Man's Dog thanked Mik-api and gave him a horsehair bridle he had made the previous winter. He left the old man's lodge feeling pure and strong.

But he was back the next day, this time with some real-meat that his mother had given him. The two men ate and talked, and then White Man's Dog left. But he came back often, always with food, for he had never seen any provisions in the old many-faces man's lodge. Mik-api lived alone on the edge of camp and received few visitors. He performed healing ceremonies throughout the winter, elaborate ceremonies to drive out the bad spirits, and White Man's Dog grew fascinated with his powers. He had never paid much attention to heavy-singers-for-the-sick. Their way seemed like magic to him, and he was fearful to learn too much. But sometimes as he and Mik-api talked, the old man would mix up his medicines or sort through his powerful objects and White Man's Dog did not see much to be afraid of.

One day Mik-api asked White Man's Dog to prepare the sweat lodge, and that was the beginning of the young man's apprenticeship. As he repaired the willow frame and pulled the blackened hides in place, he thought of his actions as a favor to Mik-api. He built up a great fire and rolled the stones into the hot coals. He carried a kettle of water into the sweat lodge. He added more wood to the fire. He felt strong and important, and he was glad to help the old man.

When Mik-api and his patient, a large middle-age man with yellow skin, were settled in the sweat lodge, White Man's Dog carried the large stones with a forked stick into the lodge. He set them, one by one, into a rock-lined depression in the center. Then he stood outside and listened to the water explode with a hiss as the many-faces man flicked it on the stones with his blackhorn-tail swab.

Sometimes Mik-api would go into the sweat lodge alone to purify himself when he had to go to a person who was gravely ill. White Man's Dog would hold Mik-api's robe while listening to the old man sing and pray. He was always surprised at how thin and pale Mik-api was. He always reminded himself that he would have to bring even more meat next time. He had taken to accompanying Mik-api to the sick person's lodge, carrying the healing paraphernalia. Mik-api would clear the lodge and step inside. White Man's Dog would wait outside for as long as he could, listening to the singing, the prayers, the rattles and the eagle-bone whistle. Often these healings took all day, sometimes more. Eventually, White Man's Dog would go to his father's lodge to eat or nap, but he would come back to see if Mik-api needed anything.

Later, in Mik-api's lodge, as he tended the fire, White Man's Dog would watch the frail old man sleep his fitful sleep and wonder at his power. But the young man had no thought to possess such power. He was just happy to help.

One day while Mik-api was sorting through various pigments he said, "Now that we have changed your luck and you have proven yourself a great thief of Crow horses, you must begin to think of other things." Often Mik-api teased him, so White Man's Dog waited for the joke. And it occurred to him that the others had quit teasing him so unmercifully. He was no longer the victim of jokes, at least not more so than any of the others. No one had called him dog-lover since the raid on the Crows. He hadn't really noticed it until now, but the people seemed to respect him. He felt almost foolish with this knowledge, as though he had grown up and hadn't noticed that his clothes no longer fit him.

And now Mik-api was telling him about a dream he had the night before. "As I slept, Raven came down to me from some-place high in the Backbone of the World. He said it was behind Chief Mountain and there he dwelt with several of his wives and children. One night as they were bedding down he heard a great commotion in the snow beneath their tree, and then he heard a cry that would tear the heart out of the cruelest of the two-leggeds. When Raven looked down in the almost-night, he could see that it was a four-legged, smaller than a sticky-mouth but with longer claws and hair thicker than the oldest wood-biter. The creature looked up at Raven and said, 'Help me, help me, for I have stumbled into one of the Napikwans' traps and now the steel threatens to bite my leg off.' Well, Raven jumped down there and tried to pull the jaws apart, but they wouldn't budge. Then he summoned his wives and children to help, but nothing would make those jaws give." Mik-api stopped and lit his pipe with a fire stick. He leaned back against his backrest and smoked for a while. "Then Raven remembered his old friend Mik-api, and so he came last night and told me of his sorrow. We smoked several pipefuls and finally Raven said, 'I understand you now have a helper who is both strong and true of heart. It will take such a man to release our four-legged brother. My heart breaks to see him so, and his pitiful cries keep my wives awake. If you will send this young man, I will teach him how to use this creature's power, for in truth only the real-bear is a stronger power animal.' Then my brother left, and when I awoke I found this dancing above the fire." Mik-api handed White Man's Dog a pine cone. It was long and oval-shaped and came to a point at one end. "I believe this came from Raven's house up in the Backbone."

White Man's Dog felt the pine cone. It had hairs coming out from under its scales. He had never seen such a pine cone. "How will I find this place?" he said.

Mik-api broke into a smile. "I will tell you," he said.

◻   ◻   ◻

Red Paint sat outside her mother's lodge in the warm sunshine of midmorning. Her robe, gathered around her legs, was almost too warm. Her shiny hair was loose around her neck, framing a bird-bone and blue-bead choker. Her light, almost yellow eyes were intent on the work before her. She had passed, over the winter, from child to woman with hardly a thought of men, although judging by the frequency with which they rode by her mother's lodge, the young men had thought plenty about her. It was clear that when or if Yellow Kidney returned, he would be besieged with requests to court his daughter. But for now, as she bent over her beadwork, she was concerned with other things. Her mother, Heavy Shield Woman, had become so preoccupied with her role as Medicine Woman at the Sun Dance that she hadn't noticed her two sons were becoming boastful and bullying to their playmates. One Spot had even tried to kill a dog with his bow and arrow. And, too, Red Paint was worried about a provider. Although White Man's Dog still kept them in meat, she felt that one day he would grow weary of this task. Without a hunter, they might have to move on to another band, to the Many Chiefs, to live with her uncle, who had offered to take them in.

She held up the pair of moccasins she had been beading. She had taken up beadwork for other people, particularly young men who had no one to do it for them. She was good and her elaborate patterns were becoming the talk of the camp. In exchange, the young men gave her skins and meat, cloth, and the Napikwans' cooking powder. They brought her many things for her work, they tried to outgive each other, but she paid attention only to their goods. Now she looked for flaws in the pattern on the moccasins. She wanted them to be perfect. They were for her mother to wear at the Sun Dance ceremony. She stretched her neck and allowed her eyes to rest on the figure astride the gray horse moving away from camp in the direction of the Backbone. The white capote that the rider wore blended in with the patches of snow and tan grass. Beyond, the mountains looked like blue metal in the bright light. Red Paint bent once again to her work, sewing the small blue beads with an intensity that made her eyes ache.

In a draw just below the south slope of Chief Mountain, White Man's Dog made his camp. He built a shallow lean-to of sticks and pine boughs and covered the floor with branches of fir. He had enough branches left over to cover the entrance. Then, in the dying light, as the sun turned Heart Butte to the south red, he gathered the wispy black moss from the surrounding trees and balled it up. He struck his fire steel into this ball until he coaxed a yellow flame. He piled on pieces of rough bark stripped from the lower dead twigs of the trees and soon had a fire. He put several twigs on the fire and sat back. Even three moons ago he would have been afraid to be alone in the mountains of the Backbone. As he watched the chunk of meat on a tripod before him sizzle and splatter the fire, he felt comfortable and strong. The fat real-bears would still be sleeping in their dens and the bigmouths would be hunting in packs on the plains.

The young man thought about the following day, for it would be the most important in his life. He knew where to find the four-legged trapped in the steel jaws. Mik-api had given him good directions, and the spot was less than half a day distant. He put the hood of his capote over his head and felt the hunger gnawing at his belly. If his luck stood up, he would find the spot behind Chief Mountain, release the four-legged and be back to this site by nightfall. He was certain that the animal was a wolverine. Mik-api would not call it by name, for to name another man's power animal would rob that man of its medicine. So Mik-api had pretended dumb. But White Man's Dog knew that the skunk-bear was the only animal as fierce as the real-bear, although smaller. He took the roasted meat off the fire, and when it cooled he cut off a small piece and placed it carefully in the fork of a tree a short distance away. Then he ate greedily, for it was his first food since morning. The yellow fire reflected off the silvery needles of the firs around him.

The croak was so deep and close, he thought he had been awakened by his gut rumbling. It took a moment to realize he was not in his father's warm lodge. He pushed aside the boughs covering the entrance and looked out into the gray light. He had slept well in his small shelter, but now his breath told him that it was very cold—and still. He heard the croak again and looked up into the trees. The sky was lighter above them. The granite face of the great mountain loomed through the trees, and the yellow light of Sun Chief struck the very top. He rolled out and stood up, and there in the pine where he had placed the meat sat a fat raven.

White Man's Dog ate a piece of cold meat and the patient raven watched him. When he had finished and gathered up his gear, the raven flew away through the trees, away to the west into the mountains. White Man's Dog looked down into the clearing where his hobbled horse grazed. There was enough grass showing through the snow and a stream nearby. He turned and followed the raven.

The shiny black bird led him up into the mountains, following a game trail on the side of a deep ravine. The winds had scoured the side, leaving only an occasional drift of snow behind rocks and downed timber. Then the bird flew up and across a massive slide of scree, dipping and bobbing its effortless way through the late morning sun. It disappeared over the top of a ridge. The way was harder for White Man's Dog, for although the scree was mostly frozen and offered firm footing, sometimes it gave way and he slid some way down the slope. Four times he slid off the hardly-there trail; each time took a little more effort to climb back up.

Finally he stood at the top of the ridge, sweating and panting, and looked around. To the south and west he could see Heavy Shield Mountain and, at the base, Jealous Woman Lake. Beyond, he could make out Old Man Dog Mountain; then, south again, Rising Wolf and Feather Woman—all mountains of the Backbone—and he prayed to Old Man, Napi, who had created them, to guide him and allow him to return to his people. He looked down the other side of the ridge and saw the raven, sitting in a snag beside a pothole lake that was covered with snow. Below the lake, in a grove of quaking-leaf trees, he made out the shiny ice and open water of a spring that led away to the north. "Oh,

Raven," he cried, "do not lead me too far from my people, for the day approaches its midpoint." At that, the raven glided down to the shiny ice and lit on a rock beside the bubbling dark hole of water.

The footing was good on this side of the ridge, and White Man's Dog trotted down on a slant, now one way, now the other, until he was circling the lake, his heavy fur moccasins leaving a soft flat imprint in the wet snow. He slid down the steep incline on the far side of the lake. The snow was firm, but going back would not be easy. Once down, he pulled his musket from its tanned hide covering and tapped some powder in the barrel from his blackhorn flask. Then he heard the raven call to him. He was sitting on a branch of one of the delicate quaking-leaf trees not fifty paces ahead. "You do not need your weapon, young man. There is nothing here to harm you."

White Man's Dog felt his eyes widen, and his heart began to beat like a drum in his throat. Raven laughed the throaty laugh of an old man. "It surprises you that I speak the language of the two-leggeds. It's easy, for I have lived among you many times in my travels. I speak many languages. I converse with the blackhorns and the real-bears and the wood-biters. Bigmouth and I discuss many things." Raven made a face. "I even deign to speak once in a while with the swift silver people who live in the water —but they are dumb and lead lives without interest. I myself am very wise. That is why Mik-api treats me to a smoke now and then."

White Man's Dog dropped his weapon and fell to his knees. "Oh, pity me, Raven! I am a nothing-man who trembles before your power. I do not wish to harm my brothers. I was afraid of this place and what I might find."

"It is proper that you humble yourself before me, White Man's Dog, for in truth I am one of great power." Raven allowed himself a wistful smile. "But my power is not that of strength. Here you see your brother, Skunk Bear, is caught in the white man's trap and I have not the strength to open it. In all of us there is a weakness." Raven dropped down out of the tree behind a patch of silvery willows. "Here," he croaked.

White Man's Dog crept around the willows and saw a large

dark shape in the white snow. Behind it the spring gurgled out of the earth's breast. The wolverine lifted his head, and his eyes looked darkly at the young man.

"So you see how it is," said Raven. "He has been trapped for four days, and now he is too weak to cry out. You may release him."

"He will not bite me?"

Raven laughed, the harsh *caw! caw!* echoing around the white field. "You are his enemy for sure, but even Skunk Bear has a little common sense."

White Man's Dog approached the animal from the rear. The big spring trap had bitten the left hind leg. The reddish-brown hair was caked with blood, and White Man's Dog could see gnawed bone where the wolverine had tried to chew his leg off. He must have been too weak, for the bone was still in one piece. White Man's Dog placed the trap on the tops of his thighs and pushed down with all his strength on the springy steel on either side of the jaws. The jaws gaped open and the leg came free. With a hiss the animal tried to scramble away but he only dug into the snow. He showed his teeth but the head drooped and finally rested on his forelegs.

"Throw him some of your real-meat, for it has strength in it to fix up this beast. I brought him some pine cones but he is not equipped to dig out the seeds. In four days he has eaten only one mouse who got too curious." Raven hopped over to the trap and looked at it. "You see, this animal has a weakness too—he is a glutton and cannot live long without food."

White Man's Dog watched the wolverine chew off bits of the meat and swallow them. He marveled at the animal's long thick fur with the dirty yellow stripes along the flanks. The claws that held the meat were as long as his own fingers.

"And now you must get down the mountain. I have medicine that will fix up this glutton's leg. I would guide you down but my wives are irritable with lack of sleep. If they had their way they would pluck out this creature's eyeballs at the first opportunity. You may leave a little of that meat for them. This time of year the pickings are lean."

White Man's Dog thanked Raven and as he turned to leave, he

glanced at the wolverine. The animal was watching him with a weak ferocity.

"By the way," called Raven, "when you enter your close-to-the-ground house tonight, lie on your left side, away from the entrance. Dream of all that has happened here today. Of all the two-leggeds, you alone will possess the magic of Skunk Bear. You will fear nothing, and you will have many horses and wives. But you must not abuse this power, and you must listen to Mik-api, for I speak through him, that good many-faces man who shares his smoke."

7

It was late winter, that time when the willows turn color and begin to bud. All along the Two Medicine River the red and yellow spears lit up the days and made people think of the first-thunder moon and of breaking winter camp to follow the black-horn herds. Men walked about and smoked and talked of their spring visit to the white trader's house on the Bear River. The hunting had been good, and within the lodges lay piles of soft-tanned robes. Some of the hunters would acquire the long-coveted repeating rifles. It was a time of anticipation and rest for the hunters, of feasts and games for all.

It was also a time of restlessness, and when the three young riders approached the village from the south, they could feel the intensity of the watchers' eyes. They drove twelve horses before them, and all the horses were big and strong. Even from a distance one could see that they were the kind the Napikwans used to pull their wagons.

Fast Horse recognized Owl Child's white horse with the red thunderbirds on each shoulder. Owl Child rode nonchalantly until they were close to the village. Then he dug his heels into the horse's flanks and galloped over. He carried across his lap a many-shots gun in a beaded and fringed scabbard. He also had a short-gun tucked in his belt. Many in the camp were afraid of him, for he had killed Bear Head, a great warrior, the previous summer in an argument over a Cutthroat scalp. Owl Child was a member of the Many Chiefs band led by Mountain Chief, one of the most powerful leaders of the Pikunis. Even at that Owl

Child was something of an outcast, feared and hated by many bands of his own people. Fast Horse looked upon him with awe, for of all the Pikunis, Owl Child had made the Napikwans cry the most.

"Haiya!" Owl Child rode slowly through camp. "How is it you Lone Eaters stay in camp when the others are out hunting and raiding our enemies? Small wonder you Lone Eaters are so poor!" He rode up to the lodge of Three Bears, who had just emerged and stood wrapped in a three-point blanket. "Ah, Three Bears—we have just returned from the south. We come with horses we found on the other side of Pile-of-rocks River. We are on our way to the Many Chiefs camp on the Bear. But now we are hungry, for we have ridden far and fast."

"Did those horses belong to someone else?" said Three Bears.

"They were wandering by themselves and we thought to take care of them before they got lost and starved to death."

"Do those horses have the white man mark on them?"

Owl Child laughed. "We didn't notice any brand on them. Perhaps they are wild horses."

"Who is with you?" Three Bears' eyes were not good for distance.

"The brave warriors Black Weasel and Bear Chief."

"Then they are stolen from the Napikwans."

"What difference does that make?" said Fast Horse, who had walked over from his father's lodge. "The white ones steal our land, they give us trinkets, then they steal more. If Owl Child has taken a few of their horses, then he is to be honored."

"It is so, Fast Horse." Owl Child laughed. His eyes glittered. "It is the Napikwans who bring it on themselves. If they have their way they will push us into the Backbone and take all the ground and the blackhorns for themselves."

Three Bears turned to Fast Horse. "We do not want trouble with the whites. Now that the great war in that place where Sun Chief rises is over, the blue-coated seizers come out to our country. Their chiefs have warned us more than once that if we make life tough for their people, they will ride against us." He pointed his pipe in the direction of Owl Child. "If these foolish young men continue their raiding and killing of the Napikwans, we will all suffer. The seizers will kill us, and the Pikuni people will be as the shadows on the land. This must not happen."

"Then you will not invite us to feast with you?" Owl Child's face had turned hard with disappointment. "Mountain Chief has great respect for you, Three Bears. He is not used to such slights."

"It is not him I slight, Owl Child." He called into his lodge for his women to make up a packet of meat. "He is a wise man and he will know the truth of my words. If the Pikunis are to survive we must learn to treat with the whites. There are too many of them for your kind of actions."

"Someday, old man, a Napikwan will be standing right where you are and all around him will be grazing thousands of the whitehorns. You will be only a part of the dust they kick up. If I have my way I will kill that white man and all his whitehorns before this happens." He looked at Fast Horse, his eyes the gray of winter clouds. "It is the young who will lead the Pikunis to drive these devils from our land."

Three Bears handed up the packet of boiled meat to Owl Child. "It is done," he said, and turned and entered his lodge.

Owl Child laughed, a brittle laugh in the early afternoon silence, and urged his horse into a trot. "Come visit, Fast Horse," he called back. "We will show you what real Pikunis do to these sonofabitch whites." Then he was galloping to rejoin his comrades, who had continued to push the horses east toward the camp of Mountain Chief on the Bear River.

White Man's Dog sat with Mik-api outside the old man's lodge. They had been enjoying the warm sun and talking about the properties of horses, how the long-ago people acquired them from the Snakes and how the Indian ponies differed from those of the whites.

White Man's Dog stirred the pot of berry soup he had brought his old friend. It was beginning to steam. "Our horses have smaller shoulders and their asses aren't so big. It's true they do not have the endurance of those big old elk-dogs that the white man runs." He laughed at his usage of the long-ago term for horses. Then he sneaked a look at Mik-api. The many-faces man was slumped against his willow backrest, his mouth open, his snores almost sighs in the warm air. White Man's Dog brushed a fly away from his friend's hair and then thought, The first fly of spring, winter is truly over. Like the others, he was anxious to go to the trading fort on the Bear River. He and his father and brother had almost a hundred robes to trade, most of them unscarred prime cows. He had his mind on a many-shots, like the one Yellow Kidney carried on the raid.

He stopped stirring the soup. On the raid he had come to know Yellow Kidney, and it didn't seem possible that he was no longer among his people. Although the raid was successful—even now he could look out downriver and see his horses grazing among others—he felt that the loss outweighed any number of Crow horses. Something bad had happened on that raid, something White Man's Dog could not get out of his mind. But he didn't know what it was that had happened, and he didn't know how far-reaching the effects could be. Yellow Kidney was dead or captive or wandering. Fast Horse had not come near White Man's Dog since the morning of their talk. It was bad to lose trust in a friend like Fast Horse, but when young men got together and talked of raids, of war parties to gain honor, the name of Fast Horse never came up. The others had come to feel, like White Man's Dog, that Fast Horse had somehow been responsible for Yellow Kidney's fate.

But lately another concern had begun to agitate White Man's Dog—the Crow youth he had killed. When the news of this deed had gotten around camp, many of the men had honored him with scalp songs. His father had given him a war club he had taken from the Crows. And his brother and the other young men looked at him with respect. But White Man's Dog could not get out of his mind the look of fear on the youth's face as he rode down on him. He could not forget the feeling in his arm as his scalping knife struck bone in the youth's back. He should have stopped the attack then, but the youth would have warned the village. He had no choice but to kill. . . .

Then there was the dream. When he told the dream of the white-faced girls to Mik-api, the old man had grown silent. He smoked a long time. He smoked far into the night. Sometimes he dozed, other times he hummed, but always he would return to his smoking. Finally he tapped the pipe out and told White Man's Dog to go home and sleep, then prepare the sweat lodge in the morning.

After their purifying sweat, Mik-api led White Man's Dog into his lodge. He made the youth lie down and pretend to sleep. He took a root of tastes-dry and dropped it into the boiling water over the fire. After a while he dipped a bowlful and passed it under the nose of White Man's Dog, making his patient inhale the sharp steam. Mik-api then pounded some alum leaves and sticky-root in a wooden bowl. All the while he chanted and sang purifying songs. When the mixture had been pounded into a paste, he dipped his fingers into the pot of boiling water, then scooped the paste onto his fingertips and placed them on White Man's Dog's body. The young man flinched, but the steady pressure of Mik-api's hands against his chest made him relax. Four times Mik-api applied the compound. Then White Man's Dog slept, and while he was sleeping, Mik-api pulled an eagle wing from his medicine parfleche. He made motions of the eagle flying with his hands; then he struck the young man several times all over the body with the wing. As he burned some sweet grass and passed it over the body, he sang the purifying song, the gentle hooting, of the ears-far-apart. Finally he blew several shrill notes over his patient with his medicine whistle, and a yellow paint dripped from the end of it onto the forehead of White Man's Dog. Mik-api fell back on his haunches and said, "It is done."

When White Man's Dog awoke, he felt that he had been to another world and had returned. He propped himself up on his elbows and he felt light and free. He had dreamed of eagles and felt almost as though he had flown with them. He felt vaguely disappointed to be in this lodge lying on this robe. A voice nearby entered his ears.

"I have driven the bad spirit that caused your dream from your body. You will not be troubled anymore."

White Man's Dog looked across the fire and saw the dark eyes of the many-faces man. It was night.

"But I could not kill it. I could not see the dream clearly enough. I know it was a dream of death, but more than that I cannot say. I fear that the spirit is out there, floating, waiting to attach itself to another one of our people."

Now White Man's Dog stirred the berry soup and thought of that night many sleeps ago. He was relieved to be rid of the dream, the burden of it, but the fact that the spirit was still free troubled him. And, too, he felt that he had let Mik-api down in not telling the dream completely or correctly enough. He had not given enough to allow the many-faces man to work his magic.

He shook the memory out of his head and leaned forward to taste the soup. As he did so, he glanced between two lodges to the home of Yellow Kidney's family. The two boys were playing with a small animal, a gopher perhaps. Red Paint was on her knees, moving her arms and upper body back and forth. White Man's Dog could just see white hair on the edges of a skin. Red Paint was rubbing brains and grease into a deerskin to make it soft. As he watched her body arch back and forth over the skin, he forgot about the berry soup. He felt his penis begin to stiffen and he cast a quick glance in the direction of Mik-api, but the old man snored on. Red Paint was now back on her heels, wiping her hands on a calico rag. She was slender but the top of her loose buckskin dress had some shape. Her tight black braids just brushed the tips of her breasts as she worked the greasy mixture from her hands.

"She's getting to be a real woman," said Mik-api.

White Man's Dog grabbed the spoon and stirred the soup quickly. "Ah, you're awake. Good. It is time to eat this."

"It's a pity that one so young and handsome can find no one to hunt for her. What is she now, sixteen, seventeen? Her winters ride well on her. You can see how she has filled out."

White Man's Dog looked at her as though he had just noticed it.

"Yes, she is a woman and of the marrying age," continued Mik-api. "I suspect one of our fine young men will see that she gets everything she needs. Most of our young women this year are ugly. It seems to go in cycles. Some years all the young women are as beautiful as the doe. Other years they look like old magpies. Such a one as Red Paint would stand out in either case."

White Man's Dog looked at Mik-api, but the old man was looking into the distance, to the greening hills. He dished up two bowls of the hot soup and the men sipped it, watching a pair of white-headed eagles circling in the blue sky. They made White Man's Dog think of the dream in which he had joined them.

"How did you become a many-faces man, Mik-api?"

Mik-api didn't speak right away, but White Man's Dog had become used to waiting. He poured himself another bowl of soup, then sat back to watch the eagles.

"I am now of seventy-four winters but I wasn't always old. Once when I was a young man, not much older than you, I had my heart set on becoming a great warrior and a rich man. I learned the ways of the war trail and once went with a group into the country of the Parted Hairs. We were just out to enjoy ourselves, to look at new country and to take a few horses. We took two horses and then we fought all the way back to see who got to keep them."

Mik-api laughed softly. "There were fewer horses in those days. Each one was a precious possession. Some things were harder then, some things easier. There were very few of the Napikwans—it was when I was a youth that the first white men appeared in this country. They came up the Two Medicine River not far from here, and first they tried to treat with our people, then they tried to kill us. We grew frightened of their sticks-that-speak-from-afar and ran away, and then they ran away. I never saw these particular creatures, but you can imagine how different they looked to those who did. Our brothers, the Siksikas, had already seen these white people north of the Medicine Line. They were a little different and spoke a different tongue.

"Some winters later, more of these Napikwans came into our country, but they stayed in the mountains and they trapped the fine-furred animals—wood-biters, mink and otters. I remember seeing them sometimes, but they remained in the mountains and didn't bother us. Many of them were as furry as the animals they trapped. They always stunk like mink and so we avoided them. But a few of our less-fortunate girls went to live with them, and we didn't see much of the girls after that. I think these men hated each other, for you never saw two of them together, and our women who went with them became little more than slaves. I don't know what the trouble was, but you never saw children around their dwellings. At first we thought these Napikwans were animals and incapable of reproducing with human beings. But they were intelligent like human beings and they piled up many furs. Gradually they left the mountains and went away. They were not like these Napikwans today who live on the plains and raise their whitehorns. We could live with those first ones." Mik-api sipped his soup, lost in thought. Two yellow dogs walked tentatively up to the soup pot and sniffed. White Man's Dog shooed them away.

"Now I forget my story. Ah, yes, you ask me when I became one of the many-faces. It was in that season of the falling-leaves moon and I had been hunting in the mountains where the Shield-floated-away River begins. I had been lucky, and as I packed out one late morning I had a long-legs and a small sticky-mouth, gutted and cleaned, across my packhorses. I had killed these animals because my family wanted a change from the blackhorn meat. It was brushy all around and the riverbed was sandy, so I was riding down the middle of the river, singing my victory song. I was young then and somewhat foolish. I sang so loudly and the horse made so much noise sloshing through the water that I didn't hear anything else. But then I stopped to admire a grove of the small quaking-leaves. They had not yet lost their color and they were golden against the rock wall behind them.

"As I sat there in all that beauty I started to sing a song I had made up for my girlfriend, but I heard something else, a kind of wailing that reminded me of a puppy, but I knew no dogs lived around there so I guessed it must be a young coyote or a wolf. I dismounted there in the water, for I had always wanted one of these creatures for a pet. I took my lariat and crept into the bushes, but the wailing had stopped. I listened for a long time but it never started again. Just as I was about to leave, I saw some broken grass at my feet. Farther along I found the place where the thing had entered the brush. There was a trail of willows that did not stand straight. I took my knife in hand and followed the bent willows some way away from the river. Then I saw something dark ahead, and as I crept closer I could see that it was a man. He lay on his back, his head propped against a rock, a knife in his right hand. I was off to one side and I thought to sneak up and lift the man's hair. But then the man flopped his head in my direction and I saw who it was. 'It is Head Carrier!' I cried out, for it was he who later became the great warrior of the ghost shirt now worn by Fast Horse. But he was a youth then, a year older than I. As I ran through the brush I saw him lift his head and knife at the same time. Then he recognized me. 'Oh, Spotted Weasel,' he cried—for that was my name then—'I am killed by the murderous Snakes.' With that he closed his eyes and rolled over.

"I ran to him, for I was sure he had passed to the Sand Hills. He had two broken-off arrows in him, one in his side and one in the guts. I pulled back his shirt and listened to his heart, and I could hear a faint murmuring. Then I rolled him onto his side. The arrow in his ribs had passed through his body and the arrowhead was sticky with blood. I managed to tie my lariat around the shaft and, with a great deal of effort, pull it through his body. But the arrow in his guts had not come through. I brought him water and made him drink but he couldn't take much. I bathed his wounds as best I could and I held him and cried. Along came dusk, and he opened his eyes and said in a weak voice, 'Go away, Spotted Weasel, let me die like a warrior.' I protested, telling him I would take him home so he could die with his people. 'No,' he said, 'I do not want my parents to watch me die. I want to die here, alone.'

"And so, still weeping, I left him there and wandered back into the brush. I could hear his death song getting fainter behind me. I found a slough and sat with my head in my hands. Oh, I was sad. All around me the green-singers were tuning up. I had never liked frogs, but as I cried I became aware of the beauty of their song. It filled me with so much sadness I thought my heart would fall down, never to rise, and I cried louder. Soon the biggest of the frog persons came up to me and said, 'Why do you weep when all we mean to do is cheer you up? Are you not grateful to us?' And so I told him about my friend, Head Carrier, who lay dying. Frog Chief said, 'I understand how it is with friends. But you people sometimes play with us and kill us for no reason. You are very cruel to your little brothers.' And I cried, 'Oh, underwater swimmer, if you will help me now I will tell my people to leave you alone. Never again will a Pikuni harm his little brothers.' So Frog Chief signaled me to be patient and dived into the slough.

He was gone for a long time. Seven Persons had begun to sink in the night sky when he came up again. He carried deep in his fat throat a ball of stinking green mud. He was exhausted, and I helped him crawl out on the bank. After a while he said, 'I had to go to the home of the chief of the Underwater People. He was reluctant to help, but after I told him your vow he gave this medicine to me. Now take it and smear it on the wounds of your friend.'

"I ran back to Head Carrier shouting and whooping, for I knew he would be glad to see me. But when I got there he was cold and stiff and his eyes stared up at the stars. Now I knew he had gone to the Shadowland. Without much hope I smeared the stinking mud on his wounds, then fell into a deep sleep. A small time later I felt something cold on my face, and when I woke up there stood Head Carrier, dripping wet. 'Wake up, you nothing-man,' he said to me, 'you have slept half the morning and I have already been swimming.' I sat up and looked at him, for I was sure he was a ghost who had come to torture me. But he said, 'When I woke up this morning I had the strangest feeling that I had gone to that place no man returns from. I dreamed that I had been killed off by the Snakes. And when I looked down I had some stinking stuff all over my body, so I went down to the river and washed it off.' I looked at his body and there was not a mark on it.

"Later, at a big ceremonial, I told this story to my mother's sister, who was a healing woman among the Never Laughs band.

'Foolish young man, why didn't you tell me of this sooner?' she said. 'Now I will teach you all the ways of healing, for you are truly chosen.' So I became a many-faces and so I am."

White Man's Dog sighed. The white-headed eagles were gone.

"Later still, I received some real medicine from the Black Paint People, but that is another story." Mik-api's voice trailed off.

White Man's Dog thought he saw a look of pain in the old man's eyes and it surprised him. He hadn't thought of Mik-api as having emotions anymore. He had thought many-faces men were beyond such frailties. The pained look had startled him but it pleased him as well. It pleased him to know that Mik-api still lived in the world of men.

O N   T H E   D A Y before the Lone Eaters were to strike camp and
journey to the trading house on the Bear River, Fast Horse sat
alone behind his father's lodge, staring up at the Beaver Medicine
bundle, which hung from a tripod. It was a large bundle, the size
of a blackhorn calf, and its rawhide covering was yellowed and
cracked. He had taken to sitting there by himself, day after day,
looking at the bundle, trying to feel its power. His father, Boss
Ribs, had kept the bundle for as long as he could remember, and
both his father and he assumed that one day the bundle would be
passed to him. His father had been waiting until Fast Horse was
old enough, and patient enough, to learn all the songs and rituals
associated with the objects in the bundle. All the living things in
the country of the Pikunis had given their songs to the medicine
bundle, and the power contained within was immense. But only
if the ceremony was done right. And so Boss Ribs had been in
no hurry to begin the teaching of his son. The time would come
soon enough.

But all that had changed now because Fast Horse had changed.
He had become an outsider within his own band. He no longer
sought the company of the others, and they avoided him. The
girls who had once looked so admiringly on him now averted
their eyes when he passed. The young men considered him a
source of bad medicine, and the older ones did not invite him for
a smoke. Even his own father had begun to look upon him with
doubt and regret. As for Fast Horse, the more he stared at the
Beaver Medicine, the more it lost meaning for him. That would

not be the way of his power. His power would be more tangible and more immediate.

Cold Maker—he scoffed at Cold Maker. One day, on one of his solitary, unsuccessful hunts, he had dismounted and challenged Cold Maker to do him in, to kill him on the spot; he had nothing to live for. At first, he had trembled, but when nothing happened, he grew louder, more angry. At the time, he wanted to die, he welcomed death, he wanted Cold Maker to clutch his heart in his icy fingers. He sang his death song and waited. Nothing. And then he grew bitter and he hated his people and all they believed in. They had no power. They were pitiful, afraid of everything, including the Napikwans, who were taking their land even as the Pikunis stood on it. Only Owl Child had power and courage. He took what he wanted; he defied the Napikwans and killed them. He laughed at their seizers and chiefs when they threatened revenge. And he laughed at his own people for their weak hearts.

As he stared at the scabby medicine bundle and thought these things, Fast Horse began to hear voices, shouts, and he saw some children running toward the east edge of camp. There was always a lot of commotion in camp, especially when visitors arrived, and Fast Horse thought they were probably hunters from one of the other bands. Out of mild curiosity, he stood and walked in that direction.

By the time he reached the edge of camp, there were already fifteen or twenty people standing there, talking among themselves. "I don't recognize the horse," said one. "Nor the strange blanket with which he hides his face," said another. "He is not from one of our camps," said a third.

The horse was small and white, with dark scars showing through the hair. It walked with a slow, awkward gait, as though it had been ridden into the ground at one time and had never recovered.

When the figure was a short distance from the camp, he slid his right leg over the horse's neck and jumped off. The horse lowered its head and began to eat the spring grass.

Fifty paces from the group the thin figure stopped and shook his head. The blanket fell away from his face, and the woman beside Fast Horse sucked in her breath. The face was gaunt, the skin stretched tight over the bones and deeply pocked. The man held his blanket over his arms in front of him. The people stared silently.

"Ha! Don't you recognize me, Lone Eaters? Have I been away so long, have I changed so much?" The man laughed. "You, Eagle Ribs, don't you know me?"

Suddenly Eagle Ribs, who had been at the front of the group, shouted and dropped his musket. He ran to the man, crying, "It is you! It is you!" He hugged the thin figure and called back to the people, "It is Yellow Kidney! He returns to his people!" In his excitement he had knocked the blanket from his friend. And now he saw the women put their hands to their mouths and cry out. The men stared. "What is this? Wretched Lone Eaters! Do you not recognize your brother?" He turned to his friend, and Yellow Kidney held up his hands. Where there had been fingers now there were none. Eagle Ribs started back. His mouth was open as though he had been caught in the middle of laughter, but no sound came out.

The people ran forward, past the dumb Eagle Ribs, to touch and embrace their brother. There was much crying. Two of the women ran toward camp to tell Heavy Shield Woman that her man had come home. A boy of ten winters picked up Eagle Rib's musket and tried to hold it to his cheek. Fast Horse was gone.

"This then is my story. You, Eagle Ribs, you, White Man's Dog, know the truth of what I am about to tell. But you don't know the all of it." Yellow Kidney looked at the men of the various groups of the All Friends society. They had smoked, and then they had eaten, and now many of them filled their short-pipes. The big lodge was heavy with the smell of meat and smoke. Three Bears burned some sage in the fire to sweeten it up. Then he too sat back. The women who had served the men were gone.

Yellow Kidney told of the journey to the Crow land, of the cold walking nights, of the lack of meat, and of the moment he sent White Man's Dog with the other young men to steal some of the grazing horses. "Then I sent Eagle Ribs in one direction and Fast Horse in another. There were fat buffalo-runners tied up all through the camp. The camp itself was as large as the valley, four hundred lodges at least. There were Napikwans there too, traders or hide hunters. They were thick with the Crows, many of them sitting at fires in the camp. But finally it grew quiet. We had let the last of the drunken revelers wear themselves out. I pulled my robe up over my head and walked into the camp. Young Bear Chief and Double Runner have seen me do this before. I walked boldly among the lodges until at last I was standing in the middle of the camp, beside the great lodge of their smoking societies. There I looked about, and it did not take me long to find what I was looking for. Night Red Light looked down from a hole in the clouds and I saw clearly, not twenty-five paces away from where I stood, the tipi of the blue buffalo. As you know, this is the lodge of our old enemy, Bull Shield, who has made the Pikunis cry many times. I approached his lodge with caution and there, tied to the lodgepole, was the most beautiful black horse I had ever seen. Now if I had been alone on this raid, I would have gone into the lodge and cut Bull Shield's throat. Oh, how I wish I had! But I was responsible for the young men who were with me, so I decided to take the horse and leave. As I cut the lariat, I whispered in his ear. Then I began to lead him away. He was eager to come with me. One could tell he was an intelligent animal.

"But we had not gone a hundred steps before I began to hear a loud noise at the edge of the camp. I lowered the robe from my head and turned my ears in that direction. The small wind was behind me and so I could not hear distinctly. My ears turned as big as the wags-his-tail's and soon I heard words, and when I could make them out they were fierce words indeed—'Oh, you Crows are puny, your horses are puny and your women make me sick! If I had time I would ride among you and cut off your puny woman heads, you cowardly Crows'—said in the tongue of our people as clear that night as I tell you now."

As if by magic, all the men quit smoking and swung their heads in the direction of Eagle Ribs.

"No, no." Yellow Kidney laughed. "Eagle Ribs is a brave and wise horse-taker. He knows the consequences of such action. It was not his voice I heard that night."

"Fast Horse!" It was out of his mouth before White Man's Dog could think.

Yellow Kidney's dark eyes locked on his. After a moment he said, "It will be known. There is time."

"Where is Fast Horse?" said Three Bears. "He is a member of the Doves. He should be here." He nodded in the direction of the Doves, who sat the farthest away. Two of them stood and slipped out the entrance.

"I heard the first stirrings of excitement in a nearby lodge, and so I drew my knife. When a man emerged, carrying a short-gun, I stepped close to him and drove my knife into his heart. Then I began to hurry away, still leading the black horse, to the north edge of the camp. Three men ran past me, then another two, and I began to feel that my luck would hold, that I would be able to mount the black horse and ride off toward the Napikwans' wagons and there turn west to rejoin my comrades. But I saw a group of men beside a lodge, talking excitedly, and one pointed at me. I knew that I had been found out, so I dropped the horse and ran behind a tipi and ran some more. I heard shots being fired and more men yelling. Three men were running in my direction but they hadn't seen me yet, so I ducked into a lodge. I had my knife ready to strike the dwellers. As my eyes adjusted to the dim light of a night fire I saw several bodies along the walls, but none of them stirred. I began to think they were just piles of robes when on the far side I saw a figure rise up and throw the robe back. I had made up my mind to attack but I saw that it was a young girl. She just looked at me and her eyes were heavy with sleep. I thought it odd that the other figures had not been awakened by the gunshots. But this thought was erased quickly by the sounds of voices outside the lodge. I know enough of the Crow tongue to understand that they were saying I had come this way, that I had passed by. I had no choice but to try to hide so I crept over to the girl, put my hand over her mouth and crawled into the robe with her. I had just pulled it over our heads when I heard the flap being opened. There was a long silence as the observer passed his eyes over the robes. Than a couple of shots rang out a way off and I heard the flap drop shut.

"After a while I took my hand from the girl's mouth but she lay there with her eyes closed. I felt under the robe and she was naked and her skin was hot. I felt her breasts and her belly and they were hot and damp. I couldn't understand because the fire was hardly big enough to see by. It was cold in that lodge, but she was naked and sweating. The mind does funny things when it is confused, and I began to feel a stirring of excitement for this hot girl. By now all the commotion was at the other end of the camp. I found her there between the legs and entered her—not without some difficulty, for she was only on the verge of becoming a woman. When I had had my pleasure, I rolled away, and that's when it hit me that she hadn't moved, hadn't made a sound, only lay there with her eyes shut. I became afraid at these unusual circumstances, so I crept to the fire and took a burning stick. I pulled the robe back and looked at her. I had seen it before, some winters ago when our people were struck down, when half of the Lone Eaters perished. There on her face and chest were the dreaded signs. I had copulated with one who was dying of the white-scabs disease."

For the second time that night White Man's Dog spoke without thinking. "My dream! My dream!" He covered his mouth in horror, but the words were unmistakable in the silence of the lodge.

Rides-at-the-door looked sharply at his son. Several of the other men murmured their disapproval. It wasn't good for a young man to interrupt his elder, especially during such an important account.

White Man's Dog felt his face burn with shame; but more than that, he felt a heaviness come into his heart that made him weak, unable to speak even if he wanted to.

Yellow Kidney looked across the fire. "You heartless ones! Do not chide this young man. He acquitted himself bravely and wisely against the Crows. And now I hear from Heavy Shield Woman that he hunted for my family in my absence. He is a good young man, and I thank him before you members of the honor societies."

But White Man's Dog had not heard Yellow Kidney's words. He knew too well what had happened in that lodge. He had been there in his dream and the girl, the white-faced girl, had lifted her arms, not for him but for Yellow Kidney. Why hadn't he told Yellow Kidney of his dream? Such a dream would have been a sign of bad medicine and they might have turned back. Yellow Kidney would still be a whole man, not this pitiful figure. . . .

It had grown quiet in the big lodge as the men watched Yellow Kidney fumble for his pipe and tobacco sack. The beading on the sack was of a different pattern from those used by the Pikunis. With his fists Yellow Kidney was able to dip his pipe into the sack and fill it. He held the pipe in the palm of his left hand and held a blunt twig in the crease of his other palm, tamping the mixture. One of the younger men picked a burning stick from the fire and came forward to light the pipe.

"Thank you, Calf Shirt. And now you, like the others, wonder what happened to my hands to make them thus." Yellow Kidney puffed on his pipe and looked around the lodge. He had the calmness of a man who has lived through the worst of it and questioned the worth of survival. He removed the pipe with a stubby scarred hand and continued. "As I said, my mind was very confused and I became frightened. I began to move around to the various robes and I threw them back and saw by the light of my fire stick that they were all young girls, dead, and covered with the white scabs. Oh, I was frightened. I dropped the burning stick and rushed out of there, not caring what I would encounter. Anything was better than that death lodge. As I stood outside, trying to keep my guts down, I noticed that it was snowing heavily. This end of camp was still quiet. I thought my luck would hold, in spite of what I had seen and done in that lodge. I thought the snow would add to the confusion and help me to escape. But then I saw two young men come toward me from a tipi off to my right. In my haste, I had left my robe inside the death lodge. It didn't take them long to recognize me as an enemy and one of them hurled a lance at me. I managed to duck out of the way, but the other had a musket, and as I turned to run I heard a blast and my right leg buckled. I had been shot in the thigh. And now they were upon me and one of them grabbed my hair and I felt cold steel against my forehead. They meant to scalp me.

"I must have fainted, for the next thing I knew I was surrounded by our enemies, and they were talking and laughing. But one of them was angry and argued with the others. Although I had only seen him twice before, I recognized this angry man. It was Bull Shield and I knew he wanted me for himself. I spit at him and called him a Crow dog-eater; then I began my death song, for I knew that they would now kill me. And I wanted to die a good quick death, scorning my enemies. How I wish it had been so! Several of them rushed at me with their knives and they would have killed me but for a strange thing—the angry Bull Shield bade them to stop. He had become calm and thoughtful. He spoke some words to the others. I could not understand them, for I sang loud in their faces. Four of them picked me up and carried me to a nearby big-leaf log. There they placed my hands against the rough bark. Bull Shield then unsheathed his heavy knife and began to saw my fingers off, one by one. At first I tried to be silent to show that it did not bother me. My hands were numb because of the cold. But then the pain hit the warm parts of me and coursed through my body like lightning. I nearly bit my tongue off. Then I screamed like a real-lion and fainted again.

"When I woke up I was sitting astride a scrawny white horse, my legs tied under its belly. They had looped the reins around my neck. I had gotten sick, for as my chin rested on my chest I saw the foul outpouring of my stomach frozen to my shirt. When I had the strength to lift my head, my eyes fell on Bull Shield. He was now wearing a full headdress and he had a repeating rifle propped in the snow at his feet. Then he signed to me: Go and tell the Squats-like-women this is what the mighty Crows do when they send their girls to steal our horses. One of them hit the bony horse on the rump, and they all set up a war cry as I left their camp in the driving snow."

There was a great outcry of sympathy for Yellow Kidney and a stronger berating of the Crows for this humiliation. Even Three

Bears, who had long since left the hot words to the younger ones, expressed his anger. "Before this coming season of the high sun ends, we will make the miserable Crows to pay. Many of our brothers from the other camps will ride with us when they learn what has happened to Yellow Kidney. We will punish them severely." All in the lodge vowed they would join the war party. Some wanted to leave the next day, but it was agreed that they would go after the Sun Dance encampment. Three Bears wanted all the Pikunis to learn of Yellow Kidney's fate.

During the heated exchange, Riders-at-the-door had watched his son slip out of the lodge. He had been watching his son during Yellow Kidney's story, and he didn't know what to make of it. White Man's Dog had sat with his head down, apparently not even listening. Rides-at-the-door had seen this attitude before, and he didn't want to think he had seen it in his son; it was the attitude of one who has done a bad thing. And it had to do with Yellow Kidney's sad story. Now White Man's Dog had slipped out like a dog that had stolen meat.

"But go on, Yellow Kidney, tell us how you survived your misfortune," said Wipes-his-eyes, head of the Doves society. He was married to one of Yellow Kidney's sisters.

"It is difficult to remember what I did those first couple of sleeps, Wipes-his-eyes. The Crows had taken my capote—I remember seeing it on one of those who struck my horse—but they had tied one of the white men's blankets around my shoulders. All that day and the next I kept fainting. But my scabby little horse—the one you saw me arrive on—kept wandering. One night I awoke to find us standing in a grove of spear-leaf trees. My horse's head was down but he was not eating. I knew that he would soon collapse and then we would freeze to death. But the dawn came and I saw we were down in the valley of the Elk River. The snow had stopped, and the wind which had plagued us on the plains was no longer blowing. As I lifted my head to look around at my last day in Old Man's world, I saw on the other bank a small village. My head cleared and I saw smoke rising from the smoke holes of their lodges. I knew that it could be a party of Crow woodcutters or hunters, but I felt it would be better to die there than to live more hours of death. So I raised my horse's head and urged him forward. As we crossed the Elk River, I felt the cold water around my knees and twice the horse stumbled. Then I thought it would be better to drown. But we made it across and I rode right into the center of that small camp. I was too weak to cry out, and so I waited for them to come out of their lodges. Once again my head went black and this time I thought I saw my shadow slipping away. Ah, it was peaceful. I felt my body grow warm and cold at the same time. Then I was flying over the white plains, and ahead I saw the Sand Hills. I began to cry, for I saw the long-ago people standing before their lodges with their arms outstretched. But then they turned their faces away. I cried to Old Man to release me, for I wanted to join my father and my grandmother and my eldest son who died of the coughing sickness. They stood there with tears in their eyes. But then they too turned away and the Sand Hills hid themselves.

"I awoke in a darkened lodge with a strange man leaning over me. After a time I asked him if I was in the Shadowland, but he shook his head and signed to me that he did not understand my tongue. Then he made the sign for Spotted Horse People. I had been there for five sleeps. They had taken me in and were in the process of curing me. I didn't understand this last part and so I lifted my hands to sign to him my confusion. Then I saw my hands. They were wrapped in bundles of the white man's cloth and I remembered what had happened. Oh, I cried bitterly, for I had lost my ability to draw a bow, to fire a musket, to skin the blackhorns. I would be as useless as an old dog, and I not yet thirty-nine winters! I began to speak to the man again, to plead with him to retrieve my fingers, but again he made a sign that he didn't understand. Then he got up and went out of the lodge.

"It turned night and I lay there thinking of my Heavy Shield Woman, of my sons and daughter. I could never hunt for them, and I wanted to die right there rather than let them see me. I began to pity myself. I cried and cried and I asked Sun Chief why he didn't let his wretched Yellow Kidney die. What had I done to offend him so? Then I vowed that if he would let me die and give me back my fingers, I would hunt on behalf of all the old ones in the Sand Hills, since I could not hunt for my own family in this life.

"My crying and pleading were interrupted by the appearance of an old woman. She carried with her a medicine sack. She had a kind face and she wore her gray hair loose beneath a blackhorn-skin cap. She knelt beside me and gave the sign for medicine woman. There was a pot of boiling water behind her. She then unwrapped my hands and held them close to her face. They were very sensitive to air and I could even feel her breath on them. I drew them back and looked at them myself. They were black and puffed up like a bladder full of water. But beneath the black scabs I could see the pink new skin beginning to form. She made a paste of pounded-up bear grass and crow root and a leaf I didn't know. She sang a healing song and chewed some buffalo food and blew it on the wounds. Then she applied the paste and wrapped my hands in new cloths. One could tell by her presence that she was a practiced healer. She never smiled, but the kindly look did not leave her face. I fell asleep dreaming of my own dead grandmother.

"I continued to recover, drinking broth and eating of the wags-his-tail and prairie-runner meat they brought me. Then a few sleeps later I awoke in a sweat with a fearful pounding in my head. Then I began to get cold and my teeth chattered so I thought they would shatter. I tossed all night in such agony. When the medicine woman came to see me in the morning I had calmed down a little. But she looked at my face and her mouth fell open for I had begun to develop the little red sores. I saw them on my arms and I felt them around my mouth, and again I was besieged by the fever and chills. My body began to buck with such fury I was powerless to stop it. The old woman hurried out and returned with two older men. They had strips of rawhide in their hands. After they had tied me down, the woman signed that all of them had lived through the last plague of white scabs. They would not get it again. But by now I was tortured by red sores which were bursting all over my body and I was terrified of dying such a horrible death. This went on for how long I don't know because I was out of my head. I saw many things during my ordeal, things that would drive a healthy man out of his mind. Perhaps Old Man was being merciful in allowing me to die at last, but I had to question his method. Many times I returned to the Sand Hills only to be drawn back right on the edge. The only peace I knew was when my relatives smiled at me.

"Then one day I returned to the lodge. I was awakened by Sun Chief's warmth as he lit up the walls. Then I smelled a meat broth and I got a little hungry. I pulled myself up on my elbows and looked at my body. It was covered with a pale salve. Many of the white scabs had dropped off and I could see the angry scars. It was there, that day while looking at my scars and my hands, that I knew why I had been punished so severely. As you men of the warrior societies know, in all things, to the extent of my ability, I have tried to act honorably. But there in that Crow lodge, in that lodge of death, I had broken one of the simplest decencies by which people live. In fornicating with the dying girl, I had taken her honor, her opportunity to die virtuously. I had taken the path traveled only by the meanest of scavengers. And so Old Man, as he created me, took away my life many times and left me like this, worse than dead, to think of my transgression every day, to be reminded every time I attempt the smallest act that men take for granted." The energy had gone out of Yellow Kidney's voice and he sat motionless, looking down at the fire. The lodge was as quiet as death, except for the occasional *pop* of the pitchy wood. Outside, in the black night, a wind came down from the north and rattled the ear poles of the lodge. The tight skins around the lodgepoles flapped and the fire flickered, then blazed.

Three Bears spoke a prayer to all the Above Ones, thanking them for the return of their son, then said softly, "The spirits can be cruel, Yellow Kidney, but in their way there is a teaching." He looked at the younger men of the lodge. "Did you find Fast Horse?"

"No, his father has not seen him since midday," said one of the Doves.

"When he is found, tell him we would talk with him." Although it wasn't said, there was no doubt that it was Fast Horse's loud boasting that caused these bad things to happen to Yellow

Kidney. But the men respected Fast Horse's father. The Beaver Medicine was the most powerful of the bundles and Boss Ribs had kept it well. Now his son would be punished. Many of them hoped that Yellow Kidney would exercise his right to revenge his mutilation, to kill Fast Horse. If that didn't happen, they would probably banish the young man. That way, Boss Ribs could save some face.

Before they left, the men renewed their vow to make war on the Crows. It was decided they would do this in the moon of the yellow grass. They would make Bull Shield pay for his cruelty.

Three Bears called to Rides-at-the-door to stay when the men filed out. He lit his pipe and leaned back. His stiff back pained him badly and he needed to rest for a moment. Finally he said, "Why did White Man's Dog leave in the middle of Yellow Kidney's story?"

Rides-at-the-door looked at Three Bears, but the old man had closed his eyes. "I think he heard something that startled him. I don't know. It shamed me to see him leave."

"Perhaps he was just upset. Yellow Kidney is a pitiful man now. I don't know what he will do."

"I was afraid he would come back this way. As he said, he would be better off dead. It pains me to say it but I wish he had not come back. I fear more bad things will happen."

"Do you think he will attempt revenge—on Fast Horse?"

"Right now I don't think he knows. He pities himself and thinks only of his misfortune. Soon, though, he will begin to think of Fast Horse."

"It could set off something. Such bad blood in a small group like the Lone Eaters could go hard on everyone."

Rides-at-the-door thought for a while. He knew what should be done but he didn't like to say it. Boss Ribs was a friend of his and had already suffered much. Finally he did say it. "Fast Horse should be banished—tonight, if we can find him. The sooner he is gone, the sooner people will quit talking about him and Yellow Kidney. Perhaps we can prevent this revenge before Yellow Kidney has a chance to think of it."

"I feel as you do, Rides-at-the-door. Perhaps you can talk to

Boss Ribs, persuade him to banish Fast Horse himself. If it can be done quietly, without commotion, our people will be able to forget this problem and get on with their affairs. There are some hotheads in this camp. We must cool them down."

"How I pity Boss Ribs! He has already lost two wives and three children to the Shadowland. To banish his own son—"

"Talk to him. Tell him it must be done for the good of his people—and for the safety of his son." Three Bears sat forward, and the pain made his eyes water. He knocked the ashes from his pipe. "One more thing. Heavy Shield Woman's man is back, thus fulfilling her prayers. I would like White Man's Dog to ride among the other bands and tell them of her vow to be Medicine Woman at the Sun Dance. He can start in the morning."

Rides-at-the-door had known Three Bears all his life and thought he knew the direction of the old man's mind, but Three Bears many times managed to catch him off balance. "Why White Man's Dog?"

Three Bears began the painful task of getting up. "I trust him," he said simply.

"What about our journey to the trading fort? The people expect to leave in the morning," said Rides-at-the-door, helping the old man to his feet.

"We can delay it a couple of sleeps. We must feast the return of our good relative, Yellow Kidney."

In spite of his concern for his son's action that night, Rides-at-the-door had to smile at his old friend's way of always trying to make things right for his people. That is why he is a chief, thought Rides-at-the-door.

9

THE NEXT MORNING WAS COLD, and a light rain ticked off the lodge skins. Beneath the roiled clouds the prairies looked as green as the waters of the Two Medicine River, and the first flowers had opened up. White Man's Dog led the gray horse from the herds toward camp and didn't notice that his moccasins were soaked through or that the smoke hung heavy and low over the lodges. Nor did he notice the man who approached from camp, until he felt the horse tug back against the lead. He lifted his head and saw his father, and he stopped.

Rides-at-the-door didn't waste words. "I want to talk about last night," he said. "Something about Yellow Kidney's story troubled you and now it troubles me. I want you to tell about it."

And so White Man's Dog told his father about his dream, about the girls in the death lodge, and about how Yellow Kidney had suffered so horribly because of the dream.

"If I had told Yellow Kidney about the dream before we raided the Crows, he would have seen the wisdom in turning back. These things wouldn't have happened to him. If I had been smart enough to see. . . ." The words trailed off and hung in the wet thick air.

Rides-at-the-door looked down toward the river. It had begun to run higher the last several sleeps as the snow melted in the Backbone. Soon it would be off-color, rushing, rolling large stones in its powerful course down the valley. During these times one or two boys would be lost from the camps, never to be seen again. Rides-at-the-door used to worry about his sons, both White Man's Dog and Running Fisher, but those concerns now seemed mild and far away.

"You blame yourself," he said. "You think by telling Yellow Kidney your dream all the bad things would have been averted. It is natural to feel this way. But what if you had told him? Men, even experienced warriors, do not always listen to reason when they are close to their prize. It is like a fever. The closer to the prize, the more the fever obscures the judgment. The world is thrown out of balance. Some things become too important, other things not important enough. It is true that you should have told Yellow Kidney about your dream, and it might be true that he would have turned back. But I believe that it would have been too late. Already the world was out of balance. You were too close to the Crow camps to see reason and so you proceeded, knowing the risks. No, do not blame yourself. At most, you made an error in judgment. I'm afraid your friend, Fast Horse, made this catastrophe with his hotheaded boasting."

"It shames me to say this, but I would have gladly blamed him. I did blame him. Now I am not sure."

"His actions speak for themselves."

"Mik-api performed his medicine on me to drive the spirit that caused the dream from my body." White Man's Dog studied the lariat in his hands. "It made me feel good to be rid of it. I felt free for the first time since the horse-taking. But Mik-api told me that the spirit was still out there, waiting to attach itself to another of our people."

"That can happen if the spirit is not completely understood." Rides-at-the-door looked at his son. "But you must not think of yourself as the cause of this spirit. It was already out there and it chose to enter your body. Some spirits are too strong to eliminate. They pass from one body to another, and then another. They must be dealt with each time."

"What about Yellow Kidney? Could the same spirit have entered him?"

"The same spirit that caused you to dream also caused him to enter that death lodge."

"And Fast Horse?"

"No. I think it is the nature of Fast Horse to be loud and boastful and to hurt others. Some men are just like that."

"What will happen to him?"

Rides-at-the-door was a head taller than White Man's Dog, a big man with a broad upper body. But as he sighed, his shoulders slumped and his face fell. "I am going to see Boss Ribs now." He stared, slack-jawed, somewhere over his son's shoulder. At that moment he was much older than his forty-seven winters. "Three Bears would have him banished from the camp of the Lone Eaters. I am to deliver the message to Boss Ribs."

Rides-at-the-door stepped forward and embraced his son awkwardly.

"I am glad in my heart that you have done nothing wrong. And I am ashamed of myself for thinking that perhaps you had. Let your heart quit this dream and its consequences, for you are as blameless as this river when it sometimes carries away one of our boys."

As White Man's Dog watched his father walk back toward camp, he felt both lighter and sadder. He had grown up with Fast Horse, and now his friend would be banished. A part of himself would go with Fast Horse, never to return. But it hurt as much to see his father go to carry out his painful task. Rides-at-the-door and Boss Ribs had grown up together too and had remained close all their lives. Many times Boss Ribs and his sits-beside-him wife had feasted in his old friend's lodge. Now, even if Boss Ribs understood the necessity of his son's banishment, he would not forgive Rides-at-the-door for bringing the message. Fathers and sons would all suffer.

Double Strike Woman handed her son a bowl of broth, then sat back and continued her instructions. She had a list of names that he was to greet in all the camps he visited. He was to deliver messages to several of them. He was to bring back messages, to listen politely, to speak with respect. And he was to collect as much gossip as he could.

"How else am I to keep up? We don't visit other camps the way we used to. When I was a girl we visited all winter long. We'd go from camp to camp and people would welcome us. My father was an important man among the Hard Topknots. We knew everything that was happening."

Striped Face, Double Strike Woman's younger sister and Rides-at-the-door's second wife, was braiding her sister's hair and listening. "Our father was not an important man. He was not a chief and nobody listened to him," she said.

"You didn't know him like I did. Wherever we went, people respected him. He was a leader in his own way."

Kills-close-to-the-lake sat on the other side of the fire making up White Man's Dog's sack of meat. She was a shy girl, slender, a year younger than him. She was also his near-mother. He had been surprised a year ago when his father took her for his third wife, but she was the daughter of a man who had been unlucky and poor all his life. Rides-at-the-door had taken her for his wife as a kindness to the man. Now she was little more than a slave to the two other wives. As he watched her finish the packet, some of the old mixed feelings he had about her began to rise and he tried to concentrate on the argument between his mother and her sister. On the one hand, he wished Kills-close-to-the-lake had never come to live with them, for she was unhappy in this lodge and had brought a tension to it; on the other hand, White Man's Dog was excited by her and the tension that existed between them. Sometimes he caught her looking at him and knew she was seeing something in him. For his part, he spent most of his time avoiding looking at her, because it excited him and he was sure everybody could see this.

Now his mother was addressing him again. "As you know, Crow Foot's people are camped below the joining of the Two Medicine River and the Bear River. I want you to take this tobacco to him and tell him that his cousin, Rides-at-the-door, and his wife, Double Strike Woman, wish him and his wife well and hope that he will accept this pitiful gift. While you are there I would like you to take a good look at his daughter, Little Bird Woman. Talk with her, make jokes with her and, if you can arrange it, walk with her. You are my son and I think it is time you settled in your own lodge." She smiled and added, "Crow Foot is a powerful man and would make a good father-in-law."

White Man's Dog did not conceal his surprise. "But she was not even a woman the last time I saw her."

"That was two winters ago, the winter of the coughing sickness. I think you will find her much changed. She has good hips, that one. She would bear you many children." Double Strike Woman winced when Striped Face yanked on her braid. "Oh, you no-good one! The way you abuse me. If you weren't my sister I would throw you out and let you go live with the Napik-wans."

White Man's Dog listened to them fight but he was thinking about what his mother had said. She too wanted him to set up his own lodge! He felt his spirits rise at the thought of his own wife and his own family. But he wasn't thinking about Little Bird Woman, or even such a one as Kills-close-to-the-lake. As he had so often in the past two moons, he saw himself seated in his own lodge, lying against a backrest, smoking. And across the fire, he saw the calm face of Red Paint as she bent over her beadwork. There would be no other wives in the lodge, only Red Paint and their son.

The entrance flap opened and Running Fisher entered, followed by Rides-at-the-door. Running Fisher was soaked, his shirt and leggings dark on his shoulders and thighs. He looked at White Man's Dog and grinned. "While you have been in here gossiping with the women, I have been out gathering the news."

"What news?" said Double Strike Woman. She pulled her head away from her sister's fingers. "Here, come sit here. Put this robe over your shoulders. Kills-close-to-the-lake, gave him some of that broth."

Rides-at-the-door shed his wet blanket. White Man's Dog glanced at him, then held his glance, trying to read his father's face. There was no expression to interpret, but the eyes seemed a little brighter than they had earlier that morning.

"It is said that Fast Horse has quit camp," said Running Fisher. "He took his things and left during the night."

"Oh, poor Boss Ribs! But why?" Double Strike Woman put her fingers to her cheeks in an expression of shock.

Running Fisher looked at his mother. He was used to her overreactions, but his voice had a tone of disgust. "Haven't you heard? Fast Horse is the cause of Yellow Kidney's misfortune. It is Fast Horse who caused the Crows to discover him."

"Do they say where Fast Horse has gone?" said White Man's Dog.

Running Fisher grinned again at his brother. "To join Owl Child and his gang. He is going to kill Napikwans and steal their wealth. Owl Child has been waiting for him."

"How is this known?"

"The Marrow Bone saw him leave. He was riding night herd, and he talked to Fast Horse."

White Man's Dog looked at his father.

"It is true," said Rides-at-the-door. "I talked with Boss Ribs. It seems Fast Horse has banished himself."

"Then he is no longer a problem to the Lone Eaters. We should be happy that he is gone." White Man's Dog didn't feel happy.

Neither did Rides-at-the-door. "I'm afraid he will be a bigger problem than ever if he joins Owl Child's gang. They're no good. They think that by killing Napikwans they gain honor. All they will do is bring the blue-coated seizers down on all of us. These seizers will rub us out like the green grass bugs."

"Some day we will have to fight them," said Running Fisher. "Already the whitehorns graze our buffalo grounds."

"Perhaps someday that will come to pass, my son. But for now it is better to treat with them while we still have some strength. It will only be out of desperation that we fight."

"I know you are right, my father. But I am afraid for the Pikunis. Last night I dreamed that we had all lost our fingers like poor Yellow Kidney."

"It is good for you to be concerned, White Man's Dog. But you must remember that the Napikwans outnumber the Pikunis. Any day the seizers could ride into our camps and wipe us out. It is said that already many tribes in the east have been wiped away. These Napikwans are different from us. They would not stop until all the Pikunis had been killed off." Rides-at-the-door stopped and looked into the faces of his sons. "For this reason we must leave them alone, even allow them some of our hunting grounds to raise their whitehorns. If we treat wisely with them, we will be able to save enough for ourselves and our children. It is not an agreeable way, but it is the only way."

"You bet it is not agreeable," said Double Strike Woman. "Soon those stringy whitehorns will drive our blackhorns out of the country. White Grass Woman says they are mean and will eat anything, even children!"

"I think it is White Grass Woman who would eat anything," said Running Fisher. "She is as fat as the real-bear when he goes to sleep in the winter. I'll bet she could eat a real-bear too—at one sitting."

"You nothing one! You mock my best friend and now you come dripping all over. Go sit over there. Give him some more of that broth. It's bad enough that this one"—she pointed to White Man's Dog—"is going out in this weather. We don't need two sick sons."

Running Fisher laughed and moved away to his sleeping robes. He leaned back and picked up some arrow shafts he had hardened over the fire. He selected one and felt its waxy smoothness with his fingers. Then he sighted down its length for straightness, his eye traveling on until it came to rest on his brother. He studied his brother's face as White Man's Dog listened to some final instructions from Rides-at-the-door. There was a calm intelligence there that Running Fisher had not noticed before. It was not the face of the young man that Running Fisher had once pitied for his bad luck. At that time Running Fisher was the lucky one, the one who had stolen two horses and a musket from the Cutthroats. He was the one who would one day become a great warrior. But now White Man's Dog seemed the chosen one and Running Fisher had come to envy him. As he watched White Man's Dog fill his rawhide sling pack, he couldn't help feeling that his brother's successes somehow diminished him. He would have to do something to gain much honor, but what? He could join a horse-taking party; there would be many parties going out now that winter was over. Or he could wait for the war party against the Crows. But that would not occur until after the Sun Dance.

He watched Kills-close-to-the-lake skirt the fire to hand White Man's Dog the sack of meat. Rides-at-the-door and his two other wives were talking among themselves on the far side of the fire.

Only Running Fisher saw the girl touch his brother briefly on the shoulder. Only he saw the quick glance and the quick looking away, the flush on White Man's Dog's face. But when he looked back at the other group, he saw Striped Face looking directly at him, a small grin on her face.

On the third day of his journey, White Man's Dog stood on a bluff overlooking the trading house on the Bear River. It was built in the shape of a rectangle, a series of squat buildings arranged around a central trading area. The log structures looked heavy and dark to White Man's Dog. In the dusty yard five men stood around a pair of horses laden with robes. He recognized Riplinger, the trader, and Old Horn of the Grease Melters. Another Napikwan, a young one in a black hat and dark clothes, squatted a few feet away. Two young Pikunis, perhaps Old Horn's sons, stood with their arms folded.

An arrow's arc to the east lay the camp of the Grease Melters. In the late morning sun the lodges looked as white as doeskin. Most of them were made of the white man's stiff cloth. White Man's Dog knew that some of the Lone Eaters would trade robes for the cloth. It was easier to piece together, would shed the water well and was lighter than the blackhorn hides. He had smelled the cloth once and it reminded him of unclean bladder. It made him smile to think of these Grease Melters living in their bladders on the edges of the trading forts. He would not want the Lone Eaters to live this way.

He had visited three bands, the Black Doors, the Small Robes and Crow Foot's people. He had not talked to Little Bird Woman but he had looked her over at the evening meal. She was chunky, attractive and lively. Her round face seemed always to be split with laughter. When she saw White Man's Dog looking at her, she would lower her head and play shyly with her puppy. Then, a moment later, she would be laughing and joking with her brothers.

She would make a good wife, thought White Man's Dog as he looked down on the trading house. She is cheerful and strong and handsome in a stout way. He knew that she had worn her elkskin dress just for him, and he wondered if his father and Crow Foot had already talked of a union between their families. The idea didn't exactly displease him, but it added a complication he was not prepared for. If his parents had their minds set on her, he would dishonor them by not obeying their wish. And he had his heart set on Red Paint. But he had only seen Red Paint from a distance and in his imagination. It was as though she had no substance, no life other than her work. I have not even heard her voice, he thought. Had she spoken that time he had delivered the meat and she surprised him? Even if she had, he wouldn't have heard the words. Kills-close-to-the-lake had more presence in his mind than did Red Paint. Even now, he could see her body, the way she moved, the expressions on her face, her voice, even the scent of her that made him light-headed. For a year they had lived in the same lodge and had almost avoided each other, yet he knew her as well as he knew any woman. In spite of the shame he felt, he smiled ruefully. I don't know any woman, he thought, not the way a man should. I am a nothing-man and all the women see it. They think I am only lucky to take the horses from the Crows.

As he swung up onto the gray horse's back, he thought of the vow he made to Sun Chief, the vow to sacrifice at the Sun Dance if he returned from the raid safely. He had returned and so he would fulfill that vow. But perhaps Sun Chief would favor him in another way, would allow him to become a good man to be trusted and respected by all the people. He was sick to death of being the puny wretch who desired the touch of his father's wife, his own near-mother. And he was sick of himself for thinking these thoughts while he had a duty to perform. He kicked his horse forward, and the horse was surprised by the force of the kicks.

By the end of the fifth sleep, White Man's Dog had visited all the bands but two. He camped alone this night, for he was tired of feasting and talking. He lay in his robe beside the small fire and studied the stars. It was a clear warm night and he could see the Seven Persons, the Poor Boys, the Person's Hand and Big Fire Star. He looked at them and felt better. He was not even hungry. But he was disappointed to learn that day that Mountain Chief's band had crossed the Medicine Line into the Real Old Man country, for he had wanted to see if Fast Horse was among them. Owl Child and his gang, when they were not out raiding, lived with the Many Chiefs. And Crow Foot had said that Owl Child had killed two woodcutters on the Big River near the Hole-in-the-wall. If Fast Horse had joined the gang he would be in trouble, as would all of Mountain Chief's people. Perhaps that was why the Many Chiefs had slipped across the line.

He lifted his hands as if to touch the stars. He remembered the stories told by his grandfather of the origins of the constellations. He had been young then and it all seemed simple. There were only the people, the stars, the blackhorns. Now his grandfather was dead and the Napikwans were pushing their way into the country. What would happen to the Pikunis? His father was right and wise to attempt to treat with the Napikwans. But one day these blue-coated warriors would come, and White Man's Dog and the other young men would be forced to fight to the death. It would be better to die than to end up standing around the fort, waiting for handouts that never came. Some bands, like the Grease Melters, had already begun to depend too much on the Napikwans. Ever since the Big Treaty they had journeyed to the agent's house for the commodities that were promised to them. Most of the time they returned empty-handed. And more and more of the Napikwans moved onto Pikuni lands.

White Man's Dog looked up at his hands. His grandfather had said those many winters ago that if you went to sleep with your palms out, the stars would come down to rest in them and you would be a powerful man. Many summer nights White Man's Dog had tried to go to sleep this way, but his arms grew tired before the stars could come. He lowered his arms and rolled over. The fire was down to embers, glowing softly in the moonless night.

The Black Patched Moccasins was the last band that White Man's Dog visited. They lived below the bend of the Bear River, where it turned south to enter the Big River. At one time, only three winters ago, they had been the most powerful of the bands. Their lodges were always full of meat and robes, and the men and women were cheerful and generous. Their leader, Little Dog, was head chief of all the Pikunis. He was a trusting man and chose to befriend the Napikwans, visiting them frequently in their Many Houses fort on the Big River. They, in turn, treated him well, for they considered him a valuable go-between who was able to control the more hostile of the Pikunis. For a while that was true, but the demands became too great and things ended badly.

Now the people of the Black Patched Moccasins were distrustful of any who were not of their band. For protection they had continued to ally themselves with the other bands, but their hearts had turned cold.

White Man's Dog rode through their camp and his eyes were rounded by what he saw. Pieces of fur and bone were scattered among the lodges, as though the people had dragged animals into camp, ate what they wanted and left the carcasses to the dogs. The smell of rotting flesh made White Man's Dog's eyes water. To his right he saw a lodge that was in danger of falling over. The loose skin covering was ripped and stained. A naked child, holding a piece of fur against its mouth, watched him ride by.

At last he saw the lodge he was looking for. It was painted black around the top to resemble the night sky. Yellow clusters of dots in the black represented the constellations. A broad band around the bottom was painted ocher to suggest the earth. And around the middle a procession of otters headed toward the entrance. This was the tipi of Mad Plume, who had dreamed the Otter Dream in his youth and who now presented the Otter Medicine bundle at the Sun Dance.

"Haiya! Mad Plume! It is White Man's Dog, son of Rides-at-the-door of the Lone Eaters. I have come with news." He looked around him and saw several of the people standing in front of their lodges. A large yellow dog snarled at him, but his master hit him on the head with a stick and the dog slunk away.

Mad Plume came out of his lodge and stood before White Man's Dog. He was a little man, and old now, but he stood with a straight back, cradling his long-pipe in his arms. The bowl was made of the red stone used by the Dirt Lodge People many sleeps to the east. The stem was covered with strips of otter fur.

"White Man's Dog. You look familiar. I don't see well anymore." He narrowed his eyes. "Yes, you used to sit with the other children and listen to my stories—during the summer ceremonies. Yes, you used to ask me questions."

White Man's Dog knew Mad Plume did not recognize him, but it was true that he had sat and listened to the old man's stories. Many children did.

"Tell me, how is Rides-at-the-door? I hear he has acquired himself a new wife. You're not her son? Get down off your horse and sit with me. Woman!" he called back to the lodge. "Bring tobacco. This young brave and I wish to smoke."

As if that were the signal, the people came forward and sat around the two men. They looked thin and listless and their clothes were shabby. The man next to White Man's Dog stunk, even though the river was only a stone's throw away. In some ways they reminded him of the stand-around-the-fort Indians he had encountered at Many Houses and the settlement at Pile-of-rocks River, always with their hands out when the Lone Eaters came to trade. But since the incident involving Little Dog, these Pikunis seldom journeyed to the forts. They distrusted the Napikwans as much as they distrusted the other bands.

"Ah, you see how it is, young man, with the Black Patched Moccasins. I watch your eyes and I see you wonder. Now I will tell you how it is and how it came to be." Mad Plume's wife came with a pouch of tobacco and his short-pipe. She took away the medicine pipe. "Once we were a strong people, first to join the hunt, first to take horses from our enemies and first to take the war road against them. Many an enemy trembled when he saw the Black Patched Moccasins ride down upon his village. But we were also a generous people, loyal to our friends, helpful to those who needed it. We were always friendly with the Napikwans, for we held nothing against them. And they, for their part, always treated with us fairly. Little Dog was even awarded a medallion from our White Father Chief in the east. He knew that the Napikwans possessed greater medicine than the Pikunis, for they came from that place where Sun Chief rises to begin his journey.

"One day the white chiefs came to our camp and showed us

a new trick. It was during the new-grass moon. They scratched at our Mother Earth's breast and buried seeds and pieces of plant flesh beneath her skin. Many of us were surprised, but Little Dog told us it was a good trick, for soon good things to eat would grow. The white chiefs wished us to quit the trail of the blackhorns and to grow the good things to feed upon. Little Dog and some of the others moved down to the settlement on the Pile-of-rocks River and tried to live like the Napikwans. They grew these good things and they even herded the whitehorns. But it took a long time for these plants to come up, and when they did they were scrawny things. The whitehorns were stringy and didn't taste like real-meat. After a winter of being hungry all the time, we came back and hunted the blackhorns. Even Little Dog came back after a while."

Mad Plume gestured around him.

"Why grow those scrawny things when the roots and berries grow so abundantly around us? We thought the Napikwans would leave us alone, for we had tried their way and it was no good. Still they wanted us to give up the blackhorns and plant the seeds. Little Dog tried other ways to make the Napikwans happy. When their horses were run off, he would find them and bring them back. He told our people not to kill any more of them. He told the seizer chiefs that he would deal harshly with those Pikunis that offended them. He wanted peace between the Pikunis and the Napikwans, and that was his downfall." Mad Plume chewed on his lower lip. A spasm rippled across his cheek. When it passed, he said, "The rest you know. He had brought some of the Napikwans' horses back to them and was returning to our village when he was jumped and killed by some of his own people. He was betrayed by some of his own people, and that is why the Black Patched Moccasins have become so distrustful."

White Man's Dog looked into the wrinkled face and tried to read the emotions there. For while the lips were curved into a smile, the eyes had become wet. It was as though Mad Plume remembered Little Dog both fondly and sadly. Yet there was something else there, something in the way the lips trembled, as though he wanted to say something more. White Man's Dog remembered the reason given for the killing of Little Dog, and now he wondered if some part of Mad Plume not only under-stood that reason but perhaps condoned it. The killers of Little Dog felt the head chief had put the interests of the Napikwans before those of the Pikunis. It was he who betrayed the people.

"We are a leaderless people now. I have tried my best but I do not inspire the young ones to listen. I am too old and I do not possess the strength. Look around you, White Man's Dog, do you see many of our young men? No, they are off hunting for them-selves, or drunk with the white man's water, or stealing their horses. They do not bring anything back to their people. There is no center here. That is why we have become such a pitiful sight to you."

"But why don't you move, Mad Plume? Away from these Napikwans. The Lone Eaters live a long way from them and are never tempted to fool with them. The game is thick in our coun-try. The Black Patched Moccasins would be welcome to hunt with us."

"Perhaps—it would be nice." But White Man's Dog saw the resigned look in his host's eyes. It was odd, he thought, how Mad Plume was such a respected man during the Sun Dance cere-mony, but within his own band he was powerless. White Man's Dog looked up at the figures on the Otter Tipi, a sacred tipi, and he looked around at the faces of the people, and he realized there were things he was not old enough or experienced enough to understand.

He told Mad Plume and his ragged band of his mission, and they seemed to approve of Heavy Shield Woman's vow. There was no woman among them who had made such a vow—nor among any of the bands—so she would be the Sacred Vow Woman at the summer ceremony.

"You will stay and feast with us, White Man's Dog. Your father and I have been on the war trail together a couple of times. He was a young one then, but oh, he was brave. . . ."

White Man's Dog looked around at the faces and beyond them. He saw the ragged lodge and he saw the naked child playing with the piece of fur. A dog was licking the child's face. "Yes," said White Man's Dog.

10

THE LONE EATERS had camped a short ride from Riplinger's trading house. The lodges were set up around a bend in a grove of big-leaf trees, so they were not visible to the two other bands who were also trading. Whole families were gong to the trading house, their packhorses laden with robes, and coming back with the goods that would make their lives easier. The women traded for cloth, beads, paints, white man's powder for cooking, kettles and pans, earrings and brass studs to decorate belts and saddles. The children came back with sweet sticks and knives and even some dolls. And the men acquired half-axes, files, hoop-iron, tobacco, ammunition and guns. There were not as many of the repeating rifles as they had expected, so most of them had to settle for the new single-shot seizer gun. These rifles were as heavy and long as their old muskets, but they fired cartridges, were easily loaded even on horseback, and fired most of the time. The greased shooters carried truer and farther than the old balls. There was some grumbling but most were happy to get this weapon, even at the price of fifteen prime hides.

Only a few of the important men of the Pikunis received many-shots guns. Riplinger had acquired eighteen of them, and he presented them as gifts to the chiefs and to others he deemed important. He often gave valuable things, such as saddles and guns, to the chiefs to ensure their future trade.

When Rides-at-the-door and his family entered the trading compound, Riplinger greeted him first in Blackfeet, then in the Napikwans' tongue. He enjoyed seeing Rides-at-the-door and respected him as a smart man, one who had learned the English language during the treaty years. He was one of only three or four that Riplinger knew who spoke the language. The others had learned it in boarding schools, but Rides-at-the-door had picked it up from a missionary who had spent a couple of winters with the Pikunis before heading on to the Flathead country.

But Rides-at-the-door did not particularly like any Napikwans, and so he answered Riplinger's questions with short, curt answers. He watched the trader sort through the hides, making piles according to grade. The trader's son helped him tot up the figure; then he sent the son to accompany Double Strike Woman and Striped Face to the storeroom, followed by Running Fisher and Kills-close-to-the-lake.

"Where is your other son?" said Riplinger.

"Off hunting," said Rides-at-the-door. He did not see any need to tell of White Man's Dog's mission.

Riplinger looked surprised. He hadn't known a Pikuni yet who missed a trading day. "Well, your hides are good, Rides-at-the-door. They are worth many of my goods. I'm sure your women will find what they need. But come—I have a surprise for you."

Rides-at-the-door followed the trader into his living quarters. He stood just inside the door.

"Would you like a drink?"

"I am not accustomed to it."

Riplinger snorted. It was almost a laugh, but he managed to check himself. "Well, probably for the best. Don't do anybody any good." He was digging around in a closet. "Ah, here!" He held up a many-shots rifle. He walked over to Rides-at-the-door. "For you. Over and above the value of your hides. I have the cartridges for it in the next room."

Before he turned to leave, Rides-at-the-door saw the trader's wife standing in a doorway to another room. She was a younger woman, about the age of Striped Face, and she wore a calico dress that came down almost to the floor. Rides-at-the-door could just see her shiny black shoes beneath the hem. He glanced at her face. She was smiling but there was a look of fear in her eyes.

Back in the lodge, Double Strike Woman and Striped Face

examined their new goods, sometimes exclaiming their admiration, other times speechless with awe. Even Kills-close-to-the-lake touched the new things. She smiled as she held a piece of red flannel to her cheek.

Rides-at-the-door watched them as he smoked and felt satisfied that they had made a good trade. From time to time he glanced over at the many-shots gun leaning against a tripod. Next to it rested a single-shot that he had gotten for White Man's Dog. He was satisfied but also a little worried. White Man's Dog was overdue. He should have been back two sleeps ago if he had ridden cross-country from the Black Patched Moccasin campsite. Perhaps he had decided to stay longer with one or two bands, or perhaps he had decided to try to see Fast Horse. That could be trouble. But White Man's Dog was levelheaded and took his responsibility seriously. He would return soon.

Rides-at-the-door listened to the rifle fire and realized that he had been hearing it all afternoon, a steady hail of fire as the men tried out their new weapons. He got up and walked outside. Most of the men were down by the river, firing at bushes and rocks against a cliff on the other side. Running Fisher would be among them, shooting up his ammunition at things that did not need killing. But it was necessary to get used to a new gun. Rides-at-the-door remembered when he was a young man and had gotten his musket. He had used up all his powder and balls and had to wait several moons before he could get any more. Things were harder to come by then. He smiled. Perhaps he should go down and fire his own many-shots gun to get the feel of it. Instead, he walked off toward the trees behind camp to take a piss.

White Man's Dog came that evening just as Sun Chief ended his journey. Families were getting together to feast and sing and to compare their new possessions. In the middle of camp, young men sat around a large fire, weapons across their laps, and sang wolf songs. Young women strolled arm in arm around the perimeter, sometimes doing a dance step, other times trailing a robe over the head of a young man. Running Fisher was part of a drum group, and he sang and watched the girls.

White Man's Dog led the gray horse into camp, watching the

various activities. From time to time, he heard the *pop* of a rifle or the taunting yodel of a young brave, meant to frighten an imaginary enemy.

A small boy fell in step with White Man's Dog. "What happened to your horse?"

"He stepped on a sharp rock." White Man's Dog recognized the boy as One Spot, Red Paint's younger brother. He wore only a breechcloth and moccasins. His cheeks were painted a bright yellow.

"Couldn't you ride him?"

"Not since morning. He's been lame all day."

They walked in silence for a way. Then the boy said, "I have a faster horse," and darted between two lodges to join some children who were playing with a gopher.

Rides-at-the-door greeted his son outside the lodge. He had been standing there, smoking, watching the drum group. "My son! It is good to see you."

The two men embraced and White Man's Dog knew his father had been worried. "I would have come sooner but I stayed a night with the Black Patched Moccasins. Then this horse came up lame. Mad Plume sends you his greetings."

"Ah, a good man, Mad Plume. Come inside and eat, my son. Your mother has been worried about you."

Later that night the two men walked over to the lodge of Three Bears. White Man's Dog followed his father in and when he straightened up he was surprised to see so many people present. Three Bears sat at the head of the fire, away from the entrance.

"Welcome, my son. Come here and sit beside me. You have been gone too long."

White Man's Dog looked at his father. Rides-at-the-door smiled. And so the young man sat in the place of honor and told of all the greetings that had been sent to Three Bears and the Lone Eaters. He told them of Mountain Chief's flight to Canada.

"Was Owl Child with them?"

"No one knew. But most felt he was, that the seizers had chased Owl Child and his gang to the camp of the Many Chiefs. That's why they all had to run."

Three Bears muttered his disgust. All the people fell silent. And that's when White Man's Dog noticed Red Paint. She was sitting beside her mother, a black cloth shawl over her head. He glanced at Heavy Shield Woman; then he looked around the group. Yellow Kidney was not among them. Although Red Paint was several paces away, this was the closest White Man's Dog had been to her. She was watching him.

"And what about the purpose of your travels?"

White Man's Dog looked at Three Bears as if he hadn't understood. But he recovered his wits. "I went from band to band—the only people I didn't see were the Many Chiefs—and they all expressed their approval. They were happy to learn of Heavy Shield Woman's vow and of her good fortune in having Yellow Kidney return to her. They said they knew she was a virtuous woman and would help to make the Sun Dance ceremony a success. They also said they would do anything she required of them. Many prayers were said, and many of the women said they would assist Heavy Shield Woman."

Three Bears picked up his medicine pipe. He looked at Heavy Shield Woman. "It would seem that all of our people are in agreement with your desire, sister. The way is clear for you to begin your preparations. You have witnessed the Sun Dance many times and you have seen the role of the Sacred Vow Woman. Many women would not accept such a role because the way is arduous. Only the strongest of our women have made such a vow, because one needs great strength to prepare for and carry out her duties. If you are successful, the Pikunis will prosper and enjoy favor with the spirit world. If you fail, if you are not strong or virtuous enough, great harm will come to us." Three Bears looked slowly from face to face within the circle. "We are one, sister, in our approval. Do you accept the role of the Sacred Vow Woman?"

Heavy Shield Woman did not hesitate. "I made this vow in a time of great distress. My heart had fallen down, but I told my children that their father would return to them. I don't know now if I believed it then. But I prayed to the Above Ones, to Sun Chief, to our Mother Earth, to allow my man to come home to me. My heart lightened somewhat because I knew the spirits had listened to me and took pity. They would not desert me and my children in our time of sadness. That's when I came to you, Three Bears. I knew when I talked with you that Yellow Kidney would be returned." Here, Heavy Shield Woman's voice almost faltered as she thought of her pitiful husband. "That has happened, and so I say to you, and to the others present, I am strong and glad in my heart to be the Sacred Vow Woman."

"We will smoke this pipe," said Three Bears. "We will pray for our sister's success."

Outside the lodge, White Man's Dog breathed in the fresh air and looked up at the stars. His father had stayed to talk with Three Bears. He looked at the stars and listened to the drumming and singing and he was happy. He would sleep well.

"I wish to thank you, White Man's Dog."

He turned his head to the voice and saw Heavy Shield Woman and Red Paint. He was too tired to be startled.

"I know your journey was long and you missed out on the trading. Your mother told me."

"No, I—I wanted to make the journey. It was good."

"Your words tonight set my heart at ease." Heavy Shield Woman smiled, and White Man's Dog felt the warmth of it. "There have been times when I wished another had made a similar vow. I would have gladly relinquished mine. But when I saw your face I knew there were no others and it made me happy."

"The other women, they were happy too. They said Heavy Shield Woman is one of great resolve, of great virtue, of great, great . . ."

The woman laughed at White Man's Dog's struggle for fine words. Red Paint laughed, and then he laughed. He laughed long and loud. He had never been this happy—or exhausted. His feet ached, he was weary in his bones, but being near Red Paint made even his weariness seem a thing of joy.

He wiped away the tears and Heavy Shield Woman said, "And

thank you—for hunting for us. You can't know—" She turned and walked away quickly.

Red Paint had not spoken and she didn't speak now. She stepped forward and touched his arm. She smiled but there were tears in her eyes. Then she turned and followed her mother.

"And what about you, young man? Now that you are rich and powerful, it is time for you to take a wife." Mik-api lay just inside the entrance to his lodge. The Lone Eaters had returned the day before to the Two Medicine River from the trading house, and the trip had tired him. The lodge skins were raised and he could see White Man's Dog from where he lay.

White Man's Dog sat just outside in the warm sun, rubbing an oily cloth over his new single-shot. He had been firing it earlier that morning, and he was still in awe of its power and accuracy. On his third shot, he had killed a prairie hen at a hundred paces. When he retrieved it, he found only a tangle of feathers and bone.

"As a heavy-singer-for-the-sick I encounter many people. Sometimes they want my healing, other times just to talk. They think they want me to tell them important things, but most often it's the other way around. Just the other day I was invited into the lodge of my friend Yellow Kidney. In passing he mentioned that he would be forever grateful to you for sharing your kills with his family. I told him that you were now a man and becoming adept in the ways of medicine. I told him you had acquired power much stronger than that of the other young ones, that you would one day distinguish yourself among our people. Of course, I was joking to cheer the poor man up."

White Man's Dog smiled.

"Then I happened to notice Red Paint, who sat across the lodge engaged in her beadwork, and I mentioned that it was too bad our young women seem to favor these beads over quillwork. Yellow Kidney agreed with me but said Red Paint did it for others in exchange for goods. Then he became very sad and held up his fingerless hands and said that he was worse than useless to his family, that Red Paint would grow up poor and no man would have her."

White Man's Dog turned around to face the old man. Mik-api sucked on his pipe and looked out the entrance at nothing in particular. His eyes crinkled as though he were straining to see something.

"I felt sorry for the poor man and, like a fool, said that I might know somebody who would keep her well. Of course, that person would have to hunt for the whole family now. But now that I think on it, perhaps there is nobody that rich and powerful among the Lone Eaters. Perhaps Yellow Kidney will have to seek out such a person among the Small Brittle Fats or the Hard Top-knots. I understand there are among them a few young men rich and powerful enough."

"Would you speak for me, Mik-api?" White Man's Dog heard the voice far away. His heart was too far in his throat for the words to come from him.

"Slow down, you foolish young one. You're getting as bad as me. First, you must go to your father and mother and tell them of your intentions. If they agree, I will talk to Yellow Kidney. But what makes you think Red Paint would want such a fool?"

White Man's Dog suddenly slumped back. He remembered Little Bird Woman, Crow Foot's daughter. But only Double Strike Woman had mentioned her as a possible wife. Perhaps Rides-at-the-door and Crow Foot were not aware of such an arrangement. Nothing had happened. He had not even spoken to Little Bird Woman. White Man's Dog jumped up. "I will speak with them now, Mik-api. I'll be back."

Double Strike Woman argued that it would be advantageous for the two families to be united; that Little Bird Woman was sought after by many men, young and old; that she was built to bear many children.

"Just think of Crow Foot. Many say he will be the next head chief of the Pikunis. They say he is already more important than Mountain Chief, because Mountain Chief is always on the run."

"I don't mind you wanting to marry off this young man, but next time you will consult with me before you do such a thing." Rides-at-the-door was angry. Most of the time, he left things in the lodge up to his sits-beside-him wife, but he too had been thinking of his son's future. In truth, he had been just as surprised, shocked even, as Double Strike Woman at White Man's Dog's request. He hadn't known of his son's interest in Red Paint. And if he were to be honest with himself, he would have admitted that the idea was not appealing to him, not because of Red Paint but because White Man's Dog would have to provide for the entire family.

"I only want what is best for my son," said Double Strike Woman. "If he were to marry into Crow Foot's family, he would have more opportunities."

"You can see he doesn't want Little Bird Woman. He wants to marry Red Paint. He is a man now."

"And what about Yellow Kidney? He will have to marry Yellow Kidney, too, and support him and that whole family! People will make jokes. People will say, There goes Rides-at-the-door's son, he marries whole families."

"And what about you, my son? Do you think you can take such jokes?"

"They will not joke for long," said White Man's Dog.

Rides-at-the-door studied his son.

Kills-close-to-the-lake looked up from her quillwork. She had been following the conversation intently. In the brief silence, she too studied White Man's Dog. Without thinking about it, she had been anticipating this time when White Man's Dog would leave the lodge. But she couldn't believe it was actually happening. With him gone, there would be nothing left for her. But there had been nothing anyway—only his presence and some vague hope. Now it was all gone.

"Your mother and I give you our permission, son. You may propose a marriage to Red Paint and her family. She is a good young woman and will make you happy."

White Man's Dog sneaked a look at his mother, but she was busy cutting meat. He stood and walked to the entrance. "Thank you," he said. He looked down at Kills-close-to-the-lake, but she was bent over her quillwork. "Thank you," he said again. He ducked out of the lodge and ran all the way to Mik-api's.

Four sleeps later the families got together and exchanged gifts. White Man's Dog gave Yellow Kidney three of his best horses. His father gave Yellow Kidney four horses, three ropes of tobacco and a full headdress he had taken from a Parted Hair. Yellow Kidney gave White Man's Dog four horses and a beaded shirt. He gave Rides-at-the-door five horses and a Napikwan saddle. Double Strike Woman gave Red Paint a pair of white beaded medallions for her hair. She hugged the girl briefly.

Earlier, Rides-at-the-door had presented his new many-shots gun to White Man's Dog. "You're going to have to do a lot of hunting now." White Man's Dog then gave his single-shot to his father. "Between you and Running Fisher, you now have two shots."

White Man's Dog had left nothing to chance. The day before, he had gone to the camp of the Grease Melters to look up a man who specialized in Liars' Medicine. The man constructed two bark figures—a man and a woman—and poured the magic liquid between them. That would ensure good loving. He charged his client a large packhorse he had noticed during the trade.

Now, on the twenty-third day of the new-grass moon, Red Paint moved her things into the small tipi beside the big lodge of Rides-at-the-door. That night the families and friends feasted on boss ribs and tongues and buffalo hump. One of the men had brought a tin of the white man's water, and the feast soon turned loud and boisterous. White Man's Dog drank the liquor and talked and laughed, but he was a little disappointed that Kills-close-to-the-lake and Mik-api were not there. Mik-api had said, "I am an old man. Celebrations are for the young." White Man's Dog drank some more and laughed louder. Red Paint sat beside him, twirling her feather fan. All the noise had made her shy— but more than that, she couldn't believe she was a married woman. Less than seven sleeps ago, marriage had been the furthest thing from her thoughts. She had sought only to help her mother prepare for the Sun Dance. Could it have been only seven sleeps ago that she had touched White Man's Dog's arm and smiled at him? Even then she had no thought that this might happen. And tonight—tonight they would go to their own lodge. She had thought occasionally of what it would be like to lie with a man, but there had been no reality to it. Her mother had said it would happen naturally and it would be good with the right man. Would White Man's Dog be the right man? She glanced at him and his face was shiny with sweat and oil. He sensed her eyes on him and turned. For a moment they looked upon each other; for the first time they looked into each other's eyes. Then Red Paint lowered her eyes to the twirling fan.

White Man's Dog stood and walked outside. He walked away from the lodge and stood in a small field. He smelled the fresh bite of sage grass and looked up at the stars, trying to locate the Seven Persons. His head was fuzzy with the liquor, but he became aware of a small hand on his. "The Seven Persons do not look upon us tonight," he said softly.

"They ride to the west, over there," said a voice that did not sound right to his ears. He turned and looked into the face of Kills-close-to-the-lake. Although she had not been at the feast, she was wearing her elkskin dress and rose medallions in her hair. The sharp sage grass gave way to the scent that made him light-headed. She said, "I am very happy for you, White Man's Dog. I wish you to have this." And she turned and hurried off into the dark.

He watched her until he couldn't see her anymore. Then he unfurled the object. It was a soft-tanned scabbard for his new rifle. In the faint light of the fire-lit lodges, he could just make out the quillwork thunderbird design. Then the design blurred and he wiped his eyes.

Some time between the moon of flowers and Home Days, with the high hot sun turning the grass from green to pale straw, the Pikuni people began to pack up their camps to begin the four-day journey to Four Persons Butte near the Milk River. Here, the Sacred Vow Woman and her helpers had determined to build a lodge for the Sun Chief, and here they meant to honor him with sacred ceremonies, songs and dances.

Heavy Shield Woman had purchased the Medicine Woman bundle from her predecessor, and her relatives in the camps had procured the sacred bull blackhorn tongues.

On the first day the people assembled near the confluence of the Two Medicine River and Birch Creek. Most of the bands arrived within the compass of the midmorning and midafternoon sun. As each band arrived, members of the All Crazy Dogs, the police society, showed them where to set up. Soon a great circle was formed, as the last of the bands, the Never Laughs, filled the perimeter. The Sacred Vow Woman's lodge was erected in the center and Heavy Shield Woman entered. Then the camp crier rode among the lodges, calling forth all the women who had vowed to come forward to the tongues. He beat his small drum and called for their husbands to accompany them. He stopped before the lodge of Heard-by-both-sides Woman, who had been a Sacred Vow Woman two years earlier, and called her to instruct Heavy Shield Woman in her duties.

When the chosen had been assembled in the lodge, Heard-by-both-sides Woman lifted one of the tongues above her head and asked Sun Chief to affirm that she had been virtuous in all things. All of the women did this. Then the dried tongues were boiled and cut up and placed in parfleches. Heavy Shield Woman began her fast.

The next day she led the procession to the second camp. On her travois she carried the Medicine Woman bundle and the sacred tongues. Four days they camped in four different locations, arriving at last on a flat plain beneath Four Persons Butte. Each day Yellow Kidney and the many-faces man, wise in the ritual of the Sun Dance, purified themselves in the sweat lodge.

The dawn of the fifth day, Low Horn, a celebrated warrior and scout, left his lodge, saddled his buffalo-runner and galloped down off the plain to the valley of the Milk River. As he rode, he examined the big-leaf trees around him. Across the river he spotted one that interested him. It was stout but not too thick. It was true and forked at just the right height. He looked at the tree, the way the sun struck it, and decided it was the chosen one.

When he reached camp—by now everyone was up and the breakfast fires were lit—he rode among the lodges, calling to the men of the Braves society. He ate a chunk of meat while the others saddled their horses. Then he led them back to the spot. Everybody-talks-about-him had been selected to chop it down, and he set upon it with his ax. He had killed many enemies. At midmorning, his bare back shiny with sweat, he gave a final blow and the tree groaned and swayed and toppled into a stand of willows. The men who had been waiting jumped upon the tree and began to slash and hack, cutting off the limbs as though they were the arms and legs of their enemies. Not too long ago, these would have been traditional enemies; now, more than one of the Braves was killing the encroaching Napikwans.

Heavy Shield Woman sat in the Sacred Vow lodge, her face drawn and gray with her fast. Soon it would be over, but the thought of food had become distant and distasteful. She listened to her helpers talk quietly among themselves, but the words were not clear to her ears. She prayed to the Above Ones, to the Below Ones and to the four directions for strength and courage, but each time she began her prayers, her mind drifted and she saw her husband as he had appeared at her lodge door after his long absence. She had greeted him with high feelings, with much crying, hugging and wailing. She was overjoyed to have her man return. But later, as they sat quietly, she had been surprised to feel only pity for him. He was not the strong warrior who had left camp in that moon of the falling leaves. This man was a shadow who looked at her with stone eyes, who no longer showed feelings of love or hate or even warmth. And he had not changed in the ensuing moons. He was no longer a lover, hardly even a father to his children. Was he still a man? Had a bad spirit taken him over? But she, Heavy Shield Woman, had changed too.

Her thoughts were interrupted by the entrance of Heard-by-both-sides Woman and her husband, Ambush Chief. He carried the Medicine Woman bundle and would serve as ceremonial master during the transfer. When all the helpers, clad in gray blankets with red painted stripes, had seated themselves, Ambush Chief began to open the bundle, praying and singing as he did so. The first object he held up was the sacred elkskin dress. He sang of the origin of the garment while the women put the dress on Heavy Shield Woman. Then they draped an elkskin robe over her shoulders. One by one, he removed the sacred objects: the medicine bonnet of weasel skins, feather plumes and a small skin doll stuffed with tobacco seeds and human hair; the sacred digging stick that So-at-sa-ki, Feather Woman, had used to dig turnips when she was married to Morning Star and lived in the sky with him and his parents, Sun Chief and Night Red Light. She and Morning Star had an infant son named Star Boy.

Ambush Chief told of the time So-at-sa-ki, while digging turnips, had dug up the sacred turnip, creating a hole in the sky. She looked down and saw her people, her mother and father, her sister, on the plains and she grew homesick. Night Red Light, upon hearing of her daughter-in-law's act, became angry, for she had warned Feather Woman not to dig up the sacred turnip. Sun Chief, when he returned from his journey, became angry with Morning Star, for he had not kept his wife from doing this, and so he sent Feather Woman back to earth to live with her people. She took Star Boy with her because Sun did not want him in his house. She also took the elkskin dress, the bonnet, the digging stick. She and her son rode down the wolf trail back to her people, and she was happy to be with them. She hugged them and rejoiced, for she was truly glad to be home. But as the sleeps, the moons, went by, she began to miss her husband. Each morning she would watch him rise up. She shunned the company of her mother and father, her sister, even her son, Star Boy. She became obsessed with Morning Star, and soon she began to weep and beg him to take her back. But each morning he would go his own way, and it was not long before Feather Woman died of a broken heart.

As Star Boy began to grow up, a scar appeared on his face. The older he grew, the larger and deeper the scar grew. Soon his friends taunted him and called him Poia, Scar Face, and the girls shunned him. In desperation he went to a many-faces man who gave him directions to Sun Chief's home and whose wife made Scar Face moccasins for his journey. After much traveling, he reached the home of Sun Chief far to the west. Sun had just returned from his long trip across the sky and he was angry with Scar Face for entering his home. Sun Chief decided to kill him, but Night Red Light interceded on behalf of the unlucky young man. Morning Star, not knowing the youth was his son, taught him many things about Sun and Moon, about the many groups of Star People. Once, while on a hunt, seven large birds attacked Morning Star, intending to kill him, but Scar Face got to them first, killing them. When Morning Star told his father of this brave deed, Sun Chief removed the scar and told the youth to return to his people and instruct them to honor him every summer and he would restore their sick to health and cause the growing things and those that fed upon them to grow abundantly. He then gave Poia two raven feathers to wear so that the people would know he came from the Sun. He also gave him the elkskin robe to be worn by a virtuous medicine woman at the time of the ceremony. Star Boy then rode down the wolf trail to earth and instructed the Pikunis in the correct way, and then he returned to Sun's home with a bride. Sun made him a star in the sky. He now rides near to Morning Star and many people mistake him for his father. That is why he is called Mistake Morning Star. And that is how the Sun ceremony came to be.

While Ambush Chief related this story of Scar Face, three helpers were building an altar near the lodge door. They stripped off the sod and dry-painted Sun, Moon and Morning Star. They painted sun dogs on either side of Sun's face to represent his war paint. Then the helpers chanted and shook their rattles to pay homage to Sun and his family. When they finished, Ambush Chief stood and lifted his face.

"Great Sun! We are your people and we live among all your people of the earth. I now pray to you to grant us abundance in summer and health in winter. Many of our people are sick and many are poor. Pity them that they may live long and have enough to eat. We now honor you as Poia taught our long-ago people. Grant that we may perform our ceremony in the right way. Mother Earth, we pray to you to water the plains so that the grass, the berries, the roots may grow. We pray that you will make the four-leggeds abundant on your breast. Morning Star, be merciful to your people as you were to the one called Scar Face. Give us peace and allow us to live in peace. Sun Chief, bless our children and allow them long lives. May we walk straight and treat our fellow creatures in a merciful way. We ask these things with good hearts."

Before they left the lodge, the helpers with brushes obliterated their dry paintings, just as Sun had removed the scar from Poia.

Red Paint stood next to her husband and watched the procession. The ground was already becoming dusty from the people and horses. Earlier the people had been busy setting up their lodges, getting water from the clear, deep creek that came out of Four Persons Butte, gathering firewood. But now they were all here, watching the procession, moving to the beat of a single small drum. Red Paint was shocked at how old and bent her mother looked. She wasn't even certain that the woman was her mother. Her face was hidden by the hanging weasel skins. Two helpers held her up.

The procession circled halfway around the unfinished Medicine Lodge. Then they entered a sun shelter to the west of it. Here, the tongues were distributed to the sick, the poor, the children, to all who desired such communion. The women who had vowed to come forward to the tongues opened the parfleches and distributed pieces to the faithful. Heavy Shield Woman, weak from her lack of food, watched the people chew the tongues and she prayed, moving her lips, without words.

It was nearly dark by the time the men of the warrior societies began the task of erecting the center pole of the Medicine Lodge. With long poles they advanced from the four directions, singing to the steady drumbeat. With rawhide lines attached to their poles, they raised the cottonwood log until it stood in the hole dug to receive it. Heavy Shield Woman watched the proceedings with prayers and apprehension, for if it failed to stand straight, she would be accused of not being a virtuous woman. But it did stand, and the men began hurriedly to attach it to posts and poles around the perimeter of the lodge. Younger men began to pile brush and limbs over the structure. Now Heavy Shield Woman sighed and slumped into the arms of two of her assistants. They carried her back to her lodge, where the hot berry soup awaited her. She could break her fast.

For the next four days the weather dancers danced to the beat of rattles against drum. Warriors enacted their most courageous exploits and hung offerings on the center pole. For each deed they placed a stick on the fire until it blazed high night and day. In other lodges Sacred Pipe men and Beaver Medicine men performed their ceremonies for those who sought their help.

All day and into the night, young men in full regalia paraded their horses around the perimeter of the enormous camp. The All Crazy Dogs had a difficult time policing the grounds. But they had discovered none of the white man's water in the encampment, and for that they were grateful. Sometimes they even had time to enter into the stick games that were being played. Throughout the night, the taunting songs of the various sides increased in volume as the stakes grew higher. During the day there were many horse races. Bands raced against each other, societies had their own horses and riders. The betting was heavy and some men lost their entire herds and possessions, even their weapons. Fights broke out over the close races and the All Crazy Dogs moved in, scattering the participants in all directions. And always there were the drums, the singing and dancing.

White Man's Dog awoke at dawn one day with a terrible dread in his heart. He had eaten and drunk nothing the previous day and he could hear his stomach rumble. He sat up in the robes and his body was wet with sweat. The days and even the nights had been hot, but this sweat had nothing to do with heat. He sat up and listened to the steady *thunk! thunk! thunk!* of a single drum. It was the only sound in camp and it was not a call to celebrate but to let the people know where they were.

White Man's Dog looked down at Red Paint. Her loose dark hair fell down around her shoulder. He touched the soft skin. His hand was rough and dark, and it seemed to him that the hand and the shoulder were made of two different substances. He was awed by the power of their lovemaking, and as he looked at her neck and shoulder he was filled with desire. The quiet camp seemed far away to him as he lay back down and reached for and fondled her breasts. He wanted her to wake up and he wanted this dawn to last. But then the thought of the day's ceremony entered his mind and his desire left him.

He stood at the back of the perimeter of lodges and peed. To the east, the first streak of orange crossed the sky. He smelled the prairie grass and the sagebrush and the sweet mustiness of the horses who watched him. He listened to the clear song of the yellow-breast crouched in the grass to his right. Two long-tails flew through the sky toward Four Persons Butte, their black-and-white bodies bobbing lightly through the morning sky. He looked back toward the camp. Most of the outer lodges were unpainted, or had simply painted designs of ocher earth, black sky and yellow constellations. The sacred tipis of Beaver, Blackhorn, Bear and Otter were on the inside of the perimeter, facing the Medicine Lodge. As he watched the sky lighten, the wisps of smoke grew fainter. White Man's Dog stood in the quiet dawn, his heart beating strong with all the power of the Pikunis. He felt ready for the ordeal ahead of him.

Mik-api sat back on his haunches and looked down at White Man's Dog. They were in a brush shelter just to the side of the big Medicine Lodge. The black paint dots trailing from the corners of the young man's eyes glistened in the dappled sunlight. Mik-api looked satisfied. He and two other old men, Chewing Black Bones and Grass Bull, had painted White Man's Dog's body white with double rows of black dots down each arm and leg. On his head they placed a wreath of sage grass and bound the same grass around his wrists and ankles. As the tear paint dried on his cheeks, the old men prayed that he would acquit himself well so that Sun Chief would smile on him in all his undertakings.

Then they led him into the Medicine Lodge and he lay down on a blanket on the north side of the Medicine Pole. He heard a man on the other side recite war honors, and he felt the hands of Mik-api and Grass Bull on his arms. Chewing Black Bones knelt over him with a real-bear claw longer than a man's finger. The man reciting war honors stopped. White Man's Dog looked into Mik-api's eyes and bit his lower lip. He felt the searing pain in his left breast as Chewing Black Bones pierced it with the bear claw. His breathing made a hissing sound in the quiet lodge. Again he felt the claw pierce his flesh, this time on the right breast. His eyes were squinted tight but the tears leaked from them. And now he felt the sarvisberry sticks being pushed under his skin and he looked down and saw the rich blood pouring down onto his arms. Mik-api and Grass Bull helped him up and held him as Chewing Black Bones attached the rawhide lines that hung from the top of the Medicine Pole to the skewers in his breasts.

"Now go to the Medicine Pole and thank Sun Chief for allowing you to fulfill your vow."

White Man's Dog approached the pole and thanked Sun for helping him on his raid and for protecting him. He asked for forgiveness for desiring his father's young wife and he saw Kills-close-to-the-lake that night running from him and he asked her forgiveness too. He felt his head get light and he almost collapsed with pain. He thanked Sun for his fine new wife and vowed to be good and true to all the people. Finally, he asked Sun to give him strength and courage to endure his torture. Then he backed away from the pole and began to dance. He danced to the west, toward the lodge door. He danced to the drum and rattle. From somewhere behind him he heard the bird-bone whistle of a many-faces man, and he felt the sticky warm blood coursing down from his wounds. Then he heard the drum speed up and he danced harder, pulling harder against the lines attached to his breasts. He danced and twisted and pulled and when he thought he couldn't stand the pain the left skewer broke loose, swinging him around to his knees. He bit his lip until he tasted blood mixed with the salty tears running down into his mouth over the black painted tears. He pushed himself up to his feet again and danced to the east, away from the door. He leaned away from the Medicine Pole and jerked his body back and forth, but the second skewer would not give. His head was fuzzy with red and black images and only the pain kept him there in the lodge. Then he saw the dawn and the long-tails and the patient horses. He heard the yellow-breast singing in his ears and then it turned into a voice, loud and deep, and it recited the victories it had gained over its enemies. Raven flew into the lodge and sat down between Red Paint and Kills-close-to-the-lake. One more step, he cawed, think of Skunk Bear, your power—and he felt the other skewer pull free and he fell backward into the darkness.

Mik-api rose and cut the bloody skewers from their rawhide tethers. Small strips of flesh hung from them. He carried them to the Medicine Pole and laid them at the base. "Here is the offering of White Man's Dog," he said. "Now he is for certain a man, and Sun Chief will light his way. His friend Mik-api has spoken to you."

White Man's Dog slept that night by himself a good distance from the encampment of the Pikunis. His wounds were raw and swollen and his stomach had become a small knot, for he had still not eaten. In the distance he could hear the thundering rumble of the drums as the dancing picked up. He lay in his robe on the flat ground and watched Seven Persons and the Lost Children in the night sky. To the east, Night Red Light had risen full over the prairie. Once he saw a star feeding, its long white tail a streak across the blackness.

Then he was dreaming of a river he had never seen before. The waters were white and the sky and ground glistened as though covered with frost. As he watched the white water flow over the white stones, his eye caught a dark shape lying in the white brush. Then he was down beside the water and the wolverine looked up at him with a pitiful look.

"It is good to see you again, brother," he said. "I have got myself caught again and there is no one around but you."

"But why is it so white, Skunk Bear?" White Man's Dog had to shield his eyes from the glare.

"That's the way it is now. All the breathing things are gone—except for us. But hurry, brother, for I feel my strength slipping away."

White Man's Dog released the animal for the second time.

Skunk Bear felt of his parts and said, "All there. For a while, brother, I thought I was a shadow." Then he reached into his parfleche and took out a slender white stone. "For you, brother. You carry that with you when you go into battle, and you sing this song:

"*Wolverine is my brother, from Wolverine I take my*
     courage,
  Wolverine is my brother, from Wolverine I take my
     strength,
  Wolverine walks with me.

"You sing that loudly and boldly and you will never want for power."

White Man's Dog watched the wolverine cross the river and amble up the white bluff on the other side. Near the top, the animal turned and called, "I help you because twice you have rescued me from the Napikwans' steel jaws. But you must do one other thing: When you kill the blackhorns, or any of the four-leggeds, you must leave a chunk of liver for Raven, for it was he who guided you to me. He watches out for all his brothers, and that is why we leave part of our kills for him."

"He will be the first to eat of my kills," called White Man's Dog. "Good luck, my brother!" But Skunk Bear had disappeared over the top of the bluff.

As White Man's Dog turned to leave, he saw in the glittering whiteness a figure approaching the river. He became frightened and hid behind a white tree. As the figure passed, he saw it was a young woman dressed in white furs and carrying two water bladders. He watched her dip the bladders into the river until they were full; then she hung them from a branch and took off her furs. She was slender but her breasts and hips were round. She stepped over the stones to the water's edge, arched her back and dove in. She came up and swung her long hair, and White Man's Dog became rigid with desire for her. He wanted his arms around her smooth brown back and he wanted to lay her down in the white grass. As he approached the riverbank, he began to take off his clothes and he heard a song which seemed to come from him. The young woman turned and looked at him. It was Kills-close-to-the-lake. She made no attempt to cover herself.

White Man's Dog quickly turned away.

"Are you afraid of me?"

"No, I am afraid for myself," he said.

"Why? Do you desire me?"

"I can't say. It is not proper."

"Why not? This is the place of dreams. Here, we may desire each other. But not in that other world, for there you are my husband's son."

White Man's Dog looked at her, and he felt nothing but desire. He tried to feel shame, guilt, but these feelings would not come.

"You may desire me, if you wish. Nothing will happen. You may lie with me, if you like." She moved out of the water and stood before him. She looked into his eyes, and he saw Kills-close-to-the-lake for the first time. He saw the hunger she had kept hidden, he saw her beauty, and he saw her spirit.

So they lay down in the white grass together, their bodies warm and alive. He covered her breasts with his hands and pressed his mouth to her slender neck. He smelled her familiar scent and knew it was her. She moved beneath him and pulled him down and he closed his eyes. He felt her fingers tracing worlds on his back, and then he slept.

White Man's Dog awoke with his cheek against the damp dawn grass. At first he didn't know where he was. He was all alone and it frightened him. He sat up quickly and felt the sudden pain of his chest. He looked down and saw the strip of trade cloth that had been wound around his torso. Beneath the cloth he saw the leaves and the salve, and he remembered the events of the previous day. He was weak with hunger, and he fell back on his elbows. Sun was not yet up, but he saw Morning Star on the eastern horizon and, above him, Mistake Morning Star. He shook his head as though the whiteness of the stars had blinded him or reminded him of another place.

When he awoke the second time, Red Paint was kneeling beside him, his father and mother standing behind her. Red Paint smiled at him and helped him up and held him tenderly to her. Her hair smelled of sweet grass, and he whispered in her ear, "You are my woman, Red Paint, and I will always be your man." He felt her lips move against his cheek but he couldn't make out the words.

He turned and touched his mother, holding her away from the pain. She looked anxiously into his eyes.

"I am proud of you, my son," said Rides-at-the-door. "Mik-api tells me you did not cry out once."

"Mik-api is kind," said White Man's Dog.

Rides-at-the-door laughed and hugged him vigorously. He let out a howl and then he laughed too. As White Man's Dog gathered up his robe, he saw a small object fall out. It was a white stone almost as big around and long as his little finger. He tucked it into the strip of cloth around his chest and caught up with his wife.

Mountain Chief stood before the gathered people. He was a tall man with a long handsome face creased by the winds of many winters. His shirt and leggings were made of antelope skin with dyed quill trim down the arms and legs. Weasel-skin pendants hung from the neck and shoulders. His bonnet was made of thirty eagle feathers standing upright from a folded rawhide headband, decorated with red flannel and brass disks. He raised his arms and the people fell silent.

"Haiya! Listen, my people, for I speak to you with a good heart. Once again we have constructed the Sun Lodge in the way we were taught by our long-ago people. Let it stand to remind passersby that the Pikuni are favored among all peoples. We have smoked the long-pipes together and are at peace with ourselves. Many have left presents for Sun Chief, and some among us have fulfilled vows made in times of trouble. Our children have learned much of the good way. Heavy Shield Woman and her helpers have shown our young girls the way to virtue. Our young men have listened to the wisdom of their chiefs. I believe our father, Sun Chief, is satisfied with us. He will bring us rain at the proper time so that the grass grows and the berries ripen. He will cause the blackhorns to be thick and everlasting upon our land. He will heal our sick and take pity on the poor. . . ."

White Man's Dog heard the sound of horses off to the right, in the area of Mountain Chief's band's lodges. He stole a glance and saw several young men sitting on their horses. He recognized Owl Child and Black Weasel and Bear Chief. The rigidity with which they sat, as they listened to the head chief, made White Man's Dog tense. They had not been around during the ceremonies. Some thought they had remained north of the Medicine Line after Mountain Chief's band fled up there. Others heard they had gone far south to the country where the Napikwans dug the yellow dust. But here they were, proud, arrogant, ignoring the people who glanced out of the corners of their eyes, dividing their attention between these intruders and their chief. Just as he was about to turn back to Mountain Chief's speech, he glimpsed the black legs and head of a horse on Owl Child's far side. He watched for a while and soon the horse, with a shudder, moved forward a couple of steps and he recognized Fast Horse. Like the other riders, he wore face paint and earrings and a Napikwan shirt, gartered at the elbows. His hair was tightly braided with pieces of red flannel. It had been two moons since White Man's Dog had seen him, and he looked leaner in the face and harder in the body. He seemed to listen to the speech but his face gave away nothing.

White Man's Dog stood and slipped behind a near lodge. He circled the inner lodges until he could see the backs of the riders. Then he walked forward slowly until he was standing beside the black horse. It was a good, strong animal but it wasn't the horse Fast Horse had stolen from the Crow camp. White Man's Dog looked up and at first Fast Horse would not recognize his presence. Then Fast Horse scratched the back of his neck, turned and looked down. He looked at White Man's Dog and a grin slowly spread across his face. It was a triumphant grin and his eyes remained hard. Then he turned his attention to the remainder of the speech, the grin still in place.

". . . I myself have never liked the Napikwans, and I say to you now I would do anything to rid this land of their presence. But many of our chiefs have spoken against me and I respect their arguments. They say that Napikwan is a way of life now. Some even suggest that we go to his schools and his churches. They say if we learn his language, we can beat him with his own words.

"As you know, the white chiefs soon will move the agency from Many Houses to the Milk River to be nearer to us. I believe this will happen before the falling-leaves moon. Already they have taken much of our land, and now they will want more. They are like the yellow-wings who hop about, eating everything in their path. Soon there will be nothing to feed upon." Mountain Chief paused and looked down at a group of children who sat near his feet. His eyes softened and he almost smiled at these young Pikunis. He lifted his head. "But I will do as my chiefs demand. We will counsel with the whites, and if they do not want too much, we will make a new treaty. My heart is not in this, but I will accede to the wishes of my people."

Owl Child suddenly whirled his horse, and in an instant the other riders followed. White Man's Dog jumped back but the tail of the black horse caught him across the face. He rubbed his cheek and watched the riders gallop out of camp and across a field and out of sight behind a rise. It happened so fast that many people saw only a cloud of dust.

Mountain Chief saw it all, and he waited until the drumming hoofbeats died away. If he had been affected, he gave no sign. He was a chief. "Now we will go our separate ways and rejoin the hunt. Let there be no bickering among you, for our plains are vast and the blackhorns plentiful. You young men keep away from the white man's water. I wish you good traveling and good hunting. Sun Chief has been honored and feels kindly toward his children. I grasp hands with all of you. My words enter your ears from my heart. Farewell."

□　□　□

As White Man's Dog helped pack the lodge furnishings on the travois, he watched the Small Robes leave the encampment. Heavy-charging-in-the-brush rode at the lead, followed by the warriors, who were singing a traveling song. Behind them came the women riding the travois horses. Children and old ones rode the travois, watching the other bands take down their lodges and pack up. The camp dogs, so boisterous during the encampment, now trotted patiently beside the packhorses. At the rear, young boys drove the loose horses, snapping pieces of rawhide at them and shouting insults.

White Man's Dog was anxious to be gone. He had learned from his father that they would head for the Sweet Grass Hills. The grass was always long there, and the buffalo caused the plains to be black as far as one could see. Also he was happy because the Sweet Grass Hills were not far from the Medicine Line. He did not like Owl Child's reaction to Mountain Chief's call for peace with the Napikwans. If trouble came, the Lone Eaters could run across the line in a day's time. The thought of running shamed him, but he now had to think of Red Paint as well as his family.

He walked over to his father's lodge to see if he could help them, but they were tying on the last of their belongings. His mother told him to get a kettle of water to douse the fire. He was glad for something to do and walked swiftly down the path to the small creek. As he neared the dam of sticks and mud, he saw Heavy Shield Woman bathing her face and arms. She was his mother-in-law now and according to custom he must not look at her face again, so he walked through the brush downstream until he came to a pool close to the bank. He lay on his belly and sucked in the cool water. He sat back and wiped his mouth. It was pleasant in the shade of the big-leaf trees, and he was glad to get away from people. He sighed and closed his eyes but he knew they would be waiting for him. He dipped the kettle full of water and turned to leave.

Kills-close-to-the-lake stood in the path. White Man's Dog realized he had not seen much of her during the encampment, but she probably spent her time with her parents, who were of the

Never Laughs band. They were camped several bands away from the Lone Eaters. As White Man's Dog looked at her face, he saw something different about her. At first he thought she looked different because he had not seen her for several sleeps. Her face was still young but her eyes were deeper, as though she had become someone else, a woman that White Man's Dog had never seen before. He started to speak when he noticed that her left hand was thickly bundled with cloth. He saw only three fingers sticking out of the bandage.

"You sacrificed a finger," he said quietly.

"It is not uncommon. It is done at the Sun Dance honoring ceremony."

"You made a vow?"

"I had a dream," she said and walked past him and knelt by the water. He watched her drink from a cupped hand and then splash water on her face and neck. Then she stood and walked a short way upstream. She leaned against a big-leaf tree and shuddered deep down. Her eyes darkened with pain as she lifted the bandaged hand to her breast.

"You should rest—for the journey."

"It was a dream about you," she said. She did not look at him. "It was the moon when the heavy snows come, but it was not cold. It was as warm as it is now. You were down here by this creek and all around it was white. You hid behind this tree but I saw you. You watched me bathe in the waters. I felt your eyes on my body and I got light-headed. I pretended I didn't notice you"—she lowered her eyes to the bandaged hand—"but then I felt something crawling all over my skin as though the water held tiny hot fleas. But when I turned to you, you were gone. In your place stood a short heavy animal with long claws and sharp teeth. He said, 'Come to me, sister, and I will show you magic.' He was the creature that lives by himself in the Backbone. All the others fear him, but I didn't. I came out of the water and let him ravish me. I didn't care; you had gone away. When he had finished, he bit this finger off. Before he left he threw the finger on the ground and it turned into a white stone. 'Let this always remind you of your wickedness, sister. You're lucky I didn't bite your nose off.'

I threw myself into the white grass and wept, for he had revealed what I had kept hidden even from myself. And it was so hopeless, this desire! I wept until all my tears, all my desires and hope, were gone and I felt lighter. I could see more clearly and I saw nothing ahead of me and I was content with this vision. I found the white stone and carried it to where you were sleeping after your torture. I placed it in the robe beside you so that you would be reminded of your good fortune."

White Man's Dog watched her run away from him. His mind was tangled with confusion. That white world she described was familiar to him. He had been there and had seen the white river. the white ground. And he had seen a dark creature and, yes, it had been Wolverine. Then he remembered the animal with white fur that had come to drink. It was a slender, lovely animal and he had watched it drink from the white waters. He had been in that world but he hadn't seen Kills-close-to-the-lake.

He felt in his small war bag that hung around his neck and he pulled out the white stone, and as he caressed it, he sang softly:

"*Wolverine is my brother, from Wolverine I take my*
courage,
Wolverine is my brother, from Wolverine I take my
strength,
Wolverine walks with me."

White Man's Dog didn't know how or why, but Wolverine had cleansed both him and Kills-close-to-the-lake. He had also given White Man's Dog his power, in the white stone and the song.

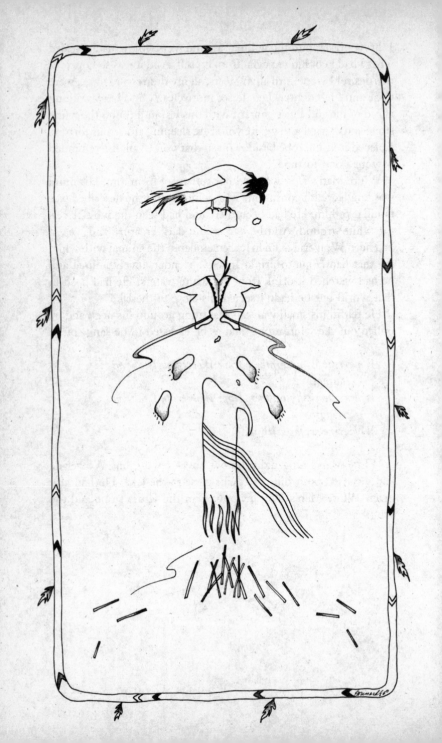

PART
TWO

II

Early in the moon of the burnt grass, not long after the Sun Dance, Red Paint sat outside her lodge resting her back. She had just fleshed a green blackhorn hide, and now it lay stretched to dry in the sun. She looked at the glistening white skin and it reminded her of the puffballs that grew in the valleys of the Backbone. She wished she was there now; the rivers were clearer and colder, the smell of pine was always sharp in the air—and the chokecherries would be ripening. Only last summer she had been a girl and had accompanied her mother and some other women up the Two Medicine River to pick the tangy cherries. It was there she had seen the round mushrooms and had picked one the size of her fist and held it against her cheek. It gave off a dry musky odor, and its skin was as smooth and hard as her own thigh. Except for the short dark whiskers on the bottom, it was as nearly a perfect thing as she had ever seen. She had taken it home to her father's lodge, but soon it became leathery and collapsed in upon itself. One day she squeezed it and it split, sending out a puff of green smoke.

In six days White Man's Dog would ride with the war party against the Crows. As she rubbed her neck and looked off to the Sweet Grass Hills, she felt again the dread that came whenever she allowed herself to think. She had tried to stay busy, but even a momentary lapse in concentration allowed that dreaded thought to steal through her whole body. She knew that war parties were part of a man's life and she knew that she should be proud that White Man's Dog had been selected to count coup on behalf of her father, Yellow Kidney. But it was because of Yellow Kidney that she felt so fearful. In her mind the Crows had grown big and fierce. She knew of their cruelty, and she was afraid White Man's Dog would become foolish in his desire to avenge her father. Last night he had told her he would look for the lodge of that treacherous enemy, Bull Shield, and bring his head back for Yellow Kidney to spit upon. She knew this was the way a man prepared himself for a war party. All the men were talking this way; she had heard her own father tell of cruelties he would inflict upon the enemy—but that was in the past now. She just wanted her husband to be safe.

Her husband. Once again Red Paint marveled that she was married and keeper of her own lodge; even more she found it unbelievable that she had come to love White Man's Dog with such heart. Now when he was away hunting, she could hardly wait for his return. And when he did return safely, she offered up silent prayers and cooked such big meals he complained that he was getting fat. Sometimes at night they would sleep away from camp under the stars, naked in their robes. They told ghost stories until both were frightened; then they made love as though the night were made only for that. Afterward, she would tell him more stories and make him laugh at her wild inventions. But the way he held her when he slept made her a little afraid—for she would never be able to live without him, without this love.

And now he was restless and he would not be at peace until he had counted war honors against the Crows. Last night he had struggled and cried out in his sleep, and she knew that he was frightened.

Red Paint unrolled another green blackhorn hide and began to stake it down. As she pounded with her stone hammer, she thought again of the chokecherries in the mountains and wished they were there now, just she and White Man's Dog. And maybe a little one inside of her. For the first time in four winters, she had missed her time to bleed. It was far too early to tell anything, but in her heart she was sure she was with child. She looked toward the lodge and saw a butterfly flitting against the stretched cover. It landed on the tied-back entrance flap. It was small and white with black-tipped wings. "Sleep-bringer," she whispered to herself.

"Daughter! Why is it you daydream when all the other women are dressing blackhorns? Let me help you." Heavy Shield Woman took the stone hammer from her daughter and quickly staked down the hide. It had been sixteen sleeps since she had been the Sacred Vow Woman, and she was recovering her strength. Red Paint looked at her face and in the bright sunlight it looked shrunken, the lines around her eyes and mouth deeper, the hollows of her cheeks shadowy. Even her strong brown fingers looked almost bony. But she struck the stakes with great force, driving them easily.

"You look different to me, Mother. Have you not recovered from your fast?"

Heavy Shield Woman stopped pounding and looked across the skin at her daughter. "It is the same as giving birth," she said. "One expects a little change. Someday soon I will appear as I was before, but I will always be different—in here." She thumped her chest.

"I want you to be strong and happy." Red Paint bent over the skin and began to work her fleshing knife over the surface, scraping away the dark meat. She wondered what the white people would make out of the robe. Once she had asked her father and he said they made big shirts and leggings out of them. He said they dressed like bears in their big towns because their skin wasn't used to the cold. But he often joked with her, so she didn't know if he was telling the truth. Yellow Kidney's lodge had once been filled with laughter.

"How is my father today?"

"Better." Heavy Shield Woman scraped a long thin strip of flesh from the hide and tossed it in the trampled grass behind her. A fawn-colored dog darted in, snatched it up and ran away. "Just this morning he made a harness for his right hand. He tied a short piece of skunk rib to it and is going to try to fire his gun with that. He can hold it, all right. He just needs a trigger-puller."

Red Paint sat back on her heels. A sudden breeze filled her nose with the scent of dry sage. "Is he going to be all right?"

"These changes take time. Already you see he is trying to become the hunter he once was." Heavy Shield Woman busied herself with a thick strand of meat. "He is a tough man, your father."

"But I mean—inside, in here, his heart."

Heavy Shield Woman did not look up. "He is not the same man. He no longer laughs, he doesn't play with your brothers or instruct them"—she ripped the scrap of meat loose—"he does not touch me if he can help it." She felt a stab of guilt, for she did not mind that part. Since becoming a Sacred Vow Woman— even before that—she had lost the desire to hold her man close. In some ways he had become a child to her. She looked after him the way she cared for Good Young Man and One Spot.

"What can we do?" said Red Paint. Her voice was a wail. "My poor mother, we must do something for him! We must restore him!"

"Do not weep, child. I have talked with Mik-api. You know his magic. He assured me that he can drive this bad spirit from Yellow Kidney, but he must have your father's cooperation. So far your father prefers to dwell in his own thoughts, to pity himself as though he were the only one whom misfortune struck."

Red Paint almost flinched from her mother's bitter words.

But Heavy Shield Woman laughed. "At least he has his hair back. I have been rubbing his head with tonic from the sharp vine. Now it is almost as thick as it once was. But he does not eat. I can't force the food down his throat, can I?"

Red Paint looked off toward the lodge. The butterfly was gone. Soon it would be too hot to work, and she looked forward to going into her lodge alone, to lie down and listen to the silence. She was tired and longed for the cool breezes that whispered down the valleys of the Backbone. She longed to be there with her husband and to lie in the lodge and listen to the cold water rushing over the stones. "I think I am growing a baby inside me," she said. She meant to add that she felt it only in her heart, but as soon as she said it, she saw the tears in Heavy Shield Woman's eyes. Her mother dropped her scraping knife and scrambled across the skin to kneel before her daughter, hugging her in her thin arms. She hugged Red Paint and wailed to the sky. Red Paint felt the tears on her own cheeks and suddenly felt happier for her mother than for herself. Perhaps a baby would bring them all closer again. Perhaps laughter would again ring out in Yellow Kidney's lodge. She looked again at the place where the butterfly had landed. If there was a baby. But she knew it in her heart, and she would tell White Man's Dog when he returned that evening.

The young warriors of Crow Foot's band galloped their horses through and around the camp. They whooped and shot their guns into the air. The puffs of smoke from the barrels were carried to the north by a strong south wind. Most of them were shirtless and their bodies were painted with war paint. Crow Foot himself wore his flowing war bonnet. His face was painted red with three black crow tracks on each cheek. He pulled to a halt before the lodge of Three Bears. "Haiya! Three Bears! Are there any Lone Eaters brave enough to take to the war road? My young men say yours are puny and would do nothing but slow us down."

Three Bears stood in his finest regalia. He too wore the flowing headdress of the Parted Hairs. His war shirt and leggings were of soft elkskin decorated with quillwork and beads. He raised his long-pipe. He was as excited as his young men. "Ah, Crow Foot, your braves are children against mine. I myself, old as I am, stand over your strongest man. If it weren't for the length of the ride, I would accompany you and count coup on those insects myself."

Crow Foot laughed. "Where's my friend, Rides-at-the-door? I suppose he is too old too."

Again the warriors galloped through camp, shouting insults and making fierce faces. But by then several of Three Bears' men had started beating on a communal drum with sticks and singing wolf songs. The songs had no words, only the attacking cries of the bigmouths. Some of the Lone Eaters had spears and shields and feinted at the riders as they galloped by.

Rides-at-the-door trotted toward the two men, wiping dust

from his eyes. His war paint was simple, a blue streak from his forehead to the tip of his nose, but his blackhorn headdress made him look big. The curly hair of the topknot had been dyed gray.

"Welcome, Crow Foot. I see you do not teach your young ones to save their shooters."

The two men embraced. "It is a good time," said Crow Foot. "Tonight we make noise. When the sun rises we will join the others who assemble at the camp of the Small Robes. Does your son ride with us?"

"Both of them. Running Fisher hasn't slept for three nights. He lies outside the lodge and watches Seven Persons take the night journey. As for White Man's Dog, he looks forward to many war honors. He is no longer a boy."

"I saw him dancing from the Medicine Pole. He acquitted himself well." Crow Foot looked at his friend shrewdly. "I hear he is married too."

"Yes, sometimes these things happen. He is married to Yellow Kidney's daughter, Red Paint." Rides-at-the-door glanced into Crow Foot's face. He hoped his friend wouldn't feel dishonored because White Man's Dog had rejected his daughter.

Crow Foot watched the mock attacks for a moment. Then he laughed. "You know that crazy daughter of mine, Little Bird Woman? That nothing-girl is going to marry into the Grease Melters. Three Suns' oldest boy. I tried to talk her out of it, but she told me Three Suns is a great chief. I don't know about her."

Rides-at-the-door smiled. He felt relieved, for Little Bird Woman was going to marry into a very important family. Three Suns was next in line to become head chief of the Pikunis.

"This talk of women depresses me. My sits-beside-me woman gives me nothing but trouble these days," said Three Bears. "Now gather up your important men and bring them to my lodge. We will smoke the pipe. I myself do not see anybody out there worth smoking with."

The booming of three different drum groups carried far into the night. Wolf songs, scalp dances and honoring songs competed with each other. The girls of the Lone Eaters sang celebration songs. Then they sang a love song that broke up into giggles. Inside the men's society lodge, the older warriors feasted and counted war honors. Before the group broke up, Three Bears passed the ceremonial pipe and offered a prayer for the party's safe return. He burned a braid of sweet grass and fanned the purifying smoke through the lodge, then declared that the pipe was empty. The men filed out, some to sleep with relatives or friends, others to stretch their soft-tanned rolls out under the stars. From one of the lodges came the last sad notes of night song. Then the camp was quiet beneath a yellow half-moon.

Red Paint lay beside her husband, her right arm and leg slung over his wide body. His right arm lay beneath her, his hand stroking the small of her back.

"Are you happy for us?" she murmured against his chest.

"Yes, very happy."

"You have been quiet these last days. You think of the war trail."

"I think of many things, but making war on the Crows is uppermost in my mind," he admitted.

"You will be successful, I think. You are the strongest of the Pikunis."

White Man's Dog slapped her butt and laughed. "Yes, but am I stronger than all the Crows?"

"You are the strongest man I know," she said. "Stronger than the blackhorns too."

"You speak with the tongue of crawls-along-the-ground, nothing-woman."

Red Paint smiled in the darkened lodge. From far off, she heard the barking and howling of Kis-see-noh-o. Soon he was joined by his brothers, and the night was pierced by their mournful howls. "The little-wolves cry to us, my husband. Are they afraid?"

"They cry to Night Red Light. She shows half her face and they want to see the rest. They are only happy when she smiles down on them."

"And you—are you afraid?"

She felt her husband's hand go rigid against her back. He sighed and said, "Yes, I am afraid."

"Of the Crows?"

"Yes—no, not of the Crows. My medicine is strong. My luck has not been better, but—"

"Then you fear nothing?"

"There is always a chance that a Crow shooter will find me. I do not fear that, for I will die an honorable death. I have spoken with Old Man and he will guide me to the Sand Hills if I am killed. No, I do not fear for myself—Old Man knows the way."

White Man's Dog shifted and held his wife in his arms. Red Paint smelled the sweet tobacco on his breath and thought they were the closest they had ever been. She began to tremble.

"I am afraid for you—and for our infant inside of you."

"I'm not certain—"

"I have never had such responsibility, and it makes me cry to think of you alone. You are a brave and good woman, Red Paint, and you work as hard as a woman twice your size. But without meat and hides you will suffer. And I must think about your family—Yellow Kidney and your mother and brothers. They too depend on me for their meat. Your brothers are a couple of winters away from hunting for their family."

"Do not go, then." Red Paint raised herself to her elbow. "Your father will understand. He is a kind and wise man."

"Ah, if only it were that easy." White Man's Dog looked away and studied his pemmican sack hung from a lodgepole. He could barely make out the red and blue designs on it. "You see, I have chosen the way of the warrior and so I must take that trail, wherever it leads. If I were to stay behind, the others would lose respect for me. For an older warrior to say his medicine wasn't good and he must not go, it would be understandable. None would question him, for that is the way. But I am a young man and my power is good."

Red Paint rolled away and looked up through the smoke hole. She could see a few stars but they were indistinct, far away. She knew he would have to go on the war party, but for the past two days, since telling him she might be with child, she had held on to the faint hope that this knowledge would make him stay. But no. He would be thought of as a coward, to be shunned by the people he cared for, perhaps even his family. Red Paint sighed.

"I think you want a boy. Yes?"

"Yes," he admitted.

"Would you want a boy named Sleep-bringer?"

"Sleep-bringer! But why?"

"Because I saw a butterfly at the very time I was thinking of a son growing inside of me. It was white with black tips on its wings. It sat and watched me, and soon I fell asleep and dreamed wonderful dreams of a proud young man who looked like you."

"Sleep-bringer. It is a fine name."

"We shall have a naming ceremony when he is born. We will ask my father to do us this honor, but just you make sure you whisper 'Sleep-bringer' in his ear."

"Kom-i-os-che is more like it." White Man's Dog laughed as he patted Red Paint's belly. "Soon he will be struggling like a worm."

"He will want to be born so he can stand on the ground-of-many-gifts and look around. He will be just like you, only shorter."

They laughed and hugged and gradually the happiness wore off and they hugged each other tighter and listened to the coyotes sing their songs to bring the moon around.

All the war chiefs were there with the exception of Tailfeathers-coming-over-the-hill. His horse had gotten too close to a black-horn bull and the bull butted the animal, causing it to fall on the chief's leg. Someone said the leg had turned around backward and that Tailfeathers-coming-over-the-hill would not walk again. He had sent his only son, Badger, in his place and there was concern for the boy's safety, for if he were killed there would be no one left to carry on the chief's tradition. But the boy insisted, and after a brief council, Fox Eyes, the head war chief, called him over.

"We know your father wishes you to accompany us, and so you shall. But you must stick with some of the experienced men and learn all you can from them. You are young and will no doubt attempt something foolish. I will keep my eye on you and on the other young ones. The first sign of foolishness, I will turn you around and you will have to explain to your father why." Fox Eyes looked around at the assembled warriors. Some were sitting on their horses, others lounged in small groups. There were over three hundred of them. Most were proven fighters. They would have to look out for the young ones. "Good luck to you, Badger. If you listen and do as you are told, you will bring honor to your father's lodge."

The camp of the Small Robes, where all the bands' warriors had assembled, was on a grassy flat near the point where the Yellow River joined the Big River. It was here that the first big treaty was signed, nearly thirteen winters ago. Fox Eyes could remember sitting almost on the exact spot where he now stood, listening to the Napikwan chief spell out the conditions of the treaty. One of the conditions was to cease making war on the enemies. But how was that possible when the enemies continued to insult the Pikunis? Were they not justified in earning the enemy's respect once in a while? And, too, the Napikwans did not honor the treaty. They spoke high words that day, but they proved to be two-faced.

Four wolf scouts sat patiently on the bluffs to the south. Fox Eyes signaled to them and they galloped off. Then he called to his war chiefs to gather their men. It had been three winters since the last such party, the winter the Entrails People and the Crows were made to cry. Fox Eyes had been a war chief then and he had killed White Grass, the famed warrior of the Entrails People. He had brought back his enemy's head on his lance, and the Pikuni women had kicked it around before roasting it on a fire. From that time, Fox Eyes became known and feared among his people's enemies.

Now as he looked down at the faces, he prayed silently to the Above Ones to make him wise and correct in his role. He wished to return these husbands, fathers and sons to their lodges. He needed no war honors and was concerned only with his leadership, for on that would their fortunes depend. He stepped forward. The brass buttons on the tunic he had taken from a slain seizer chief glistened in the high sun.

"Hear me, warriors of the Pikuni people! Sun Chief smiles down on this spot where the Small Robes choose to summer and causes all of us joy and excitement. But he also knows that a great wrong has been done to one of his children and he wishes us to punish those who would laugh at the Pikunis. For this reason we now take to the war trail. Our brother, Yellow Kidney of the Lone Eaters, is not among us, for the Crows have mutilated him and shamed us all. In his place, White Man's Dog, son of the war chief and leader Rides-at-the-door, will count the first honor against our enemy. It has always been so with our people, and so it shall be.

"There are many among us who go to war for the first time. Let them follow the counsel of their chiefs, and no harm will come to them. If their hearts are not in this, now is the time to turn back. There is no dishonor in wisdom. For those who would be foolish and seek to gain glory only for themselves, let them also turn back. In that way there is no profit." The war chief paused and stared at the groups of young men. His eyes seemed to find each of them and look directly into their eyes. Then he lifted his head. "Now I pray to the Above Ones, to the Below Ones and to the four directions to grant us success against the Crow dogs and return us safely to our families. The war chief, Fox Eyes, is heard."

The old men, women and children watched the warriors ride away. Even the dogs did not bark or try to follow. They sat silently in small packs, tongues hanging from the midday heat. Some of the men in the rear sang a riding song as the party climbed the bluffs. The horses were all painted on the shoulders and haunches, around the legs; some in the face. Fox Eyes was the first to reach the plain. He kicked his roan horse into a faster walk, not quite a trot. His feathered shield bounced against his left arm. Made from an old bull's neck skin, it was the same shield with which he had fended off White Grass's arrows. He had hated White Grass then, and it had been this hatred which gave him the strength to kill him. Now he felt a mild regret that his old enemy was no longer around. With his victory, Fox Eyes had lost something, the desire to make his enemies pay dearly, to ride among them with a savage heart. He had lived forty-three winters, and he wished to live forty-three more in peace. Two of his sons were in the party, and he worried about them. The youngest was only sixteen. Like the other youths, he would gladly follow the counsel of the war chiefs, but when they closed upon the Crows, he would ride blindly among them, seeking to kill them all, to count war honors enough to last a lifetime. This was how the young ones were killed.

Fox Eyes looked behind him. All the warriors had made the plain. They were a fearsome group, decked out in their war regalia, their painted bodies, their fastest horses. Some of them carried plumed lances and shields, as in the old days, but most carried guns. To his left rode Rides-at-the-door and, beyond him, Crow Foot and Takes-good-gun. Crazy Dog and Lone Medicine Person and Almost-a-wolf were to his right. They were good war chiefs and would handle their men well. If the Pikunis could take their enemy by surprise, it would go well for them. Perhaps then Fox Eyes could deliver his men safely home. But if the Crows learned of their party and met them with equal force, there would be much grief in the Pikuni lodges.

They followed the Yellow River south, keeping to the plain on the east side. Two sleeps away lay the Snowy and Little Belt Mountains. To the southeast, a little closer, they could make out the dark-forested Yellow Mountains. It would be easy going. Fox Eyes and his chiefs figured they would be in Crow country in six sleeps. The wolves were good, experienced men—Eagle Ribs was among them—but in this open country they would need luck to remain undiscovered. They wore no paint, no regalia, so even if the enemy discovered them, they might think the wolves were simply lone hunters. But they would be sweeping the country for distant movements, for recent fires, for blackhorn guts. They knew the signs of men and how to interpret them. But even now, thought Fox Eyes, a Crow party or their allies could be watching us from any of the surrounding buttes. A party of three hundred men was hardly invisible.

Fox Eyes called to Lone Medicine Person, who had been most recently in the Crow country. "My friend, I hear you have taken

Crow horses this season of Home Days. Did you come upon the camp of Bull Shield?"

"We passed it by. It is on a small creek between the Bighorn River and the Red Mountains. I had too many youths with me to risk taking their horses."

Fox Eyes almost smiled. Lone Medicine Person was a rangy man with a big nose and large hands. He was proud of his horse-taking ability.

"Were they many?"

"I counted eighty lodges. And there was another camp a short distance away. Thirty-eight lodges." Lone Medicine Person spat. "And the white hide-hunters were with them. Seven of the Napikwan lodges. They had many big-ears to pull their wagons. We did not wish to get mixed up with them. Their guns are big and sound like thunder. I didn't want any of my youths to piss on themselves."

The war chiefs laughed and then the men behind them laughed. Fox Eyes' big roan put back his ears in disapproval.

"And you, Lone Medicine Person—were you frightened?"

"You bet I was. Those guns can make a man's guts want to leave his body. When I get old I want to tell my grandchildren I have seen something."

"I would like to punish Shoots-near-the-water and his people," said Crow Foot. "He took some of my best horses last heavy-wind moon. He took that big horse with the spotted rump I took from the Black Paint People on the other side of the Backbone."

"Rides-at-the-door tells me you got that horse from the Liars," said Crazy Dog. "He said you had to sleep with their ugliest woman to get him."

"Rides-at-the-door tells lies that make the Liars look good. Their women are ugly, though," admitted Crow Foot.

"They make good wives for the Napikwans. I have seen the offspring—they are pink like the entrails of the slippery swimmers. Even their eyes are pink."

Fox Eyes listened to this banter with patience. The men were happy to be finally on the move against the Crows. The tension of waiting for this journey was dispelled and the men could now joke and laugh. But it would return in a short time as they neared the enemy's camps. Fox Eyes had made up his mind, and he felt a tingle of excitement crawl up his backbone. When the talk died away, he said, "I think we will punish Bull Shield. He is the strongest of their chiefs and many will cry for him. His is the head that will be cut off so that our friend Yellow Kidney may sleep well in his lodge."

Just after midday of the fourth sleep, a strange event took place. The party had ridden down a shallow coulee just north of the Elk River, keeping above a brush line that marked the course of a dry creek. The grass around them had turned golden in the late summer sun. The yellow-wings jumped and buzzed in the air before the horses. Fox Eyes had decided to await the return of the wolves at the mouth of the coulee. From there they could see the valley of the Elk River and remain unseen. The scouts would by now have located the camp of Bull Shield. On their return a strategy could be determined.

White Man's Dog was worried about his horse. Although he didn't limp, there was something wrong with his gait, as though he were favoring a leg. White Man's Dog pulled out of the dusty stream of riders and got down. The sun was warm on his back as he felt the horse's legs and bent the fetlocks to look at the hooves. He could find nothing wrong and decided it must have been his nerves. He stretched his back and looked up to the southwest. The Day Star was a brilliant pin of light in the orange sky. He hadn't noticed how bright it was this day. He adjusted his leggings, which had ridden up his crotch during the ride, and as he did so he noticed that the sky was turning gray. He shielded his eyes and peeked between his fingers. The sun had ceased to glow and a chunk of it was missing. He had not seen this happen before. He looked down the coulee and saw the last of the riders round a bend beneath a sandy bluff. He became uneasy and tried to mount his horse but the animal shied away from him. He grabbed the horse by the ear and squeezed tightly. Around him it had become dusk. The grass which just moments before had been burnt yellow now was silver and the edges of the coulee cast shadows. Again he peered at the sun, and this time he didn't have to shield his eyes. It had become a dark ball with just a rim of glowing gold. His horse had gentled some and he released the ear and stared at the hole which had replaced Sun Chief. Gradually he became aware that his whole body was trembling. The air was colder but the trembling came from within. White Man's Dog was too frightened to pray or even to think. He heard a far-off barking of coyotes in the quiet dusk. He looked around him and the grass was shimmering. A large white stone on the other side of the dry creek was glowing as though lit from within. Then, just as the coyotes began to howl, a sliver of fire appeared at the side of the dark hole. He looked away from the light, and when he looked back, the sun had begun to grow fire wings.

Soon the sun was whole again and the air warmed quickly. The coyotes had quit howling and the gray horse grazed at the golden grass. White Man's Dog remembered his grandfather telling of a similar event. That time, when Sun hid his face, the people trembled and cried. A few days later, Emonissi, the great head chief of the Siksikas, was thrown from his horse and trampled by the blackhorns.

When he caught up with the party, all had dismounted and were crouched silently in small groups. Only the war chiefs were animated, huddled together, gesturing, their voices rising and falling as each spoke his words. He saw his father's broad back, his war shirt stretched over the powerful shoulders. The gray blackhorn headdress, his war medicine, bobbed up and down as he nodded his head. He seemed to be speaking but he didn't gesture as did the others. Fox Eyes sat passively to one side as though he didn't listen to what the others were saying.

"It is a sign we cannot ignore," Rides-at-the-door was saying.

"It is a sign of catastrophe," said Crow Foot.

White Man's Dog had crept close enough to hear their words. He squatted beside Running Fisher. He wanted to ask what the leaders had said before he arrived, but as he looked at his brother, he saw a look of cold fear. The young man's eyes were staring straight ahead, at the backs of the leaders, but he seemed to see nothing. White Man's Dog touched his shoulder, but Running Fisher didn't seem to notice. It was the first time White Man's Dog had seen real fear in his brother, and he didn't know what to do.

"We have come this far—we must go on," said Lone Medicine Person.

"We are Pikunis," said Crazy Dog. "We are not afraid."

Almost-a-wolf signed his affirmation, his fist over his heart.

"What about these young men?" said Rides-at-the-door. "They are afraid now. They can't be counted on."

"We will talk to them. Those that want to turn back, we will let them."

"Did we come here to avenge Yellow Kidney? Are we going to run away like women?"

White Man's Dog watched Fox Eyes rise and walk slowly away from the group. He was halfway to the bend that hid the party from the Elk River valley when a wolf scout rode into view. His horse was lathered and winded. He slid down and walked up to Fox Eyes. It was Eagle Ribs. White Man's Dog watched the two men talk; then he looked at his brother. The fear was still there but his eyes had come back. "A-wah-heh," whispered White Man's Dog. "Take courage, brother."

12

THEY ATTACKED THE VILLAGE of Bull Shield at dawn. White Man's Dog had sung his Wolverine power song and had tied a small pouch containing the white stone around his neck. He rode between his father and Crazy Dog, slightly ahead of them. It was his honor, in Yellow Kidney's place, to strike the enemy first. The long gallop down the hill seemed to take forever. Behind him he heard the thunder of the horses' hooves and the cries and yodeling of the warriors. A steady *pop* of rifle fire increased until it seemed that Thunder Chief, Many Drums, rode with them. White Man's Dog's throat was dry in the surging wind, and his heart beat strongly in his ears. Then he was on the flat, guiding his horse with his knees, firing his many-shots gun, his wedding present from his father, blindly at the lodges. He saw a man emerge from one of the tipis clad only in leggings. He turned the gray horse slightly and bore down on him and he heard a strange animal cry that filled his heart with fear before he realized that it came from him. His horse had his head lowered in his all-out gallop, and White Man's Dog could see the laid-back ears just below his line of fire. The man raised his musket but now White Man's Dog was upon him. He felt his horse swerve between his knees as he fired at the man's chest. The man toppled back into the entrance of his lodge and lay there with just his feet sticking out. White Man's Dog looked quickly around and saw the Pikunis weaving between the lodges, screaming and firing their weapons. Out of the corners of his eyes he saw Crow warriors scrambling out of their lodges, some shooting at the Pikunis, others running for cover.

He urged his horse forward until he was near the middle of the camp. A pack of dogs raced by, cutting him off, and he felt his horse's front legs come up off the ground. He leaned forward to regain his balance and that's when he saw a black horse rearing against a lariat tied to the lodgepole of a tipi decorated with blue buffaloes. For an instant he stared at the tipi and the panicked horse. Then he slid off his own horse and trotted between two lodges. He heard someone calling to him, a voice that he didn't recognize over the din of the guns and crying and shouting. He stepped over the body of a man who had been shot in the face. The arms and legs were still trembling. He fired a shot into the blue buffalo tipi and a man appeared at the entrance. When he stood up, his headdress fell to the ground behind him. There was a wild look in the man's eyes and White Man's Dog thought he was going to run back inside. But the man gathered his courage and began his death song. In his right hand he held a short-gun; in his other hand, a feathered shield with red sharp-cornered designs. For an instant the two men looked at each other. Then White Man's Dog heard the voice again, the one who had called to him earlier. He glanced to his left and saw the blue seizer's tunic that Fox Eyes wore. He heard a *pop* and felt a warm pain in his side. He stumbled back and fell down. As he fell, he heard Fox Eyes call out the man's name. In spite of the burning in his side, he lifted his head and watched Fox Eyes ride down on Bull Shield and knew that his chief wanted to count coup, that just shooting Bull Shield from a distance was not enough. In disbelief White Man's Dog watched the short-gun come up and fire just as Fox Eyes leaned to his right for a shot. And he saw the horse shy and Fox Eyes land in a heap at Bull Shield's feet. White Man's Dog moaned and fell back. It seemed to him that he lay there for a long time—he could hear the gunfire and the screams—but when he opened his eyes Bull Shield was still advancing. Without knowing how, he found his gun, lifted it and fired. The greased shooter tore through the warrior's shield and into his chest. He shot the warrior twice more and then his rifle was empty. Bull Shield stepped back with the first shot, as if in surprise. The second and third shots caught him in the belly and he doubled over, tottered forward with little steps and fell. White Man's Dog got to his feet—the pain was less severe now—and felt his side. His hand came away bloody. He looked down at the dead man and his head felt strange, as though it were trying not to be there. Then a horse galloped up and skidded to a stop and a rider jumped off. It was Almost-a-wolf. He gathered up Fox Eye's body and hoisted it up over the saddle, arms and legs dangling on either side of the horse. Almost-a-wolf glanced at White Man's Dog; then he was on the horse, behind the saddle, and the horse was galloping off. White Man's Dog looked back for his own horse. It was not there. As he looked about he saw bodies on the ground and men engaged in fighting. Twenty paces from where he stood he saw a look of shock on Lone Medicine Person's face as a Crow knife was plunged into his stomach. A girl of not more than three winters stood crying, holding her bloody fingers to her mouth. As he watched the girl, he heard a voice behind him; then he felt a hand grab his shoulder. He whirled about and saw that it was his father leaning down from his horse. "Take his hair, son," he said.

White Man's Dog dropped to his knees over the fallen Bull Shield. He took the hair in his left hand and made a slice across the top of the forehead. Then he began skinning the scalp back as though he were dressing a deer. At the last cut, the head fell limply forward, the white patch of bone glistening in the dusty sun.

"Get up, get up, you brave!" shouted Rides-at-the-door. "Take this fine horse, this prize Crow horse!" He had cut the black horse loose, and now he handed the lariat to White Man's Dog. "My fine son, this day you are a brave!"

White Man's Dog looked at the happy face of his father, and the strange feeling in his head went away. He swung up on the horse and felt the pain in his side sharpen. Then he and his father were galloping toward the north ridge above the camp. Several of the Pikunis were there already, shooting their guns in the air, their horses skittering nervously beneath them. On both sides of them other warriors were racing for the ridge. Behind them they heard the *pop! pop! pop!* of the Crow guns. White Man's Dog looked down at the sticky scalp in his fingers. Then he leaned over the side of the black horse and vomited.

The next day, well away from the Crow camps, they stopped to rest at the edge of Big Lake, a shallow body of water in open country. There was no danger that the Crows could organize swiftly enough to follow such a large war party this far. The men were weary with the battle and the ride, and many of them stripped and swam in the warm, weedy water. Some ate their last handfuls of pemmican while others dozed. Then the war chiefs moved among them, rousting them, and soon they were riding slowly to the northwest.

Rides-at-the-door and White Man's Dog rode behind the bodies of Fox Eyes and Lone Medicine Person. They were wrapped in sleeping skins and tied over Crow horses. White Man's Dog looked behind him and counted six other bodies in sleeping robes. Thirteen men were missing and seven more were hurt badly enough that they had to lie on makeshift travois. White Man's Dog searched for Running Fisher. He rode by himself off to the side, and his eyes were distant.

White Man's Dog stretched and the pain came, but it was only a dull throb. The shooter had opened the skin and nicked a rib. He had thanked Wolverine for giving him a war wound and he thanked him for not making it too serious.

After they had traveled a short way, Crazy Dog rode back among the men. Four of them got off their horses and built a fire. Soon the flames rippled away to the south, pushed by the strong north wind. Some of the warriors rode off and returned with greasewood from a nearby ridge. The greasewood caught fire and began to crackle, and the riders dragged it along the ground behind them. Soon the grassy plains to the south were ablaze, the heavy smoke blowing ahead of the flames.

"Now we make the Crows to cry twice. Their blackhorns will leave them and become someone else's meat," said Crazy Dog. With that he laughed and the Pikunis turned their horses north, to their own buffalo ranges.

At twilight the men stopped beside a small creek flanked by dead big-leaf trees. They built platforms in seven of them and prepared the bodies for burial. It was a simple preparation—the dead men had few weapons with them, and their horses remained in the Crow camp. Crow Foot sprinkled tobacco over the sleeping skins and commended their spirits to the Shadowland. Then the bodies were laid on the platforms and a Crow horse was shot in the ear for each of them to ride in that other world.

For Fox Eyes they found a ledge beneath a tan rock high up on the side of a bluff. Two men carried his body up the steep incline, their shoulders and backs gleaming with sweat. Three others brought his knife, his pipe and his war bag. The war chiefs followed with sacrifices of tobacco and greased shooters. Below, the men sang and wept as the body of their leader was placed beneath the ledge. Fox Eyes was the only true war leader many of them knew, and now he was gone to the Sand Hills, killed by the enemies.

White Man's Dog stood and watched the burial and thought of the afternoon a few days before when Sun Chief hid his face. And he thought of Fox Eyes riding down on Bull Shield instead of taking the simple shot that would have killed the Crow. White Man's Dog couldn't shake the feeling that Fox Eyes knew he was going to die, perhaps even wanted to. Only great chiefs died when Sun hid his face.

13

RED PAINT TRACED THE RIDGE of the war wound with her fingers. It was almost as long as her hand and was healing to a deep liver-colored stripe. She sat in the bright lodge beside her sleeping husband and watched the shadow of a spear-leaf limb sway against the south wall. The sun, even at its midpoint, was low in that direction. The nights had become cooler and the days shorter. In less than a moon, the leaves of the trees would begin to turn. She liked this season, for it promised nothing. The summer hunt was over, they had plenty of meat, and now they could be lazy until the blackhorns began to grow their winter coats. Red Paint wanted more than anything to go to the mountains of the Backbone. She wanted to pick the last of the chokecherries and swim in the cold streams. If they rode straight across from the Sweet Grass Hills, it would take them less than four sleeps. Her body tingled with excitement as she saw the sparkling water, the dark stones, the deep green of the scented trees. She was so thankful to have her husband safely back. And she had not bled for two moons running. She was certain now that she carried another life inside her. Once again she counted on her fingers and once again she came up with the many-drums moon, a powerful moon, the moon her son would be born. It would be a son and it would make her husband happy. They had to go to the valleys of the Backbone to celebrate alone this new son! But first she had to tell her husband that this son was surely on the way.

"Wake up, Fools Crow!" She hit him on the shoulder. "Fools Crow!"

He rolled onto his back and rubbed his eyes. His head hurt. "Fools Crow! Fools Crow!"

He opened his eyes and looked at Red Paint. With great effort he propped himself up on an elbow and rubbed his head. He had drunk too much of the white man's water the night before, in the big lodge. He suddenly sat up. At the naming ceremony!

"Yes! Fools Crow, the great warrior!" Red Paint laughed. She handed him a bowl of water and he drank greedily. "It is midday, time to wake up."

"Fools Crow," he said.

"That is you, my husband."

Fools Crow. The naming ceremony. Three Bears had named him Fools Crow after hearing how he had tricked Bull Shield into thinking he was dead and then risen up to kill the Crow chief. But was that how it was? The story of how he had earned that name had been greatly exaggerated, despite his initial protests, until many thought he had tricked the whole Crow village, that his medicine contained some magic that made another man's eyes see wrong. The story of how Fools Crow had killed and scalped the man who had mutilated Yellow Kidney was even more embellished. Now Fools Crow had made the man cry, had laughed and spit on him, had made love to his wife, then killed him and stuffed his bloody genitals in his mouth. The men of the warrior societies laughed and kidded Fools Crow, but in their eyes he had become a man of much medicine.

If only he hadn't drunk the white man's water. He remembered sneaking out of the big lodge three or four times and drinking the harsh liquor out of a tin with some others. He remembered with shame how he had acted out his encounters with both Crows, how he had made the warriors laugh and moan with the ups and downs of his confrontations.

Now he heard Red Paint, and she was talking about their son. "He will want to walk in the forest with us, to swim with us, to pick the cherries with us."

"Our son will come with us?"

"To the Backbone. He is already with us." Red Paint stood and walked to the other side of the lodge. She bent down and came up with a long soft-tanned bundle stretched over a willow frame. "See?" she said. It was a cradleboard.

Fools Crow smiled and forgot about his aching head for a moment.

"It belonged to my mother. She carried me in it, then Good Young Man, then One Spot. Now she gives it to us."

"When will our son come out to look around?"

"Moon of many drums. It is the best time."

Fools Crow walked around the fire. He took the cradleboard from his wife. It was made of elkskin and decorated with a single wild rose. He touched the skin, and Red Paint moved closer to him and put her arm around his waist.

"What is this talk of the Backbone?"

"Can we go there? Now? In the morning? I can pack right now."

He looked down at his wife and his heart jumped. He was ready to go. It was a perfect thought, just him and Red Paint. They could pick chokecherries. He would hunt the white bighead and the bighorn. They could stay through the falling-leaves moon, until Cold Maker's breath turned frosty.

"Two sleeps," he said. "We will get ready tomorrow and leave at dawn the day after." He hugged Red Paint to him and felt her heartbeat, or was it the pounding in his head?

Red Paint slipped out of his arms and ran to the entrance. "I will tell my mother!" Then she was gone.

Fools Crow. Fools Crow. He was beginning to like the name. If only he hadn't drunk the white man's water. He remembered dancing on the scalp of Bull Shield and the men shouting. And then he remembered Yellow Kidney, who sat quietly, impassively, as he often did these days. After the dance, Fools Crow had held up the scalp and boasted, "There is your Crow brave, this puny hair that sickens Fools Crow!"

Now the young man groaned loudly and dropped to his knees. He rolled onto his back and closed his eyes as an older memory crept into his heart. He had boasted to Yellow Kidney in the same manner that Fast Horse had boasted to the Crows the night Yellow Kidney was captured and mutilated. He had belittled his father-in-law without thinking, and he knew Yellow Kidney had lost face forever. His humiliation was complete.

Fools Crow wept and cursed himself for being wicked, for drinking the liquor, for killing Bull Shield, for allowing the others to think he had tricked the Crow. Fools Crow was his name now, but he hadn't earned it. The Crow had fooled himself into thinking White Man's Dog was dead. Then a thought crossed Fools Crow's mind that caused him to stop weeping. The bad spirit that Mik-api had driven from the body of White Man's Dog—it was still out there, Mik-api had said so—perhaps it now found the body of Fools Crow. Perhaps it didn't know that both bodies belonged to the same man. Perhaps it was now making Fools Crow do wicked things. Perhaps Mik-api could heal this newly named man.

As he stared at the shadows the ear poles were making on the high walls of the lodge, Fools Crow felt a drumming in his body. He lay there almost dreamily watching the shadows as the sound entered his ears. He heard the beating hooves, then the shouts of men, the patter of children running. He jumped up and ducked through the entrance, his many-shots gun in his hand.

Across a wide plain to the southwest he saw a column of Napikwans loping toward the camp. One of the men leading them carried a lance with a colored cloth tied to its tip. As they closed, Fools Crow saw the blue uniforms of the seizers. He began to walk, then trot to the lodge of Yellow Kidney, for Red Paint was there visiting her mother. Then he saw her and Heavy Shield Woman standing by a robe they had been tanning. They were watching the seizers.

The column came at a leisurely pace, leaving a trail of dust that blew to the south. All the horses were bays, their deep red intensified by dark streaks of sweat on the shoulders and flanks. One of the leaders shouted and the column came to a halt as one. They were not more than a hundred paces from the perimeter of the camp. Fools Crow could see the dark sweat circles under the riders' arms. One of the horses whickered and shook his head. The bit jingled in his mouth, the only sound in the afternoon air.

"They are many and big like the tall stones of Snake Butte," whispered Red Paint with awe.

Fools Crow recognized the scout, Joe Kipp. He was a halfbreed who knew the Pikuni tongue and had often led the seizers north from their fort on the Pile-of-rocks River. His father had been a trader among the Pikunis for many years. Fools Crow remembered Joe Kip as a young man who joked with the warriors and teased the women.

"Will they kill the Lone Eaters?" said Red Paint. "They have a cruel look about them. I do not like that seizer chief."

"Hush," said Heavy Shield Woman. "Don't put ideas in their heads. Look, they dismount."

Joe Kipp and two of the seizer chiefs had gotten down from their horses, but the others sat motionless, their rifles across their laps. There were more than eighty of them, by Fools Crow's count. Many of them had whiskers and their blue shirts were dusty. One of them took his cap off and wiped his forehead with his arm. Another yawned, a large dark hole in his sunburned face. Another said something to him and he sat up straight.

The two chiefs with Joe Kipp walked stiffly, almost uncertainly, the way men do when they have spent a long time in the saddle. One of them had many yellow stripes on his arms. The other wore a white head-cover that shaded his eyes, but Fools Crow could see that he had a hairy face. He was buttoning the top buttons of his tunic. A long knife jangled against his thigh.

"Haiya!" shouted Joe Kipp. "Where are my friends, Three Bears, Rides-at-the-door, Boss Ribs! Ah, there they are, the great chiefs of the Lone Eaters!"

"How is it that the Napikwan speaks our tongue?" said Red Paint. She had seen very few white men in her life. "He does not look like the others; yet he is not like a Pikuni. Perhaps he is of the Liars. He has those kind of eyes."

"His father owned a trading house many sleeps east of here. Often we traded with them when we were over that way," said Heavy Shield Woman. "His mother was of the Dirt Lodge People. Now this young Kipp is a wolf for the seizers."

Fools Crow left them and walked cautiously to Three Bears'

lodge. His father glanced at him. Three Bears stood unsmiling, his blanket wrapped around his shoulders. In his hand he held his long-pipe.

Joe Kipp held out his hand and Three Bears took it. Kipp smiled and clasped hands with Rides-at-the-door and the others. Then he gestured toward the seizers and said, "This is the Captain Snelling of the Pile-of-rocks River and his war chief, John Gates."

Kipp turned to the two men and said something in their language. The Captain Snelling stiffened and bowed slightly, his blue eyes fixed on Three Bears. The striped-sleeve lifted his arm to rub the back of his neck and nodded. He wore a pink garment under his blue shirt. Above the button, a mat of curly red hair caught the sun.

Three Bears motioned for the men to sit. Several of the Pikuni men had appeared and they sat in groups around the seizers and the chiefs.

"We will smoke," said Three Bears. "Tell your seizers that the Lone Eaters smoke with them. We welcome them into our camp."

"The Captain Snelling is honored," said Joe Kipp. "He rides far and his business is urgent, but he would welcome a smoke with the fine Lone Eaters." Kipp turned to the seizers and spoke the strange language. The striped-sleeve shouted to the mounted men and they relaxed in their saddles but didn't dismount or sheath their rifles.

After the pipe had gone around, the seizer chief unbuttoned the top three buttons of his tunic and spoke. He said many words to Three Bears. Joe Kipp looked nervously from the seizer chief to Three Bears and Rides-at-the-door.

Fools Crow wondered if Joe Kipp knew that his father spoke the Napikwan language. Rides-at-the-door had sat in on many of the negotiations with the Napikwan chiefs, and Fools Crow had heard him speak with the traders. But now he sat with a blank expression. Maybe this Napikwan spoke a different tongue, or perhaps Rides-at-the-door didn't wish to acknowledge the words yet.

The seizer chief fell silent and wiped his forehead with a red cloth.

"My friends, a bad thing has happened," said Joe Kipp. "Seven sleeps ago the white man, Malcolm Clark, was killed. You know this man as Four Bears, husband of the Pikuni Cutting-off-head Woman. He has lived and traded among you for many years. He is much respected by the white bosses for his knowledge of his red brothers. Now he is murdered and his spirit passes to the Shadowland. This makes the bosses of the great lodges at Many-sharp-points-ground very angry—"

The seizer chief interrupted Joe Kipp and again spoke for a long time. The longer he spoke the sharper became his voice. At one point he pressed his thumb into the palm of his hand and moved it back and forth. Then he stopped and glared at the chiefs.

Rides-at-the-door leaned close to Three Bears and said something. Fools Crow could see his lips move but he couldn't hear what his father was saying. Three Bears continued to stare at the seizer chief.

"The big bosses have sent this chief to track down the murderers. There were witnesses. Malcolm Clark's daughters and son saw this thing happen. The son was wounded and left for dead, but the Great Spirit was looking out for him. Now he identifies Owl Child and Bear Chief and Black Weasel as the men who killed his father."

Fools Crow felt his heart quicken. He wondered if Fast Horse was among the murderers. It was less than a year ago that Fools Crow and Fast Horse had gone on the Crow raid to gain honor and wealth in the traditional way: Fast Horse, who would one day become the keeper of the Beaver Medicine, who had always been smart and ambitious. It wasn't the fact that he might have helped kill the white man that bothered Fools Crow. This Malcolm Clark was known as a two-faced man, a bully, a dangerous fool who had little regard for the Pikunis. His death caused Fools Crow no sorrow. But Owl Child was also a bad man. He had killed one of his own, Bear Head, when the two men argued over the scalp of an enemy. Owl Child had lied and tried to claim it, but many in the party had seen Bear Head bring down the enemy. Now Owl Child wandered about with his gang, threatening the Napikwans and stealing their horses—and Fast Horse had become a part of it. He had turned away from his own people.

They could kill us now and their bosses would be pleased, thought Fools Crow. Sun Chief favors them with strong medicine.

"It has become known to the white chiefs that Owl Child and his men are with Mountain Chief's band, that they hide with their relatives. I have told this seizer chief that Mountain Chief has crossed the Medicine Line, but this pup is bull-headed"—Kipp almost smiled—"and wishes to know if the people of the Lone Eaters band know where he is. I know my friend Three Bears is a good man and it pains me to speak to him thus. It is with a straight tongue that I tell him Joe Kipp wishes him and his people no harm." Kipp's eyes changed to a glittering hardness. "But you know how the Napikwan thinks, and it will go hard for you if you try to deceive him."

Three Bears leaned toward Rides-at-the-door and said, "How is it with the seizer chief that he smokes with us, then threatens to harm us when we welcome him?"

Rides-at-the-door had his back to Fools Crow. He spoke, then shrugged his shoulders.

Three Bears knocked the ashes from his long-pipe. He looked at the seizer chief and spoke. "As you know, Joe Kipp, I have known your father for a long time. I traded with him and he always treated me fairly. I watched you grow from an infant to a man, and I always had a liking for you. Now it saddens me to see you consorting with this rude long-knife. There are better ways for you to put food in your mouth. But you have chosen this way and so I will tell you what I know. It does not sadden me to hear of Four Bears' death. The Pikuni people have long since cut the rope with him. He is a two-faces. He talks to us one way and to the Napikwans another. Now he is dead and we lose no sleep. Owl Child is no better and it does not surprise me that he has killed Four Bears. Bad blood has always existed between them—ever since Four Bears beat him in front of his own people. Owl Child swore revenge and he has taken it. That is no business of the Lone Eaters. But it troubles me that this long-knife has nothing better to do than threaten us. All the time the Napikwans trespass on the Pikuni territory. Their whitehorns threaten our blackhorn ranges. It is known by Ka-ach-sino, the great Grandfather in the east, that his children who were here first desire to live in peace with the Napikwans. He has promised us that this should be so. He has promised us that we would be treated fairly and we would be rewarded for the lands we have given up. He has promised us rations. But so far the Pikunis see nothing. His agents give us nothing, though we have knocked on the door many times. Is this how he would have us treated?

"No, tell your seizer chief here that the Lone Eaters have not seen Mountain Chief or Owl Child. The Lone Eaters attend to their affairs and wish to be left alone. Tell him the pipe is empty."

As Joe Kipp talked with the Captain Snelling, Fools Crow noticed that the striped-sleeve had set his eyes hard on Three Bears. He wasn't listening to Kipp's words. He had heard it all already.

14

FOOLS CROW SQUEEZED THE TRIGGER and quickly pumped another shell into the chamber, but there was no need. The white bighead collapsed where he had stood, then rolled over and off the narrow granite ledge. He hit the long slide of scree at the top and slid all the way to the bottom. The report of the shot echoed in the high bowl, followed by the harsh slide of thin jagged shale. Then it was quiet. From this distance the white animal looked like a piece of summer snow. Fools Crow stood up and flexed his legs. He had been stalking the animal for most of the morning, and his body was sore from the climbing. He breathed deeply and looked around at the gray mountains. He hadn't known how good it would be for him and Red Paint to get away from the camp of the Lone Eaters. The visit by the seizers had only heightened a tension that had existed since the Sun Dance, since Mountain Chief's speech and Owl Child's reaction to it. So many Napik-wans, closing in all the time, made the people feel that their time on the plains was numbered. Lately, their only contacts with white people brought bad news. It saddened them that Mountain Chief, their leader, was now on the run. It angered them to think that the seizers thought he could control Owl Child, as one hob-bles a horse that has a tendency to wander. Now the seizers were determined that Mountain Chief pay for the crimes of Owl Child. This was like shooting one gopher because another gopher had bitten a child's finger. War with the Napikwans seemed unavoid-able—even Rides-at-the-door, who for so long had counseled peace, now saw war as a possible solution and had said so at the council called after the seizers had left—and so Fools Crow was glad to come to the Backbone to clean his mind, to renew his spirit. When he and Red Paint returned to their people, he would be ready to fight for the hunting ranges that belonged to the Pikunis.

They had been in the mountains for eighteen sleeps, and now the moon was approaching the time of the first frost on the plains. In the mountains, the quaking-leaf trees were already turning a faint yellow. Cold Maker would soon be stirring in his lodge in the Always Winter Land. Fools Crow had made an offering to Cold Maker soon after Fast Horse had left the Lone Eaters. He and Eagle Ribs had left camp before dawn one morning and ridden all that day to a sandy creek just on the other side of the Medicine Line. They made a fire and burned sweet grass. Then they placed two prime blackhorn hides in the notch of a young big-leaf tree. They threw wood on the fire until it blazed high; then they let it die down to a bed of red coals in the gathering dusk. As they rode back to camp in the starry night, they sang of their sacrifice and prayed that Cold Maker would find the robes adequate to clothe his daughters. The thought of them shivering in their birdskins in that Always Winter Land filled the men with pity. The coals would provide eyes for them to look down on the Pikunis and intercede on their behalf if Cold Maker became angry this winter. As they guided themselves to camp by the moonlit outlines of the Backbone, they suddenly felt an icy wind on their backs and knew that Cold Maker had come to claim their offerings.

Fools Crow took off his shirt and sat down on the trail. It was just wide enough for him to stretch out his legs. He leaned back into a shallow crevice, into the shade, and closed his eyes. He knew he should get down to dress out the white bighead, but the sun was warm and he needed a rest.

He awoke to the sound of laughter. He sat up quickly and bumped his head on a jutting rock. "Oh," he said. "Oh!" The laughter grew louder. He wiped away the tears. To the west he could see Sun returning to his home. He scrambled to his feet and picked up his rifle. "Who is it?" he said. "Who laughs at me when I am in such pain?" He spun around and lifted the rifle.

"Easy, brother," croaked Raven. "I was only laughing at what is going on below. Have a look."

Fools Crow leaned over the ledge. At the bottom of the scree he saw a large dark shadow haloed with silver. Just before it entered the timber he caught a glimpse of white hair. The white bighead!

"Ah, ah!" Raven laughed. "Ah, ah! Real-bear is a thief. Look at him, as if he couldn't hunt for himself."

Fools Crow heard the animal crashing through the timber. He turned to Raven. "Why didn't you warn me sooner?"

"You think I haven't anything better to do, foolish man? I have to hunt for my wives. All day they pester me about not providing for them." Raven smiled. "As a matter of fact, I was just about to fly down there and take a piece for myself, but real-bear beat me to it."

"I stalked that white bighead all morning," said Fools Crow bitterly. "I thought to lay my head on his white fur this winter. Now I have nothing."

"Now, now. Why is it you nothing-men think only of yourselves? Look at it this way—you have made a great sacrifice to real-bear. He will not forget. Besides, he makes your power animal look like the turnip."

"You speak the truth," admitted Fools Crow. "Real-bear's power is the greatest of all the four-leggeds. He is a relative of the Pikunis. Still, I wish he hadn't chosen my bighead."

"The greater the sacrifice, the greater the reward." Raven hopped down onto a ledge at shoulder level. He ruffled his feathers and shit. Then he cocked his head and looked across the bowl toward Rising Mountain. "I have come to speak to you about another matter."

Fools Crow was surprised to see that Raven's whiskers were white, like those of an old coyote. But his eyes were dark and lively. The feet that curled over the edge of the rock were black and tough. Fools Crow blinked as though his eyes played tricks on him. When he looked again, he saw a thin band of silver around one of Raven's ankles. A pale blue stone caught the last of Sun's light.

"Nice, isn't it? Not long ago I flew down to the Always Summer Land to visit with my brothers there. One of them had taken this from the Many Bracelets People. It has great power, Fools Crow. Now I see farther than ever."

"You know my new name?"

Raven laughed softly. "When I was flying home I decided to stop and see how the Crows were faring. I'm not too fond of the men, but the women enjoy my company. They give me lots to eat, and they are nice to behold when one's eyes are sore with the wind. There is something about Crow women that makes me think of my youth. . . ."

"You saw our war party attack the camp of Bull Shield!"

"Oh, yes. You killed twenty-three men. Alas, you also killed six women and one child." Raven sighed. "Such is war."

"Then you saw me kill the two warriors!" Fools Crow exclaimed. "You saw me trick Bull Shield!"

Raven reached down and picked at the silver bracelet. It jingled on the rock, the tiny sound echoing around the basin. "I don't think you fooled him, do you? The one you got your name for?"

Fools Crow felt his face grow hot with shame. "I fell," he said weakly. "I thought I had been shot. I *had* been shot, but . . ."

Raven laughed at the young man's discomfort. "Ah, but you see how it turns out? The people don't know that, and so they speak your name with admiration. It makes them feel good that one so brave walks among them. It increases the Pikuni power. I'll never tell."

Both man and bird were silent for a moment, watching Sun Chief slip behind a jagged peak. The heat from the rocks behind them warmed their backsides.

"Your long-ago people believed that Napi, who created them and gave them life and death, lived among these mountains, that he retired here after his work was completed."

"Yes," said Fools Crow. "My grandfather said that Old Man —and Old Woman—still live in that place that gives life to Old Man River across the Medicine Line. He said that one can still see Napi's gambling place up there."

"He was a gambler, all right. After he made the first two-leggeds, he and Old Woman decided to gamble to see if your kind should live forever." Raven puffed his feathers. "I was there. He picked up a blackhorn chip and said, 'I will throw this into the lake, and if it floats, the people will die for four sleeps, then return. If it sinks, they will die forever.' So saying, he threw the chip out as far as he could and it floated. But Old Woman, who was something of a gambler too, said, 'No, let me. I will throw this rock into the water. That will determine the people's fate.' The rock sank, and so you two-leggeds die forever. Even Napi couldn't control his woman," Raven said sadly.

"But good came of it. Now people take care of themselves. And when they die, others feel sorry for them. It would be sad to die and think that nobody pities you."

"Did your grandfather tell you that?"

"He was a wise man."

"Not always." Raven laughed. "I knew him when he was a youth. Wild and reckless, that one. Of course, he was poor—he was the poorest one of the Black Doors. He reminded me a little of you when you first came to see me, poor and out of luck. I often wonder what would have happened to your grandfather if I had not helped him. . . ." Raven had a faraway look in his eyes. Then he shook his head. "But that is not what I wish to talk to you about.

"You see, seven, eight moons ago I became aware of an evil presence here in the Backbone. At first, I must admit, I didn't think of it as such. During my hunts I began to notice a lot of dead animals—real-bears, their cousins the black sticky-mouths, long-tails, real-dogs, wags-his-tails, even the flyers, white-head and Peta. In the beginning, I thought Sun Chief had chosen to smile on his poor relative. I brought the meat home to my wives and we gorged ourselves. Unlike you two-leggeds, we ravens prefer the meat of the meat-eaters; it has more tang. After several days, my wives became worried and asked me to find out what was the matter with these creatures that they couldn't hold onto life. I told them to shut up and enjoy the bounty, but they persisted in their demands." Raven wiped his beak under his wing. "By this time my belly was so big I couldn't fly very well. I begged my wives to let me rest up, but the cruel things pushed me out of the tree and said I couldn't come home until I had solved this riddle.

"Well, although my guts were aching with surfeit, I began to scout around, and it didn't take me long. The second day out I came upon a clearing filled with berries. There, in the center, a large real-bear was stripping the bushes into his mouth. It was disgusting the way his muzzle was covered with purple juice, but I decided to ask him if he knew what was going on. Just as I began my descent, he stood up and looked around. As you know, the real-bear has weak eyes but his nose is keen. He began sniffing the air, and that's when the Napikwan jumped up and shot him four times with his many-shots. That was natural enough. The two-leggeds are always killing for meat and hides. I settled in a tree and waited for the Napikwan to dress him out. I confess, the smell of blood had made me hungry again. I was anxious for some guts, but the Napikwan walked up to Real-bear and shot him once more, this time in the ear. Then he swore in this peculiar language and walked away, leaving his kill.

"For three more sleeps I followed this strange Napikwan that leaves his meat. He killed a long-tail, a bighead, three real-dogs and five wags-his-tails. He even tried to kill your brother, Skunk Bear, but I flew ahead and warned him. In anger, the Napikwan took a shot at me, scared the shit out of me, so I left. But for many moons now the hunter kills animals until they become scarce. I fear he will kill us all off if something isn't done.

"It was more than good fortune that brought you to me. I was flying over this bowl when my eye caught sight of the white bighead lying at the bottom of the slide. I thought, Oh, the crazy Napikwan kills another of my brothers. You see, I have become afraid even to go down and pick carcasses. Look how skinny I have become. My wives call me coward and pick on me. Then I saw you up here, sleeping in the warm sun, and I knew Sun Chief had sent you."

Fools Crow frowned. He looked at Raven and saw that it was true that he had become thin and ragged. Now his eyes didn't look so sharp and he seemed much older than the time he had led Fools Crow to the trapped wolverine. He pitied the old bird. "What can I do?" he said.

Without looking at his companion, Raven said, "You must kill the Napikwan with your many-shots gun."

Fools Crow shuddered, as though the evening air had turned to winter. To kill a Napikwan! Had not the seizers warned the people? Hadn't his own father spoken against making trouble with them? He thought of Owl Child and Fast Horse and their gang, but they were different. They had nothing to lose, they were hardly Pikunis anymore.

"I can't do it," said Fools Crow, defeat coloring his voice.

"Would you have all your brothers killed off, then?"

"But surely Real-bear could sneak up on him and—"

"This one is different. He is more animal than human. His ears can hear a leaf turn at five hundred paces. His eyes can spot a worm deep within the earth. They say he can smell a stone beyond the next ridge. No, we are no match for him—and that is why Sun Chief sends you to us. Only Fools Crow can kill this Napikwan."

"But how? Even now I tremble to think of this man. He will kill Fools Crow! Such a one would not release my spirit to the Shadowland. I would become a ghost. My people would grieve."

"But that is why Napi decided you would die forever—so your people would cry and mourn your loss." Raven smiled wryly. Than his eyes glittered with tears. "I thought Fools Crow was a man, but now I see I was wrong. He would see his brothers, the four-leggeds and the flyers, perish and not put up a fight. He would allow his people to mourn the passing of their little brothers and starve for want of meat. He would rather his unborn son—"

"No, no, do not go on, Raven! Do not speak of such things. It was a selfish coward's heart that made me tremble with fear when I learned of Sun Chief's desire that I destroy this Napikwan." Fools Crow brushed away a tear. "I will kill this one who snuffs out life so easily."

Raven looked at him shrewdly. "If your heart is not in this . . ."

"Now I hate him as I feared him before. I will kill him with a good heart. Fools Crow will put an end to this evil one."

Raven laughed. "Don't overdo it. You will need your strength for the accomplishment of this deed." He strutted back and forth on the ledge. "Such a brave one! A minute ago he is weeping with fear, and now he will rid the world of all evil!" Fools Crow could see his friend's spirits rise. He too began to laugh, and the sound of their laughter traveled far in the approaching dusk.

Red Paint, stirring the berry soup in the valley below, heard the laughter and a smile lit her face.

That night Raven visited the dreaming place of the Napikwan. The cabin was made of log and mud and was dark. It was so low and small it scarcely cast a shadow. Raven pulled down on the rawhide string on the outside of the door. The latch inside popped up and the door swung open, just wide enough for the ugly bird to waddle through. Across the room he could see coals smoldering in a rock fireplace. The inside of the hut smelled of smoke and rancid grease and the Napikwan's sour body. The greasy smell sharpened Raven's appetite but he kept his mind on his work. He hopped up on a short bedpost at the man's feet. His eyes had adjusted completely to the windowless room. He could see the big white feet pointing up at the bottom of the sleeping robe. There were three toes missing from the left one. Raven flapped his wings and flew as lightly as he could to a head post. The draft of his wings made the Napikwan's hair flutter. He stopped in the middle of a snore and licked his lips; then the air rushed out of his mouth with a whistle.

From the post Raven could see this strange man who leaves his kills, and it was not a bad face in repose. The nose was long and sculpted on the sides with shadows. The eyelashes were fine and curved, if a little crusty. The rest of the face was covered with curly hair, a shade darker than the straight sandy hair on the head. Raven looked the length of the body. The white feet were a long way away.

Now Raven leaned over and began to sing in a voice unlike his own. The notes were as sweet and strong as those of the yellow-breast, yet made no sound in the small room. The words entered the man's ears and caused him to stop snoring. The words told a story of a young Pikuni woman, lovely and graceful, a woman of such charms that she made men mad with longing. He sang of her shiny hair that hung undone to the small of her back, of her breasts so pale and firm they reminded one of the snowbird eggs, of the lean dark thighs that invited a man. Raven was beginning to enjoy his work. He sang of long soothing fingers, of skin as smooth and cool as the wet fur of otter, of eyes that made the female wags-his-tail cover her own in shame. The room had become hot and Raven began to sing the praises of her hips, her nose and toes, the delicate hair of her center. Raven stopped and wiped his sweaty brow with the edge of his wing. Then he leaned closer to the man's ear and whispered where he could find this desirable creature. Raven told him to be sure to wear his wolf headdress so that the maiden wouldn't mistake him for another Napikwan. She was so lonely she would fall in love with the first man she laid eyes on.

Raven flew down and waddled out of the cabin. He jumped up and caught the string in his beak and closed the door. Then he sighed, a long shuddering croak. He would fly directly home. He had been away from his wives too long.

Sun Chief had cleared a small ridge to the southeast and was burning off the last of the ground fog when Red Paint finished washing the berry pot, bowls and horn spoons. She sat back on her heels and watched the slippery swimmer that had stationed himself in an eddy behind a yellow rock. He would drift to the edge of the current, float downstream a short way, then return with a wag of his tail. The day before she had tossed him a couple of yellow-wings and he had darted up, his body splashing silver in the sun, to devour the insects. She had been tempted for three days now to catch him and taste of his flesh. Her own people scorned those who ate the underwater swimmers, but she had a cousin who had married into the Fish Eaters band of the Siksikas, and he had become fond of the silver creatures. He said they tasted like the young prairie chicken. She wiped her wet hands on the hem of her dress and smiled. Today she would make a bone hook. She would catch him for Fools Crow. In the solitude of the Backbone they would taste the flesh of this swimmer together.

She carried her dishes up the gentle incline to the lodge. The small meadow was filled with windflowers, bear grass and lupine. The dry odor of juniper came with a breeze. Downstream the thickets of chokecherry bushes glistened with the purple fruit. Red Paint placed her hand on her abdomen and thought she felt a slight roundness. "Sleep-bringer," she crooned. Then she slipped inside the lodge, glanced at Fools Crow, the sacks of dried chokecherries, the bundles of dried roots and leaves, and picked up her beadwork and ducked quietly through the entrance again. She walked downstream a hundred paces to her favorite sitting spot, a grassy knoll beneath a tall fir that grew apart from the forest. She sat with her legs tucked under her and looked at the tiny moccasins. She had finished the yellow butterfly on one of them. She held the soft sole against her cheek. It was made of elkskin. Fools Crow had shot a calf and she had tanned it. After cutting out the moccasins, she had rolled the skin and tucked it away. It would yield more moccasins as their baby grew.

She looked back at the lodge. She was glad that Fools Crow had gone back to sleep after their morning meal. He had tossed and turned all night as though tormented by bad dreams.

Fools Crow got up when he could hear his wife's footsteps no longer. He put on his leggings, picked up his rifle and peeked out the door. When she had settled herself under the fir tree, he hurried out and around the other side of the lodge. He had tethered the horses a good way upstream, out of sight. He trotted the few paces to the edge of the timber. Once in, he began to circle higher until he came to a patch of bushes a little above the top of the fir tree. From here he could see both upstream and downstream and the hillside across the meadow. He settled down to wait.

He had wanted to warn Red Paint, but Raven had said not to alarm her, for she would give away the trick by her actions. As he squatted behind a red bush he looked down at the back of his wife. She had grown more beautiful in the days since their marriage. It was a beauty that had to do with the way she moved, the way she walked, even the way she sat. Her face and body had not changed, except for the slight swelling of her abdomen. Maybe that was it. Fools Crow had seen women who were with child become more serene, more womanly, more desirable. But they also became heavier, more centered on the ground, as though to move would break their tie with Mother Earth's spirit. Red Paint was light and swift, as graceful as the prairie-runner in her stride. Her body was firm and yielding, her hips wide and strong. When he watched her bathe in the stream, Fools Crow knew he was married to a woman who turned other men's heads. Now he felt ashamed that this beauty would spring the trap.

Just before midday Fools Crow saw the Napikwan approach from upstream. He walked unhurriedly, without fear, into camp. His long stride reminded Fools Crow of the big-nose who lived in the swamps. The Napikwan walked straight to the lodge and pushed the flap back with his gun barrel. He knelt and looked inside. Then he stood and looked first upstream, then across, then downstream. He was the biggest man Fools Crow had ever seen. In his fringed jacket and leggings, with his wolf headdress, his bushy beard and hair, he looked like a molting blackhorn bull, half in and half out of his winter coat. His gray eyes stopped, and Fools Crow knew he had spotted Red Paint. The Napikwan stood still for a moment; then he walked back to the edge of the timber.

From his vantage point of seventy paces up the hill from Red Paint, Fools Crow could not see the man's upper body, but by laying his chin on the ground he could see the long striding legs moving silently toward him. Then the legs stopped and spread slightly. The gun butt rested on the ground between them. Fools Crow grew frightened for Red Paint. Suppose Raven was wrong. Suppose the Napikwan's heart was not filled with lust, but instead with hatred. He had killed many animals for no reason; suppose he now wished to kill a human. Fools Crow glanced at Red Paint. She sat quietly, unaware, her slim back bent over her beadwork. Then he looked back toward the legs. The rifle butt had disappeared. The legs had shifted, so that the left one was now pointed toward Red Paint. The Napikwan was perhaps fifty paces below and to the right of Fools Crow. Thick branches still hid the man's upper body, but in the hot dry air, the warrior could hear the Napikwan's breathing. There was a hard edge to it as though the man had the winter sickness.

Fools Crow knew the trick had gone wrong. The Napikwan was truly more animal than human. He had sensed the trap, and now he was silently taunting Fools Crow to come out of hiding. Of course, he had looked into the lodge and seen the warrior's possessions. Raven had told him in his dream that Red Paint would be alone. Now he was using Red Paint, the threat of harm, to make Fools Crow show himself. Oh, thought the warrior, oh, not only is the Napikwan stronger, but he is smarter than Fools Crow as well. He began to tremble. He wanted to shout to Red Paint to run, but the man was in easy range to drop her with one shot, should she move. Fools Crow lifted his rifle. His only chance was to shoot the man's legs out from under him. But as he sighted down the barrel, the legs moved back behind the trunk of a pine. Fools Crow lifted his head, then sat up slowly. He wiped his damp palms on his leggings. The big Napikwan is more than animal, he thought. He is a spirit who sees without seeing. Again Fools Crow wiped his palms on his leggings, but this time they weren't damp. Nor were his hands trembling.

He stood, crouching, glancing about. There was a tree on the edge of the brushy clearing. If he could reach that he would have a better angle to get off a killing shot. The sun was hot on his bare back and sweat trickled down his ribs. Then he was running, dodging the red bushes, trying to see both the Napikwan and the ground before him. Suddenly he heard a *boom!* and fell to the ground. He lifted his head, spitting dirt, and saw a fresh chip in the tree that had been his goal. He panicked. His only thought was to get to Red Paint before the Napikwan tired of the game and decided to kill her. He was running down the slope, shouting to her to get away, but she didn't move. She watched him come near with a questioning look in her eyes. Her mouth was open as though she were about to speak. The next shot lifted Fools

Crow off his feet and spun him around. He came down hard on his back and slid until he was stopped by a small pine. He pulled himself up and leaned back against the tree. His breathing was raspy. Then at the same time, he heard Red Paint scream and the Napikwan shout something in a slow singing voice. He continued to sing as though he were boasting, mocking the Pikuni warrior. Fools Crow looked at his shoulder. A piece of flesh had been blasted away just below the shoulder bone. It was matted with dirt and grass. His rifle lay on the slope two body lengths away. He heard the Napikwan laugh and then another *boom!* The small tree snapped in two above his head. Fools Crow leaned back and breathed deeply and saw a red wall come up behind his eyes. He felt sick and weak. He closed his eyes and called out to Sun Chief, to Wolverine, his power, to give him strength, to let him die with honor. Slowly, almost silently, a sound entered his ears. As the sound increased in volume, the red wall behind his eyes receded. Now he saw the slope clearly, the red bushes, the slender yellow grasses—and his gun. The sound was in his head and in the small meadow surrounded by the great mountains of the Backbone. The sound flowed through his body and he felt the strength of its music in his limbs, in his hands, in his guts, in his chest. He sprang to a crouch, then made a dive for his weapon. A *boom!* kicked up a patch of duff inches from his head. But the music had reached his heart. The weapon was in his hands, against his cheek, and he watched the greased shooter leave his rifle and he watched it travel through the air, between the trees, and he saw it enter the Napikwan's forehead above the startled eyes, below the wolfskin headdress, and he squatted and watched the head jerk back, then the body, until it landed with a quivering shudder in the bear grass, the lupine, the windflowers. Then the sound was no more. Fools Crow's death song had ended.

15

THREE BEARS LIT the ceremonial pipe, puffed, then passed it to his left. Each man smoked the pipe until it reached the entrance. Then it was handed back, unsmoked, to Three Bears, who gave it to the man on his right. Again each man smoked until it reached the entrance. Three Bears retrieved the pipe, refilled it, and the ceremony was repeated.

The fire had warmed the council lodge, and most of the men had let their blankets fall behind them. The odor of sweet grass hung in the smoky air. Outside, a sharp north wind rattled the ear poles and luffed against the lodge skins.

"And now we will listen to Fools Crow," said Three Bears.

Fools Crow took a deep breath and told them about his and Red Paint's journey to the mountains, their days of hunting and picking berries, his killing of the white bighead and its theft by the real-bear, Raven's visit and fear, Fools Crow's fear, the trick and the killing of the Napikwan who leaves his kills. As he spoke he realized the unlikelihood of his story but he persisted, for it was important that no detail, no event, be left out. Once he glanced at his father and saw a look of consternation on the long face. Three Bears looked into the fire.

When he was finished, Fools Crow removed his shirt and looked at each man. There was a murmuring of voices as the men stared at the wound. Although it had almost healed, there were rounded ridges of flesh around the concavity. Fools Crow had instructed Red Paint in the preparation of roots and leaves. The paste had taken away the pain, and in just eight sleeps the scar tissue was firm.

Fools Crow could see the skepticism on the faces. He heard one man say, ". . . shot himself." He looked across the fire to Mik-api, but the many-faces man was mixing something on the earth before him.

Three Bears cleared his throat and the lodge became silent. "Our young friend has had quite an adventure," he began. Several of the men laughed, but the laughter died quickly under the stony eyes of the old chief. "If this is the truth, then we must counsel with seriousness. To kill a Napikwan is worth little laughter." With that, he passed the ceremonial pipe down to Mik-api. The medicine man held the pipe and dipped a brush into the mixture in the small bowl at his feet. The men watched him paint the stem a dull red. From somewhere in the camp came the steady thump of a drum, as in an owl dance. One of the men nearest the door leaned forward to throw another stick on the fire.

Mik-api passed the pipe back to Three Bears. Shadows flickered on the wall behind him as he lit it. The pipe was handed down to Fools Crow. All the warriors watched as the young man held the pipe, for to smoke this red-painted pipe with a deceiving heart surely meant that one's days were numbered. Fools Crow put the pipe to his lips and sucked in the smoke. He puffed the pipe three times, each time blowing the smoke up into the warm air over the fire.

Now the men began to talk excitedly. One of them pointed to Fools Crow's wound, and those around him said, "Ahhh!"

Three Bears took the pipe and knocked it against a stone in the fire ring. The red ashes fell to the ground.

"Fools Crow knows the power of this pipe and he smokes it with a true heart. Now we must deliberate."

And so the men argued about the killing of the Napikwan. To most of them it was a good and just act, for the white man had been killing off all the animals, thus depriving the Pikunis of their food and skins. Some felt that the killing of a Napikwan was no worse than the killing of a wolf with the white-mouth. Young Bird Chief, who was popular with the militant members of the band, suggested that now was the time to kill them all off, one by one or all at once. Several around him shouted their agreement.

Rides-at-the-door got to his feet and they fell silent. His voice was low and flat, as though his mind were occupied with something other than what he said. "Let us put an end to this foolish talk. Many of you are too young to remember our previous conflicts with the Napikwans.

"My own father, Fools Crow's grandfather, was killed many winters ago in a pointless raid on one of the forts on the Big River east of here. Many of you have also lost relatives in the long-ago. At that time the Pikunis did not know the power of the Napikwans. They thought to drive out these strange creatures, so they loosed their arrows and lances, rode into battle with axes and knives and were killed mercilessly by these new sticks-that-speak-from-afar. Many women and children were left to cry. It became apparent to our long-ago chiefs that they must make peace with the Napikwans, or the Pikunis would disappear from their mother's breast. It has been almost thirteen winters since the big treaty with the bosses from the east. I remember the council on the banks of the Big River. At that time the Pikunis gave the Napikwans some land in return for promises that we would be left alone to hunt on our ranges. We were satisfied, for our ranges still extended beyond where sky touches earth. We in turn promised that we would leave the white ones alone. Four winters ago, we signed a new paper with the Napikwans, giving them our land that lies south of the Milk River. Again, we promised to let them alone. We thought that would put an end to their greed. Last year they brought us a new paper and our chiefs marked it. We were to get commodities to make up for our reduced ranges and our promise to live in peace with them. Our chiefs were to receive some of the white man's money. These things never came to pass. And so we have every reason to hate the Napikwans."

The warriors began to speak at once, their voices filled with anger. Young Bird Chief stood and the talk died away. "You say well, Rides-at-the-door. We know you speak the truth and we respect you as a coming-together man. But sometimes we think you and the other leaders do not see with the sharpness of your hearts. Do you not notice the whitehorns grazing on Pikuni soil to the south and east of us? Soon the Napikwans will take that land from us. Did you not see how the seizers, led by Joe Kipp and the Captain Snelling, rode undisturbed right into our camp on our own land? Did they ask permission, send kind requests and gifts? No, they demanded we tell them the whereabouts of Mountain Chief's people so they could kill them off. How long before they turn on the Lone Eaters and decide that we too are insects to be stepped on? Are we to go quietly to the Sand Hills, to tell our long-ago people that we welcomed death like cowards? That is not the way of the Pikunis. If we must go to the Shadowland, we will go with our heads high, our spirits content that we have fought the Napikwans to death."

The men of the council gestured and murmured their agreement. Even Fools Crow found himself joining in assent, thinking that perhaps the leaders did not see the peril before them. And he remembered standing beside the black horse during Mountain Chief's speech, looking up into Fast Horse's face. That grin Fools Crow had seen was not so much a grin of cruelty but of contempt. Contempt for the leaders and the people for trying to appease the Napikwans, for trying to live in peace with them even as they treated the Pikunis like insects to be stepped on, just as Young Bird Chief had said. As he looked around at the faces, he saw many of the older men, including his father and Three Bears, staring down at the fire. Fools Crow pulled his robe over his back and listened to the howling wind. He didn't like what he had seen.

"There are many who would join us. Mountain Chief would surely lead us. We could count on the Hard Topknots, the Small Brittle Fats, the Small Robes, the Never Laughs among our number. Many Kainahs and Siksikas would join us. Others would see our numbers and join in." Young Bird Chief was now addressing all the warriors in the lodge. "With such a war party, we could drive the Napikwans from our lands. Once again the Pikunis, Kainahs and Siksikas would be feared by those tempted to live among us. As Old Man created this land and created us, so must we defend it until we are no more. It is right. Young Bird Chief has spoken to you."

Rides-at-the-door had listened to Young Bird Chief with an

open mind. In many ways the young brave was right. Napikwan had his hands around the Pikuni throat and was tightening his grip. Soon there would be nothing left of the people but their strangled bodies. Would they not be justified in joining the spirit of Owl Child and his gang in their growing resistance to the whites? Perhaps if the Pikuni numbers were strong, they could drive the Napikwans from their land—or at least obtain an honorable treaty. Wouldn't that be better than sitting like old blackhorn bulls, waiting for the end? Even as he thought this, Rides-at-the-door knew how it would be. The Napikwans would use the excuse of war to exterminate the Pikunis. He felt obliged to speak again.

"Haiya! Listen to me, warriors. Much of what Young Bird Chief says is as true as the stem of the medicine pipe. Our hearts are full of anger, and I have no doubt we could inflict a great blow on these Napikwans. It would not be difficult to drive these individuals from our lands. Perhaps we could burn down the trading forts and the white settlements. Many scalps would hang from our lodgepoles. It would make our people feel good to do these things. It would make me feel good, for no one hates the presence of the Napikwans more than I. In my youth I was a member of Bird Rattler's party that killed the steamboat men on the Big River. I fought the seizers at Rocks Ridge Across and stole their big-ears. Boss Ribs and White Calf"—he gestured in the direction of the two men—"were with that party. But that was long ago. There weren't many of the Napikwans in those days.

"But now things are different. The great war between the Napikwans far to the east is over. More and more of the seizers who fought for Ka-ach-sino, the great Grandfather, have moved out to our country. More come still. If we take the war road against the whites, we will sooner or later encounter great numbers of them. Even with many-shots guns we couldn't hope to match their weapons. Or their cruelty. We have heard what they did to our old enemies, the Parted Hairs, on the Washita: rubbed them out. So too would they do to the Pikunis. We are nothing to them. It is this ground we stand on they seek. These four-leggeds they would have for their own meat. Our women and children would wander and starve—those that were left." Rides-at-the-door paused and looked into the faces of the warriors. He could see fear. But he was not done. "Sun Chief favors the Napikwans. Perhaps it's because they come from the east where he rises each day to begin his journey. Perhaps they are old friends. Perhaps the Pikunis do not honor him enough, do not sacrifice enough. He no longer takes pity on us.

"And so we must fend for ourselves, for our survival. That is why we must treat with the Napikwans. You are brave men, and I find myself covered with shame for speaking to you this way. But it must be so. We are up against a force we cannot fight. It is our children and their children we must think of now."

Rides-at-the-door's final words hung in the smoky lodge. Even Young Bird Chief, who had thought to deny Rides-at-the-door's estimation of the Napikwans' strength, could not refute the gravity of these words. The distant drum continued its monotonous beat. A woman called for her child, the sound of her voice ragged and harsh above the wind.

Three Bears lifted his eyes from the fire. "Are there any here would deny the wisdom of Rides-at-the-door? You all know him as a brave men, a man who would lead this party against the whites if there was any chance of success. It has taken great courage to speak these words to you, and so we should listen with our heads, although our hearts say otherwise. It is natural for the Pikuni men to wish to fight. We have always fought our enemies. We now engage in the biggest fight of all—the fight for our survival. If we must do it without weapons, so be it. But if the Napikwans mistake our desire for peace for weakness, then let them beware, for the Pikunis will fight them to death. That too is natural." Three Bears filled his pipe. "Are there any others who wish to speak on this matter?"

One or two of the men shifted, but none took up the offer. The smoke hung gloomily above their heads.

Three Bears turned to Fools Crow. "Young man, you have done a brave and good thing, for surely this Napikwan was possessed of evil spirits. As Sun Chief honors you, so do your people." Three Bears glanced around the circle. "But let there be no more killing of the Napikwans. Let the Lone Eaters be known as men of wisdom who put the good of their people before their individual honor." He pulled his blanket tighter against the draft that sifted between the lodge skin and liner. "Now tell us, brave one, did you lift this Napikwan's hair?"

Fools Crow dug into his robe, then held up the wolfskin headdress. "Just this, Three Bears. I thought it was his hair." He placed the large cap on his head, the wolf's head resting atop his own. The men nudged each other and began to laugh.

"Ah, ah, you bad one," said Three Bears. "See how you frighten your comrades?"

"I have a woman who looks like that," said Young Bird Chief.

The warriors laughed, and the wind rattled the lodgepoles far over their heads. The mournful drum had stopped.

16

FOOLS CROW RODE HARD behind the big cow, knees clamped tight around the black horse. The blackhorn ran with her head down, her eye rimmed with white, her tongue lolling out of the side of her mouth. Her short legs were a black blur beneath Fools Crow's line of vision. The drumming of her hooves sounded hollow on the short-grass prairie. When he got even with her shoulder, he raised the rifle to his cheek and fired. The shooter entered the blackhorn's body just behind the shoulder and the front legs collapsed. Her momentum caused her to skid several paces on her chin. Then she rolled onto her left side, her back legs still kicking. She bellowed once, then lay quiet.

The rest of the small herd disappeared over the lip of a ravine. Fools Crow reined his horse in and watched them stream up the other side. The black horse panted lightly, but Fools Crow could feel the rib cage expand and contract between his legs. He turned in the saddle and looked behind him. The other cow lay like a black stone some five hundred paces back. In the distance he could see Red Paint and Heavy Shield Woman leading their packhorses toward the first blackhorn. It had been several sleeps since he had killed blackhorns. The thought of boss ribs and back fat made his mouth water. The hides were not yet prime, but they were thick and sleek. They would bring a fair price.

Fools Crow ejected the spent shell and sniffed the faint smell of gunpowder. He looked up at the sky. The clouds were lower and puffier today, driven south like gray bighorns by Cold Maker. There had been a snow cover at dawn. It was gone now, but the longtime-rain moon had passed. Soon the snow would come to stay. Fools Crow tightened the belt of his capote and turned away from the wind. To the south he could make out the pale outline of Sun Chief behind a high thin cloud. He thought again of that hot day when Sun had hidden his face. He had thought of it many times with an increasing sense of dread. The people always said when Sun Chief hides his face a great chief will die. Fox Eyes, the great war chief, had died, and the people thought that was the end of it. But perhaps they were wrong, he thought, perhaps they were mistaken. He felt a mild tingle of fear in his backbone. To question Sun Chief was not good, but he couldn't help the feeling that came over him, the thought that had been growing in his head. Perhaps Sun was angry with the Pikunis and meant to strike them all down. Hadn't Rides-at-the-door, his own father, said that the people were no longer favored by Sun? Wasn't it true that Sun Chief no longer cared whether the people lived or died? Perhaps he had sent the Napikwans to rub them out. The Pikunis were small in his eyes. Only the Napikwans were large enough to attract his pitiless gaze.

Fools Crow looked mournfully about him. He scanned the prairies and horizons. Like all the Pikunis lately, he had taken to looking often into the distance, not for game, but for the enemy, the Napikwans, the seizers. He was certain in his heart that the seizers would return, this time not for talk but for war. He remembered how the striped-sleeve had watched the parley between the leaders of the Lone Eaters and Joe Kipp and the seizer chief. Even now he could almost smell the hatred in the man's eyes, like the acrid scent in a cornered weasel. But since shooting the big Napikwan in the Backbone, Fools Crow was no longer afraid of them. They were only men who could be killed with their own weapons. He looked down at the many-shots gun. He knew that he could kill more Napikwans, and in spite of what his father said, he looked forward to it. Still, it gave him no joy. Why had Sun Chief deserted the people?

Fools Crow was about to turn back, to help Red Paint and her mother load the meat and hides on the packhorses, when something caught his eye to the southeast. He squinted but he could not make out the size and shape of the object. It could be a lone blackhorn, he thought, or a dark rock. Perhaps a bear. Or a rider. Most of the Lone Eater men were off hunting to the southwest, near the rims of Yellow Paint Coulee. This rider, if the object was that, was not of the Lone Eaters. Then who? The Never Laughs band was camped to the south, near the big bend of the Bear River. Perhaps this rider was of the Never Laughs, perhaps with news.

Fools Crow turned his horse and galloped back to the small knoll where the two women were butchering the cow. He addressed only Red Paint, cautiously avoiding his mother-in-law. They had the hindquarters off and were working at the ribs. Heavy Shield Woman continued to split the ribs with a small ax while Fools Crow and Red Paint talked. She feigned indifference, but as soon as her son-in-law expressed concern that the rider might be hostile, she began to drag a hindquarter toward the packhorses. Fools Crow helped them load the horses, finally covering the meat with the wet hide. Then the women mounted their horses and turned toward camp, leading two of the packhorses. Fools Crow watched them go, then glanced up at the lightless sun. They would make the camp well before dusk.

He led the other packhorse to the downed cow, which he quickly gutted, setting the liver and emptied stomach off to one side. Then he got back on his horse and rode to a rock outcropping on the edge of the cutbank coulee. He could see, on a gentle slope to the south of him, the sliding prints made by the blackhorn herd he had chased earlier.

The figure was that of a man on horseback, and he was riding directly toward Fools Crow. He looked behind the rider but the prairies were empty to the horizon. He got down off the black horse and levered a cartridge into the chamber of his rifle. The wind ruffled the two raven feathers in his hair.

He did not recognize the rider. The heavy buffalo coat and wide-brimmed hat hid the man's features. The horse was a large bay. The saddle was a white man's saddle. The man was hunched forward into the wind, his hat pulled low.

Fools Crow held his rifle at his waist. He couldn't tell if the man had spotted him. He was less than a hundred paces away, on the other side of the shallow ravine. The man stopped his horse and lifted his head. He looked around him, as though he had just woken up. His buffalo coat parted and Fools Crow saw the short-gun in the man's hands. Both men stared at each other across the ravine. Then Fools Crow let out a whoop, jumped on his horse and rode down into the ravine. The black horse jumped a dry wash and scrambled up the other side. The man looked wary but sat on his horse patiently.

"It is you," cried Fools Crow, looking into the dark, close-set eyes. "Fast Horse, you have returned!"

Fast Horse grinned at his old friend, baring his clenched white teeth, more a grimace than a smile. His face looked ashen, but Fools Crow thought it was because of the gray light.

"You look about the same, dog-lover," said Fast Horse. "Perhaps a little fatter. They tell me you are married now."

"To Red Paint, daughter of Heavy Shield Woman and Yellow Kidney." Fools Crow saw the flash of pain in his friend's eyes and wished he hadn't mentioned Yellow Kidney.

After a pause in which Fast Horse turned in his saddle and scanned the prairie behind him, he said, "And a new name. They tell me you fool the Crows now. Is this true?"

"So you say." Fools Crow rubbed his nose in embarrassment.

Fast Horse laughed, but the deep voice had an edge to it. "Your luck has changed, my friend. You are no longer the sad-faced dog-lover of this time a winter ago."

"You are different too. You no longer dress like the Pikunis." Fools Crow had been studying his friend's dress—the buffalo coat, the dusty black hat, the white collarless shirt, the gray wool pants. Fast Horse wore moccasins, but he had a pair of Napikwan boots tied to his saddle. His face, lean and tight-lipped, retained that look that Fools Crow had noticed at the Sun Dance ceremony.

"I have been places," said Fast Horse. "I have been to the whiskey forts beyond the Medicine Line. I have been to that place below Many-sharp-points-ground where the Napikwans dig the yellow dust. Now I return from Many Houses fort on the Big

River." Fast Horse smiled. "And now I'm afraid I am shot." He lifted the buffalo coat from his left side. He had tied a heavy cloth around his ribs but it was caked with blood. "Here is where it came out."

Only twice on the journey to the camp of the Lone Eaters did Fast Horse speak again. Once he asked about his father in such a way that Fools Crow knew he was apprehensive about his reception in camp. Another time, after a long coughing fit in which he spit up a mouthful of foamy blood, he said, "I am shot by the fool Napikwans." The rest of the time he hunched low in his saddle and appeared to doze.

It was dusk by the time they arrived in camp. As Fools Crow led his friend to Boss Ribs' lodge he noticed how quiet all the lodges were. Three dogs had come out to meet them as they approached camp, barking and howling, but now they trotted silently beside the horses. A woman with an armload of firewood watched them pass. But he saw no children about, no men standing in small groups, gossiping. It had become a winter camp.

Fools Crow got down from his horse and called into the lodge for Boss Ribs. Then he helped Fast Horse down, but the young man's legs were as weak as a baby's. He fell and Fools Crow caught him and laid him gently on the ground.

Boss Ribs came out, followed by his two wives, neither of which was Fast Horse's mother. She had been killed by a real-bear while berry picking. Boss Ribs knelt beside Fools Crow and looked down.

"He's been shot." Fools Crow drew away the coat, exposing the bloody cloth.

Boss Ribs looked down at his son, who lay with his eyes closed. If Fools Crow had expected to see Boss Ribs exclaim or weep, he was disappointed. The older man said to his wives, "Help me carry him inside."

As Fools Crow hurried down to Mik-api's lodge, he wondered at Boss Ribs' reaction to his wounded son. He realized he had never come to know this keeper of the Beaver Medicine. When Rides-at-the-door told him of the many crazy things he and Boss Ribs had done when they were young, he had never been able to imagine Boss Ribs running a herd of horses through the camp of some Entrails People back in the days when the Pikunis were friendly with them. Or pissing from a ledge onto a Cutthroat scout who had fallen asleep. Fools Crow only knew him as his friend's father, a serious quiet man who opened his Beaver Medicine bundle with each new moon and who kept the winter count.

Fools Crow sat near a far wall of the lodge all night, watching Mik-api make his medicine. Boss Ribs and his two wives sat together, opposite Fools Crow. Mik-api did not like to have a sick one's family in the lodge because it thinned the concentration of the medicine. A bad spirit, as it made up its mind to leave the body, would sometimes see the family, become frightened and jump back in. But Mik-api made an exception in this lodge. Boss Ribs was a spirit man and his wives helped him with the Beaver Medicine ceremony.

Mik-api performed the healing ceremony as though only he and Fast Horse were in the lodge. The only time he looked away from the youth was when he needed something from his bag or told Fools Crow to boil water or grind leaves. He seemed to be in another world as he chanted and sang and beat the small stretched skin with his blackhorn-scrotum rattle. Once he stood up and circled Fast Horse, swooping and diving, imitating the eagle's flight, blowing on his eagle-bone whistle. Then he dropped to his knees and fanned Fast Horse's body with an eagle wing. He blew the whistle over the body, and a thin yellow stream of paste dribbled on the chest and stomach. He put away his eagle things and applied a third compress on the wound. He held the compress tightly until all the liquid oozed over the wound. All the while he chanted, "Eagle spirit, heal this body, each death makes me poor."

Fools Crow awoke in the gray light of winter morning, startled out of a dream of mountains and berries. He stirred the small fire and added more wood. Mik-api was still bent over the limp body, praying in a language that Fools Crow had heard before in Mik-api's healing ceremonies. It was the language of the Black Paint People, who taught him his medicine. Mik-api's gray hair hung loose around his face. He looks like an old woman, thought Fools

Crow, so drawn and wrinkled. Even his hands are bleached and withered, like an old skin thrown away to the rain and sun. It was hard to believe that the shrunken old man possessed so much magic. Fools Crow settled back to watch, to learn.

Again, Fools Crow was awakened out of a dream, this time by a sharp moan. He sat up quickly. The lodge was light and quiet. Mik-api was gone. Boss Ribs and his wives were gone. Fools Crow scrambled to build up the fire.

Fast Horse lay with his eyes open. His face was gray and bloated. At first, Fools Crow thought he was dead, but as he looked down in dread, he saw his friend blink his eyes. He knelt beside the face and touched it with his hand. The cracked lips moved but no sound came out. The eyes closed.

Fools Crow dipped a cloth into the warm water over the fire. He wrung it out and bathed his friend's face. He dipped a cup of water before he remembered that Mik-api, another time, had told him not to give water to one who had been gut-shot.

Mik-api must have gone to his own lodge to sleep, thought Fools Crow. He hated to wake the heavy-singer-for-the-sick, but he knew that Mik-api would want to know that Fast Horse had opened his eyes. He pulled the robe up under his friend's chin; then he ducked outside the flap and almost knocked Mik-api over. Mik-api was wearing a fur cap over his damp hair.

"I was having a sweat with Boss Ribs and his wives. They'll be along shortly."

"He opened his eyes."

"That is a good sign, but we must not hope too much." Mik-api entered the lodge. "There is poison in him yet."

"Do you think he can drink? I'll bring some broth—"

"Not this one. We had better starve him today." Mik-api smiled wearily. "But you can bring me some."

As Fools Crow walked away from the lodge he heard the rattle begin. He was halfway to his own lodge before he realized that he was walking through snow up to his ankles. He looked up to the sky and saw that the clouds had white edges to them with jagged patches of blue between. He breathed sharply through his mouth and a puff of steam curled out. He was very hungry.

On the third morning after his return to camp, Fast Horse woke up and saw his father looking down at him. The lodge was bright and warm, and Fast Horse knew he had been here before. He smelled smoke and robes and broth and they were familiar, like the face. He recognized the firm chin, the wide cheekbones, the thin mouth. He knew the brass and feather earring, the braids wrapped in weasel skins. He even knew the way his father sometimes cleared his much-broken nose by puffing bursts of air through it. It was when he looked into the eyes that he grew uncertain of himself. Had he ever seen those eyes before?

"You have been gone a long time," said Boss Ribs.

Fast Horse didn't know if he meant his spirit or his body. He had been gone a long time in both.

"I have prayed for you."

Since his return or since he left? Or before both? Had his father always known he would turn out like this?

"Last night I brought in the Beaver Medicine. When you are well, I hope you will assist me."

But why? Didn't his father know he no longer believed in the Beaver Medicine or in anything Pikuni? He had been to the whiskey forts and he had lain with a girl with yellow hair, with skin as white as snow. He had killed three Napikwans and stolen their yellow dust.

"Mik-api healed you with his magic. He drove the evil spirit from your body and made you whole again. Your friend, Fools Crow—you knew him as White Man's Dog—helped Mik-api."

Now Fast Horse recognized those eyes, the pain in them. He had seen it when his mother died and when his near-mother died, then that winter when three of Fast Horse's brothers and sisters died of the coughing sickness. It was a young, almost frightened look in the eyes that contrasted sharply with the tough wrinkled face.

"I know you have been sick in the spirit for some time, my son. I noticed it but I said nothing, hoping I was wrong. This sickness came out on your raid on the Crow horses. It has persisted since then. It has made you choose bad companions and do bad things with them. And now it has almost cost you your life."

Fools Crow must have told him it was a Napikwan that shot me, thought Fast Horse. Did he tell him how it happened? Did I tell Fools Crow how it happened?

"But I think this sickness was in you before, much before the raid. I saw a change in you and, although I didn't care for it, I thought it was natural. Boys change when they are on the edge of manhood. I thought your loud boastfulness was a way of declaring yourself. I thought your cruelty to the other youths was a way of establishing your place among them. I thought when you had seen a little more of life you would outgrow these bad traits, you would become a man among his brothers. This is how we Pikunis live. We help each other, we depend on each other, we fight and die beside each other. There is no room for the man who despises his fellows."

Fast Horse turned away. He could not look any longer into those eyes.

"I am afraid you have become such a one. The sickness has made you look down on your own people. You no longer follow their ways. You ignore their most sacred traditions. And yet, Mik-api, through his Pikuni medicine, has healed your body. The medicine, whether you believe in it or not, still works on you."

Fast Horse remembered nothing of the healing ceremony— only waking up in the morning and seeing Mik-api, head bent, pounding monotonously on his small drum. Later, he saw Fools Crow looking down at him.

"Mik-api healed your body but not your spirit. The sickness is too deep within you for such a simple ceremony." Boss Ribs smiled, and it was a sad but hopeful smile. The young, frightened look had gone out of his eyes. "That is why I want you to assist me in opening the Beaver bundle. There is great power in that bundle. We will open it, and I will teach you its ways. There are four hundred songs that you will have to learn. There are stories and proper ways of acting them out. I do not expect you to learn it all at once, but the power of the bundle will heal your spirit. Once again, you will join your people. Ok-yi, son, welcome."

Fast Horse closed his eyes and thought of that time, when he was five or six winters, that the real-bear killed his mother. She was picking berries with some other women. He stood at the edge of the thicket and watched the almost serpentine slide of speed as the real-bear came out of nowhere to knock his mother down, shake her until her body was as limp as her skin dress, then drag her off. It happened so fast that for years all he could remember was his mother's slender neck in those slavering jaws. But now the whole scene came to him, and if he could have cried, if he had any tears left in him, he would have. He was too tired. He wanted nothing more than to roll over and sleep in peace. The sound of his father praying kept him in the lodge.

Red Paint had fleshed and scraped the blackhorn hide and now sat waiting for the stones to heat up. In a pot beside her, she had mixed the grease and brains with which she would begin her tanning. She looked at her hands and was surprised to see how red and rough they had become. They were no longer the hands of a girl. Her knuckles seemed larger and the fingernails had dark crescents of grease beneath them.

She sat back and watched Fools Crow and Fast Horse walk down by the river. Fast Horse was healing, but he was gaunt and his walk was fragile. The bulky buffalo coat covered his body from neck to midway down his calves. His head looked small, and his hands pale and narrow. Beside him, in his white red-trimmed capote, Fools Crow gave the appearance of burly health, of color and strength. Although half a head shorter than his companion, his width and low gravity made one think of the real-bear. Even his gait furthered that impression.

Red Paint watched the two friends. As a girl she had had a crush on Fast Horse, as did most of the other girls. He was tall, handsome, haughty and seemingly indifferent to their attentions. For a year she had dreamed of making love with him. And she dreamed of carrying his child, serene amid the jealous stares of her friends. In her dreams their lodge was made of the whitest skins and her dress was covered with elk teeth and ermine tails. He was a great warrior and hunter, and he sighed with pleasure when she braided his hair in the morning. Then they would make more love and have more babies and he would never take another wife. Sometimes, in her dreams, he would die a tragic but good death, and people would point to her, her hair cut off and legs slashed in mourning, and say what a noble woman she was. And every night his spirit would return from the Sand Hills and they would make love and have still more babies.

Now Red Paint felt her tummy and thought that the baby was that of Fools Crow, one that none of the girls dreamed about. He was always just the one with Fast Horse. Red Paint remembered being jealous of him.

It was all changed. She was married to Fools Crow and loved him and sought only to be a good wife to him. About Fast Horse, she felt a kind of pity. Since his return, the camp of the Lone Eaters had become divided. Some wanted him turned out as soon as he was well. A few even wanted him killed for his betrayal of Yellow Kidney. But there were many who remained loyal to Boss Ribs and wanted to forgive his son, to welcome him back as they would welcome back one who had been to the whiskey forts and associated with the loose girls and bad Napikwans.

Red Paint didn't know what to think. Her pitiful father still stayed apart from the others of the band. He ate, he slept, he sat in his lodge or wandered by himself on the prairie. Red Paint had been in his lodge, beading with her mother, when they received the news that Fast Horse had returned. She had watched Yellow Kidney's face, half afraid that he would grab his gun and kill the young man. But he simply sat there as though the words did not enter his ears. He had looked at his mutilated hands as though they did not belong to him. The camp crier had said Fast Horse was wounded and would die before Sun came up. Perhaps that was the only revenge her father needed.

But Fast Horse didn't die and Red Paint didn't know what to think. As she watched the two friends down by the river, she couldn't help feeling that perhaps he should have died to give everyone peace of mind.

She looked to the Backbone. The granite faces above the dark forests seemed to watch over the winter camp of the Lone Eaters.

Red Paint had enjoyed the summer in the Sweet Grass Hills, but she always felt unprotected away from the Backbone. Now that the big Napikwan had been killed, she could once again think of the mountains as sanctuary. It was good to be back at the winter camp on the Two Medicine River.

Red Paint spread the greasy mixture on the stiffened hide. Then she took one of the warm stones from the edge of the fire and began to scrub the hide with it, working the grease in. The stone felt good to her cold red hands. She was glad that Fast Horse hadn't died.

17

THE SNOW LAY BLUE AND DEEP on the land in the dark
before dawn, and in those places where the Two Medicine
slowed and eddied the ice groaned and cracked beneath its
weight. The twenty-six lodges of the Lone Eaters stood among
the big-leaf trees and willows, quiet as the world around them.
Only the smoke arising from each lodge betrayed the life of the
people sleeping inside. A sudden hard wind during the night had
piled drifts behind the lodges and trees.

One set of tracks blemished the perfect cover. It led away from
a large lodge near the center of the camp. On almost any other
day the women would have been up, building up the fires, carrying water and wood, moving quietly to and from the river. The
men and children would be asleep or awake, reluctant to leave
their sleeping robes until the smell of cooking meat became too
strong to resist. Then they would dress and walk out beyond the
perimeter of the camp to piss, to look about, to think of the day's
activity. Then they would return to the lodges, where the meat
and broth would be ladled out and consumed with great appetite,
men first. Afterward, a smoke, and then the ceaseless round of
visiting. Some of the men would go off hunting, or just exploring,
always with their weapons. The women would prepare hides or
continue with bead- or quillwork and gossip. The children would
throw stones into the river or play with dolls or sleds.

But on this day, the day after the first big blizzard of the winter,
even the women snuggled deeper into their robes and slept.

Fast Horse laid his saddle and provisions down in the knee-deep snow. He put the saddle blanket on top of the saddle and his gun on top of that.

With bridle in hand, he walked among the horses of the vast herd, speaking gently to the skittish ones. A few of the horses had dug away the snow and were feeding on the short grass beneath. Most of them stood, half asleep, rumps to the gentle but cold wind. Fast Horse moved among them, clucking and soothing, until he came to his bay. The horse was not as wary as he would become later in the day. Fast Horse slipped his arm around the bay's neck, then eased the bit into his mouth. The horse was strong with a straight back, big shoulders and rump. Because the horse had once belonged to a Napikwan, he was used to the bit and did not fight the cold steel. Fast Horse led him through the herd to his possessions.

He felt a twinge of pain as he threw the saddle on the horse's back, but the wound was almost healed. He had eaten a lot of meat in the past several sleeps since he had decided to live, and although he still walked stiffly, he felt strong enough to leave the camp of the Lone Eaters. This time for good.

He had heard from a Grease Melter that Mountain Chief's people had come down from the country across the Medicine Line and were wintering on the Bear River. Owl Child and the others would probably be with them. Fast Horse missed his friends and the way they moved around the country, acquiring things. Once he had taken three pouches of the yellow dust from a miner on his way to the town at Many-sharp-points-ground. He knew the dust was valuable, but he felt best about making a fool of the digging-man. Owl Child had made him throw away the scalp. If they were ever caught, it could be used against them.

Fast Horse had learned much from Owl Child about the Napikwans and their laws, about the seizers and their movements. Owl Child seemed to have a knack for attacking in one part of the country while the seizers searched for him in another. He knew which settlement was well protected, which wagon train was alert and ready for them. He knew which ranches were vulnerable.

Until the last time. Fast Horse tied his bundle onto the back of the saddle, slung his rifle into the scabbard and clambered stiffly aboard the big bay. He skirted the village to the south, staying in the valley just below the swell of the plain. It was light enough to see the lodges clearly, the smoke rising from them. He heard a puppy bark, the sharp *yap* carrying in the wind that blew toward him. There was nothing in camp for him anymore, nothing about the life the Lone Eaters lived that appealed to him. The thought of hunting, of accumulating robes, of the constant search for meat seemed pointless to him. There were easier ways of gaining wealth. Raiding other tribes, stealing their horses, was a waste of time. Just a few Napikwan horses were worth more than whole herds of Snake or Cutthroat animals. As for women, there were enough who hung around the forts. And there was the Napikwan woman with the yellow hair. She had fought good for a while, but after that first night away from her people she had settled down. Fast Horse had never seen a body that white. Even the hair of her sex was light. She was fat and her face was covered with brown spots, but Fast Horse could not forget the yellow kinky hair of her center. He didn't even mind much that Under Bull had gotten her man's boots away from him. He had another pair. After the second day they had released the naked woman, but by then she didn't seem to care where she was or what she was going to do. Fast Horse shifted in the saddle to accommodate his stiffening penis. He would get himself another Napikwan woman, this time one who wasn't so fat.

The horse walked easily through the powdery snow, and Fast Horse thought again of the Napikwan who had shot him. He had a ranch south of Many Houses fort on the Big River, just above Rocks Ridge Across. Owl Child had scouted the ranch that afternoon, pretending to be lost. He counted sixteen horses. He said the man was alone with his wife and two daughters. That night they made their raid, riding into an ambush. Fast Horse was almost pulled from his horse by the rancher, a large redheaded man, but he managed to kick the man to his knees and ride away. No more than fifty paces from the corral, he heard the bark of a rifle and felt the sharp burn of the shooter in his back. He felt immediately hollow inside and gasped for air. He had cried out with pain and surprise, but after that, when he opened his mouth no sound came out. He rode hard and he heard the volley of shots and he didn't know what had become of Owl Child and the others.

The wound had bled that first night as he rode north and west, but he had wrapped it with strips of torn-up shirt and by morning the bleeding had stopped. He rode for another day and night before he saw Fools Crow. The wound had become a painful tightening in his back, but the cold kept him in and out of consciousness. He knew that the Lone Eaters were hunting near the Sweet Grass Hills, for he had heard them planning during the Sun Dance ceremonies. He knew if he could make it to his father's lodge, he would live. And he did live. And now he would rejoin Owl Child and go take his revenge on the big redheaded man. He would make the man die many times.

He pulled the collar up on the buffalo coat. Before rounding a bend he looked back. The village of the Lone Eaters looked small and insignificant in the blue snowfield.

Fools Crow sat in the warm tipi studying the Beaver Medicine bundle. It was large and bulky, the size of a sleeping blackhorn calf. Usually it would be resting on a platform behind Boss Ribs' lodge so the people would be aware of its power. Once Fools Crow had watched Boss Ribs perform the ceremony. It was long and complicated. Fools Crow had sat from morning to dusk watching the holy man and his helpers perform the songs and prayers and dances. It had been opened during the new moon of the burnt grass. At one point, Boss Ribs had called to him and burned sweet grass and rubbed the smoke over his body. It was a blessing from Beaver Chief. It had been done to help Fools Crow, then White Man's Dog, shake his bad luck. There had been other blessings bestowed on other members of the Lone Eaters, but White Man's Dog had felt honored to be a small part of the ceremony.

"I see you are interested in the Beaver Medicine, Fools Crow," said Boss Ribs.

"I was remembering that day I witnessed the ceremony three winters ago. It made my eyes go round."

"Ah." Boss Ribs laughed. "It was performed exactly as Beaver Chief instructed Akaiyan in the long-ago. Beaver Medicine is the oldest and holiest of our medicines. It is the power of our people, my young friend. Let us smoke."

Both men filled their short-pipes and smoked for a while. Fools Crow was not comfortable. From time to time, he thought to speak, but the look in his host's eyes told him to hold his tongue. He glanced around the lodge. After he had sat down with Boss Ribs, the women and children had disappeared. He thought it a curious thing. He had often visited the lodge because he was so close to Fast Horse, and the family had always treated him as one of them—except for Boss Ribs, who had always held himself away from the chattering and bickering that went on around him. Now the two men were alone and the lodge was quiet.

Boss Ribs was a tall, loose-jointed man with a sad face. Although he was a rich man and the keeper of the Beaver Medicine, many in the camp pitied him, for he had lost two wives and three children. Some even questioned his role as keeper of the sacred medicine since he had encountered so much misfortune himself. Fools Crow had heard Young Bird Chief say, "How can he help the Lone Eaters if he can't help himself?" The other young men agreed that it was a curious thing. But Boss Ribs performed the ceremony correctly and well, and the power did help the sick ones, the poor ones, and Fools Crow knew that he was highly respected among the elders.

Finally Boss Ribs set his pipe down next to his tobacco pouch. He leaned back against his willow backrest and pulled a robe over his legs. He closed his eyes for a long time. Fools Crow thought the man was tired, so he packed his own pipe away. Just as he started to rise, Boss Ribs said, "I will tell you the story of the Beaver Medicine."

Fools Crow noticed that there were fire shadows dancing on the walls of the lodge. It had gotten dark outside.

"In the long-ago, before the coming of the elk-dogs, there lived two brothers: orphans, they were. The younger was named

Akaiyan. He lived with his brother, Nopatsis, and his wife. Now this wife was a cruel one and she didn't like Akaiyan in their lodge. Many times she told her husband to cast him out, but he always refused. He knew what it was like to be young and alone, and he said there would always be a place for Akaiyan in his lodge.

"One day Nopatsis went out hunting, for they were low on meat and had been living for some time on gophers and mice. When he returned he found his wife with her clothes torn and her legs bleeding. She told him that Akaiyan had attacked her and roughed her up. This was a lie, of course, for Akaiyan was a gentle young man. But Nopatsis, perhaps because he was tired of his wife's constant badgering, became very angry, and in a few days he devised a plan to rid himself and his wife of his younger brother. It was during that time of summer when the ducks and geese lose their feathers. Nopatsis said to Akaiyan, 'Let us go to the island in the big lake and collect feathers for our arrows.' So off they went, and when they came to the big lake, they built a raft and floated on it to the island. Now, Akaiyan, being unaware of his brother's treachery, walked around the island, picking up feathers until he had quite a bundle, as many as he could carry. When he returned to the raft it was gone and he saw his brother paddling to the far shore. He cried out and begged his brother to come back for him, but the brother merely laughed at him. 'You can spend the winter on your island, and in the spring when the ice melts I will come back for your bones,' said Nopatsis.

"Akaiyan thought he was going to die, so he sat down and wept and beat the ground with his hand. He called to Sun Chief, to Night Red Light, to Morning Star to help him. He prayed to the Underwater People to save him. Oh, he was sad. He didn't want to die alone on that island without even a wife to mourn him. He pitied himself and cried all the more. Soon, though, he gathered up his courage and decided to make the best of it. He collected more feathers for a bed, cut down tree limbs for a shelter and killed ducks and geese for his meals. He skinned these birds and made himself a warm robe of their pelts.

"One day he came to a small pond where he saw a beaver lodge.

He lay down and wept, for it was approaching the moon of the first snow and he had no home of his own. Soon a little beaver came out of the lodge and said, 'Come in, you wretched one, my father would talk to you.' With that the beaver jumped in the water and Akaiyan followed him. They swam into a long dark tunnel, and the only way Akaiyan could see was from the little bubbles the beaver made with his tail. Just when he thought his lungs were about to burst, his head popped up and he was in a big dark lodge. When his eyes became adjusted, he looked around and saw many beaver children and a mother and father. This father was as white as the snow goose and bigger than any wood-biter Akaiyan had ever seen. He knew this must be Beaver Chief. He began to shiver in fear, but Beaver Chief told him to settle down and tell him why he had been crying. When Akaiyan told his sad story, Beaver Chief took pity on him and said he could live with them all winter. With that, his wife closed up the lodge.

"Akaiyan stayed with the beaver family. They slept all around him and put their tails over him to keep him warm. All winter Beaver Chief taught him things, many great things. He taught the young man the roots and herbs, the leaves and bark that our people still use for healing. He taught him paints and rituals that could be used for healing the sick. He gave Akaiyan tobacco seeds, which our people later made grow and now use in ceremonials. Above all, Beaver Chief taught him the songs and dances, the acting, that would accompany the magic of these wonderful things. It was a good winter for Akaiyan. He learned much and he grew to love the beaver family and think of himself as one of them, for he had never had a family of his own.

"One day, when seven moons were up, Akaiyan heard the ice breaking on the lake. It would soon be time to leave the good beaver family. He began to gather up his things, but Beaver Chief told him to wait awhile, for he knew that the bad Nopatsis was returning to the island to search for his younger brother's bones. Akaiyan hid behind a tree and watched his brother paddle the raft to the island. He had a big smile on his face, for he had become a cruel one. Akaiyan watched him jump off the raft, singing to himself. When his brother disappeared into the trees, Akaiyan paddled the raft to the other shore. Many moons later, when he returned to the island, Akaiyan found his older brother's bones not far from the beaver lodge.

"Now the young beaver who had found Akaiyan and brought him into the lodge missed his new brother. One night he came to Akaiyan in a dream and told the young man that he would teach him even more wonderful things, so the next day Akaiyan returned to the big lake and, sure enough, there was the little beaver waiting for him. Together the two brothers made their way back to Akaiyan's village, and when Akaiyan told the people who the little beaver was, they raised a great cry and were happy to see him. All that summer the little wood-biter taught the people the songs and dances and prayers of the beaver family. Akaiyan of course had already learned these things, so he assisted in the teaching. One day, the little beaver told Akaiyan that it was time for him to leave. He had taught the people and now he missed his family. Akaiyan was sad, but he knew how it is with families. Before he left, the young beaver gave the young man a sacred pipe. He said, 'Whoever smokes this pipe will remain in good health. Put this in your bundle, Akaiyan, and let it be the first thing you lift out when you perform your ceremony.'

"That spring Akaiyan invited all the four-leggeds, the flyers, the underwater swimmers, the things that crawl along the ground, to add to the power of the bundle. Many of them offered their skins and the songs that went with them; some just their songs or dances. Every spring Akaiyan returned to the beaver family and Beaver Chief would give him something to add to the bundle—a headdress, an eagle-bone whistle, a sacred tobacco planting stick—until it became as large as you see it now. Akaiyan became a great Beaver Medicine man and raised his own family and lived for many years. Before he died he handed the bundle down to his son. It has been handed down ever since."

Fools Crow drew a deep breath and sat back. He looked at the Beaver Medicine bundle, which lay not more than three paces away. His head almost hurt from his fierce listening. He had heard the story of the origin of the medicine when he was a child. It was one of his grandfather's favorite stories. But this telling was different. It came from the lips of the man who was the keeper of the bundle, who had learned the ways of the medicine the same way Akaiyan had learned it in the long-ago. And there lay the bundle, filled with magic and power.

"Mik-api tells me you are becoming wise in the ways of medicine," said Boss Ribs.

"I have helped Mik-api and he has taught me many things. There is so much to learn, sometimes I think my head is not capable of absorbing it all."

"You are young. There was a time when I thought I would never learn the ceremony of the Beaver Medicine. Once you understand, it becomes easier." Boss Ribs sat forward suddenly and looked down into Fools Crow's eyes. "Once you commit yourself to such knowledge, there is no turning away."

Fools Crow was surprised at the edge in Boss Ribs' voice. It was as though the older man was warning him, but he hadn't committed himself. He liked Mik-api and he liked the medicine, but he did not think of himself as the old man's successor. Until now he hadn't thought of himself as anything but a hunter. His warring and raiding were not unusual for a Pikuni. He had killed the Napikwan more out of fear than for honor. No, he was a blackhorn hunter, a provider of meat and skins, nothing more.

He looked at the fire and said, "What is it you wish of me, Boss Ribs?"

Some children ran by, leaving a trail of laughter in the shadowy lodge. Each man remembered that he had been a child once, had laughed the same way, at nothing but his own joy.

"What is it you wish?"

Boss Ribs rubbed his eyes and sighed. "I would like two things from you, young one. First, tell me what it was that changed my son so—that turned him away."

Without hesitation, Fools Crow told the father of Fast Horse about the raid on the Crows. He left nothing out. He described Fast Horse's dream in detail, the search for the ice spring, the anger of Cold Maker, the frustration of his friend. With some reluctance, he told Boss Ribs of his son's careless treachery that led to Yellow Kidney's discovery and mutilation. He knew Boss

Ribs had heard that part, had probably lived with it in dreams, but he wanted to tell it right, perhaps to clarify it in his own mind.

"Fast Horse did not fulfill the vow he made to Cold Maker. He was afraid of what he had done to Yellow Kidney. He was afraid that Cold Maker would consider him unworthy—and harm him." Fools Crow was guessing, but he had given it a lot of thought.

Even when he had recovered from his wounds, Fast Horse had never mentioned the Crow raid to Fools Crow. During their walks together, Fast Horse had spoken of things from their childhood, the places he had been, the things he had seen. Once, on the bank of the Two Medicine, as they were watching Sun Chief return to his home, Fools Crow told him about the Napikwan in the mountains, how afraid he had been of the giant man, how he thought he was going to die a shameful death. He had hoped such an admission would bring Fast Horse to open up about his own shameful behavior on the raid, but his friend just laughed and said there would be many more Napikwans to kill. Then, the night before Fast Horse left again, he came to Fools Crow's lodge. Red Paint went off to gather wood in the snowy night, but Fools Crow knew she would go to her parents' lodge. Fast Horse came close to thanking his friend for saving his life. The feelings were in the air like smoke, but the words would not come. There was a moment of silence and Fools Crow thought his friend would finally say something about the long-ago raid, perhaps as a favor to him. Fast Horse had looked keenly at him and there was pain in his eyes, but as he did so often, he laughed and talked of the women he had met on his war trail. Impulsively, Fools Crow had cut him off with the suggestion that Fast Horse should talk to Boss Ribs, that his father could help him; at the very least, go see Mik-api. Both were great medicine men and could cure a man of whatever it was deep inside that troubled him. Fast Horse had flared with anger and said their magic was no good for him. Then he left the lodge that night and left camp the next morning.

The sound of Boss Ribs' voice interrupted his thought. "I know my son has done wrong. He has shamed himself and he has shamed me. Worst of all, he is responsible for turning a brave into a pitiful thing. I can never look Yellow Kidney in the eye for shame. Perhaps Fast Horse deserves to carry this burden with him wherever he goes."

A dog barked close by, followed by an angry curse and a thump.

"But he is my only son. You know of my losses, Fools Crow, you know how Fast Horse lost his mother when he was a young child. Sometimes, I think I am cursed with this Beaver Medicine. Sometimes, I think I do not perform the ceremony well enough, that I anger Beaver Chief. But the people come to me and I make them well! Yes, through Beaver Chief I cure their illnesses, heal their wounds, their spirits. I return sons to mothers, wives to husbands, brothers to sisters. I thank Beaver Chief for these blessings every day. I pray to him to carry the evil spirit from my son's heart. But when I ask for myself, he does not listen. I think sometimes that the keeper of the bundle is the only one who does not benefit. Many times I have thought to sell it. Rich men from all the bands would wish to possess it, for it makes them powerful." Boss Ribs smiled at Fools Crow. His eyes glistened.

"But always in my heart I knew that I would pass it to my only son, even if it meant misfortune for him too. Now it seems he has created his own. If he is not stopped in this course he has chosen, it will only be a matter of time before he is dead—and not honorably. I have become a foolish old man, but I think there is a chance that we can save him before this happens."

Fools Crow had been stirring the fire. Now he looked up at Boss Ribs. Although he had heard every word, he found his mind drifting, his thoughts shifting from Fast Horse to his own brother. Running Fisher had become sullen in the same way that Fast Horse had after the raid. Something had happened to Running Fisher that day Sun Chief hid his face. Fools Crow remembered the fear in his brother's face and tried to remember if he had seen him during the battle in the Crow village. The fighting had been so heated, and Fools Crow himself had been so scared—

"Go after him, Fools Crow. Find him and bring him back. Get him away from that treacherous gang. I will begin to instruct him in the ways of the Beaver Medicine. He will learn that it is his destiny as well as his duty. Tell him his father begs him, his people beg him. There can be no turning away!"

Fools Crow looked into the young, frightened eyes of his friend's father, and the look alarmed him. He thought of the many times Boss Ribs had opened the Beaver Medicine, how the people came to him in despair and left with hope in their hearts, how the young ones learned the ways of the old rituals by observing him and his sacred helpers, how the unhealthy ones gained strength through the medicine. Fools Crow glanced at the medicine bundle. The outer covering was of stiff rawhide. The painted red designs were faded by weather, barely noticeable, much less intelligible. Inside was the power of the Pikunis. "This magic is no good for me"—that's what Fast Horse had said. And Mik-api had said, "I can't heal a man who doesn't have the heart for it." What good would it do to bring Fast Horse back?

"I will look for him," said Fools Crow. The weakness in his voice irritated him. He had wished to be more positive. "I will find him and bring him home."

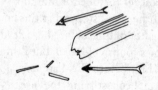

PART
THREE

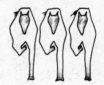

18

THE WARM CHINOOK WIND had blown for two days and a night. While the snow was still heavy in the ravines, cutbanks and valleys, most of the hills of the plain were yellow with sparse grass. A small herd of blackhorns grazed on the slope of a ravine to the west. Most of them were old bulls, no longer important to the larger herds. Their coats were ragged and reddish in color. One bull lay in the sun, his eyes closed, his large head nodding in sleep. His withers were gaunt and his tail was crusted with shit. A single fly, hatched by the warm winds, crawled over the mucus in the corner of his eye. The bull did not know where he was anymore. His breath came in harsh gasps, but he did not care that he was dying. A black-and-white long-tail, perched on his rump, picked at the crusty scabs with great care.

Owl Child sat on his horse on the south side of a steep hill. The snow was slushy beneath the horse's hooves. Wind ruffled the two hawk feathers tied in the mane between the horse's ears. Owl Child had one leg up, crooked around the saddle horn. He was working on his rifle. A cartridge had jammed in the breech and he was trying to free it with his knife. He could just get the tip of the blade beneath the lip at the base of the greased shooter, but every time he twisted the blade it would slip off. "Sonofabitch," he swore. He knew several of the Napikwan words, but this was the one he liked best.

"Sonofabitch," said Crow Top.

Owl Child looked up from his work and grinned. Then he felt the knife blade catch again. This time he wedged the knife against the thick barrel and eased the cartridge out. It popped loose and fell into the slushy snow.

"Sonofabitch!" shouted Crow Top, and the other men laughed.

Owl Child jacked another cartridge into the chamber. It slid in easily. Owl Child beamed. "Fast Horse, how is it this Crow Top speaks like a Napikwan, yet he is the blackest of all the Pikunis?"

Red Horn, Star and Black Weasel laughed again. Their horses, awakened by the rough sound, shifted uneasily beneath them. Only The Cut Hand did not laugh. He was ill with the white man's disease. He had drunk half a jug of whiskey two days ago and the poison was still in his guts.

Fast Horse lay on his buffalo coat on the side of the hill. The three-day ride down from Mountain Chief's camp had exhausted him. He looked up at the small fleecy clouds scattered throughout the blue. "He must have learned it from that fat white woman."

"Ah, she was good," said Crow Top. "She taught me many things. Someday I will learn that language; then I will teach you good."

"Perhaps you should go to the white man's school. They teach you to sit off the ground. That way you know where your ass is."

Crow Top leaned closer to Owl Child, his hand near his mouth. He whispered and both men laughed.

"This one wants himself another white woman," said Owl Child. "He says they are better than his hand, even better than his dog!"

Star and Red Horn teased Crow Top. The Cut Hand leaned over the side of his horse and heaved, making belching sounds, but nothing came out. He wiped his mouth and groaned.

Owl Child slid off his horse and walked over to Fast Horse. He looked down and said, "And what do you want, old woman?"

"You know what I want."

"And when you kill this Napikwan you will feel better?"

"I have thought how I will kill him, little by little. I will cut off little pieces. . . ."

Owl Child looked off toward the west. Most of the old bulls had passed over the crest of the yellow hill. Only the sleeping one remained on the slope. He was lying on his side, surrounded by long-tails. Any other time Owl Child would have practiced his shooting—to put the old one out of his misery—but not now. They were too close to the ranch. He knew what Fast Horse was feeling inside. He too wished to teach this redheaded Napikwan a lesson. But Fast Horse had only been wounded. He hadn't been humiliated as Owl Child had been that day long ago when he had been struck down with a whip and slapped before his own people. But now Owl Child was revenged. He had made Malcolm Clark pay. He had killed him in his own house. The sight of Four Bears Clark lying in his own blood, his women screaming in the other room, had filled Owl Child with great pleasure. It should have been enough but it wasn't. There were other Napikwans as evil as Four Bears. Owl Child felt his face grow hot as he heard the words again that Clark had called him: a dog and a woman. All the Napikwans would pay for those words. And to think his own cousin, Cutting-off-head Woman, had married Four Bears and had let this bad thing happen to Owl Child. To think that many of the Pikunis had disapproved of Owl Child's revenge. They were the women—letting the Napikwans steal their lands, kill off their blackhorns, marry their women. They thought that by humbling themselves they could appease the whites. Owl Child spat. They would pay too, he thought. They would pay good, but not at the hands of Owl Child, for he would have nothing to do with them. Only Mountain Chief and a few others knew that the white men were evil two-faces. But that was not Owl Child's worry. No, he was on his own and liked it that way. Owl Child would make a name for himself that would make them all, Pikuni or Napikwan, tremble to hear.

As he looked off toward the dying bull, he heard the soft drumming of hooves like muffled thunder. He reached his horse in ten steps, leaped into the saddle and sat tensely, rifle butt resting against his right thigh. Out of the corner of his eye he saw Fast Horse scrambling to his feet.

The two riders appeared over the rim of the hill. Owl Child watched them ease their horses down the soft earth slope, kicking up mud and slush. Bear Chief and Under Bull slowed their horses to a trot. Owl Child settled back in his saddle.

"How is it?" he called.

"The man works in his corral, shoveling manure. His woman sits on the steps of the lodge with two little ones. Easy for us." Under Bull was breathing hard. His nose ran.

"How about the horses?"

"In a wire pen behind the corral. Sixteen we counted."

"No other Napikwans?"

"We looked around. No others."

Owl Child turned to Fast Horse and grinned. "There is your Napikwan. Like an old cow in the corral."

"I am ready," said Fast Horse. The tiredness had left his bones. "I will make him cry many times before Sun returns to his lodge."

Owl Child and the others laughed. "Then let us not keep him waiting. He gathers manure for the evening meal."

Fast Horse rode beside Owl Child, his big bay two hands taller than the white horse with the red thunderbirds on his shoulders. This was what the Lone Eaters did not know about, he thought, this urgency, this ease with which one could make his enemies pay. He glanced back at the riders. The Cut Hand, at the rear of the small column, was leaning over his horse again.

Fools Crow had followed Fast Horse's tracks that first day out. It had been easy in the deep snow. But that night as he lay asleep in a shelter under a cutbank surrounded by rosebushes, the chinook winds began to blow. By morning the snow level in the high places had lowered considerably. Fools Crow sat on his heels outside the shelter and ate the boiled meat that Red Paint had packed. The sky was light enough so that he could see it would be a clear day. The small puffy clouds were riding the wind northeast.

By midday he was nearly to the point where the Two Medicine joins the Bear. The grass showed yellow through the thin layer of snow on the hills to either side of him. Large chunks of ice floated in the eddy of the confluence. Fools Crow found a dry rock and sat and smoked. There was no hope of following Fast Horse's trail now. But he didn't need to. He knew Fast Horse would ride up on the rims overlooking the valley, keeping out of the deeper snow. Mountain Chief's camp was not far. He would reach it sometime in the afternoon of the next day. And he knew that either he would find Fast Horse there or somebody would know where he had gone.

He had enough boiled meat to last this night and the next morning. Then he would have to start living on the pemmican or stop and kill something. He chewed on the cold belly fat that Red Paint had thrown in as a treat and suddenly, unexpectedly, felt excited. He was enjoying himself. He had not been without another person for some time. He did not feel sad or lonely because Red Paint or his father or another hunter were not with him; instead, he felt the freedom of being alone, of relying only upon himself. He remembered his first lone hunt as a youth, the giddiness with which he stalked the deer for a whole day, the thrill he felt when he held its liver in his hands, still warm and steaming in the winter air. He had never felt so free.

The thought came into his mind without warning, the sudden understanding of what Fast Horse found so attractive in running with Owl Child. It was this freedom from responsibility, from accountability to the group, that was so alluring. As long as one thought of himself as part of the group, he would be responsible to and for that group. If one cut the ties, he had the freedom to roam, to think only of himself and not worry about the consequences of his actions. So it was for Owl Child and Fast Horse to roam. And so it was for the Pikunis to suffer.

He stood and walked over to the joining of the two rivers. As he watched the silent seam filled with ice chunks and froth, he knew he would find Fast Horse. But could he talk him into returning to camp, into giving up this freedom? Fast Horse had changed, and Fools Crow knew his task was hopeless. His own feeling of freedom deserted him. As he looked into the ice-clogged seam of the two rivers, he felt again the weight of responsibility. He had promised Boss Ribs to bring back his son, and that's what he would try to do. He tossed a chunk of ice into the seam and it joined the other chunks, indistinguishable, heading downriver.

The camp of the Many Chiefs lay in a bend of the Bear River not far east of the Medicine Rock. The Medicine Rock was red and lay halfway up a bluff on the north side of the river. Many said there was life in that rock and made offerings to it. Fools Crow had placed a small brass earring at its base but did not linger. He noticed feathers and shells and a finger ring around it. Such offerings assured safe traveling.

Fools Crow followed the valley east to the camp. It was not a large camp, some twenty-seven lodges scattered on both sides of the slow clear river. Less than three moons ago there had been forty-four lodges, but many had moved away when they heard that the seizers were looking for Mountain Chief. The river had cut deep here, and the lodges lay between tall dark bluffs over which the cold north winds passed. Big-leaf trees and stands of willow marked the curve of the river, just above the cracked black gumbo of the bed.

Fools Crow urged his horse across a shallow riffle to the side where Mountain Chief's lodge stood, surrounded by others. On a small bluff behind the lodges, children slid down the slope on their buffalo-rib sleds. The snow had long since turned to black slush and the sleds moved slowly. A pack of dogs trotted out to greet Fools Crow. Others stood barking beside the entrances to the lodges.

Mountain Chief's tipi was made of twenty-five skins, the largest in the village. The top and bottom were painted black and red and yellow in stripes and jagged lines. Red horses circled the middle. Fools Crow saw a handsome woman hacking meat from a bone near the entrance. He recognized her as the chief's sits-beside-him wife. She looked up, pushing the hair from her face with the backs of her hands.

Fools Crow slid off his horse. "I am looking for the great Mountain Chief. I would speak with him about an important matter concerning Boss Ribs, keeper of the Beaver Medicine."

"You are of the Lone Eaters."

"I am the son of Rides-at-the-door, war chief of the Lone Eaters."

The woman smiled. "And your mother is Double Strike Woman, formerly of the Hard Topknots. We grew up together. That makes you White Man's Dog or Running Fisher."

"Fools Crow. I used to be White Man's Dog."

"Then you are welcome, young man, whatever your name is."

Fools Crow blushed. The woman was teasing him.

"You come to talk importantly with my husband, then?" She stood. She was slender and as tall as Fools Crow.

"Yes," he mumbled.

"He is down at the river with two others." She pointed in the direction where the river made a sweeping loop, north to south, before heading east again. She smiled again. "I think they are gambling."

Fools Crow thanked her and walked off in the direction she had pointed.

"Say hello to your mother," she called. "Tell her Little Young Man Woman greets her."

Fools Crow thanked her again. He liked this woman who joked like a man. She was well named.

At the edge of the camp he heard giggling behind him. He turned and found that he was being followed by three little girls. One of them was holding a puppy. He raised his arms and growled at them and they ran off, their small buckskin dresses flapping around their ankles.

The trail led through a narrow strip of willows, set down from the camp level. He met a young man dressed only in leggings and moccasins who eyed him warily, without speaking, until he was past. His naked upper body was wet.

Three men stood in water up to their waists, talking. Suddenly one of them dipped beneath the surface and kicked his legs out of the water. He paddled a short way from the others, then stood in chest-high water. He shuddered like a horse, his white teeth gleaming in the afternoon sun. He caught a piece of ice that had floated into his hair and threw it far out into the river. The other two men laughed. Then one of them caught sight of Fools Crow and nudged his companion. Fools Crow stepped forward and identified himself. The man who had swum away from the others ran his hands through his loose black hair, squeezing the water out. He waded slowly to the bank.

"I am Mountain Chief," he said. "What brings you to our camp, young man?"

Fools Crow watched him step up onto the grassy bank. His legs, up to mid-calf, were covered with black gumbo. Fools Crow had often seen Mountain Chief at the summer encampment and had always thought of him as an old man. But now, looking at the naked, water-beaded body, he realized that Mountain Chief possessed the tautness of a young warrior. Only his weather-marked face gave the impression of age.

"Boss Ribs sends me to look for his son, Fast Horse. He would have Fast Horse return to his lodge. He thinks his son is with Owl Child."

Mountain Chief dressed slowly, pulling on his leggings, tying the blue breechcloth around his middle. As he pulled the cotton shirt down over his head, Fools Crow could see an ugly scar under his right armpit.

"It is true Owl Child lives among us, but he is gone more that he is here. When we returned from the Real Old Man country to our winter camp, he kept on going. He is not among us."

"How long has he been gone?"

Mountain Chief called to the two men who were still in the river. They looked at each other. One of them said, "Ten, twelve sleeps."

"Did Fast Horse come here?"

"Three sleeps ago. He too was looking for Owl Child." The man glanced at Mountain Chief, but the chief was looking across the river to the black buttes. "He stayed the night."

"Did he say where he was headed?"

The man was silent for a moment. Finally he said, "He stayed with the family of Bear Chief. They might know."

Without looking at Fools Crow, Mountain Chief said, "Have you seen the seizers on your journey?"

"No. I come directly from the camp of the Lone Eaters. No sign of them along the Bear." Fools Crow looked up at the weathered face. In his clothes, Mountain Chief looked older again. "They came to our summer camp in the Sweet Grass Hills two moons ago."

Mountain Chief looked at him. "Were they looking for me?"

"Yes."

"What did your chiefs—what did Three Bears tell them?"

"That the Lone Eaters had not seen Mountain Chief since the summer ceremony. They knew that you had crossed the Medicine Line into the Real Old Man country. The seizer chief was very angry. He wishes to make Mountain Chief pay for the killing of Malcolm Clark."

Mountain Chief laughed but his eyes were hard.

"He holds Mountain Chief responsible for the acts of Owl Child," said Fools Crow.

"His business is with Owl Child, not me. It was Owl Child who killed Four Bears."

"The Napikwans wish revenge. They would have all the Pikunis killed off, blameless or not. They go after you because they say you harbor Owl Child and are pleased with his acts. They say you would make the Napikwans cry."

"That is true," admitted Mountain Chief. "If the other chiefs had hearts like mine, we would take to the war road. We would drive these white near-men out of our country. We would slaughter their animals like insects. We would burn up their square houses and cause all trace of Napikwan to disappear. Our long-ago people would once again recognize this land. It shames me that they grow restless in the Sand Hills because their children do nothing." Mountain Chief looked up at the sky. "We have become a nothing-people."

Beneath the warm sun, out of the wind below the bluffs which sheltered the camp, Fools Crow felt a chill run through his scalp. He had heard this powerful chief speak his mind, and it went to his heart. It troubled him that his own father and Three Bears, and most of the Lone Eaters, counseled peace with the whites. Yet either way it seemed that the Pikunis were being driven into a den with only one entrance. What did Sun Chief ask of them? Why did he ignore the prayers of his people?

"Tell me your name again, young man."

Fools Crow gave it and said farewell to Mountain Chief. He hesitated a moment, but the chief was once again looking to the black bluffs to the north. He turned and trotted through the willow strip and up the incline to the camp.

He learned from Bear Chief's father that Bear Chief had gone with Owl Child and several other young men. They rode south, he wasn't sure where, but someplace on the Big River, perhaps Rocks Ridge Across. Fast Horse had followed them.

Fools Crow rode up a dry wash to the bluffs south of the camp. He stopped and looked back. He didn't really know why, but he was glad to be away from there.

She was a bony woman, and at first Owl Child thought she was the redheaded man's mother. Her face was hard and lined and her brown hair hung limp and dirty. She was naked to the waist and her whiteness almost hurt his eyes. Only her neck and large knobby hands reflected a life of sun and wind and dirt. Her breasts, small and low, were flanked on either side by a harsh definition of ribs. She looked beyond Owl Child toward the corral.

At first she had screamed and screamed when she saw Fast Horse standing over her husband, emptying his rifle into the limp body. Crow Top and The Cut Hand had held her while Star slapped her face and ripped her dress down to the waist. He clubbed her below the ear with his fist and she fell to the ground, her last scream caught in her throat. They dragged her inside the small cabin, shutting the door on the two children, who held each other and sobbed.

When she came out, she did not try to cover herself up. She did not scream. She did not seem to notice the small boy and girl who gathered folds of her skirt in their pudgy hands and held their faces skyward, their wailing a monotonous *ahhhh* in the late afternoon.

Now Owl Child looked at her and felt nothing at all. Her upper lip had puffed, and there was a long scratch below her left breast. Owl Child looked behind her. Crow Top drew his finger across his throat. The Cut Hand was drinking out of a jug.

Perhaps they should kill the woman, thought Owl Child. It would be best not to leave a witness. And she is ugly. But there was something in her passionless stare that made Owl Child feel she would be better left alive. To tell the other Napikwans what she saw. Yes, she would tell them she had seen something. And when they saw that nothing-look in her eyes they would become frightened.

"You tell them Owl Child did this to you. This is how he treats with the belly-crawlers." He knew she didn't understand him, but that was all right. The message would be delivered.

Under Bull and Bear Chief had the Napikwan's horses out of the corral and ready to drive. They watched Fast Horse study the red hair in his hands. But Fast Horse was not happy. He had wanted the Napikwan to die more, piece by piece. He had been cheated by his own rage. He tucked the red hair into a pocket of his buffalo coat, which was tied to the saddle behind him. Then he watched Owl Child and the others leave the bare-earth yard and ride toward him. Under Bull and Bear Chief started the horses. "Sonofabitch." He had done it too fast.

19

DOUBLE STRIKE WOMAN cut many chunks of meat the size of her fist from the hindquarters that lay on a piece of rawhide near the wall of the lodge. Her friend White Grass Woman was coming to feast, along with her husband, Skunk Cap. She hummed as she worked, a gentle sleeping song that she used to sing to Running Fisher and, before him, White Man's Dog. She still couldn't get used to the name Fools Crow, just as many years ago she couldn't feel comfortable with the name White Man's Dog. She had to smile when she thought how he had acquired that name. He was nine winters, and he had taken to following an old storyteller around—Victory Robe White Man. One day one of the men saw the storyteller alone and said, "Where is White Man's dog?" and the name stuck. Double Strike Woman had never liked it. In the lodge, sometimes, she still called him Sinopa, his birth name, but she knew better than to embarrass him with a child's name when they were with others. He had changed so much in the past year, so fast. One day he was a sullen youth, in and out of love, unlucky in all his endeavors. The next day he was a man, married, soon to be a father, counting war honors and a great favorite of Mik-api. Now he was a presence in camp, the kind of man the others asked about.

But Double Strike Woman was worried about him and angry with him. Once again he had sneaked out of camp, this time to get that no-good Fast Horse. Just when things are going good for him, she thought, he does this foolish thing. It wasn't just Fast Horse, it was that whole gang of killers he ran with. They were so vicious they would kill one of their own and not think twice. Why hadn't he thought more about his own family? She cut the last chunk of meat, then rewrapped the hindquarters in the raw-hide. The worst part was she had had to hear it from White Grass Woman. How did that woman hear everything? She always had the latest gossip. Somehow she was able to dig it out of people. Even as they were telling her their troubles or secrets, they knew she would hurry off to gossip about them. Perhaps they felt it was better to tell this great cow of a woman and have it become common knowledge than to let it seep out slowly to become twisted and malicious. White Grass Woman was in great demand among the Lone Eater wives. Perhaps, thought Double Strike Woman, that is why she is so fat.

She padded over to the entrance and stuck her head out the flap. Striped Face knelt over a large stone. She had a stone ham-mer in her fist. Several cracked marrow bones lay beside the stone.

"Are you getting it all out?" Double Strike Woman called to her sister. "Here, this one here—there is still some in this end."

"That is too near the knuckle. I can't crack it. Now leave me alone."

Double Strike Woman laughed. She was glad that Rides-at-the-door had taken Striped Face for his second wife. Striped Face had been a wild girl, and their parents thought she would be too much for any young man to handle. They feared that she would never get married. It took a lot of talking by Double Strike Woman to convince Rides-at-the-door that she needed help around the lodge. But Striped Face was attractive in a belligerent way. Her small tough body and mocking eyes made men uneasy—but in-terested. Rides-at-the-door had thought he would have a hard time of it trying to keep her from straying, but once she moved into the lodge, she changed. She still enjoyed flirting with men around the camp, but it had become harmless on her part. Mostly, she liked to tease Rides-at-the-door, to make him angry and aroused enough to take her into the small lodge, where they would struggle among the robes. The first time this happened, Double Strike Woman had felt strange; not betrayed, exactly, but forgotten, as though she were no longer principal wife but a thing, a cow that suckled the two infant sons. She had felt old, even at the age of twenty-four winters. Her heart was a heavy thing beneath her full breasts. But when they came back to the big lodge in the morning, she saw in Rides-at-the-door's eyes that she was still his sits-beside-him woman. That night she gave him one of her breasts, and the strength between them grew.

The winters have gone by, thought Double Strike Woman; my sons are now young men who seek their own way. She frowned as she thought of Running Fisher. What had gotten into him lately? She still couldn't understand why he had moved out of the lodge. He never talked anymore. Sometimes when she asked him a question, he only looked at her, as though his mind wandered out on the prairies. The other day when she had taken him a special meal of stuffed intestines, she had found him lying in his robe, staring up through the smoke hole of his small lodge. Rides-at-the-door said he was having trouble because his older brother had become successful in many ways. It was natural to be jealous, and it would soon pass. But why did he have to quit the lodge? She missed her sons, the laughter and teasing, the fierce scoldings she gave them when they reached too far. Double Strike Woman sighed and ducked back into the quiet lodge. Kills-close-to-the-lake looked up and smiled. She was cutting new neck-hide soles for a pair of winter moccasins.

Kills-close-to-the-lake, the third wife of Rides-at-the-door, sat far from him. She dipped some marrow from the bowl and sucked it off her fingers. There seemed to be three conversations going on most of the time, but when White Grass Woman mentioned a name they all stopped talking and listened intently. Even the men did not want to miss the latest story about Two Stab's wife, or about Big Wolf Medicine and the stolen gray horse, or about the young man from the Grease Melters who had been seen around Motokis' lodge. White Grass Woman reported these incidents in a fine bitter voice, followed by a rich, rolling laugh when she reached the end of a story. Then the voices would begin again, a loud hum of laughter and anger, sometimes at the same time, and Kills-close-to-the-lake would return to her own thoughts.

She was the daughter of Mad Wolf, a poor man of the Never Laughs, on whom Rides-at-the-door had taken pity. The two men were cousins in a distant way and they were members of the same society, the All Crazy Dogs. Many times at the Sun Dance ceremony they had sat together and talked. In spite of his name, Mad Wolf was a gentle man, given to moments of sorrowful silence. He was neither a good hunter nor a warrior, but Rides-at-the-door found a quality in him that he liked, a trustworthiness that made one want to confide in him. Once Rides-at-the-door was to the point of asking Mad Wolf to take his family and live at the agency at Many Houses. There he could ingratiate himself with the Napikwans, work for them and perhaps gain some information that would be useful to the Pikunis. But such a move would destroy those very qualities that Rides-at-the-door liked.

It was at the summer encampment the summer before this last one that Mad Wolf expressed concern for his only daughter. He had no dowry to offer, so it was unlikely that a young man would take her as wife. She would grow old and bitter in her father's lodge. In a moment of pity and generosity, Rides-at-the-door said he had no need of more wealth. He offered to take the girl into his lodge as his third wife. She was sixteen at the time. There was no ceremony, only an exchange of small gifts. Rides-at-the-door gave his friend an old ball-and-powder gun, and Mad Wolf gave him a somewhat battered real-lion skin with painted designs on the tanned side. So Kills-close-to-the-lake left the encampment with the Lone Eaters. She had been desperately unhappy to leave with the stranger and his two other wives but she had little choice in the matter.

". . . and so that skinny thing had to move into the lodge of her son-in-law. Can you imagine the trouble they must be having trying to avoid each other?" White Grass Woman rolled her eyes.

Kills-close-to-the-lake listened to the laughter with a nervous flutter in her stomach. Her throat was dry, and the small amount of meat she had eaten threatened to come back up.

Once again she tried to convince herself that it was all right, that it was not even her doing. She glanced across the circle to Rides-at-the-door. In the time they had been married he had taken her to the small lodge only four or five times. He treated her more as a daughter, and his other wives treated her as a necessary but uninvited presence. Double Strike Woman ordered her about, and Striped Face often mocked her timidity—especially when Striped Face came back after spending the night with Rides-at-the-door in the small lodge. She would sit across the fire sewing or drinking broth and look up from time to time to grin silently at the young girl.

White Grass Woman was telling yet another story, but Kills-close-to-the-lake felt that all were conscious of her presence and her thoughts. She saw herself again that first time it happened. It was dusk and she was walking down to the river to fill a kettle. A light snow had fallen, and she could hear the squeak of it beneath her moccasins. As she passed the small plain tipi set apart from the others, she heard her name being called in that familiar voice. Now she knew she had recognized a tension in the voice and knew she should have kept walking. But she had stopped and turned slowly. She saw him standing by the entrance, a load of firewood in his arms. As she entered the tipi, she saw him bend over and she heard the brittle clatter of the wood dropping on the hard earth. He was talking in a spirited way, but she didn't remember the words. When he turned she looked down at the buckskin leggings she had made for him, the red trade-cloth that covered his groin. When she looked up she saw the firelight dancing on his strong teeth. He was laughing in that thin, nervous way she had heard so many times around her husband's fire.

She tried to recall exactly how it happened, those first few moments in the tipi, but all she could remember was being shoved down on the blackhorn robes and the feeling of his cold fingers inside of her. She had struggled, but he had forced her back with his forearm across her shoulders. When his harsh breathing had subsided, she stood and smoothed her dress down over her leggings, picked up the brass kettle and continued down to the river. There she washed herself in the cold water. It wasn't until the next morning that the shock wore off and she felt a warmth in her thighs. She felt her heart beat fast and realized that she wanted a man of her own, wanted him more than anything she could imagine. And she would go back again, and again, for as long as he wanted her.

She felt dizzy and almost sick from the laughter and the heat in the big lodge. She looked across the fire at White Grass Woman, who had the marrow bowl set on her great breast. Her chin was greasy and her small eyes glittered with delight. Her husband, Skunk Cap, was telling a story that had the others whooping with laughter. Striped Face was bent at the waist, spearing a piece of meat from the wooden slab, her other hand over her happy mouth.

Kills-close-to-the-lake slipped quickly out the entrance, walked a short distance away and raised her face, breathing deeply the chinook wind. Seven Persons was partially hidden behind a ragged cloud illuminated by the half-full moon. She stood still and listened to the talking and laughter in the lodge. They had not missed her. She walked to the path that led down to the river. She wove her way among the lodges, glowing with evening fires. Some were quiet; others contained the noises of feasting that went on every night in the camp. She stopped behind one lodge to let two women pass. She didn't see their faces. Then she was on the path which snaked between two patches of wild rose. Once beyond them she could see the plain tipi set back among the big-leaf trees, thirty paces from the path. She picked her way through the long damp grass, holding the hem of her dress. She stood beside the entrance and listened for the sound of voices, half hoping to hear them. She heard only the rippling of the river as it descended a riffle to a smooth bathing pool. Off to the southwest Early Riser glittered yellow-white in the night sky. Kills-close-to-the-lake breathed deeply and ducked down through the flap.

Running Fisher lay against a backrest, studying the markings on an arrow. He glanced up, and she saw his young smooth face clearly in the firelight. At seventeen, he was one winter younger than she. He smiled, and then he laughed that high nervous laugh that sounded like wind through a quaking-leaf grove.

"You have returned. What's the matter—did you leave something last time?"

She wanted to answer in that same mocking tone but when she opened her mouth a dryness caught in her throat. She stood just inside the entrance, her legs trembling. She tried to smile.

"Come here, then—where it's warm." Running Fisher held the robe back. He was naked from the waist down.

With a thin cry that she didn't hear, she slipped beneath the robe. He sat up and pushed her dress around her waist. He undid her leggings and pulled her moccasins off. He smiled down at her and said, "You are shivering. Is it cold out? Would you like me to build up the fire?"

With a shudder she pulled him down and felt his warmth growing against her thigh. His fingers stroked her and she bit her lower lip in an effort to keep from crying out. At that moment he was everything she possessed in the world, and she gave herself to him.

Striped Face limped back to camp, muttering in pain. Once she stopped and lifted her dress to look at the knee. She rubbed the roughened skin and held her hand to the moonlight. The blood was dark and warm on her fingers. She cursed the stone she had tripped on and the stone her knee had hit. This is what you get, she thought, for being so nosy. But the wound was not bad, not as bad as she had thought. It was only the cold air that made it sting so. She lowered the hem of her dress and walked on.

She had been right, though. She had seen something and heard even more. In spite of the pain, she smiled. To think it had been Fools Crow that she had suspected! When he lived in his father's lodge, she had seen the way they looked at each other, the way they touched by accident, the way her cheeks flushed on those rare occasions he spoke to her. At the Sun Dance encampment she had spied on them down by the creek. Although they kept their distance from each other, Striped Face could feel the tension in the heavy summer air. She had been sure they were lovers, but she could never catch them. It had been a disappointment when Fools Crow moved out of the lodge to marry Red Paint.

Ah, but this one! Running Fisher, the proud one—the one who never acknowledged Striped Face—satisfying his lust with his own father's young wife! This was better, for in truth she liked Fools Crow.

And she pitied Rides-at-the-door; if the news got around camp he would lose much honor. To be betrayed by a wife was one thing; to be betrayed by a son was another. But together! Striped Face frowned. She too would lose honor to be married to such a man. They would all be talked about and laughed at. She thought of White Grass Woman's great rolling laughter and became angry. And she grew angrier at the injustice of her own situation. She had been virtuous although it hadn't been easy. When the drunken hunter of the Hard Topknots had carried her into the bushes, she had fought him. Her heart wasn't in the fight —her struggle became a struggle against herself as well. And there were others, but she hadn't allowed herself to submit. Her knee began to throb as the stinging lessened and she thought of those men, and she knew again the power she felt when she turned them away. Even her husband—when she was in the mood for teasing, she made him ask, almost beg to come to her. Oh, he treated her roughly when she finally yielded, but they both knew that she had the power.

And now she had real power over Kills-close-to-the-lake and Running Fisher. She was pleased with herself for having the cunning to follow the young wife when she left the lodge. She just had a feeling. Her face burned when she recalled the sounds of their lovemaking. She had stood outside the tipi, hidden in a thick stand of willows, scarcely three paces from where they carried on. She had felt her own legs grow weak, as though each moan and cry were her own. She had closed her eyes and imagined that she could see them, could smell the juices of their coupling. Suddenly it had become quiet and when she opened her eyes, she saw the warm glow of the tipi and heard a dog bark. She had felt heavy and weak as she picked her way through the willow to a clearing by the river. She was going down to wash her face when she stumbled over the river rock and hit her knee. That had brought her to her senses.

But now she was again filled with desire, and vaguely irritated that it should be so. As she neared the big lodge she wondered if Double Strike Woman would be sleeping with Rides-at-the-door. She grinned with heat. There would be no teasing tonight.

20

FOOLS CROW HAD TAKEN to traveling cautiously now, for he was in the country of the Napikwans. There were ranches along the Big River and others scattered on the bluffs above. Each year there were more, and they became harder to avoid. He stayed well away from the buildings, but sometimes he had to ride through the herds of whitehorns. They were scrawny things with wide horns and long faces. Sometimes they would run from him, but other times they would just look up, chewing thoughtfully, their dark eyes questioning this strange man. Most of the time he kept to the low points, the ravines and cutbanks, as he made his way south.

On the third day after leaving Mountain Chief's camp, Fools Crow noticed a change in the air. The southwest wind vanished and the sky took on a hard, gray look. The sun seemed to move away from the land until it became a pale disk that one could look into without fear. It grew colder, and Fools Crow belted his capote tighter around his waist and put the hood up. He found his fur mittens and drew them over his icy fingers. The chinook was over and, all around, the land hardened up to a dirty yellow. Cold Maker had ended his brief nap.

That afternoon Fools Crow lay on his belly on a hill overlooking Rocks Ridge Across on the Big River. From here he could see far into the distance, but his eyes were trained on a small group of buildings some five hundred paces beyond the base of the hill. There is no life there, he thought. But still he waited, until Sun lay on the shoulders of the Backbone. He studied the corrals and the fields beyond them, but he saw no trace of animals. The buildings squatted dark and still in the weakening light.

And then it was dusk and Fools Crow rode his black horse down from the hill. He stopped between the house and the corral, his repeating rifle ready across his thighs. Then he rode over to the three steps leading up to the door of the house. The house was set back on an incline, the front of it propped up with logs. Antlers, bleached white, hung over the door. Off to his left, fifty paces away, he saw a long dark shape. He rode over to it. It was a black-and-white dog, his shoulder crushed and matted with dried blood. He lay with his mouth open and Fools Crow could see that most of his tongue was gone. He looked down at the dog's cuts, which were hanging from his open belly. The long-tails had eaten most of them away.

When he finally figured out how to open the door latch, Fools Crow stepped inside the room. It was dark and he stood while his eyes adjusted. Then he saw hundreds of jagged white objects on the floor. He picked one up and it was smooth and slick on both sides, like a milky ice shard. He dropped it and it rang on the wood surface. He picked his way over to the sleeping platform. In the center of the white cloth he made out three dark stains. He bent over and smelled them. The odor was faint but unmistakably blood. There was also blood on the soft white headrest at the end of the platform. Fools Crow straightened up and looked around the room. Three large wooden objects lay on the floor, cloth things flung from them. Napikwan clothes. Then he saw the eating platform and the seats lying on their sides, some of the legs missing. He remembered Rides-at-the-door's description of these objects from that time he had eaten with the Grandfather's chief at the agency. He picked up another shard and noticed its round edge. Rides-at-the-door had also described the round shiny things they ate from.

He walked down to the corral and entered the horse shed, but it was empty. He opened the back door and stood in the pasture full of frozen horse turds. He began to shake in the cold, dark night; he couldn't stop it. He felt himself surrounded by ghosts of Napikwans and expected to be touched by them. He looked back to the horse shed and the house and they were filled with ghosts, waiting for him. The ghost of the dead dog sat not more than ten paces from him in the corral. The ghosts of horses watched him from beyond the poles. Fools Crow tried to move, couldn't, then could. His body felt light as he jumped the corral poles and raced toward his horse. Without breaking stride he leaped onto the horse, his feet already kicking the horse's ribs. The black horse leaped forward and galloped away from that Napikwan ranch, his hooves beating loudly over the frozen ground, his neck stretched and his eyes wild. Fools Crow could see nothing ahead of them, he couldn't remember the terrain, so he closed his eyes and hung on.

That night he slept in a rabbit run under a patch of rosebushes far from the Napikwan homestead.

Yellow Kidney sat at the back of the lodge and watched his sons, One Spot and Good Young Man, harden arrow shafts over the fire. They had peeled the sarvisberry sticks and trimmed and scraped them smooth with stones. Good Young Man was thirteen winters and his brother was eleven. They had learned much the past summer from Fools Crow, their brother-in-law. He had taught them to select the right woods for their bows and arrows. He had given each of them a horse, good strong horses, and they had learned to ride well. Good Young Man had killed his first blackhorn, a yearling calf, and had made a quiver and saddle from the hide. White men's saddles had become popular among the men, but Fools Crow had taught the youth how to cut the wood frames and how to stretch and sew the rawhide over them. Then Fools Crow had taken the saddle down to the river and, with a laugh, had thrown it into the swift current. Good Young Man had jumped in right after the saddle hit the water, but it had taken him some time to catch up with it. They flung it over a dry-meat rack, and two days later the sun had shrunk it over the wood forms. Now Good Young Man was a hunter, but he looked forward to the many-drums moon when Fools Crow said he might take him on a horse raid against the Entrails People.

One Spot was envious but admired his older brother. He would have to wait until next summer to bring down his blackhorn. He hadn't had the strength to drive an arrow deep into the thick-hided animals this past summer. So far all he had killed were fool hens, gophers and one porcupine. He was serious as he rubbed down a hardened shaft.

Yellow Kidney smoked his short-pipe, not aware that the stubs of his right hand were fondling the tobacco pouch that the Spotted Horse People had given him. Since he had returned, he handled the pouch often. It was greasy and soft and the painted designs were less distinct. As he watched his sons, he again thought of his leaving, and this time it did not fill him with so much pain. Fools Crow was good to them. He would see to their upbringing. As for Heavy Shield Woman, she was content in her role as Sacred Vow Woman. The young girls revered her and the men treated her with respect. Yellow Kidney felt the familiar tightening behind his eyes. They had not been man and wife since his return because he was a near-man. No longer did the sight of her body fill him with thick longing. When they slept together, it was only to keep each other warm.

Yellow Kidney no longer felt any desire toward women. He looked at them, the young pretty ones, with the eye of an old man, remembering what had once been. But he did not have the comfort of growing old. He had been young, and now he was old. His sons were like grandchildren. Because they were good boys, they talked to him, brought him things and sat near him, their eyes watching his face expectantly. But he had no stories for them. What had happened was over.

The only real memory he possessed was of those days and nights in the Spotted Horse camp, waiting, wishing to die. Many times, while sitting in the lodge or walking out on the prairies, he saw the faces of the spirit-people as they reached out to him; he heard his own voice cry out to Old Man to allow him to join his grandmother and eldest son in the Sand Hills. He would have gladly died then, a pitiful creature without honor.

But lately he had been thinking about the people in that Spotted Horse camp. There had been only nine lodges in that camp on the Elk River. Except for four or five hunters and their wives and children, all the other people were old. The camp itself was permanent, the hunter going out from there and always returning. It was pleasant in that camp; the old people sat around and told stories and made medicine. Yellow Kidney realized he had been sent to that camp to recover from his misfortunes. The old people had taken care of him and he gradually became one of them, sitting around day after day, learning enough of their tongue and signs to feel included. He had been at peace with himself, and with the people.

"Aaiii, you boys should be out in this weather. Your friends are in the small meadow, playing hoops and sticks!" Heavy Shield Woman had entered the lodge, a water bucket in one hand and a large piece of tripe in the other.

"We do not play anymore," announced One Spot. "We make arrows for the hunt."

"And when does this hunt take place, young man?"

"Next snow—when we can track the blackhorns."

Heavy Shield Woman laughed. She set the bucket on a flat stone near the fire. Her gaunt cheeks were red. "And you, Good Young Man, do you wait for this fabled snow too?"

He had been notching one of the sticks. He looked up and was surprised to see how thin his mother looked in her bulky robe. "We will play," he said.

"We will play," said One Spot, as though he had just thought of the idea. He looked at his father. Then he jumped up and got his stick and hoop.

Yellow Kidney smiled as he watched the boys duck out through the flap. The lodge was suddenly quiet. As he watched his wife pound the tripe, he thought, I love them but I will not miss them.

That night Yellow Kidney gathered up his weapons and the pemmican bag he had stuffed and hidden earlier. He took from a lodgepole the parfleche which contained his war paints and owl feather medicine. He put his short-pipe and tobacco pouch into the parfleche. At the door he looked back and studied for the last time the sleeping forms of his wife and sons. One Spot was almost unnoticeable in his robe. Good Young Man slept with his bow and arrows within reach. He is well named, thought Yellow Kidney. He looked at his wife. Her dark loose hair was half hidden by her sleeping robe. She will comb and braid her hair as always in the morning, he thought. He hoped she would be happy that he was gone.

He walked quickly away from camp. He greeted Seven Persons and Night Red Light. He glanced at the Lost Children and a cold chill ran through his body. But he felt strong and alive and his pace was fast as he climbed up from the river bottom. For the first time in many moons he felt as young as his thirty-nine winters. He felt that he could walk all the way without stopping. The cold air made his teeth ache, and he realized that he was grinning. The nearly eighty horses he left behind would now be the property of his sons. White Man's Dog—he laughed—Fools Crow would see to it that they became good warriors, just as he had shown Fools Crow how to take the Crow horses.

At the top of the bluff he began to run, a slow steady lope, over the smooth rolling prairies. His bad leg felt strong. He headed south and east, away from the Backbone, away from the camp of the Lone Eaters, the land of the Pikunis. He didn't think of anything but his destination. He would find that camp of Spotted Horse People.

Crow Top spotted the rider first. He had been sitting on a ridge watching the horses, which grazed in a draw. A short way down the draw the men were resting beneath a single spear-leaf tree, its bare gray branches angling up to the sky. Beyond them the dark earth of a blackhorn wallow contrasted sharply with the yellow grass quivering in the steady north wind.

They were tired and they didn't talk. They had ridden all the way down to Other-side-deep Creek, where they had picked up another nine horses to go with the sixteen they had taken from the redheaded Napikwan. None of them looked forward to the long journey to the trader's fort on the Saskatchewan, but twenty-five horses would bring a good price.

Owl Child was dozing when he heard Crow Top's shout. He had become irritable in the past two sleeps. Many in his party had wanted to go on south to the ranches around the White Stink Springs. There were many horses there and new country. Owl Child had made the mistake of telling them about the time he had gone there and saw the small gray animals with curly hair so thick a man lost sight of his hand before he touched the body. They had wanted to see these strange creatures, maybe eat one. Fast Horse had argued with him, and Owl Child didn't like that. He didn't like a lot of things about Fast Horse. He stirred, then stood, his legs stiff from all the riding.

"Saiyah! Saiyah!" Crow Top was motioning from the top of the ridge.

Now all the men were on their feet. The Cut Hand had a pained look in his eyes. He had been kicked in the thigh by one of the Napikwan horses. He wanted to kill them all.

Owl Child left Red Horn, Black Weasel and Under Bull to watch the herd; then he and the others climbed to the ridgetop. The wind was stronger and colder up here, and Crow Top stood with his robe pulled tightly around him.

"He's down a draw now, over there."

The men waited, and then they saw the dark figure appear over a swell. He was coming from the direction they had come. The herd had left a wide trail.

Bear Chief had the best eyes.

"Who is he?" said Owl Child.

"Not Napikwan. Ah, he wears a capote beneath his robe. His horse is black." Bear Chief rubbed his eyes. "The wind makes my eyes wet."

"We will greet him," said Owl Child. "Crow Top will wait here and tell us which direction this rider takes. Keep low, you black Pikuni."

"Wait," said Fast Horse. "I recognize him."

"Then we will greet him for you, near-man!"

Fast Horse stood and waited for the rider to see him. Bear Chief hesitated, looking at Fast Horse, then scrambled down the ridge after the others.

Crow Top hunkered down. "Who is this rider who trails us?"

Fast Horse did not answer. He wondered what Fools Crow wanted.

A short while later he saw the small party ride swiftly between two hills. The draw curved around behind Fools Crow, who had been riding with his head down. But now he stopped and stood in his stirrups, stretching his legs. His eyes swept the horizon until they locked on Fast Horse and Crow Top. He sat back in his saddle and lifted the horse's head.

Then Fast Horse saw the riders come up behind him, riding fast, their rifles pointing in the air. He heard four small pops as the wind drove the explosions away from him. Fools Crow whirled his horse, but the men had surrounded him, their rifles pointing now in his direction. They all sat silently on their horses for a moment, then the riders put their guns away.

Fast Horse trotted down into the draw to wait for them. He could feel the pebbles of the blackhorn trail through his thin soles.

By the time Owl Child and the others returned with their guest, a light snow had begun to blow down from the north.

"This Fools Crow calls himself a friend to Fast Horse." Owl Child's voice had a mocking ring in the gusting wind. "He says you used to play dolls together, that you are 'sonofabitch' together."

Fast Horse looked up at Fools Crow. He became angry at his old friend. "He is of the Lone Eaters."

"Perhaps he wishes to make you new moccasins. We hear the Lone Eater men are good at women's work."

Fast Horse said nothing as the others laughed.

"We will camp tonight at Meat Strings. You and this Fools Crow can catch up. I'm sure you wish to gossip now."

The snow came harder and the big flakes, after their swift horizontal flight, began to stick on the ground. Fast Horse and Fools Crow watched the men drive the horses to the top and over the ridge. Then the clattering of hooves was gone and the draw was silent again.

Fast Horse turned and said angrily, "What is it you want?"

Fools Crow didn't answer right away. He studied his friend's face and saw that they were truly not friends anymore. They had chosen different lives, and the burning eyes told him that the break was as final as death. He felt no sorrow inside himself.

"Your father sends me after you."

Fast Horse turned and walked a few steps away, his back to Fools Crow and the blowing snow. "And what does my father want now that you have found me?"

"He would have you return to his lodge. He misses you."

"I don't miss him—or the Lone Eaters."

"He is your father and he misses you," repeated Fools Crow.

"Does he know what I do?"

"He knows you ride with Owl Child."

"And what does he think?"

Fools Crow looked beyond Fast Horse to the spear-leaf tree and the blackhorn wallow. They had become hard-edged in the blowing white snow. "He thinks you should come home and learn the Beaver Medicine. He thinks that is more important than killing off the Napikwans and taking their horses."

Fast Horse turned with a scornful look, but Fools Crow continued.

"I see what you and Owl Child and that gang do. Two sleeps ago I found the Napikwan ranch on Rocks Ridge Across. I found blood."

Fast Horse laughed, but it was a thin dry laugh that did not carry far. "You feel sorry for the Napikwans? You think we make them cry too much?"

"Soon the Pikunis will cry—when news of this attack reaches the ears of the seizers."

"Perhaps Owl Child is right. The Pikunis wear the dresses of women. They no longer have the heart to kill off these treacherous insects that steal their land."

"You, Fast Horse, you have become the heartless insect, for you would betray your own people."

"Ha! Who betrays who? Those who would seek to drive them from our land or those who would chew meat until there is nothing left?"

The two stood rigidly, their eyes locked for that moment. A

gust of wind rattled the limbs of the spear-leaf tree, high up. Fools Crow, perhaps because he was tired and not thinking well, felt an unfamiliar hatred building in his chest, and he would have fought his childhood friend to the death if Fast Horse had given him an excuse. But Fast Horse suddenly laughed.

"It is not worth it, dog-lover. I see what is in your eyes and I tell you it would be foolish."

The moment passed and the fight went out of Fools Crow. He was helpless and ashamed of his sudden rage. As he walked to his horse, he felt his fists unclench. He breathed deeply and let the air out slowly.

"What am I to tell Boss Ribs?"

Fast Horse followed him partway. He had his black hat pulled low against the wind. "Tell him you couldn't find me," he said almost kindly.

Fools Crow stepped into the stirrup and hoisted himself slowly into the saddle. He felt empty, and he was glad to be going home. He missed Red Paint. He longed for the peace of the lodge, the quiet of the winter camp.

"I found you. I told Boss Ribs I would find you and bring you back. But now I think he is better off not knowing what you have become." Fools Crow turned his horse away, then stopped and looked back at Fast Horse. "Tell me—after the Crow raid you changed—what was it that made you—"

"Hateful?" Fast Horse tried a scornful laugh but he didn't look at Fools Crow. A gust of wind flattened the hat brim against his cheek. "I will tell you the truth. Cold Maker betrayed me. He promised to make me a powerful one, but he didn't keep his word."

"But what of your dream?"

"I was sure I would find the ice spring. In my dream I saw it as plain as I see this snow. I knew if I drank from it I would become a powerful many-faces man, perhaps the most powerful one of all—Fast Horse, who makes Cold Maker do his bidding. It was all there in my dream. It was a power dream such as few men know."

"And Cold Maker betrayed you?"

Fast Horse looked troubled, as though he still did not believe what had happened to his dream. "I did something—something to offend Cold Maker."

"It was because of Yellow Kidney."

"No! He walked into that camp. He was foolish to take such a risk. He caused his own bad luck."

"But you yelled. You caused him to be discovered." Fools Crow lifted the reins. "You caused him to become a pitiful man."

"He shouldn't have gone into the camp," said Fast Horse bitterly.

"I will tell Boss Ribs I couldn't find you."

"He was a foolish man!" shouted Fast Horse.

But Fools Crow urged his horse up the trail to the ridgetop. He was tired of it all. He had found Fast Horse and now he could forget him as something important in his life. He turned his face into the folds of the capote. The driving snow burned his exposed cheek.

21

As Yellow Kidney struck the flint and steel into the small pile of moss, he remembered his father's story of Seco-mo-muckon and the firehorn in the long-ago. At that time there was no flint and steel, and a young man was selected to carry the firehorn from camp to camp as the people moved. Seco-mo-muckon was such a young man. It had been in the season of the new-grass moon, right after the first thunder, at which time the keeper of the Sacred Pipe unwrapped his bundle and performed the ceremonies. As is the custom, the Sacred Pipe man prayed to the Above Ones to allow them good weather for traveling and hunting. He prayed to Sun Chief and to Thunder Chief to keep the people healthy and safe from the hazards that surrounded them. After the ceremony the people felt good and feasted for three days. Then they decided to move camp to a spot on the Yellow River where the game was plentiful.

On the morning of the move, Seco-mo-muckon packed the firehorn with moist, rotten wood. He found a good coal and placed it deep in the blackhorn receptacle. Then he filled it with damp moss and plugged it with a piece of wood. Four times that day he added moss to the firehorn to keep it burning. He was a good young man, and the people felt safe entrusting their fire to him. On this journey, Seco-mo-muckon ran ahead of the people, for he knew the camping spot on the Yellow River and he thought he would build a good hot fire before the rest arrived. As he hurried along, he thought to himself that one day he would be keeper of the Medicine Pipe and keep the people safe, just as

Awunna now did—for in truth Awunna liked this young man and had hinted that he was destined for big things.

Seco-mo-muckon, with this thought in mind, entered a long shallow coulee not far from the Yellow River. Ahead of him, he could see a grove of big-leaf trees that drank from the deep waters of the earth. All about them he could see thousands of small yellow things. He thought they were last autumn's leaves caught in a whirlwind, but as he approached, he saw they were butterflies. The trees were covered with yellow butterflies, and they flew out in their dipping, flitting arcs, only to return to land on the rough bark. Seco-mo-muckon thought he had never seen anything so beautiful. He stopped and lay down to rest and watch the butterflies. As he lay on the soft new grass, a butterfly landed on his nose and he fell into a deep happy sleep. He dreamed many dreams, but the one that appealed to him most was the one where he saw the Medicine Pipe bundle lashed above the entrance to his lodge.

When he woke up, the butterflies were gone. Sun Chief glowed in the western sky above the Backbone. Seco-mo-muckon jumped up and ran as fast as he could, but when he reached the bluffs above the Yellow River, he saw the people setting up their lodges on the other side. He was angry with himself for falling asleep and letting them pass him by. Then as he started down the bluff he felt the firehorn and noticed that it was cool. In panic he opened it and put his finger inside. The fire was out. He cursed and cried and beat his head with his fists.

When he had settled down he looked across the river. Nobody had seen him yet, so he sneaked off, downstream. He swam across the river a little way from the shallow fording place. When he walked into camp, dripping wet, the people came out to greet him and were glad to see him alive, for there were many enemies around. The women fed him and brought him dry clothes. The men clapped him on the back and tousled his hair. Then they listened to the story of how Seco-mo-muckon had been captured by the Underwater People, how mischievous Otter had grabbed him by the leg as he forded Yellow River and pulled him down to the home of Underwater Chief. They became frightened when he told them that the Chief was angry because Awunna had not prayed to him during the Medicine Pipe ceremony. To make the Pikunis pay, he released the coal from the firehorn and warned Seco-mo-muckon that if his people did not treat the Underwater People with more respect, they would drown all the Pikuni fire and they would have to eat raw meat and freeze in the winter.

When he had finished his story, the people grew angry and cursed Awunna for being negligent and angering the spirits. That night Awunna stole out of his lodge and placed the Sacred Pipe bundle over the entrance to Seco-mo-muckon's lodge. Then he left camp and was never seen again.

Yellow Kidney smiled to himself as he remembered his father's manner of pretending to end the story here, despite the protests of Yellow Kidney and his sisters. He would grin at their indignation over Seco-mo-muckon's treachery. When he became satisfied that they had learned the lesson, he would tell them how Seco-mo-muckon was killed that moon of ripe berries by a bolt of lightning thrown down by Thunder Chief.

Yellow Kidney finally got the punk to burn after several tries. He had gotten used to having no fingers, but most things were still difficult. He had learned to tie knots with his teeth and hands, but they were seldom tight enough. The trigger-puller he had rigged out of a curved bone worked, but it hampered his ability to reload quickly. Still, he was pleased that he could get along. Since leaving the Lone Eater camp, he had been finding more and more that he could do things if he did them deliberately and without haste. He had been gone for six days, two of them in this war lodge, waiting out the blizzard. As he listened to the wind rattle the limbs and pine boughs and the grainy snow sift through the dry leaves, he felt a contentment that had been lacking in the past several moons. And the thought occurred to him again, as it had the previous night, that he felt almost capable of going back to his wife and children. The few sleeps away had changed his thinking about himself. He no longer felt that it was necessary to go to the camp of the Spotted Horse People to die. He had lost much honor with his own people, but he no longer felt pitiful and worthless.

He put some larger sticks on the fire and it flamed higher. He placed his hands over the warmth, and the sight of his stubby fingers no longer filled him with hopelessness. He sat back on his bed of freshly cut pine boughs and undid the strings of the pemmican sack with little difficulty. He scooped out a handful and threw it into his mouth. The large drifts around the war lodge would keep it warm. He thought the wind had dropped. Perhaps by morning the blizzard would end. He lay back beneath the robe and watched the smoke rise. He was not far from Cut-throat country—four or five days at the most. He felt strong and cunning. He had always been one of the best horse-takers among his people.

He dozed off. His last thought was of the fire. He must not let it go out again. Then he dreamed of Seco-mo-muckon and the people who trusted him. The wind blew through the pines above the war lodge and Night Red Light showed her face briefly, then disappeared.

It was around midday of the second day since leaving Fort Benton on the Missouri River that the two riders began to worry. They had slept the first night at the ranch of a friend, and it was there that they learned of the death of Frank Standley. He had been killed and scalped a few days earlier by a party of Blackfeet. His wife had been beaten and raped and still did not have a clear idea how it happened. She and her children had been brought to the fort, but the two men hadn't seen her there.

The wind had picked up again, bringing more of the low clouds down from the north. They were still a day and a half from their ranch on the Teton. Now it didn't look like they would beat the weather home. The big one turned in his saddle and glanced back at the three packhorses. They walked with their heads down, exhausted from that last struggle with a drift. Their bellies were beaded with ice and their tails were heavy with frozen chunks of snow. One of the packs had begun to slip. The horse, a five-year-old with big bones, swayed to the right, grunting with each step.

The man swore and dismounted heavily. They were on a long table of land and the snow was not deep. He took off his buffalo coat and flung it over the saddle. Then he walked back and studied the pack. The load had shifted under the canvas. He lifted the covering and saw that a sack of flour had edged down too far. The pressure on the crosstree had caused it to bite into the horse's side. With a great effort, the man lifted the frame and looked at the wound; it was bare and red and bleeding around the edges. The man looked through the supplies lashed under the rope. At last he found the flowery piece of cloth he had bought for his wife. He pulled it loose and ripped off two large squares. Then he folded them and squeezed them under the frame. The wind blew through his flannel shirt and long johns as he pulled the cinch tighter. They would have to find someplace to spend the night, then redo the pack in the morning.

As he walked back to his horse he thought of the grove of pines on the south slope of Bad Horse Butte. It couldn't be more than three hours away. He cursed again. He had wanted to make Sid Colby's place by nightfall. His wife was a good cook. But there was an old war lodge in that pine grove, and they had plenty of hardtack and jerky and coffee. And some dried apples they had treated themselves to. He looked over at his son, who was nearly fifteen. Well, he can tell his kids that he slept one night in a war lodge—but not with Indians. There wouldn't be anybody there this time of year. But it might be nice to run into some, after what they did to Frank Standley and his wife. He thought again of that red curly hair that always reminded him of St. Louis, of civilization. Now it was in some Blackfeet's war bag. What a hell of a thing, he thought, as he urged his horse forward. He cursed as he felt the first snowflakes hit against his bearded cheek. He pulled the collar of his buffalo coat up. What a hell of a country.

They made better time than he would have guessed, and it was still light when they dropped off the table into a large basin. Less than half an hour away he could see the pine grove. It was more extensive than he had remembered, covering almost the entire length of Bad Horse Butte, but as they closed the distance, he could see the chimney in the gray face of the butte. The war lodge would be just below it. A swirl of wind blew snow in his face and under the collar of the coat. It was getting worse, and he was getting more and more grateful for that bit of shelter up ahead. He glanced out of the corner of his eye at his son, who was leading the packhorses. He had a scarf over the lower half of his face and a beaver cap pulled down low over his forehead. The big man could see the exhaustion in his son's eyes. We'll be home by tomorrow nightfall and then he can tell his mother all about the trip. She'll be mighty relieved. Might even begin to make up for having to rip up her pretty cloth. Still, it's a damn stupid thing to run out of supplies in the middle of winter.

Suddenly he reined up and motioned for his son to do the same. It couldn't have been, he thought. It was just a gust of wind in the pines, blowing the powdery snow around. Then he saw it again, but he couldn't believe that it was smoke. Not in this weather. A person would have to be a damn fool to be out here. But the man's son pointed to the place where he had seen the smoke. It was there, all right—someone was in the war lodge.

They weren't more than four hundred yards from the edge of the pine grove. The man pointed to a dark ravine that started low and led up into the trees. "Wait there," he said. "Take the horses and stay put until I come for you."

The son nodded and kicked his horse in the ribs. The pack animals lifted their heads in protest, but he got them moving. The lanky horse with the sores grunted in pain. Then the snow blew up around them and they disappeared from sight.

As the big man rode toward the war lodge, he gradually became aware of a thought that had been playing around the edges of his mind. It had started well over a year ago when he heard that Charles Ransom, a rancher over on the Sun River, had been killed out in his fields not six miles from Fort Shaw. He hadn't known Ransom, but the incident concerned him, made him aware of his own family's isolation. He had welcomed the move of the Blackfeet Agency from Fort Benton to the Teton River. It was only four miles from his place and there were white men there. Not many, but he believed in safety in numbers, no matter how small. Now, with the death of Frank Standley and the rape of his wife, the big man had been filled with dreadful thoughts. Standley had lived well south of Blackfeet country, among other whites. It had seemed they were beyond striking range.

Now the thought was centered in his mind. He pulled up just inside the pine grove and slid his rifle out of its scabbard. He levered a round into the chamber, then climbed down. He tied his horse to a sapling. I want to kill an Indian, he thought, as he began his stalk of the war lodge.

Yellow Kidney had been out that morning, during a rare lull when the wind let up and the snow had quit falling. He found a small clearing in the pines, filled with fresh elk tracks. They had been drifted in, but the imprints had been made only a short time before. A whole herd of elk had drifted through, probably while he was eating his pemmican before deciding whether he would move that day. He had followed the tracks a short way, but he knew he would not catch up with them. From the length of their stride, they had a destination and were in a hurry to get there. Yellow Kidney smiled ruefully, for he had missed a feast and enough meat to get him away to Cutthroat country. He had made up his mind to go there and take some horses, then return to his family. He wanted to watch his sons grow up, to help them become men. He knew that things would never be as good as they once were, but he did like to share the lodge with Heavy Shield Woman. They could live together, grow old together.

And he wanted to live to see his grandson. He wasn't supposed to know that Red Paint would soon deliver a little one, but he had heard them talking. Sometimes, they seemed to forget that he was there. He wanted to give the infant a name, and he had the name picked out. The second day after leaving the camp, he had seen a blackhorn cow and her late calf grazing on a hillside a good distance away. His first thought was to sneak up on the animals and bring them down. But then he noticed that the calf was yellow and as big and strong as any he had seen. He found himself filled with admiration for the yellow calf—as though its strength and young life somehow embodied all that he had believed in before he became pitiful—and his own life suddenly seemed worth preserving. He thought he might kill the animal anyway and, with the right sacrifices, take a lock of hair for his war bag. He was certain that this calf had been presented to him by Sun Chief as a token of forgiveness. Perhaps the Great Spirit thought he had suffered enough for his transgressions in the Crow camp.

But then the yellow calf lifted his head and looked right at Yellow Kidney, and the warrior knew that he could not kill him. Instead, he would take his name away for his grandson. Yellow Calf. A strong name, one that would someday be spoken with fear in the camps of the enemies.

Yellow Kidney squatted beside the drifted elk tracks and spoke the name to himself. Then he felt the wind increase and knew the snow would not be far behind. On his way back to the war lodge, he came across a patch of wild rose and managed to kill a rabbit. As he skinned the rabbit, he felt the fleas crawling up his hands, seeking the warmth of his body, and he hurried as best he could. The rabbit was a skinny one, but it would make a good meal.

That evening he roasted the rabbit on a spit over the coals. It was his first fresh meat in seven sleeps. Although the blizzard had gathered force in the afternoon, he felt in his bones that it would end by morning. He turned the rabbit a quarter turn and sat back against the backrest he had constructed out of willow and sinew, a project that took him all of one day. He was satisfied. He had even managed to twist and wrap his hair.

He didn't see the barrel of the rifle as it poked through the thick pine bough covering the entrance. And he didn't feel the slug that tore through his chest just below the wishbone. The second and third shots were meaningless because his heart had already exploded. The backrest was spattered with blood but otherwise unharmed. The slugs had gone between the willow sticks.

The big man entered the war lodge tentatively and grimaced at the smell of gunpowder and smoke. He was surprised by the warmth of the small fire. He looked briefly at the warrior, who was lying on his side, a long otter-wrapped braid flung across his open eyes. Then he noticed the rabbit on the spit. He squatted on his heels and pulled the marten cap from his head.

He didn't see his son, bent over at the entrance, staring at the hands of the Indian. They lay in a peculiar position, down by the crotch, both palms up, side by side. But there was something even odder about them than their position. The son looked at the back of his father's head and the scrawny carcass over the fire. He turned and within three long steps he mired in a snowdrift and fell forward, vomiting up the pieces of hardtack he had chewed on while waiting for his father to return.

22

MIK-API SAT CLOSE to the fire, a blackhorn robe draped over his thin shoulders. He had been smoking his pipe and watching Red Paint prepare the evening meal. There was a certain effort in the way she stood up or bent over, and she often put her fingers to the small of her back and stretched. Once she looked up and caught his eyes and smiled, but her face was flushed and a little heavier than he remembered. Was she really getting older—so soon?

In many ways she reminded him of his own wife of long ago: the slender limbs, the way she walked on the balls of her feet, the pensive, almost scowling concentration on the intricacies of her beadwork. But mostly it was her voice, a surprisingly low yet soft voice, that brought the image of his wife into the lodge. As she worked, Red Paint talked about simple things—the thickening of the ice on the river, a lame horse she had seen that afternoon on the ridge above camp, the rough condition of her hands. Mik-api listened, but his thoughts were wandering to another time. She was a Black Paint girl who had been captured when the Pikunis were at war with them. Mik-api had met her at the trading house at Many Houses fort in the days before the Napikwans turned against the Pikunis. She had been a slave then, and Mik-api's mother was against their courtship. They had only been married two winters when she died, and that was long ago, but Mik-api could remember everything about her. Later, after the Pikunis and Black Paints became friendly, he had gone to their camp on the other side of the Backbone and met her family. Her father had been a many-faces man and had taught Mik-api his ways. The powerful medicine he now used came from the Black Paint People, who were renowned for the effectiveness of their healing ceremonies.

It had been more than forty winters since his wife died, and Mik-api had never remarried. He concentrated on his medicines, and as word of his success spread, he found himself too busy to think of a wife and family. And he had noticed a strange thing: As his powers increased, men began to talk less and less of their attractive daughters. Young women who, some years before, thought of him as a real catch no longer found excuses to meet him on the path or bring him food or clothes in gratitude for some small favor he had done them (mostly salves, he thought now with a smile, to rub on their faces or bodies). By the time he was thirty-five he knew he would not marry again, that the opportunity would not present itself because the people somehow feared his powers. Perhaps it was because it came from the Black Paints, or perhaps he had changed or had been changed by his gift for healing. Sometimes he regretted his solitary life, and sometimes lately he thought of taking some old woman as a sits-beside-him wife, but more often he enjoyed the quiet of his lodge, surrounded by his medicines, living out the ceremonies in his mind. In truth, he was satisfied with his memories of his Black Paint wife. Those two winters they had shared, even her agonizing death and his helpless rage, would never leave him.

"You are a long way away, Mik-api."

"I have been thinking. . . ." He came back. "There is something different about you."

"Go on." She smiled. But her face grew red.

"I am an old man but I am not blind." Mik-api rubbed his jaw thoughtfully. "What is it, now?"

"It is the fire—it makes me hot." She dropped some belly fat in the pot, and it hissed as she stirred it to coat the bottom. She had six large chunks of bighorn meat on a flat stone beside her. She grimaced and leaned back against her heels, her fingers kneading the small of her back.

Mik-api saw then what it was, what he almost suspected. The

round tummy was barely noticeable in the loose folds of her dress, but he saw it. I am getting stupid in my old age, he thought, not to have known. And his mind flashed briefly to the image of his own wife as she lay naked on the robe, the runny red eruptions on her swollen belly. She didn't even have a medicine man—he had died already of the white-scabs disease.

"Then you are with child," he said.

Red Paint laughed. Was it that obvious, even in her loose skin dress, or was Mik-api that perceptive? "It's a secret," she said. "You are not supposed to know."

"But why?"

She suddenly frowned. "He—he was not to know. It was to have been a surprise."

"Fools Crow?" Mik-api was genuinely surprised.

Red Paint placed the pieces of meat into the pot and stirred them with the wooden paddle. Then she sat back and looked at Mik-api. "My father. We were going to have him name the child." She lowered her eyes to the browning meat. Why had he left? Why had he deserted his family, her mother and brothers? But these were not the real questions that had been troubling her, that had been making her feel increasingly guilty. Why had she not told Yellow Kidney that she was expecting a child? He would have stayed for that. And why had the Above Ones made her life one of happiness and contentment and his one of misery and despair? Did they not see the injustice in that?

"My father has been gone for sixteen sleeps," she said quietly.

Mik-api looked into the fire. He didn't say anything about the dream he had been having the last three nights. As happened to him often now, the dream was not complete. His dreaming power had begun to fail him, but he saw the fleeting images of the war lodge, the elk herd that moved past in the twilight and the horses that waited in the draw. Yellow Kidney had not appeared in the dreams but he seemed to be a part of them. Perhaps tonight Nitsokan, the dream helper, would reveal Yellow Kidney. Mik-api was afraid of this revelation. He had a bad feeling.

"He will be found," he said, and almost said more, but a flurry of cold air carried away his thoughts.

Fools Crow stood just inside the lodge, his robe almost white from the blowing snow. He wiped his nose with the back of his hand.

"Ah, Mik-api, you honor our lodge."

"It has been too long," said Mik-api. He looked at Red Paint and smiled. "Much has happened with you since we last talked. We haven't had a good visit since we doctored up Fast Horse. How is he?"

Fools Crow frowned. "His wound has healed; he is all right that way." He sat down and held his hands over the fire. "Why do you ask?"

"I heard a rumor," said Mik-api. "I had a visitor, and he told me you had gone off to find Fast Horse."

"No one was to know that. Boss Ribs wanted it kept a secret. Who was this visitor?"

"One who flies far and sees many things. He says he is a friend of yours." Mik-api chuckled at Fools Crow's startled expression. "He says you always leave part of your kill for him. But tell me, did you find Fast Horse?"

"He wouldn't return with me." Fools Crow figured that Raven had told Mik-api that too. "He is happy with his life of making the Napikwans cry. It is in his blood, the blood you kept from leaking out of him."

Mik-api sighed. It was not the first time he had healed up a foolish man.

"Now there is news in camp that some Napikwans were killed —some hunters—and Three Bears is worried that the whites will take revenge, perhaps try to strike us and drive off our horses."

"Do they say it is Pikunis for sure?"

"It is always Pikunis with them. Three Bears thinks it is Owl Child and his bunch."

"Fast Horse rides with them once more," said Mik-api. He sighed again as though he realized the effort of doctoring Fast Horse had been wasted. But it was more than that. "I have a feeling it will go hard on us when the winter breaks. I think even before the many-drums moon we will see the seizers again."

Red Paint poured the dried crushed chokecherries and water

in with the browned meat. Her hand trembled but her face did not change. She did not want her husband to see her fear. He had been back for six sleeps since his confrontation with Fast Horse and he had said little about it, but now she knew just how bad things were. Owl Child and Fast Horse were still killing Napikwans, and now the Napikwans would come after the Lone Eaters before the many-drums moon. Only a few moments ago she had been thinking of her life as one of happiness and contentment. Only her father's suffering seemed a reality. Now all that was changed for her, and for the first time she feared for the future of her family and her people, of Fools Crow and herself. But mostly she was afraid for Butterfly. He was to be born in the moon of many drums. Would he live to be born? Would it be better to be born and killed or killed inside of her?

"What is it, Red Paint?" Fools Crow took the paddle from her hand.

She looked down and saw that the kettle had tipped. The stones were wet and steaming where the stew had spilled. She looked at her hand and it was red. "I felt our infant move," she said. "Butterfly is with us."

Fools Crow laughed and hugged her tightly to him, but Red Paint was looking at Mik-api. He was smiling, but his eyes were dark and troubled.

Three days after the blizzard ended, the scout, Joe Kipp, sat on his horse overlooking the camp of the Lone Eaters. It was one of those still, clear, cold days, but the sun was brilliant and faintly warm on his back. Because the temperature hadn't really changed, the snow was light and powdery, and from where he sat, high up on the bluff, he could look back and see the slightly undulating tracks of his horse in the white landscape. No other animals had yet moved on the plain, preferring to stay in the shelters of the trees and valleys. He looked toward the mountains, which began their ascent less than half a day's ride from where he sat. He had killed a bear in a stand of timber along the Two Medicine River when he was a youngster, the small black kind the Pikunis called sticky-mouth. From here he could see that patch of pines and firs. He smiled wistfully. Life was less complicated in those days. In fact, he had hunted with some of these very Lone Eaters and they had respected him. Not anymore, especially not after today.

Kipp looked down at the camp, and it looked much the same as it did back in those days—almost the same number of lodges arranged in the same way, people walking back and forth to the river, children and dogs chasing each other. These people have not changed, thought Kipp, but the world they live in has. You could look at it one of two ways: either their world is shrinking or that other world, the one the white man brought with him, is expanding. Either way, the Pikuni loses. And Kipp—well, Joe Kipp is somewhere in the middle—and has a job to do. He slipped a big gold Ingersoll from his waistcoat pocket and sprung the lid. One o'clock. He could deliver his message to the Lone Eaters and make the Hard Topknots' camp by nightfall. He looked upriver to the big horse herds, the reds, blacks, grays, the painted ponies. These Blackfeet, he thought, are some horse-takers. He started down the bluff. A group of children stood at the edge of camp, watching him.

That night, the members of the Braves, All Crazy Dogs, Raven Carriers, and Dogs and Tails societies met in the big lodge to discuss this latest proposal from the seizer chiefs. None of the young men's societies were present, and Rides-at-the-door breathed a sigh of relief, for they would surely have put up a fight out of pride and stubbornness.

Although Kipp had only hinted at it that afternoon, Rides-at-the-door knew that the proposed meeting had to do with Owl Child's depredations and probably the number of stolen horses in the camps, Napikwan horses. The seizer chiefs wanted to meet with the Pikuni chiefs, and little good would come out of it.

And so the warriors discussed the proposal. This time there were no shrill arguments, no accusations, no bluffs, no conclusions. The men seemed bewildered, almost fearful, and by the time they smoked a final pipe, the only thing they had decided was to send a rider to the other camps to learn how they were handling Kipp's message.

Rides-at-the-door walked Three Bears back to the old chief's lodge. Night Red Light was almost full in the clear black sky, and the stars danced around her.

"I do not wish to make such a journey down to the agency. I see no good in it." Three Bears sounded tired, and he watched his breath go away from him. "These Napikwans think that we can control our young men. It is not right. I know there are many Napikwan horses in our herds—I myself am against such foolishness—but what can we do? As for Owl Child, what can any of us do? He is slippery like the underwater swimmers. Besides, Mountain Chief would never allow us to hand Owl Child over to the Napikwans. That's what they want, isn't it?"

"Perhaps the seizer chiefs will understand that our power is limited. Joe Kipp says their head chief is a good man and is aware of our predicament."

"And you trust Joe Kipp?"

"No," admitted Rides-at-the-door, but he felt a small sorrow in his heart because he once had. Joe Kipp's mother was of the Dirt Lodge People to the east and Joe Kipp had grown up at his father's trading post, where his only friends were Pikunis. He had changed horses.

"I'm afraid he represents the Napikwan interests," said Three Bears. "But what do you think, my friend, about this council?"

"I fear these seizer chiefs' motives. It seems simple enough— to meet with the Pikunis, to council, to come to an agreement. But I think it might be a plan to gather our chiefs in one place and kill them or hold them hostage. The agency is on the edge of our territory. It would be easy to sneak enough of the seizers in to capture our chiefs."

"Those are my thoughts." Three Bears stopped and laughed. "Listen to you, Rides-at-the-door! You, who have always counseled peace with the Napikwans. I think you sound more like one of Owl Child's gang. Next you would have us capture this Napikwan chief so our young men could practice their scalping on him."

"It was in my mind." The other laughed. "It would not displease me to have this seizer's hair hanging from my lodgepole."

"That is why I lean on you for advice, my friend—you have the blood of a warrior flowing through a peace-talker's body. Now, what do you advise?"

"Wait. Until the other bands have received Joe Kipp's message. It is important to know what Mountain Chief and Heavy Runner think. As you know, they are as different as the real-bear and the prairie chicken. Mountain Chief wishes to deal harshly with the Napikwan, while Heavy Runner would seek to clean their longshoes. The other chiefs fall in the middle and could perhaps be persuaded one way or the other."

They had reached Three Bears' lodge. They listened a moment to a woman singing. "My youngest daughter. She is the only one left to marry off, but she is getting older and has the withered leg. It will not be easy." Three Bears bent to enter the lodge; then he stood and turned. "If this council at the agency takes place, can I count on you to speak for the Lone Eaters? I have no heart for this matter."

"It would be an honor—but I would speak only those words that came from Three Bears himself." Rides-at-the-door laughed with little humor. "But I have it in my mind that the Pikunis are invited only to listen. We are being squeezed, Three Bears. I'm afraid this is the latest trick, perhaps the last, to gain our lands without fighting. The seizer chief will certainly demand the impossible. I think he will try to divide the Pikunis between those who would follow Mountain Chief and those who would line up behind Heavy Runner. Already, they attempt to solidify their friendship with Heavy Runner."

"You do not agree with his—"

"Desire to please the Napikwans? No. Heavy Runner would have us give away everything for a few blankets and a tin of the white man's grease."

"He thinks they would take care of us, that we should put our fate in their hands," said Three Bears.

"And Mountain Chief would like us to fight. Either way, we will lose." Rides-at-the-door looked up at the night sky. He felt old suddenly and envied the stars their distance. "We will lose our grandchildren, Three Bears. They will be wiped out or they will turn into Napikwans. Already some of our children attend their school at the agency. Our men wear trousers and the women prefer the trade-cloth to skins. We wear their blankets, cook in their kettles and kill the blackhorns with their bullets. Soon our young women will marry them, like the Liars and the Cut-throats."

"Perhaps it is useless to resist?" Three Bears looked keenly into the eyes of his friend and adviser. He was alarmed to hear this kind of talk. But he needn't have worried, for even as Rides-at-the-door delivered his harangue, he had begun to anticipate the seizer chiefs' demands and seek ways of countering them. It would require compromise, but he had no intention of counseling the Pikunis to give in. One thing did trouble him—suppose he wasn't allowed to enter into the talks? He wasn't a head chief or a band chief. He had no right to be heard, and the head seizer chief would undoubtedly be unyielding in his demand that only chiefs be present. The only chance he had was the knowledge that the chiefs valued his ability to deal with the Napikwans, as he had proven in the past. He spoke the strange language and had clarified many points in the previous treaty discussions. If the moderate chiefs showed up—those somewhere between Mountain Chief and Heavy Runner—they would seek his counsel and even desire him to speak for them in some instances.

"We must resist them," said Rides-at-the-door, "but we must also give them something—even if we have to kill Owl Child ourselves."

"That would give some among Heavy Runner's band great pleasure; it was one of their people that he killed. Bear Head's relatives would welcome the chance. But who would be foolish enough to go to Mountain Chief's camp and demand that he turn over Owl Child? And would this be enough to satisfy the seizer chiefs? What about the Napikwan horses?"

"They will have to understand that the return of the horses

would be impossible. Most of them have already been sold to the traders north of the Medicine Line. If the seizers insist on this point . . ." Rides-at-the-door threw his hands up to the night sky, as though the stars were horses out of reach.

"Then we may have to join Mountain Chief's side. We will not align ourselves with Heavy Runner," said Three Bears. Only a moment ago his back hurt and his feet were cold, but now he spoke with determination. "We will not become like the white-horns that these white people herd from one place to another. I will tell you this, my friend—if the Napikwans do not respect our lands and our people, I will lead the first war party against them. I am an old man and I see things I do not like. It is clear to me that our days of following the blackhorns where we choose are numbered. I see the signs all around me. Many of our young men go off on their own. They do not listen to their chiefs. They drink the white man's water and kill each other. Some of our young women already stand around the forts, waiting to fornicate with the seizers for a drink of this water. They become ugly before their time, and then they are turned out like old cows to forage for themselves. It is bad for our young people and it will get worse. The Lone Eaters are lucky. We live many sleeps from these places of ruin. But the day will come when our people will decide that they would rather consort with the Napikwans than live in the ways our long-ago fathers thought appropriate. But I, Three Bears, will not see this day. I will die first."

23

I T   W A S   A   S U N N Y   W I N D L E S S   D A Y, and the seven children pulling their blackhorn-rib sleds to a steep hill beyond the horse herds talked and teased each other. The two girls, at twelve winters, were the oldest. They had been sent to keep an eye on the younger ones, but they were not happy, for the five boys made jokes about the size of their breasts and the skinniness of their legs. One Spot, in particular, was cruel to them. He liked these times when he didn't have to follow his older brother around, and so he bullied the younger boys and made the girls chase him. He boasted of his hunting skills and rubbed snow in another boy's face. When one of the girls hit him with a small skin of pemmican, it stung his cheek but he didn't cry. He called the girl Skinny Weasel and he liked her, although she was a year older than he was. She liked One Spot's brother, Good Young Man, but he was more interested in hunting than girls. He was off hunting the bighorns with Fools Crow now near the Backbone. They would be gone for two or three sleeps. One Spot picked up a handful of snow and threw it at Skinny Weasel. His cheek stung but he liked her.

None of them noticed the wolf that had emerged from behind a clump of drifted-over greasewood until he was fifty paces to the side of them. He was large and gray and his eyes were golden in the brilliant sun. Snow clung to one side of him as though he had been lying down. As he walked, his tail drooped and dragged on the deep snow, and a sound, somewhere between a growl and a grunt, came up from his chest.

It was this sound that Skinny Weasel's girlfriend heard, and when she looked over she saw the animal's gait was shaky and listed to one side. He had his head down, his tongue hanging almost to the snow. Then she saw the whiteness around his mouth and thought he had been eating snow. Her first impulse was to turn and run, but then the wolf began to veer away from them. She watched him out of the corner of her eye as the wolf circled behind them. Then she said something to Skinny Weasel in a low voice and the girls stopped and turned. It was at this point that one of the boys let out a cry of fear, for he had just seen the wolf.

The wolf looked up at them and coughed and bared his fangs, making chewing motions as though he were trying to rid himself of a bone or hairball. He watched listlessly as the children ran, all but One Spot, who stood in the deep snow with his hands on his hips. He taunted the bigmouth with a war song that he had learned from Fools Crow.

The other children stopped near the base of the big hill and turned to watch. The wolf covered the thirty paces with such speed that they didn't have a chance to cry out a warning. By the time One Spot had turned to run, the wolf was upon him, knocking him face down in the snow, standing over him, growling, the hair on his back standing up and shining in the sunlight. The children screamed as they watched the wolf attack the bundled-up child. He struck repeatedly at the blanket, his low growl now a roar of fury. At last he found One Spot's head and sank his fangs into the exposed skin behind the ear. The child screamed in pain and turned over, only to feel a fang knock against his cheekbone, opening up the skin. Then the fangs were twisting and pulling at the cheek, gnashing into the soft flesh. One Spot felt the wetness and the hot breath. He saw for one brief instant a yellow eye and a laid-back ear—then he sank into the snow and the red darkness.

Skinny Weasel was crying as she watched the wolf stagger away. In his charge and attack, he had used up the last of his energy. Now his throat was swollen shut and the saliva hung in long strands from his mouth. He began a wide circle, veering always to his right, his eyes glazed, his breath coming in harsh barks, his tongue and tail once again hanging and dragging on the snow. Skinny Weasel watched him disappear behind a stand of willows near the river; then she ran to the limp form in the snowfield. When she rolled him over, she bit her lips to keep from screaming. A flap of ragged skin lay back over One Spot's eye, exposing the clean white bone of his cheek. One earlobe hung from a thin piece of skin and there was a large mat of blood in the hair. She thought she heard a rattle deep in the boy's throat. With a shudder, she placed the flap of skin down over the cheekbone. Then she and the others lifted him onto a sled. Skinny Weasel's girlfriend covered him up with her own blanket. Then the two girls pulled the sled through the deep snow back toward camp. The sun was high and the sweat was cool on the girls' bodies.

By the time Fools Crow and Good Young Man returned from their hunting trip four sleeps later, One Spot was able to sit up and take some meat. But most of the time he lay in his robes and thought of the yellow eye and laid-back ear, the harsh breath and snapping teeth. Every time he closed his eyes, he saw the bounding wolf and cried out in his weakness and pain. Heavy Shield Woman had slept little, despite the fact that Red Paint and another woman had taken over the nursing of her son. Now she sat in a listless trance and thought of the many things that had happened to her family. She didn't really think much, but images of Yellow Kidney and Red Paint and Good Young Man entered her head and they all seemed far away, as though she had lost them all. Even when she looked down at One Spot, in one of his moments of peace, she saw the black pitchy substance that held his cheek in place and thought that he had gone away from her too. Only Red Paint was there to talk with, but Heavy Shield Woman didn't talk. She had begun to wonder about her role as Sacred Vow Woman at the Sun Dance ceremonies. Had she done something wrong? She thought she could not be a virtuous woman, for she felt no happiness or peace since her husband was returned to her. She felt a day-to-day barrenness of spirit relieved only by moments of pleasure at the antics of her sons and Red Paint's swelling belly. She knew she would never see Yellow Kidney again and that thought almost gave her relief, but then she would think of the happiness they had shared, the times they had lain together, the pride in his eyes each time she delivered him a child, and she would become consumed by a restless, quiet fury. Many times she thought of going to Three Bears and telling him what was in her heart and renouncing her role as medicine woman. In her mind she had already done so. Now when the girls looked to her for guidance, she averted her eyes and said nothing. She began to avoid them, for she was sure they would see in her eyes what she felt in her heart.

Fools Crow and Good Young Man rode into camp with the carcasses of two bighorns. Fools Crow had a set of horns for One Spot tied to the frame of a packhorse. He rode first to his own lodge and dumped one of the bighorns in the snow beside the entrance. Then he led the other packhorse to Heavy Shield Woman's lodge, kicking a black dog in the ribs when he became too curious. As he loosened the rawhide strings that held the animal down, Red Paint emerged from her mother's lodge. She came forward and squeezed his upper arm and smiled. She called a greeting to her brother, Good Young Man, who sat exhausted on his horse, ready to drive the packhorses back to the herd. Wearily he rolled onto his belly and slid off the horse. He had planned to return to the camp in triumph because he had shot one of the bighorns with Fools Crow's rifle, but now he felt the stiffness in his legs and butt and wanted only to lie down and sleep.

But Red Paint motioned him close, and then she told them about One Spot's encounter with the wolf. Even as she said that he was all right, her voice shook and she looked at the snow at Fools Crow's feet. Good Young Man ducked into the lodge.

Red Paint looked into her husband's eyes. "The children he was with think the wolf might have had the white-mouth. They say he was acting funny, walking sideways in a big circle. They think he had the foam on the mouth, but they couldn't tell if it was that or if he was eating snow."

"Did he breathe different?"

"Skinny Weasel said it was like a harsh bark in his throat."

"Maybe it was a bone stuck."

"Maybe," said Red Paint.

"Is your mother in the lodge?"

"She is out gathering firewood."

Fools Crow entered the lodge, with Red Paint right behind him. Good Young Man knelt beside his brother, holding his hand. One Spot looked at Fools Crow; then he grinned.

"I sang my war song," he said.

"But did you have your weapons?" Fools Crow got down on his knees and ruffled the boy's hair.

"No," the boy said sheepishly.

"Haiya! What warrior goes out empty-handed?"

"He would kill this bigmouth with his bare hands. He would be a great warrior," said Good Young Man.

"If I had my knife—"

"If he had his knife! Listen to him talk!" Fools Crow laughed. "And now you have your first battle wounds. Let me see." Fools Crow leaned over the boy's face. The patch of skin held by the black pitch looked a pale purple and was slightly swollen. He almost lost his whole cheek, thought Fools Crow. As it is, it will always be swollen and discolored, but it will at least be there. The earlobe was completely bitten off and would cause no trouble. But behind the ear, in a patch of cut-off hair, there were several puncture wounds. The whole area was an angry red, except for the small white circles around each fang mark. These were draining, but the area was swollen and tender-looking. It scared Fools Crow to look at these wounds, but he didn't say anything.

"He has nightmares," said Red Paint. "He gets very little sleep because of them."

"Sleep-bringer will visit soon. All warriors have bad dreams after battle. They will pass." Fools Crow looked down at One Spot. "You must not think of this wolf as your enemy. He did only what wolves will do. The bigmouth is a power animal, and if he visits you in your dreams, it is only because he wishes to help you. Someday he will become your dream helper."

"When I am old enough for my seeking?"

"Yes. Then he will come to you and give you some of his secret medicine. But for now, you must think of him as your brother and treat him with respect. Do you understand that?"

"But why did he attack me?"

"This one was—sick. I think he didn't know what he was doing. But wolves are unpredictable. It is best to leave them alone, even if they are our brothers—like the real-bear."

"Will I have a scar forever?"

"Do you remember the story of Poia—Scarface?"

"Yes. He came from Sun Chief and instructed our people in the Sun Dance. Afterward, Sun Chief made him a star in the sky, just like his father, Morning Star."

"But before that he was a boy just like you, with a scar on his face."

"But the people laughed and scorned him!"

"In those days, the people were not wise. Now we honor Poia. Of all the Above Ones, he is most like us, and so you must think of your scar as a mark of honor. You will wear it proudly and the people will be proud of you. And they will think highly of you because you did not kill your brother, the wolf." Fools Crow laughed. "We will tell them you took pity on this bigmouth."

One Spot thought for a moment, his dark eyes narrowed and staring up at the point where the lodgepoles come together. He heard some children run by but he didn't envy their freedom. Finally he said, "Yes, I took pity on my brother. Bigmouth will come visit me when I am older and I will welcome him. But if I had my weapons, I surely would have killed him."

One Spot did not get over his dreams, but now, instead of attacking him, the wolf turned away or stopped, sometimes lifting his lip to growl, other times simply staring at the boy through golden eyes. But he always kept his distance, and One Spot, in spite of his fear, began to look forward to the wolf's visits, for he was memorizing every aspect of the animal, from his silver-tipped fur to the way his long ears flickered when One Spot shouted at him.

For seven sleeps he dreamed of the bigmouth, and on the eighth day he was well enough to walk down to the river to throw rocks. Good Young Man stayed with him, never leaving the lodge to play with friends or even to visit Red Paint and Fools Crow. Together, he and his mother had skinned and quartered the bighorn. The meat was strong but good and would last a long time. Heavy Shield Woman also seemed to be recovering her spirit. For the first time in many sleeps she went to visit a friend who lived on the other side of camp. The friend was happy to see her, for she had been concerned about Heavy Shield Woman's misfortunes. They ate and talked until well after dark and the friend noticed that Heavy Shield Woman smiled and laughed more than she had in some time—since the days Yellow Kidney, then a whole man, and she had come to feast. When the friend's husband came home, with a fat blackhorn cow he had killed on the cutbank, Heavy Shield Woman remembered that she had not fed One Spot and Good Young Man. She looked up at the stars as she hurried along the icy path to her lodge, and the cold air was fresh in her chest.

When she entered, Good Young Man looked up anxiously. He was kneeling by his brother's side. "One Spot seems to be sick again. He seems to have trouble swallowing. He moves his jaws and is thirsty all the time but he can't drink."

Heavy Shield Woman ran to One Spot and sank to her knees. His forehead glistened in the firelight and his throat seemed to jump and quiver on its own. He looked up at her and his eyes were wide with fear. He tried to speak but the effort made him swallow and he cried out in pain. In panic he began to thrash around under the blackhorn robe. Heavy Shield Woman held him and spoke soothing words to him, but he didn't seem to hear or know her.

"Good Young Man, put on the water to heat—build up the fire first—then run for Fools Crow and Red Paint. Run fast."

One Spot had quieted down a little, but when Heavy Shield Woman looked down at him, she saw the saliva bubbling around his mouth. His eyes were dark and unseeing.

When Good Young Man returned with Fools Crow and Red

Paint, Heavy Shield Woman was mopping the sick boy's face with a cloth dampened in the warm water. Suddenly One Spot began to tremble violently and make noises in his throat. He tried to kick the robe off, but Fools Crow held his legs.

"It is the white-mouth," he said. "The wolf has him."

"Oh, I feared it!" Heavy Shield Woman moaned as she remembered how a girlfriend had died of a fox bite. She had never forgotten it and now she was seeing it again.

"Red Paint! Hold his legs while I get Mik-api."

Fools Crow was gone for a long time. Red Paint helped her mother hold down the struggling boy. He did not recognize either of them, but the strange noise in his throat seemed a cry for help. Red Paint sank back on her heels once when her brother suddenly stopped and held himself rigid. She wiped the sweat from her forehead, and only then did she realize that she had been crying.

At last, Fools Crow entered the lodge. His chest was heaving and his face was crimson.

"Where's Mik-api?" Red Paint held her breath.

"I searched the camp. Somebody thinks he is visiting the Hard Topknots."

He looked down and Heavy Shield Woman was looking up at him with a blankness in her eyes. He suddenly thought that he had not looked at her this way since he had married Red Paint; nor had she looked at him. But now this taboo seemed far less important than the bad spirit in the boy they loved.

"We need a green hide," said Fools Crow. "Mik-api once told me how he did this."

Heavy Shield Woman looked down at her son, who was beginning to stir again. A trickle of blood from the crescent scab on his cheek ran down his neck. She wiped the saliva from his mouth. She looked up at Fools Crow and thought to question his ability as a medicine man—he was only an apprentice—but the dark shining in his eyes stopped her. He seemed to be somebody she had not known before.

"Morning Gun has just returned from his hunt," she said. "He brought back a blackhorn."

Fools Crow ran across a small icy field to Morning Gun's lodge. He told the hunter what he needed, and the two men began to skin the blackhorn. They worked quickly, not caring if they punctured the skin or left too much meat on it. When they finished, Fools Crow draped the skin over his shoulder and began to trot back to Heavy Shield Woman's lodge. He was surprised to see so many people standing around. They had been talking among themselves, but he hadn't heard a word.

The two women undressed the struggling, kicking boy while Fools Crow spread the green hide, skin side up, on the other side of the fire. Good Young Man helped him clear away the spot. Fools Crow clapped him on the shoulder and squeezed. Then he helped the women carry One Spot over to the hide. He was taken aback by the strength in the small body and understood how much effort it had taken the women to hold him down. But they managed to lay him on the smooth cool skin, with his arms pinned to his sides, and roll him up. Only his head stuck out of the shaggy bundle. Red Paint looked down and could not believe that the contorted face, the white foamy mouth which uttered such strange harsh sounds, belonged to her younger brother. But she knew that when a bad spirit entered one's body, the body no longer belonged to the person. And so, as she looked at the face she grew calm, for she felt that, now the spirit had been trapped, her husband would drive it away with the medicine he had learned from Mik-api. She helped her mother to the far side of the fire and squatted to watch.

Fools Crow, who had stopped by his lodge for his parfleche of medicines, took out a small bundle of braided sweet grass. He lit one of the braids and captured the smoke in his free hand. He began to chant and to rub the smoke over the out-of-his-body boy and himself. He chanted with his eyes closed, and the steady rhythm of his voice, like a heartbeat, seemed to place the boy under a spell. One Spot stopped struggling and the noise in his throat subsided. Fools Crow chanted:

"I take heart from the sacred blackhorn.
Where I walk, the grasses touch my feet.

I stop with my medicine.
The ground where my medicine rests is sacred."

Then he removed a burning stick from the fire and touched it against the shaggy hide. There was a hiss and the lodge was suddenly filled with the stink of burning hair. Heavy Shield Woman started, but Red Paint held her close. Still chanting, Fools Crow burned off more of the curly hair. He did this several times until the hair was black and crinkly; then he turned the boy over. The movement made One Spot cry out. But now Fools Crow began to pass the burning stick over the green robe, lighting long strips of hair, and the smell made Red Paint feel faint. She looked beyond her mother to Good Young Man, but he was watching intently, mesmerized by the moving stick of fire. Again Fools Crow turned the boy over until he was lying on his stomach. The boy made no sound and Red Paint became frightened.

Fools Crow stopped to wipe One Spot's sweat-drenched head. He looked into the boy's eyes, but they were opaque and without recognition. Then he turned him again and burned off the last of the hair.

When he had finished, Fools Crow threw a bundle of sage grass onto the fire to purify the air. As he did this, he said a prayer to the Above Ones to take pity on the boy and restore him to health. He asked the Medicine Wolf to take pity on the boy and to forgive him. Then he instructed the women to unwrap One Spot and bathe him with warm water. While they did this, he took some sticky-root and tastes-dry and ground it up into a paste. The women placed the small limp body on a robe and Fools Crow swabbed the paste on the boy's throat and mouth. They covered him with another robe.

Fools Crow sent the two women back to his own lodge, there to prepare some meat and broth. He said he would send Good Young Man to fetch them when they were needed. Heavy Shield Woman was reluctant to leave, but Red Paint talked her out of the lodge. The sudden draft of cold air swirled through the space and dried the sweat on Fools Crow's face. The lodge smelled of burnt hair and sage and sticky-root.

Good Young Man built up the fire and gave Fools Crow a

drink of water. He dipped another cupful and looked question-ingly at his younger brother, but the medicine man motioned the youth to sit on the other side of the fire.

For the rest of that night Fools Crow beat on his small neck-hide drum. His stick was made of ash, rounded at one end, feathered at the other. He accompanied the slow beat with a monotonous song:

> *"Medicine Wolf walks with me.*
> *Medicine Wolf is my brother.*
> *Medicine Wolf enters me.*
> *Medicine Wolf is my helper."*

Fools Crow sang this song over and over and Good Young Man eventually fell asleep. Just before dawn he was awakened by a harsh growling and snapping. He sat up and saw Fools Crow, down on all fours, circling the body, swinging his head from side to side, growling and snapping his teeth at One Spot. He made three circles, sometimes feinting in to snap, other times growling low in his throat. Then Fools Crow wandered off to a bed near the tipi liner. He circled around and around four times, then lay down and curled up like a wolf. He closed his eyes.

Sometime after first light, Good Young Man awoke again and it was quiet. He threw back the robe and sat up. Fools Crow knelt beside One Spot, but now he was hunched over, his head down. Good Young Man watched his broad back move up and down with his breathing. Then he slid his legs from beneath the robe and tended to the fire. It was nearly out, but he coaxed a flame out of some dry twigs. When he had the fire crackling, he crept around and looked down at the face of his younger brother. In the half-light of dawn, the face looked pale and shiny, like the belly fat of a blackhorn. Only the skin on the cheek that had been torn away had some color. It was a dull purple, fading to bright pink along the scar. Good Young Man got down on all fours and looked closer. He looked at the chest beneath the robe. Nothing moved. He became frightened, and in his fear he blew on the face. The eyes seemed to move beneath the lids. He blew again, and this time the eyes opened and the brows came down in irritation.

24

THE PARTY THAT MOVED through the cold gray sunlight toward the Four Horns agency on the Milk River spoke very little. They had picked up a wagon track that only three winters ago had not existed but now cut deeply into the earth. The men rode two abreast, bundled up in blankets or capotes. Beneath their outer garments, they wore their finest leggings and shirts and winter moccasins. Most of the men wore fur caps and mittens. Heavy Runner alone wore trousers made of blue trade-cloth. He also wore a bronze medallion that had been presented to him at the last treaty-signing by the representative of the white Grandfather. That and the quillwork design that ran down the outside of his trousers were his only ornamentation. He carried his medicine pipe stem, wrapped in soft elkskin, in his arms.

Beside him rode a Kainah band chief, Sun Calf, a large man with close-set eyes above a large nose. Heavy brass hoops hung from his long earlobes and a white bone breastplate covered his chest. He was not an important chief, but many of the Napikwans took him to be so because of his impressive appearance.

Behind them rode two other Pikuni chiefs, Big Lake and Little Wolf. Big Lake had once been respected by all the Pikunis, but after throwing in with Heavy Runner he lost influence with most of the young warriors and many of the other chiefs who did not trust the Napikwans. Little Wolf was the leader of a small band of Pikunis who possessed little power, but he was the keeper of one of the Sacred Pipe bundles and thought himself an important man.

Rides-at-the-door rode behind them, listening to the squeak of saddles and the occasional shudder of a horse. He was not happy and he knew the seizer chiefs would not be happy, for this group was small, only the ones expected to show up, whether for a handout or a treaty-signing. He had hoped that some of the chiefs who sat somewhere between Heavy Runner and Mountain Chief would join them, but their messengers were firm in their refusals. It is a waste of time to be here, thought Rides-at-the-door. I do not speak for anyone. But he could interpret and at least get the seizer chiefs' message clear. He could take that message back, so the other chiefs would know where they stood. But he already knew where they stood. And the head seizer chief would take their absence as a sign of hostility. And that would give the Napikwans an excuse to deal harshly with the Pikunis and Kainahs. It was clear to Rides-at-the-door that this would be the last of the friendly meetings with the Napikwans, the last chance to reach an agreement that would prevent the seizers from taking control of the Pikuni lands and fates. The only hope this small group of chiefs had—and they had discussed it—was to stall off the seizer movements until spring. Maybe things would quiet down by then. Maybe Sun Chief would think differently about these invaders then.

Rides-at-the-door looked ahead at the back of Heavy Runner. He had a heavy Napikwan blanket draped over his head. He was a good-hearted man who wanted peace for his people, and Rides-at-the-door respected him for that. Even Mountain Chief did not question Heavy Runner's desire to do what was best—even necessary, in his opinion—for the Pikunis. But this very desire had led him to believe that the Napikwans too wanted what was best for the Indians. He could not see that they only wanted the land, the blackhorn ranges on which to graze their whitehorns, and that the Pikunis were obstacles to the fulfillment of this goal. Heavy Runner was a good man but the wrong man to lead this party.

Rides-at-the-door turned in his saddle and looked behind him. Seven young men—three from the Kainahs and four from Heavy Runner's band—rode alertly, their eyes sweeping the country through which they passed, as though every tree, every hill, every stand of willow concealed fierce eyes that watched them ride into a trap. Even their horses were nervous, dancing behind the more placid animals of the chiefs, heads held high and back, tails arched. They were young horses and, like their riders, ready for any kind of action.

They were riding through the big-leaf and spear-leaf trees along the Milk River. A few winters ago, it had been good hunting for long-legs and wags-his-tails and, before that, bighorns, real-lions and sticky-mouths. With the settling of the Napikwans, these animals had moved into the Backbone, which loomed above the riders to the west. Rides-at-the-door looked over at Ear Mountain and, below it, Danger Butte. His people still used the war lodge on the butte. Unlike the others, it was built of logs and then covered with brush. The Snakes also used it on their raiding parties against the Pikunis. Once Three Bears and his party killed five Snakes there, and Three Bears had named his second wife Strikes-the-Snakes-below-the-Ear in honor of the occasion.

Now the wagon track moved just outside the big-leafs and began a long curve to the east and south. To the left, the riders could see the low log buildings of a ranch. Four horses held their heads high over the corral rail, watching them. In front of the house, just off the step, stood two children, a boy and a girl, both blond. The girl, nine or ten winters, wore a long tight blue coat. Her thin black-stockinged legs looked like burnt twigs. The boy, a little older, wore a wide-brimmed hat and a brown coat. They both watched the riders with awe.

After the warriors rounded a bend, Heavy Runner pulled up and the others did the same. Before them lay the agency buildings, the squat rectangular structures that the Napikwans seemed to favor. In the center of these outbuildings stood a much larger one, built in the shape of a U with a narrow entrance at the mouth. This log building contained the offices and sleeping places of the Napikwans, as well as the storeroom and shops. Heavy Runner had told the younger men about this place, how it was built to withstand attack, how it contained everything the

Napikwans would need, including a deep hole in the middle where they could get water out of the earth. He had told them of the school inside where the big-headed man could teach them many things. He had taught Heavy Runner how to make his name with a stick that squirted black juice.

Now Heavy Runner looked toward the entrance. There were two seizers, one on each side of the gate. A short distance away stood two white lodges, the kind the seizers pitched when they were traveling. But there were no horses and no other people. Heavy Runner was disappointed for he had expected a ceremonial greeting. He liked the way these seizers lined up on their horses and blew their brass pipe. Once, at the big treaty on the Big and Yellow rivers, they had rattled their drums, a fierce thundering roll that had the people ducking behind each other for cover. Heavy Runner had realized then that the Napikwan warriors possessed great medicine.

The gates opened and five men, dressed in the long coats of the seizers, passed through and into one of the white lodges. Heavy Runner turned to the small group and said, "We will ride in with honor. These seizers know how powerful the Pikunis and Kainahs are and they will welcome us with good hearts. Let us meet them with the same."

With that, Heavy Runner kicked his horse lightly in the ribs. The animal, impatient at being held back that crisp winter morning, broke into a trot and the others followed. They rode across a large snowy field, staying two abreast in the ruts of the wagon trail. The young men behind the chiefs had to hold their horses to the pace, but they too were tempted to break into headlong flight, not necessarily toward the agency buildings.

The soldiers at the gate caught sight of the party at five hundred yards and called to the men who were warming themselves by a stove in one of the tents. They tumbled out, buttoning their coats and checking their weapons. One of them, a hard-looking man with red hair, gave an order and slipped through the gate into the agency compound. The rest assembled before the gate, their rifles across their chests.

The sun was high and gray and even Heavy Runner felt un-

easy as the party reined in before the soldiers. The young Napikwans looked tense and held their weapons tightly. One of them
was turned slightly so that his rifle was pointed at Heavy Runner.
Heavy Runner held up his hand in greeting; then he made the
sign for Blackfeet people, but the seizers looked confused.

"We are the chiefs of the Pikunis and Kainahs. We have come
to council with your chiefs. I am Heavy Runner."

The seizers did not respond.

Rides-at-the-door eased his horse between Heavy Runner and
Sun Calf. Sun Calf looked at him with some annoyance, for he
had been trying to stare down the seizers.

Rides-at-the-door spoke to the young man with two stripes on
his sleeve. "These chiefs of the Pikunis and Kainahs would speak
with the chiefs of the seizers. They have been invited."

The young man looked up at the broad, fierce Indian face. He
was surprised to hear his own tongue coming from such a man.
He had only been out west for three months and had not encountered the Indians before. But he had heard stories of savagery and
deceit and was not about to let his guard down. The corporal
thought this man who spoke English was about to play some kind
of trick on him.

"We have our orders to secure this gate," he said.

"Your chiefs wish to see us."

"The General is being notified. We will know in a moment if
it is all right for you to pass." He looked past the chiefs to the
young men who sat with their rifles in their arms. It was bound
to be a trick. The sight of these braves, with their paints and
ornaments, their weapons at the ready, filled the corporal with
apprehension. They seemed larger than white men, and their
impassive faces were filled with hate. There was no telling how
much damage even a small party could do.

Rides-at-the-door translated the corporal's words, and a look of
consternation passed over Heavy Runner's face. He was well-
known to the Napikwan chiefs. They had always treated him
with the hospitality due a chief. Could this signal a change?
Perhaps he had led this party into an ambush; perhaps behind that
gate stood a hundred seizers, ready to burst forth, rifles roaring

with thunder. But no—this was simply a mix-up to be endured with dignity and patience.

And so the two groups of men waited for several tense moments without speaking but with eyes focused on the slightest movement, with ears tuned to the click of a safety being thrown off or a cartridge being levered into a chamber. But the only sound was the clang of metal on metal from within the compound.

Finally the gate creaked open and the redheaded sergeant led three officers out of the structure. Two of the officers wore their longcoats, but the third stood before the warriors in his tunic and a fur cap. He was a tall, wiry man with dark hair and mustache and a long limp beard that covered only his chin. His blue eyes had a tired look, but they were hard with disappointment as they swept over the small group of Indians. He had expected too much, and as his eyes finally fell on Heavy Runner, he knew the council would be worthless. A thin smile crossed his lips, and he strode forward to shake hands with the chief. Worthless, he thought.

After the somewhat cheerless greeting, the mounted warriors were led into the courtyard of the agency. Several soldiers stood at ease in the center beside the well. As the warriors dismounted, they placed their weapons in a rack. The young men relinquished their rifles reluctantly after Heavy Runner set the example. Rides-at-the-door looked around him and hid his surprise at the amount of activity going on. Several Napikwans stood outside the compound doors watching them. Off to his right, partly obscured by a wagon, two women were gesturing with delicate motions. Then he heard the familiar clang of a man striking metal. He had watched such a man down at Many Houses fort and had marveled at the way the man made a rim for a wagon wheel, heating and pounding the iron until it came together in a hoop. For some reason the sound comforted him. If the Napikwans were engaged in such activities, they must think this occasion was not far out of the ordinary. He looked up the pole beside him and saw the red and white flag with the patch of blue in the corner. The white sharp-pointed designs on the blue represented the many territories conquered by the Napikwans. This had been explained to Rides-at-the-door many winters ago by a white many-faces man who had come to camp with the Lone Eaters. He wore a black robe and the Pikunis called him Long Teeth. So long ago, thought Rides-at-the-door. Long Teeth had been different from these Napikwans. He wanted nothing from the Pikunis but a knowledge of their ways and the opportunity to paint their faces on thin white skins he kept in his parfleche. Many of the people were afraid to sit for him, for fear that he would capture Nitsokan, their dream helper. But most trusted him, and for a short time the Pikunis thought that the Napikwans came to them as friends. But Long Teeth himself had told how they conquered all and he did not seem proud.

The redheaded man with the stripes on his sleeve stood before Rides-at-the-door. "The General says you will be allowed to sit in on the meeting, but you will not be allowed to take an active part in the discussions."

"You know I speak your language?"

"We've met before. I saw how you listened."

Rides-at-the-door suddenly remembered the man. He had been present when the seizers were riding after Mountain Chief the previous summer. He had been with Joe Kipp and the seizer chief. And he remembered how the striped-sleeve had listened to the talk between the chiefs.

"And you speak the Pikuni tongue."

The striped-sleeve almost smiled. "I learned it from Little Dog back in the days on the Sun River—when he tried his luck at farming. Before your people killed him."

Rides-at-the-door ignored this last statement. "Who is this General?"

"General Sully? Why, he's in charge of Indian policy in this territory—at least, for now." This time the smile came.

The two men followed the chiefs and a pair of escorts toward one of the doors. Rides-at-the-door turned and looked at the seven young warriors who stood in a clump by the wagon. They were staring after the procession. The two women who had been gesturing were gone.

The room was long and low-ceilinged. Light entered through

two small windows that looked out onto the courtyard. The sun was low to the southeast. The chiefs stopped and stared at a small creature which lay in a square of sunlight. It had pointed ears and a long tail and was licking the inside of a front leg.

"Get that damn cat out of here," said General Sully. "And don't disturb us."

The chiefs watched as one of their escorts scooped the animal up and carried it out. The other man followed him. Rides-at-the-door had been in this room before. It was here he had eaten with the agent and his family. But he felt uncomfortable under the low ceiling, and the plank floor was springy under his feet. He wished they could have met in the iron-pounder's lodge, for it was on the ground.

Now the seizer chief spoke to them, motioning with a sweep of his arm for them to sit on the square platforms with legs. Heavy Runner, with a broad smile, sat at one end of the table and told the other chiefs to do likewise. "Coffee," he said, using the Napik-wan word.

General Sully laughed and instructed the striped-sleeve to bring the pot of coffee that was resting on the barrel stove in the corner.

While they waited for the sergeant to pour the coffee, General Sully spoke in low tones to the other two officers. Rides-at-the-door couldn't hear what they were saying, but he could see that they were not pleased. One of the Napikwans at the other end of the table, a short man with a trim black beard, seemed especially agitated. He talked and gestured sharply toward the chiefs with a sheaf of papers in his hand. Rides-at-the-door had not caught his name, but he knew from the way the man dressed and the way he spoke to the General that he was not one of the seizers. At last he sat back, with an exasperated sigh, and the sergeant put coffee cups with steaming black liquid before each man. Then the sergeant sat down by the elbow of the General.

The chiefs watched Heavy Runner take a sip of the coffee. He made a face and spoke to Rides-at-the-door.

"He wishes the white sand to make it sweet." Rides-at-the-door spoke Pikuni to the sergeant.

After the chiefs had doctored the bitter liquid, General Sully spoke, at first with a faint smile. It soon disappeared and a look of concern came into his eyes.

Then the striped-sleeve spoke: "General Sully wishes to thank Heavy Runner and his chiefs for the honor of their presence. He knows that Heavy Runner"—here the sergeant glanced down at a piece of paper—"and Sun Calf of the Kainahs and Big Lake and Little Wolf of the Pikunis are friends to the American people. And he extends the greetings of the Grandfather, who lives in that place where the sun rises. It is for the Grandfather that the General speaks.

"However, the General would also desire that his disappointment be known to you, because he had expected more of your chiefs to show up. It is only through the cooperation of all the Pikunis and Kainahs that these great issues before us can be resolved and peace attained. And that requires face-to-face talk with the chiefs. Again, he would like to emphasize his disappointment that your major chiefs chose not to attend."

Heavy Runner had been sipping his coffee, but this last statement made him look up. He was not foolish enough to think that he was as influential as Mountain Chief, but he was a major chief with many followers. The striped-sleeve seemed to be finished, so Heavy Runner cleared his throat. "It is good for the Pikunis and Kainahs to get together with their brothers, the Napikwans. I, Heavy Runner, one of the major chiefs of the Pikunis, speak for all, with a good heart. It is our desire to live in peace with the Napikwans, and so it shall be, for we know that peace is in the hearts of our brothers."

After the sergeant had interpreted Heavy Runner's words, the General nodded, then looked down to the papers on the table. He studied them for a moment, then looked up. His eyes had lost any warmth they might have possessed. "As you are no doubt aware, there are two main—three main points of contention. If the first two are resolved, then the third takes care of itself. I have been instructed by my superiors to enumerate these points and to elicit a promise from the Pikuni and Kainah chiefs that they will assist in all ways possible to attain justice. If the chiefs refuse, I have been instructed to remind them of the grave consequences of their actions. And the consequences will indeed be serious."

The General kept his eyes on the papers before him as the sergeant spoke the strange tongue of these red men. He pulled on his beard, vaguely aware of the impatient breathing of the marshal who sat on his left. Sully had dealt with the Indians many times in the past and had learned the value of patience. Still, he wanted this meeting to be as brief as possible, for he knew that it would be fruitless to parley seriously with this small a representation of Blackfeet. Sully was also aware that his reputation would suffer, for he had instigated this meeting with the expectation that, if successful, it would avoid the great conflict that his colleagues pressed for. Sully's moderate stance had already earned him a reputation as an "Indian lover" with the territorial politicians, the press and his fellow officers. Already the wheels were in motion for an action designed to punish the Blackfeet severely. This meeting could have made such an action unnecessary and, as an added benefit, would have enhanced Sully's reputation as a man who brought peace to the northern plains. But now he realized that that was not even true—the people of Montana Territory wanted not peace but punishment. They wanted to run these red Indians right off the face of the map, push them into Canada or, failing that, kill them like wild animals. It was an emotional issue for the people, a practical one for the politicians and bankers. They wanted to open up the Blackfeet land for settlement. Sully knew that he was a hindrance and, furthermore, that the deck had been stacked against him from the start. Even if all the chiefs had shown up, it would not have changed the simple fact that the Blackfeet were to be eliminated by any means possible, or at least forced into a position they would never peacefully accept. Sully shook his head, a rueful smile hidden by his mustache. The only question now was, who would be eliminated first—he or the Blackfeet? He was suddenly aware that all the eyes in the room were on him. He picked up the papers.

"Point one: I have here a warrant for the arrest of Owl Child, Bear Chief, and Black Weasel in connection with the murder of Malcolm Clark and the near-fatal assault on his son, Horace. The government of the United States, as represented by Marshal

Wheeler here"—he indicated with a toss of his left hand the short bearded man—"requires the assistance of all the Blackfeet peoples in bringing these fugitives to justice. They are to be handed over and dealt with in the white man's court of law, for it is against the whites that they have committed their depredations."

General Sully studied another piece of paper while the sergeant interpreted to the chiefs. He was aware that the chiefs had begun to talk among themselves. From their excited whisperings he knew that they had now become aware of the seriousness of the proceedings. He glanced up and noticed that the other Indian, Rides-at-the-door, was leaning into the small circle and talking in a calm voice. Sergeant Gates had said he knew the English language, but Sully hadn't expected the respect with which the chiefs were listening to him. He motioned Gates closer.

"Just who is this Rides-at-the-door?" he said.

"A Lone Eater, sir. They are somewhere in the middle, but Kipp thinks they lean more toward Mountain Chief. Rides-at-the-door is one of their chiefs—war chief, I believe. He has negotiated with us before. He's a cunning one."

"I see," said Sully. His spirit began to rise for the first time since he had seen the pitifully small group of chiefs outside the agency compound.

"Captain Snelling thinks he is one of the tribe's principal advisers—behind the scene, so to speak."

Sully looked down the table. Rides-at-the-door was looking at him. Their eyes locked for a moment, then Sully lowered his eyes to the paper.

"Point two: It is estimated that in the past six months nearly a thousand head of livestock, mostly horses and mules, have been stolen from the citizens of the Territory of Montana—not to mention a good number stolen from the United States Army. It is a further requirement of the United States Government that these animals be returned to their rightful owners immediately." Sully put the paper down and looked up. "We know that many of these animals have been driven north and sold to the traders on the Saskatchewan in Canada. It is, of course, illegal for these traders to buy property stolen from citizens of the United States, but until now there was nothing we could do about it. As you shall see, we are about to remedy that problem.

"What concerns us now is the return of all horses in the possession of the various bands of Blackfeet, be they Pikunis or Kainahs. Therefore, we charge you now with the return of said horses. And we will expect results within two or three weeks—let us say, within a moon. You will begin this operation immediately as a sign of your good faith."

Heavy Runner started to say something after these words were spoken by the sergeant, but Sully cut him off.

"Point three: I also have here a general indictment of all the Blackfeet people in reference to the harassment and killing of the citizens of this territory. Many deaths have occurred in the past six months, the result of your raiding villains. Men, women and children have been forced to live in terror of Blackfeet threats against their lives and property. Traders find it unsafe to ply their wares among you. Miners have been shot and scalped for their earnings. Woodcutters no longer feel safe to venture out after fuel. As a representative of the United States Army, I tell you that all such activities will cease as of this moment.

"Now"—Sully leaned back and faced the chiefs directly—"it has been the history of the Blackfeet to commit these crimes and then sneak off across the Medicine Line into Canada, knowing full well that we could not pursue them into that country. There they felt secure enough to sell horses and buy whiskey and rifles and generally live high on the hog until they felt it was safe to return. Canada has long been regarded as a haven for your people because their government refused to cooperate with my government." Sully moved forward suddenly, his chair scraping on the pine floor. "It's different now. I have been authorized by my government to cross the border and bring the criminals back, and, by God, that's exactly what I intend to do."

Rides-at-the-door stared out one of the windows while the sergeant's deep voice droned dutifully on in translation. He could see only the tops of the roofs and the flag, which now hung limply from the pole. He looked at the sky beyond the flag, but he couldn't tell if it was blue or gray or white.

Mountain Chief himself, even if he were so inclined, could not meet these requirements, thought Rides-at-the-door. It was strange to think of the head chief of the Pikunis as powerless. Yet not even he possessed enough authority to stop the young men from preying on the Napikwans. Nor could he deliver up the horses demanded by this seizer chief. And certainly not Owl Child.

Heavy Runner leaned toward him. "Is it true these seizers can now cross the Medicine Line?"

"The big chiefs of the Napikwans up there live far to the east. By the time they heard of the seizers' raids, it would be too late. The seizers would deny they had been up there. Yes, I believe this chief speaks the truth when he says he would follow our people across the line."

Heavy Runner grew thoughtful. There was a long silence in the room, save for the impatient breathing of Marshal Wheeler. Finally the chief spoke. "It is as the great seizer chief says. There has been much trouble between my people and the Napikwans. It is true that many of our young men run wild, inflamed with the white man's water, desiring wealth and honor at the expense of the Napikwans. Many of these young men do commit the crimes you charge them with. For this, I am ashamed for myself and my people.

"As you know, already it has been a difficult winter—much snow and cold. It is difficult to hunt, and many of our people are cold and hungry. We have been promised food and blankets by your people, but we do not see these things. Some of our people grow impatient because of their suffering. Some of them, the young ones, take matters into their own hands, and then the trouble begins again. Some, like Owl Child, take pleasure in making the white people cry. But he is no friend to the Pikunis. Among our people he is known as a murderer and a thief—he has caused us to suffer as much as the whites. He has even killed a member of my band, and for that he should be punished. But he is a bad head and an outcast—he is not welcome in the Pikuni camps and so he should be handed over to the Napikwan chiefs.

"But how is this possible? He and his gang are seldom seen.

They leave no tracks. They do not visit our camps that we might have an opportunity to seize them and hand them over to you. Many of our people are afraid of them and so let them have their own way. No, I see no way to capture Owl Child. It would be easier to kill him as one would kill a real-lion, who would seek to—"

"That is acceptable," interrupted Sully, who understood the Pikuni word for "kill." He had been following the interpreter's commentary. "Providing you bring in the body to the fort on the Sun River."

Rides-at-the-door leaned forward and told Heavy Runner what the chief had said. Big Lake, Little Wolf and Sun Calf listened intently. Then they sat back with doubt and suspicion in their eyes. They knew that Mountain Chief would not be happy with such as drastic act. While they did not consider themselves followers of the head chief, they knew better than to make him angry.

But now Heavy Runner spoke angrily to them. Did they not see the position he was in? "You wish to see Owl Child dead as much as I do. He causes nothing but trouble!"

"Does Mountain Chief accept this?" said Little Wolf.

"In time he would see that it was the only way—the only thing to appease these white chiefs."

"I don't think he would like us to kill one of our own people to satisfy the Napikwans," said Big Lake.

"Owl Child is not one of us!" Heavy Runner turned to Rides-at-the-door. "What do you say?"

Rides-at-the-door looked down the table to the General, who was listening to the marshal. Once again, the short bearded man was gesturing toward the chiefs. The General looked up, again directly at Rides-at-the-door.

"Tell this seizer chief that we will kill Owl Child." He looked at the vacant blue eyes of Sully. "It is the only way to avoid war. And tell him we will return as many of the Napikwan horses as we can find. It is the only way."

Heavy Runner grunted with satisfaction. He turned and faced up the table to the Napikwans who were awaiting his response.

"It is decided—we shall do everything in our power to rub out Owl Child and his gang."

"But first you will do everything in your power to take them alive and turn them over to us," said Sully. A public hanging would go far to soothe the outraged citizenry. He watched as Rides-at-the-door translated.

"Yes," said Heavy Runner. "And we will see to it that the horses belonging to the Napikwans are returned. It will not be easy because my people are weak with hunger and cold. And now, some of the Pikuni bands farther down the Bear River are again touched by the white-scabs disease. Already many in the Black Patched Moccasins have gone to the Sand Hills. Many others are sure to follow them—"

Sully interrupted. He had heard Gates whisper "Smallpox." "Do you mean this disease is here—among the Blackfeet?" He had heard that it had afflicted the Crows, but the Pikunis? He turned to one of his officers. "Why wasn't I informed of this?"

"We knew nothing about it, General. This is news to me too."

"Didn't Kipp say anything about it?"

The officer shook his head.

"The white-scabs catch us when we are weak," said Heavy Runner. "We must have food and blankets if we are to survive. We must have 'coffee' medicine. Perhaps the great Grandfather would take pity on the Pikunis and provide us with these necessities."

Sully pulled on his wispy beard and looked down at the chiefs. He seemed to be weighing this new information. He sighed. "You have my sympathy, Heavy Runner, but I'm afraid that will not be possible—until you fulfill the requirements of these court orders. The sooner you do these things, the sooner you will receive your food and blankets—and medicine."

Heavy Runner listened, then said, "These things have been promised to us for many moons."

"And so you shall have them. But only after you meet my conditions." Sully did not bother to look down at his papers. "One, you shall effect the capture or death of Owl Child and his gang. Two, you shall return all horses stolen from the white people. Three, you shall cease all hostilities against citizens of the United States."

Sully picked up the papers, straightened them and began to tuck them into a leather envelope. He was through with the chiefs, except for one last speech. As he handed the envelope to Marshall Wheeler, he fixed his eyes on Rides-at-the-door. "My messengers were sent among the Pikunis and Kainahs to deliver a communication of vital importance. If more of your chiefs had attended this council, we might have avoided a conflict that can only go badly for your people. But it seems that my messengers found most of your chiefs delirious with drink and not in any condition to speak with seriousness on these matters. One of my men almost lost his life at the hands of the Never Laughs. Fortunately, they were too drunk to see straight, much less shoot straight."

The officer to Sully's right hid a grin with his hand. It was his only sign of emotion during the meeting.

"But this is a serious matter. Your people claim they want peace but they prove otherwise. My people are sick and tired of this constant raiding, this constant murder of innocent citizens. When I deliver the results of this meeting, I'm afraid they will be very disappointed. Indeed, many will wish to settle the score in a less than peaceful manner. It is out of my hands now.

"It is up to you to deliver these ultimatums to the other chiefs. And you will have to do it with great speed." He was speaking directly to Rides-at-the-door. "You must make the other chiefs, especially Mountain Chief, aware that war is imminent. Their people will be killed like so many buffalo. They themselves will be killed or brought to justice.

"It is not the wish of the United States Government that such desperate measures be taken. We are a peaceful people and we would wish to pursue a course of peace, to live in harmony with all Indian people. But we are capable, and some more than willing, to punish any Indians who would deliberately thwart that peaceful course. You are warned—and you would do well to warn those other chiefs who saw fit to ignore this chance for peace."

If Sully had expected Rides-at-the-door to give any sign that he had agreed, or even listened, he was disappointed. The warrior, who was Sully's only real chance to deliver his ultimatum to the hostile chiefs, turned to the window and looked again at the flag. But he had heard, and the seriousness with which the white General spoke had registered. He knew that many of the other chiefs, including Mountain Chief, would not trust any agreement Heavy Runner had made with the seizers. But if they were here, thought Rides-at-the-door, they would realize that their choices were ending. They would have to agree to these conditions or risk the end not only of their way of life but of themselves and their followers. He was only vaguely aware of Heavy Runner's voice.

". . . and so I ask the great seizer chief for a piece of paper with writing on it that states that I, Heavy Runner, am a friend to all whites. If your people decide to make war on the Pikunis, I would desire it to be known to them, on paper, that Heavy Runner and his followers are at peace."

Big Lake and Little Wolf also requested such a document. After a moment of thought, Sun Calf assented.

And so the friendly chiefs waited in silence while Sully scratched out a few words that would signal to all that these men had cooperated with the United States and were therefore not to be considered hostiles. The pieces of paper were signed by General Alfred H. Sully and dated 1 January 1870.

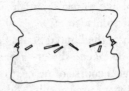

PART
FOUR

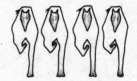

25

IT WAS ONE of the rare warm days of that winter, and the snow had melted just enough so the metal-rimmed wheels of the big wagons dug into the skin of earth and left a long, twisting, dirty trail far to the south. The sun rode close and yellow and caused the prairies to shine with a brilliance that made men wipe tears from their eyes.

The two men driving the ox teams were sluggish with the warmth and paid little attention to the squeaking of the wheels or the creaking of the loads. The metalwork of the big oxen's harnesses jingled in the warm air, but the animals too did not seem aware of the small sound in all that space. They had crossed the last of the big hills that morning and now they worked steadily in unison to pull the wagons north along the Whiskey Trail.

Three men followed the wagons, riding shaggy big-headed horses. Two of them wore long untrimmed beards, and the third had not shaved since they left Fort Benton four days ago. They were tired yet wary, and they kept their rifles within reach in scabbards by their right legs. The two shaggy ones had pistols tucked in their belts. The third wore an army holster and belt under his long gray coat.

He was still overwhelmed by this country that his companions took for granted. The rolling prairies were as vast and empty as a pale ocean, and the sky stretched forever, sometimes blue, sometimes slate. The few small groups of mountains, like islands in this sea of yellow swells, only seemed to emphasize its vastness. In the winter, when snow covered the land and lay heavy in the bottoms, the man was filled with foreboding dreams of an even larger isolation.

But he had escaped death more than once in the past several years and had come to feel that maybe his life was a charmed one, destined to go on forever whether he wanted it to or not. Many times he had wished for death, especially when he was young, a young Georgia cavalry officer riding time after time into the guns of the North. During each terrifying retreat, he thought of nothing but the comfort of the dead left behind, the end of the war come early. But the war did not last forever with him, and when he knew the end was near and sacrifice was senseless, he left camp one night and headed west. There were many fleeing men on the road, and he was almost killed in Louisiana for the horse he was riding. He survived and continued west into the Texas panhandle, where he was shocked by the serenity of the country, whose open spaces held no threat and where a man could wander with nothing on his mind but the thought of his next meal.

He worked one whole year for a rancher, building corrals and riding herd. Not once did he feel homesick, and when the war ended he hardly noticed. Whether cutting poles or wrestling calves, he worked with the knowledge that he was alive and the open country of the West had become his life. He would have stayed there forever if it hadn't been for a quiet conversation he overheard in a saloon in Pampa. He'd come in for supplies, and while his wagon was being loaded over at the feed store, he wandered down to Bevin's for a glass of beer. The first word that made him perk up his ears was "gold." Then he heard, "Lots of it, just layin' in those creek bottoms." And finally he heard, "Montana—Alder Gulch all the way to Virginia City—miles of it." He didn't even know how far Montana Territory was from Texas, but as he drove the supply wagon back to the ranch he began to think of his life. Although he liked old Mr. Styles and didn't mind the hard work, he knew that he couldn't do it forever. And, too, there was talk of rebuilding the South. His father had once owned one of the largest dry-goods businesses in Atlanta. He had become involved in politics and entertained prominent cotton people, lawyers and merchants. He prided himself on making campaigns work, on electing his new friends to local and confederacy offices, on helping them finance their electioneering. He enjoyed this new world and began to pay little attention to his business. A year and a half later, the bank foreclosed and he was left with a large town house, a small cotton farm and three children. When it came time to call in debts, he found that nobody owed him, politically or financially. Just before the war broke out, the family had moved to the cotton farm near the hamlet of Green's Gate.

And so it seemed to the young man as he drove the wagon home to Mr. Styles' ranch that an opportunity too good to pass up had been presented to him. He had often thought of his family, and he had dreamed of returning home with enough money to put his father back on his feet. He had not allowed himself to think that such a possibility existed, because it hadn't—until then.

The next day he had collected his wages and ridden north. It had taken him four months to get to the Montana Territory because he had to work along the way to keep himself fed, and when he arrived at Alder Gulch the gold was already playing out. By the time he had acquired a grubstake by working for a freight company, most of the fields had been reduced to a rubble of stone that did indeed stretch for miles, all the way to Virginia City. One thing that surprised him was the number of Confederates, men like him who had deserted the army of General Lee for the wide-open spaces of the West. Many were rough, treacherous men dug up in the last days of the war, caught and put into uniform. It was either serve or be shot. But it didn't take long to see the way the war was going and they began to leave in droves, all of them heading west—to Texas, the Arizona desert, and north to Colorado, and finally to the goldfields of Montana.

Now the man rode silently behind the whiskey wagons, oblivious to the two bearded men who rode beside him. His eyes were sore from looking at the sunstruck prairies. His lips were dry and there was a scum of saliva across his front teeth. Although the day had warmed up considerably, he huddled deep within his gray coat and thought of the hot, humid summers of Georgia. He didn't miss Atlanta—nobody will miss Atlanta because it isn't there anymore, he thought with a grin—but he did miss the farm and those days he had labored beside his father as they tried to pull it together after several years of neglect. They had just finished planting the first crop of cotton and were eating a big supper complete with a bottle of French wine his father had saved for the occasion when the Negro from Parnell's place rode into the yard on a mule and shouted that war had broken out. By the time they had reached the porch—all of them, his father and mother and two younger sisters who had been so gay only moments before—the Negro was galloping off with the urgency of Paul Revere.

The man had to take a piss but was reluctant to stop. His side ached and the insides of his thighs were chafed. He hadn't ridden this much since leaving the goldfields almost three years ago. He'd had to sell his horse at Fort Benton to pay off a gambling debt. But it was a bustling town—the farthest landing up the Missouri River for the big steamboats—and he had worked off and on as a carpenter, first for the army, then for the settling merchants and ministers and others who kept the town expanding. He liked the work and had become good at it, but when the building slowed down he had taken this job as guard for the whiskey wagons on the spot. The regular guard—if any of them could be called regular, since they were recruited out of saloons —had broken his leg in a brawl the night before the wagons were to roll. Since he was broke and had never been to Canada, and since he didn't much care what happened now that his dream of returning to Georgia a wealthy man had been thwarted, he had taken the job without hesitation.

The small caravan had started down a gradual slope to the Dry Fork of the Marias. They would pass within a few miles of Riplinger's trading post, but they wouldn't stop. Riplinger, like other legitimate traders, had little use for these whiskey runners, not because he felt their business immoral but because they took trade from him. And so the drivers knew enough to steer clear of him. They didn't need him raising hell and putting pressure on the army to stop these illegal shipments.

But on the other hand they had chosen this route because of its proximity to Blackfeet camps. Although most of the shipment was due for the Canadian posts, they were not above selling whiskey in the camps en route. Most of the whiskey was in its pure state in the sixty-three gallon hogsheads lashed down in the wagons. But there were also several kerosene tins of doctored stuff that they would sell right off the tailgate. The drovers had mixed capsicum, molasses and tobacco before leaving Fort Benton; then they had filled the tins up with river water and whiskey. There was enough whiskey to make the Indians drunk and enough water to make it profitable.

As the party descended, the drovers pulled back firmly on the brake handles to keep the heavy wagons off the oxen. The wheel rims screeched beneath the brake shoes, and the muddy snow backed up and fell off in wet chunks. Finally they were on the flat and the wagon trail followed the Dry Fork down to the Marias. They were less than two miles from the river. The oxen smelled the water ahead and began to trot, their metalwork jingling in the windless afternoon air.

The man in the gray coat spotted a small stand of cottonwoods surrounded by brush a hundred feet off the trail. He reined in his horse until the others moved ahead, then trotted over to it. He thought about the thick stands of pine in Georgia as he swung down. His sisters would be grown now. He was suddenly filled with an intense loneliness. He longed to know if they were married, if the family was still on the farm, if his father and mother ever thought about him. At that moment he would have given anything to be back home, harvesting the cotton, hunting deer, sitting down to a meal of biscuits and gravy. Even the long days behind the plow or clearing land brought a brief smile. The yellow stream of piss steamed in the warm air as the man lifted his closed eyes to the sun.

At first when he opened his eyes he felt embarrassed and angry. He glared at the figure in the dark hat and buffalo coat. Then he saw the bone choker necklace above the collarless white shirt, the single brass and feather earring dangling from the right ear. As he looked into the dark face the earlier feelings gave way to a brilliant fear, but he made no move, didn't even attempt to button his pants. Then he saw the rifle pointed straight at his breast. Oh, God, he thought, and he saw the ramshackle cabin and he was standing on the porch with his father and mother and sisters, watching the Negro riding away on the mule, shouting about war.

The single rifle shot echoed up and down the Dry Fork. Both teams stopped. The lead ox on the left of the trailing team swung his head back but the yoke prevented him from seeing the man lying at the edge of the thicket. He felt the sting of the bullwhip and heard the bellow of the teamster and he jolted forward, for an instant pulling the creaking whiskey wagon by himself. Then the others strained forward against their yokes and against the cracking whip and the wagon picked up speed.

A hail of gunfire from a chokecherry thicket to the left of the wagons snapped out. The bullwhacker in the lead wagon toppled sideways and one of his animals went down, bawling and skidding through the grassy mud as the others charged ahead in panic.

One of the men on horseback managed to pull his rifle free of the scabbard before a shell burst in his stomach, sending him back over the cantle of his saddle. His horse lunged forward and he did a somersault, landing on his feet, but his knees were already dead. The other horseman stood in the saddle of his whirling horse, firing his short-gun in all directions. When it was empty he threw it toward the thicket and spurred his horse up the shallow gulch. His fingers had just closed around the stock of his rifle when he saw the Indian riding at him. With a sudden series of yips the Indian urged his horse into a dead run. The white man had almost cleared the rifle from its scabbard when he saw the barrel of the musket swinging toward his head, and that was the last thing he saw.

Fast Horse caught the loose saddle horses, then got down off his own animal and picked up the weapons. One of the rifles was a many-shots gun. He wiped the mud from the barrel, then fired it in the air. It was a good find. He looked at the two men lying on the ground and saw that one of them was wearing a cartridge belt over his canvas coat. As he bent down to loosen it he looked into the face. The eyes were wide open and blue. The whites were red with bursted blood. As he pulled the belt from beneath the man's body, he heard a long rattle from deep within the man's chest. He drew back and looked again at the eyes. He thought he saw a flicker and knelt close to the face. He looked deep in the sunlit blue of the eyes, searching for life, and was surprised how far into the eyes he could see. But the man lay still and there was no life in him. Fast Horse had thought he wanted to take the man's hair, but those blue sightless eyes spooked him.

As he rode down the Dry Fork he grew uncomfortable. The Pikuni camps were not far away. Mountain Chief's camp was only a day's ride to the northeast. The Hard Topknots were less than that. If the seizers came upon these white men and their wagons, they would attack the nearest Pikunis. We have done a bad thing this time, thought Fast Horse. We have struck too close to the camps. He looked around, searching the horizons, but he saw nothing.

One of the wagons lay on its side and its cargo lay scattered in the muddy grass of the draw. The big whiskey barrels had burst on impact and the smell of whiskey was in the air. Under Bull and Red Horn were picking through the debris. Not far away the team was grazing. Farther down the trail, several hundred paces away, the other wagon stood upright, still attached to the oxen. Black Weasel and Crow Top were slitting away the canvas with their scalping knives. Owl Child sat on his horse, examining a bullwhip. Suddenly he lashed out with it, wrapping the tip around a wheel rim. Crow Top looked up, startled, and Owl Child laughed.

"I will use this on your hide, black Pikuni, next time you shoot one of these shit-beasts," he said, flicking the whip in the direction of the downed bull.

"He had a wild eye, that one," said Crow Top. He slit the last of the canvas free. "He looked at me and I felt my testicles climb up inside of me."

"Next time I'll shake your testicles off with this."

Crow Top and Black Weasel pulled back the canvas and whooped with pleasure. The six barrels were still lashed securely and the tins of doctored whiskey stood neatly in rows. Between the tins and the barrels there were sacks of coffee and flour and packages of trade-cloth and tobacco. There was also one large heavy crate. Crow Top popped the cap off one of the whiskey tins and drank. Black Weasel made a swipe at the tin and the whiskey erupted over Crow Top's face. As he gasped and coughed, Owl Child swung up into the wagon, laughing, but his eyes were on the crate. He began to pry up with his knife on the top boards, the smooth square nails squeaking in protest. When he had removed two of the boards, he slit the canvas underneath and dug around with his hand. "Sonofabitch," he muttered.

"Sonofabitch." Crow Top laughed.

Owl Child drew out a cast-iron frying pan, then another, then a kettle. He threw the cooking items into the grass below the wagon. Black Weasel worked on the top of one of the kegs with his axe. "This is the real Napikwan whiskey," he said. "No water, no bugs to make it bad."

Fast Horse had pulled up a few paces from the wagon and watched the three men dig through the goods. The steady chopping of the ax sounded almost peaceful. He glanced up the hill to the east and young Bear Chief waved to him. He was supposed to be on watch, but he was more interested in what the warriors were finding. Fast Horse pointed to his own eyes with forked fingers and Bear Chief held up his hand and turned away.

Owl Child had looked up and noticed this. "So you have come to claim your white woman cooking pots. What is that on your finger?"

"It is a finger ring—made from the red see-through stone. I claimed it from the one who was pissing."

Owl Child frowned. He had found a leather packet with Napikwan money and some pictures. "I'll give you this and you give me that finger ring. There is a white woman here that will make you squirt."

"You keep it. Fast Horse does not need to squirt with a picture of the white woman."

"Someday I will cut off that finger and claim the red stone."

Black Weasel yelled in triumph and dipped his cupped hand into the barrel. He drew it out slowly and held it before Crow Top. "Now I drink the clean water, not that whitehorn piss you find."

The young men dipped a kettle of the whiskey and found a dry place on the side of the draw. Crow Top had also found a sack of dried apples. The men passed the kettle and ate the apples.

"What will we do with the big whitehorns?" Fast Horse was looking down at the teams. The Cut Hand was down with the bulls, rifle in his arms, circling them. "I think that bad head wishes to shoot them all."

Owl Child yelled at The Cut Hand. Then he turned to Fast Horse. "They are no good. They are too slow to drive. Only the white man can make them go where he wants."

"What about the other goods—the whiskey?"

Owl Child chewed on a dried apple. He looked at the big barrels. "It makes me sad to think of leaving it."

"We could take some of the shiny-skins," said Crow Top.

"You would drink the Napikwans' piss too," said Black Weasel.

"You who talk look like an old woman with that headdress."

The others laughed. Black Weasel had cut a strip of flowered cloth from one of the bolts he found and had wrapped it around his head.

"Dump out one of the shiny-skins and fill it up with the good whiskey," said Owl Child.

"Ah," said Crow Top in admiration. "We will fill many with the good whiskey. Come, old woman."

Owl Child and Fast Horse watched the two men at their labors. Under Bull and Red Horn were riding down the draw from the first wagon. Red Horn wore a long gray coat. The sun had traveled far since the young men had made their ambush. It lay just above the peaks of the Backbone.

"This is not a good thing," said Fast Horse. "This time we strike too close to our people's camps." He expected Owl Child to flare up, to mock him.

But Owl Child said, "I think as you do. We have made it bad on Mountain Chief. The seizers will say he did this."

Fast Horse was surprised. "We must burn these wagons and all the goods and the Napikwans with them," he said. "We must do this now while there is light but not enough to allow the smoke to be seen. Then we must drive the big whitehorns far away, down toward Many Houses. They will join up with other whitehorns."

"Can we burn the whitehorn that Crow Top shot?"

"Perhaps we can drag him into the bushes. Then we must get away—we can cut across to Bad Horse Butte. There is a war lodge there and no Napikwans."

"We could cross the Medicine Line now." But Owl Child's voice was tentative. Fast Horse had not seen this before. He glanced over at the sharp dark face. In the fading light, the slash across Owl Child's cheek looked pale. He was only twenty-five or thirty winters, by Fast Horse's reckoning, but he looked tired. His mouth drooped and his eyes had lost that intense darkness. Perhaps he is tired from all the running, thought Fast Horse. They had not spent two nights in a row in one place. They were always driving animals or just running. Then Fast Horse had another thought, a thought which filled him with sudden apprehension: Perhaps Owl Child was losing his nerve. He had been edgy lately, sulking at times, snappish at others. His decisions seemed more impulsive, less confident. And now, striking so close to the Pikuni camps—this was a bad thing.

"It has never been my thought to bring trouble to the Pikunis. I scorn them for what they allow the Napikwans to get away with, but I do not wish them harm." There was a flatness in the voice, as though Owl Child was repeating something he had said to himself many times. "They are foolish people and they did me wrong once. I had a right to kill Bear Head, for he tried to cheat me out of a kill that day we made the Cutthroats cry—" He glanced at Fast Horse's face; he knew that most Pikunis thought it had been the other way around; but there was no sign of belief or disbelief on the face. "Now they are angry with me because I try to rid this land of the Napikwans. They hate the Napikwans as much as I do, but when I fight they say I do wrong. They would like to kill off these insects but when they get around them, the Pikunis roll over like weak dogs. Now they blame me for their weakness. They say I bring harm closer to them. Perhaps I bring them an opportunity to stand up and fight." Owl Child watched The Cut Hand circle the wagon below them. He was drinking heavily from a shiny-skin. Owl Child stood and brushed the seat of his baggy wool pants. "They are foolish, but I too am a Pikuni. Now we will burn up these wagons and drive the animals away."

As Fast Horse watched him trot down the hill, he couldn't help the feeling that Owl Child's days were counted. Whether it was nerves or fatigue, something was drawing him closer to the end. About himself, Fast Horse did not know.

26

THE WINTER CAMP of the Lone Eaters lay quiet in the valley of the Two Medicine River. The horses grazed some distance to the west and the day-riders were snuggled down in their robes, half asleep on their ponies. The only sound was the steady murmur of the river itself. The only movement was the wispy smoke coming from the lodges. There were no people outside the entrances, and the camp dogs were curled nose to tail, dozing beneath the high sun. The hunting had not been good for many sleeps, and there were few hides staked out to dry.

The two riders approached the camp from the east. They were bundled up in buffalo robes, and ice clung to their horses' fetlocks and tails. As the men rode along the river, they slumped listlessly in their saddles, unmindful of the steam that rose from the dark waters. It was the barking of the dogs that lifted the riders' heads, and then they saw the lodges and the stark gray big-leaf trees behind them. The man in the lead stopped and watched the dogs charging across the snowy field. The sun was hazy and gave off no warmth. The horses lifted their heads and watched the dogs come but there was no tension in their bodies. They too were tired. When the dogs reached them, a big red one with a blaze of white across his muzzle began to lunge at the lead rider, snapping at the foot that rested in the stirrup by the horse's belly. Suddenly the man threw open his robe and brought a rawhide quirt down across the dog's nose, sending him yelping and skittering across the wind-packed snow. The other dogs drew off and the riders urged their horses forward. By the time they reached the lodges, several men stood by the entrances with their rifles crooked in their arms. The riders stopped in the middle of camp near Three Bears' tipi.

"Haiya! My relative, Three Bears! It is Pretty-on-top who seeks you."

The men from the other lodges began to approach, their eyes all on the second rider. Although he had his buffalo robe pulled tightly around his lower face and a wolf fur cap pulled down, they had noticed the mustache and the black riding boots.

Three Bears emerged from the tipi and his breath was frosty as he spoke. "Ok-yi! My relative, it is good to see you. You are welcome among the Lone Eaters. But who is this Napikwan that comes with Pretty-on-top?"

"He is called Sturgis. He comes from Many Houses fort. He is a heavy-singer-for-the-sick among his people."

Three Bears looked up at the Napikwan. The brown eyes were wide open, without fear. "And does he come to heal the Lone Eaters?"

Pretty-on-top dismounted and motioned the healer to do the same. "It is a great sadness that brings him to us. The camps on the lower Bear River, those near Ever-shadow Bluff, are afflicted with the white scabs. The Black Patched Moccasins and the Small Brittle Fats are laid low. Many are down in the Many Chiefs band." Pretty-on-top nodded to Rides-at-the-door and Fools Crow. "Many are dead, and every day more become so."

A group of men began to talk among themselves, their voices sharp and frightened in the crisp air. Several women had joined the men and now began to cry. Many in the camp had lived through the last white-scabs outbreak. They knew that once this evil spirit entered the body there was little the medicine men could do to drive it out.

"We have feared this," said Three Bears. "We heard it was on the lower Bear near the Big River. We didn't know it was traveling so fast."

The Napikwan lowered his robe and spoke. "It is not here, then—among your band?"

Three Bears looked at Rides-at-the-door, who turned to Fools

Crow. "Ask around. Take two of the young men with you."

"Come into my lodge," said Three Bears. "We will eat and smoke and then you will tell about it." He turned to the camp crier. "Get Boss Ribs and Mik-api."

After the men had eaten, Rides-at-the-door said, "How is it that you speak the Pikuni language?"

The Napikwan healer sat against a willow backrest. There was darkness beneath his eyes. "For seven winters I was married to the daughter of Takes Gun and Otter Woman of the Black Patched Moccasins. I was healer to the seizers at their fort on the Pile-of-rocks River. Takes Gun and his family came down to farm and there I met his daughter, Blue Grass Woman. Later, I took her with me to Many Houses and there we lived as man and wife. It was my wife who taught me the Pikuni tongue."

"What are you doing among the Pikunis now? Why aren't you down at Many Houses?"

"This past season of the falling leaves, my wife grew lonesome for her people so we decided to visit before they left on their winter hunt." The Napikwan was addressing not just Rides-at-the-door but all the men in the lodge. His voice was soft, and sometimes the men had to lean forward and cup their ears. "The hunting was good and there was much feasting. Every night we ate in a different lodge. Then one day my wife scolded me because I had not brought any meat into camp. You may be a heavy-singer-for-the-sick among the Napikwans, she said, but here you must hunt or you will shame my family. Well, I took that woman at her word, for in truth I had come to feel lazy. The next morning I went out with Takes Gun and two others. We rode east until we came at last to the big bend of the Big River where it flows south. There we saw many blackhorns in the bottom of a coulee. They had not caught wind of us. Takes Gun whispered to us to get ready to run them up the hill on the other side." Sturgis smiled faintly.

"Now, although I have hunted all these years, I had never run the blackhorns and I was plenty nervous. Takes Gun had told me to spot a choice animal and take after it, to get one sure kill—then I could go after the others. We sped off, hard and fast, down the hill, whooping and hollering, and just as fast the blackhorns started running. Lucky for us, they didn't follow the coulee but started running up the hill on the other side, just as Takes Gun had wished. We overtook them quickly and I killed my first animal, a big dry cow, and two others with my many-shots gun before they gained the top of the hill and were gone. I was so excited it was all I could do to keep from going after them, but I knew they could outrun my horse on the downslope. And I had killed enough meat to satisfy myself and, I hoped, Blue Grass Woman." Sturgis stopped to light his pipe.

Fools Crow entered the lodge. He could tell by the way the men sat forward that a story was being told. He sat down quietly by the entrance.

"If I seem to go on about that hunt, you must forgive me, for that was the last happy day in my life." He cleared his throat, and the men looked at each other. "After we skinned the animals and packed our meat sacks full of the best parts, we started for camp. It took us the rest of the day, for our horses were tired and loaded with meat and hides. We arrived in camp at nightfall and went straight to Takes Gun's tipi. The only one to greet us was his youngest son. He helped us to unload the skins and meat, and when we asked him why he was so quiet, he said there was sickness within the lodge. We entered, and there on a couch of robes lay my poor wife. I knelt and laid my hand to her forehead, and there was fever there although her teeth were chattering and she said she was cold. I assured her that she would be all right, for I believed that something she had eaten didn't agree with her. I thought she had become too used to the Napikwan food and was suffering from the change in diet, for we had feasted much on the Pikuni grub. I had the young boy fetch my medicine bag, and I gave her a liquid to settle her stomach. This made her feel a little better and so I joked with her, telling her that now I bring meat she can't eat it. But she was restless that night, so I stayed up and watched her. It wasn't until morning light that I saw the small red sores on her forehead and under her hair. That day she became feverish and delirious. . . ."

A catch in Sturgis' throat made the others look away. Rides-at-the-door glanced over at Fools Crow, and the young man made a negative sign. There was no illness in the camp.

"Her tongue and throat were swollen so that she could take no water. She lived in torment for four days; then her shadow went to the Sand Hills, and there she is today."

"And what caused the white-scabs?" Three Bears said this after the exclamations died away.

"I can only guess that it came from Many Houses. Although the big boats do not come upriver after the falling leaves, there are still many Napikwans who come overland. Two or three moons ago I heard that the white-scabs had swept through the Dirt Lodge People many sleeps to the east. Then the Crows were afflicted. It is my guess that a Napikwan who had been among them brought it with him to Many Houses."

"But why does it not make the Napikwans die?"

"Some do. But their medicine men shoot them with"—Sturgis searched for the Pikuni word—"juice, a juice that keeps them safe from this disease."

"Then let them shoot the Pikunis full of this juice. There is no need for us to die then."

The men around the fire agreed. Boss Ribs held up his hand, and the others fell silent. "I too am a medicine man and I have lost kin because my medicine is not strong enough to keep my own family safe. You say there is a medicine that makes all the Napikwans come back from the Shadowland. How is this? Why did you not give this to your Blue Grass Woman? Are not the Pikunis men too?"

"Your questions enter my ears and trouble me. This medicine does not cure the white-scabs disease, it prevents it from entering the body." Sturgis glanced around at the faces. "The destroying juice does not possess any healing power, once the bad spirit enters. For those already afflicted it is too late to do them any good."

"We are to die then?" said Three Bears.

"No. I have just returned from Many Houses. They are sending for the destroying juice. It will help you, but it will take many sleeps to get here—twenty, thirty." Sturgis looked at Rides-at-the-door. "Is the sickness in this camp?"

"My son tells me no."

"We find no sickness among the Lone Eaters," said Fools Crow. "There is a child in the lodge of Sits-in-the-middle that has the winter sickness, but nothing more."

"Good, that is good. Then you must keep yourselves from contacting any of the other bands until the destroying juice arrives. You are far enough away from the others. There must be no trading, no contact with the Napikwans. I know you have relatives in the other camps and some of them will come to you, to seek shelter. You must not let them into the camp of the Lone Eaters, even if they appear well. Many of the older Pikunis will not become sick because they lived through the last outbreak. But they can carry the bad spirit. It will ride with them, on their clothes, their skin, even their horses. You must turn them away!"

Two or three of the men began to talk at once, their voices loud and angry.

"It is true, my brothers!" Pretty-on-top's words shocked them into silence. "Already I have seen families break apart. I have seen mothers leave their babies to the care of the old ones. I have seen fathers deny their sons entry into lodges. Many are moving their lodges out of camp, leaving their sick and dying. Death is everywhere and I do not blame them, and so mustn't you. I pray to the Great Spirit that this sickness does not test the Lone Eaters." He angled his head in the direction of Sturgis. "This white man here, he comes to you with a good heart. He has suffered as much as any, and yet he moves among our people, rendering what assistance he can. You men of the Lone Eaters, you know me. I have gone to the white man's school and some of you hold that against me. I have learned much about the Napikwans, and there is much about them that I do not like. But I have kept an open spirit and I do not think all of them are bad.

"This Sturgis"—he said the foreign word well—"this man married one of our people and is well-respected among the Black Patched Moccasins. Now he goes from camp to camp, helping as he can. He means us no harm, and you would do well to listen to him and abide by his words. Pretty-on-top speaks to you with a good heart."

Fools Crow had been tying knots in a piece of rawhide fringe on his legging. Now he looked up. Pretty-on-top was not much older than he was, but there was something different about him. There was a softness in his round face, a softness that extended to his limbs and belly. His short hair, cut straight across, barely reached his shoulders, and when he moved his head quickly it seemed to ripple out like the fur of a bear when he shakes off flies. Perhaps it was the dark wool pants and the white shirt buttoned at the neck or the lack of ornament; he wore nothing but the winter moccasins and blackhorn robe that would mark him as a Pikuni. But many of the Napikwans wore these things. Fools Crow looked down and tied another knot in the fringe. And then he knew what it was. He had seen a religious man once, a man newly arrived at Many Houses fort. With some other young men, Fools Crow had watched the big boat pull up at the landing. The blast of the whistle had caused his horse to break free of his tether, and when Fools Crow had caught him and ridden him back to the landing, he got there just in time to see the religious man set foot on the ground. He too was a soft man, his jowls hanging loose over the white band around his neck. When he found firm footing on the landing, he did not gawk and stretch as the others had done; instead, he dropped to his knees and lifted his face to the sky. Even the other Napikwans stared at him. Later Fools Crow had learned from one of the Liars that this was a holy man, possessor of great power. That was the last holy man Fools Crow had seen among the Napikwans, although he had heard of Long Teeth, the black robe, who had visited the Pikunis before he was born. All the elders spoke with awe of Long Teeth; some of them longed for his return. But he did not come back, and the holy man at Many Houses did not come among the Pikunis.

Now Fools Crow stared at Pretty-on-top. He knew that the soft young man had become a spirit-man in the manner of the Napikwans, and for an instant he doubted the power of the Pikuni medicine, of Mik-api and Boss Ribs' medicine and of his own puny efforts. Then a thought came to him that caused his breath to catch in his throat. Suppose this Sturgis had come to infect the Lone Eaters? He did not bring the Napikwan medicine and he knew the Pikuni medicine was weak. Perhaps he brought the sickness instead? Fools Crow watched Three Bears light his ceremonial pipe. It was much valued for the red stone of its bowl. In happier days, before the Napikwans came in great numbers, Three Bears had obtained it in a trade with the Dirt Lodge People. Now the white-scabs came from the Dirt Lodge People. Three Bears passed the pipe to his right, to Sturgis. The white man did not hesitate; he puffed three times, blowing the smoke upward, then passed the pipe on to Pretty-on-top. The young man held the pipe by the red bowl. He glanced across the circle to Mik-api, but the old man was tracing patterns on the quillwork on top of his winter moccasin. All the other eyes were on Pretty-on-top as he finally put the pipe to his lips and drew in the warm smoke. Often when a man is put to the test, the others breathe in and out with him in a kind of relief. But this time the others held their breath too long, and it was clear that they too no longer trusted Pretty-on-top. It was one thing to smoke with a Napikwan, but another to trust a Pikuni who had taken on the Napikwan's ways.

The two visitors were taken to Rides-at-the-door's smaller lodge to rest up for their return trip. The men sat silently staring at the small fire. All of them had relatives in the afflicted camps. Now each man wondered who among his own kin would not appear at the Sun Dance encampment next Home Days. And they wondered when the first survivors would find their way to the camp of the Lone Eaters. How many would come? How would they all eat? Winters were difficult in the best of times, but with so many in one place, the animals would be hunted out in a short time. All would face hunger, perhaps starvation. And if the survivors brought the white-scabs . . .

It was Sits-in-the-middle who broke the silence. "How can we turn away our own relatives? Would we see them die piteously on the edge of our camp? Would we shoot them if they tried to enter?"

"That is not our way," said Three Bears.

"But the Napikwan says we must do this." Sits-in-the-middle looked around the circle. "Even Pretty-on-top says this is the way it must be."

"Do you listen to Pretty-on-top who wears the Napikwan's clothes, who sleeps in the Napikwan's bed?"

The sudden anger of Fools Crow's voice made Mik-api look up for the first time since entering the lodge. "I do not think he is a bad man," he said. "It is true he has taken to the white man's ways, but I think in his heart he is still a Pikuni. He smokes the pipe with his brothers."

"And what about the white man Sturgis?" Three Bears addressed Mik-api, but his eyes were on Fools Crow.

"It is natural for us not to trust this man, for we have never had much luck with the Napikwans. But I find this one different. He suffers the loss of his wife. He suffers the loss of her people. The Black Patched Moccasins trusted him. Many of us know and respect the judgment of Takes Gun—he has joined many parties against our enemies. If he trusts this Napikwan, we would be wise to respect that trust."

"I feel as you do, Mik-api. I find no deceit in this man. But what he says makes my heart fall down. If his medicine will not help the Pikunis, then I fear many of us, our young ones, will go to the Sand Hills."

"Perhaps we should move camp." Rides-at-the-door spoke so quietly that the others were not sure he had spoken at all. "Perhaps we should move across the Medicine Line, to Old Man River. The Siksikas would let us camp there until Cold Maker retreated to his house in the north."

"Or we could go to the agency on the Milk River. They would have to take us in."

"I'm afraid that all the afflicted ones, the ones healthy enough to make it, will be there, Sits-in-the-middle. That direction would bring us death."

"But why must we leave our ranges? There are no blackhorns in the country of the Siksikas. We would have to eat the slippery swimmers. I would go into the Backbone and eat the bighorns and white bigheads before I would eat the Siksikas' food." Sits-in-the-middle looked at Fools Crow as if he sensed that the young man would be with him.

But Fools Crow was ashamed of himself for his outburst against

Pretty-on-top. He was there to listen, not speak, not speak so violently against one who had chosen another way. He had spoken out of place against one who was not there. But he also had been thinking about what his father had said. In some ways he agreed with Sits-in-the-middle. It would be better to winter in their own country. If they went south they could find game and be far enough away from the other camps to spend the winter untouched by the bad spirit of the white man's disease. Why then would his father suggest they go north, into the teeth of Cold Maker's fury? It was true that the Siksikas were their relatives. They would take the Lone Eaters into their country and help them. But to leave their ranges in the middle of winter . . . ?

Then it came to Fools Crow as though it had been in the fire all along, in the smoky curls that drifted straight up to the smoke hole, and he spoke again. "There, the Napikwans are not thick like ants. They do not wish to make the Pikunis cry. These seizers here will ride us down before the moon of the new grass."

Rides-at-the-door said nothing, but a look of pride softened his eyes.

The other men in the lodge let Fools Crow's words hang in the air. For the last several sleeps they had put the threat of these invaders out of their minds. They had listened to Rides-at-the-door's account of his meeting with General Sully and they had watched him ride off to council with the band chiefs at the camp of the Hard Topknots. Even Mountain Chief had been there. But when Rides-at-the-door had returned two days later, they saw the look of dejection on his face and they knew that the chiefs had rejected the seizer chief's demands. The dread they had felt then returned now and, coupled with the immediate threat of the white-scabs disease, made their world seem hopeless.

"Perhaps we should call the societies together," said Three Bears. His voice was low and far away.

27

THE WAR LODGE beneath the chimney of Bad Horse Butte looked deserted. Fast Horse and Owl Child dismounted wearily. The day had turned cold, and Fast Horse had his buffalo coat buttoned to the neck. A thin snow lay on the landscape. They had not encountered any sign of horses or humans, but Owl Child had the others scout the far side of the butte.

Owl Child stayed with the horses while Fast Horse approached the war lodge with his short-gun drawn. He came from the side toward the entrance. A large pine bough lay bulky and dark on the ground, not quite covered by the fresh snow. Fast Horse squatted beside the opening and peered in. It was dark inside the lodge and at first he saw nothing. He put his head inside, and his eyes adjusted to the dim light filtering through the boughs. He saw first the tripod with a small carcass hanging over the gray ash of a cold fire. Then he saw a long tan shape like that of a wags-his-tail. He ducked through the entrance and stood just inside. The shape lay beneath a tanned-on-both-sides robe. It was a man.

Fast Horse crept around the cold fire and poked the robe with his short-gun, but the man lay still and stiff. He pulled back a corner and saw a moccasin and legging. Then he threw the robe all the way off. It was a Pikuni man lying on his side, a long braid across his eyes. The braid was wrapped in otter. He glanced around the lodge and saw the backrest. There were three blotches of dried blood on the willow sticks, the one in the center darker, bigger. He saw a pemmican sack partially eaten away by mice. He looked down at the man again and saw the hands with no fingers. He squatted to move the otter-wrapped braid from the face but he already knew who it was; instead, he watched the hands that he had caused to become this way that long-ago night in the Crow camp. A small cold wind blew through the boughs that covered the lodge, but he didn't feel it.

28

FOOLS CROW COULD NOT SLEEP that night. Each time he closed his eyes he saw the fire in the big lodge. And he heard the voices, some loud, some strangely muted, some angry, some reasonable. All the voices entered his head and troubled him, and he could not sleep.

Red Paint rolled onto her side away from him, and he tucked the sleeping robe under her knees and over her shoulder. He allowed his hand to brush against her belly and marveled again at its round tautness. Earlier that day when she prepared to get water he had offered to help her and she had chided him. Did he want her to get fat and lazy, good only for gossip like White Grass Woman? Perhaps he preferred that fat cow to her? And when he protested, she reminded him that the other men would call him an old woman, and how could she live with such a human being? Fools Crow had smiled but the point was well taken. She would decide when she could no longer work.

He reached across her body and pushed a couple of sticks farther into the fire. Then he lay back and stared up at the flickering shadows on the tipi walls.

All the men's societies had been represented. Because these societies encompassed all the bands, many of the important society chiefs were not among the Lone Eaters. The Raven Carriers had only one member in the camp. He was a man of fifty winters and was known as a stubborn man even among the other Raven Carriers. His name was Heavy Elk, and it was he who spoke first after Three Bears had explained their situation.

"I have many relatives among the Small Brittle Fats and Small

Robes. One of my daughters is married into the Never Laughs people. You know her husband, Many Spotted Skins. He is a chief and a strong man among the Raven Carriers. He has many scalp locks hanging from his war shirt. How can I refuse him the safety of my lodge? Am I to tell my daughter that she is not welcome in the camp of the Lone Eaters? If we cross the Medicine Line, my relatives will come here and die, and when they go to the Sand Hills they will tell the before-fathers that Heavy Elk ran away when they needed him." He looked around the lodge. He had an intense, angular face and many of the men looked away from him. But others murmured their assent.

The council went like that all night. First they were against moving, then they were in favor of it, back and forth, until the speakers reached an exhausted impasse. Three Bears and Rides-at-the-door spoke, but their words carried little weight in the heated talk. Mik-api did not speak, for this discussion had nothing to do with many-face men. If their medicine had worked against this white-scabs disease, the fierce arguing would not have been necessary, for few of the men in the lodge were inclined to run away from the Napikwans. Fools Crow was surprised at this. It was as though the men had decided, individually and without thinking about it, that they would not allow the Napikwans to drive them from their land. Fools Crow was also surprised and puzzled that his father did not press this issue. Once, during a lull while the men smoked, he almost spoke to his father to ask him why he didn't point out the advantages of crossing the Medicine Line. But his father's jaw was rigid and Fools Crow knew that he was running out of patience with his own reasonableness and the reaction to it. Fools Crow had seen this new attitude during the past eight sleeps, since his father had returned from the meeting with the Pikuni chiefs. It seemed that the people did not want to give in to the Napikwans in any way—they did not want to return the Napikwan horses, they did not wish to turn Owl Child over to the seizers, they had no desire even to discuss the presence of the Napikwans. Either they felt that the Napikwans would go away if they ignored them, or they were ready to fight when the time came.

In the end nothing was decided, and that was the way it had

been lately. As Fools Crow lay in the shadowy lodge, listening to his wife's sleeping breath, he felt the impotence that had fallen over his people like snow in the night. Before the coming of the Napikwans, decisions had been made. There was always the arguing, but in the end, the men had made a decision and all had abided by it. Fools Crow's grandfather had told of a much simpler life when the decisions were easier—when to move camp, when to go to the trading house across the Medicine Line, where the hunting would be best, if it was time to raid the Crow or Snake horses. Now, each decision meant a change in their way of life. And what about Fools Crow? How would he decide if he had to speak for the people? If the Lone Eaters crossed the Medicine Line, the chances were good that their country would be in the Napikwans' hands when they returned. And, too, the white-scabs might wipe out the Pikunis and there would be nothing to return to, for without their relatives the Lone Eaters would be nothing more than a small wandering band with no home.

Fools Crow shuddered and realized he was sweating. He moved away from Red Paint's body, and his eyes fell on the scalp he had taken from Bull Shield. It hung glistening in the firelight from a lodgepole. I was powerful then, he thought, my luck was good. But what good is your own power when the people are suffering, when their minds are scattering like horses in the four directions? Was Sun Chief laughing at them, not content just to abandon them? Why must he pull them apart? Why must he make them abandon each other? Fools Crow closed his eyes and listened to the voices in the lodge once again, but this time they all merged into one mumbling drone that went on and on until Fools Crow finally drifted away to the world of Nitsokan, dream helper.

29

RED PAINT STOOD BESIDE THE LODGE and watched him ride away. She watched his horse pick a way up the steep draw to the rolling hills south of camp. She expected him to stop at the top of the rise and look back but he didn't. He disappeared. She continued to watch the horizon for some time, as though by an act of will she could draw him back, but she knew that his dream had power beyond her will.

She had awakened to see him kneeling over her, and in the dim light it had taken her a moment to see the paint on his face and another moment to see that it was not a war face. The whitewash was barely thick enough to hide the natural color of her husband's skin. But it was the eyes—rather, the hollows around the eyes—that made her catch her breath. The charcoal-gray smudge gave his face the appearance of a mask. As she studied the man above her, she felt a shiver go through her bones and knew she was looking into the face of death.

He stood then and walked around the fire. His hair was loose and hung down past his shoulders. He was wearing an old skin shirt and leggings. Both were stained with grease and dirt and ash. Red Paint saw that the fringing on the shirt had been cut off. She watched him gather up his bow and quiver and the small medicine bag that he wore around his neck. He returned and again knelt beside her.

"I had a dream," he said. "Nitsokan instructs me to make a journey."

Red Paint looked up at the face, and it was difficult to recognize her husband.

"I will be gone for seven sleeps. You can move to your mother's lodge for that time."

Red Paint raised herself to one elbow. "Are you going to hunt?"

"Perhaps—later. But first I must attend to something else."

"What is it?"

"Nitsokan doesn't say. He will only guide me."

"Do you have food? There is meat—" Red Paint threw back the robe and tried to rise.

Fools Crow gently pushed her back. "I must take no food on this journey. I must come to this place as a beggar."

"Why do you paint yourself in this way? It frightens me."

"A-wah-heh, wife, take courage. I intend to come back to you as the man I am. For now, I must do as Nitsokan says. I myself do not understand, but if my journey is successful, perhaps it will help the Lone Eaters find a direction." He stood and draped a small calf robe over his shoulders. "You must pray to the Above Ones for my success and for my return. You must ask them to take pity on this poor beggar—and on the Pikuni people."

"But did your dream helper vow to return you to me?"

"Nitsokan helps all our people. He will return me to you."

"But will he know where to find me? What if the chiefs decide to move camp before you come back? I will stay! I will not leave here even if all the others go away."

"You are a brave woman, Red Paint. Pray for us and for our unborn child."

"I will pray for you, my husband, but you must promise me that you will return. You must promise me!"

Fools Crow reached the top of the rise out of the Two Medicine valley and kicked his horse into a trot. He was riding the black buffalo-runner that he had taken from the Crows. He was a big horse with a good seat and easy gait that made Fools Crow uneasy. Nitsokan had told him to come as a beggar, and beggars did not ride such fine animals. But it would take three days to reach his destination, and he didn't want to take a chance on a poorer creature coming up lame or not having the strength to get him there and back. Nitsokan had instructed him to ride for three days and three nights. The dream helper would give him and his horse the strength to endure such a trial, but it would be hard. Fools Crow knew there would be times when he would wonder if it was worth the effort, times when he would be tempted to turn back to the warmth of his lodge and his wife.

As he scanned the snowy short-grass plains stretching away to the blue mountains of the Backbone, he began to be afraid. He knew this country well, knew all the buttes and mountains, the creeks and rivers; yet this day he felt strange, and when he looked at familiar landmarks he saw them as a stranger would, in a different place, in another time. He was grateful when the sun broke above a cloudbank to the east. He was grateful that Sun Chief would watch over him one more day.

He made good time that first day and night. His horse trotted strongly beneath him, and when he looked back he saw that he had left the Two Medicine River far behind. In the last darkness before dawn, in the waning moonlight, he stood on a ridge just east of the Milk River and looked down on the buildings of the Four Horns agency. They squatted low and dark in a grassy clearing and Fools Crow thought he heard voices, but then he realized it was the sound of his own stomach. He had ceased feeling hungry sometime during the night, but now in the silence of the snowy night his stomach rumbled its complaint.

He swung himself onto the black horse and the horse began his steady trot. Fools Crow almost urged him into a lope, for now they were in the country of the Napikwans, in the wide-open country where a horse and rider would attract attention. He would not reach the eastward curve of the mountains until nightfall.

Fools Crow made a prayer to Nitsokan to help him get through this day, to pass unnoticed in this country of the enemies. But as the first light of dawn appeared on the eastern horizon, he became afraid again. Before the day ended he would have to pass near the seizers' fort on the Pile-of-rocks River. He began to think of finding a willow grove to hide in until night. He knew of such a place just to the west. He could make it before Sun had cleared the land. But as he turned the black horse, he remembered how Nitsokan had said to ride three days and three nights, without stopping. If he stopped, he wouldn't know the way or when he had reached his destination. No, he could not interrupt his journey, not for fear or hunger or fatigue, but he couldn't help the feeling of discouragement that swept over him, of knowing that the seizers could end his journey that very day. And he would never know what awaited him. Worst of all, he would not know if that which awaited him would help his people. Nitsokan had not said so, but what other purpose for such a hard ride? In spite of his fear, he had to believe that Nitsokan would bring him past the Napikwans.

Fools Crow was riding south again, sunk in his gloomy thoughts, so he didn't notice the first thin veil that softened the outlines of the land and caused the oranging of the eastern sky to dim. He was cold and tired, and he hid his face beneath his long, loose hair. He did not sleep but he was in another world, a world of warmth and plenty and happy voices. He saw the lodges of the Two Medicine River, and the children playing in midsummer water, and his own wife, singing to herself as she worked over a stretched skin. He saw the large horse herds and the outriders and the village, all in a golden light, in peace. And he saw his father and Three Bears smoking outside a lodge, Mik-api dozing beneath a green big-leaf tree, oblivious to the two puppies that wrestled at his feet. Then he saw a young man riding into camp, his horse picking his way between the tipis, the dry-meat racks, the stretched hides, the children and dogs. He led three horses, all packed with meat and skins of the blackhorns. The young man stopped before the lodge where Red Paint worked. She looked up and smiled at him. Her face was sweaty and her hands were slick with brains and grease. She smiled and Fools Crow slid down off his horse and went to her.

The black horse had been standing beside the water for some time. He did not try to graze or drink but stood patiently waiting for the rider to give him a sign. When finally the rider lifted his head, he was startled to find such a dim world. He could barely see the river, and he could not see across it. The land had vanished. In his fatigue, Fools Crow thought he was in a blizzard, but as his senses returned to him he noticed that the air was still and nothing was falling out of the sky. Then he noticed the horse, then himself—they were covered with frost. It is the work of Nitsokan, he thought. He creates the thick white air that creeps along the ground. He has hidden Fools Crow this day.

He nudged the horse and they crossed the river. Luckily it was a place where the water ran fast and it was not iced over. Only on the edges did they encounter a thin crust that broke beneath the horse's hooves. As they continued their way south, they passed within hailing distance of the seizers' fort, a dim darkness in the cloud, but all was quiet.

That night they came upon the rolling foothills of the mountains. The cloud had lifted and they stayed within the stunted pine trees on a much-traveled game trail. Once they passed so close to a herd of deer that Fools Crow could have killed one with an arrow just by shooting into their midst. The deer moved away from the trail and stopped to watch them pass. Another time, a real-bear grunted several times on the slope below them, but he didn't catch their scent.

The next day Fools Crow dreamed off and on of a winter hunt with his father and brother. They ran the blackhorns well, and when they looked back they saw several dark lumps strewn over the snowy plain. They were prime animals, and Fools Crow and Running Fisher were happy and their father smiled.

The horse trotted on without pause or hesitation. Once, Fools Crow woke up and got down to piss and urged the horse to eat in a grove of saplings, but the horse stood with head high, his eyes trained to the south, until his rider climbed wearily into the saddle. Nitsokan gives you strength, buffalo-runner, and the keen eyes to see where we are going. Does he also tell you our destination? Has he shown you what he hides from me? Then Fools Crow drifted into his dream and the horse trotted on.

The snow was a pale blue in the dusk-light by the time they reached the mouth of the canyon. Although Fools Crow had been in this country twice before, he had not noticed the canyon. The wall on the south side was made of granite with several horizontal striations too small to be called ledges. Each striation held a narrow line of snow that seemed to point Fools Crow's eyes up the canyon. The other side of the canyon was a more gradual slope covered with short gnarled pines and gray grasses. Between this slope and the small ice-blue stream that emptied out onto the flat where the black horse stood, there was a thick patch of red willows that blocked the entrance to the canyon.

Fools Crow slid down and led the horse to the willows. The snow had covered up the path, but he could just make out the small dark depressions in the snow that meant animal tracks. The light was going fast and he was reluctant to enter the canyon, but he knew this was the place Nitsokan had directed him. Still he hesitated, until the black horse raised his head sharply and pulled the reins from Fools Crow's hand. Before his master could react the horse whirled and crashed into the willow stand, the brittle branches clattering as they closed behind the animal. Fools Crow yelled but he knew that the horse wouldn't hear him over the clattering willows. Again he grew fearful, but before the feeling could overpower him, he lunged into the willows and began to follow the dark sharp hoofprints.

Although he kept to the path, the way was hard, and by the time he emerged into the openness of the valley, his face was red and stinging from the slapping branches. There was a long bloody scratch on his cheek from a broken-off branch that he had walked into, but he felt alive and alert and warm as he looked up at the sky and saw the familiar Seven Persons and the Lost Children. He looked back toward the entrance to the canyon and saw Night Red Light, almost full, hovering yellow over the plains. And when he looked down he saw his shadow before him, and he remembered the fear in Red Paint's eyes as she had seen his ash-gray face. She was far away now.

Although the valley was small, the mountains sloped away with such ease that it made the way ahead look open and inviting. The mountains on both sides were covered with large dark pines. Below the mountain to the north there was a saddle, and a leafless grove of aspen spilled down to the valley floor. Fools Crow saw his black horse near the edge of the grove, less than two hundred paces away. He trotted over to the horse and patted the powerful shoulder. The skin rippled under his hand with such energy that Fools Crow felt it go into his own body and he felt strong. As he lifted himself into the saddle, he said, "I shall call you Heavy-charging-in-the-brush from now on because you have shown me the way. That is a good name for such a war-horse."

The horse began the familiar trot with his head up and ears forward, but this time Fools Crow did not slump down into dreams, content with letting the horse lead the way. He sat with his back straight and his eyes scanning the moonlit country ahead. He knew that Nitsokan waited for him.

The small dwelling was made of logs and mud. It stood on the bank of a small river, surrounded by leafless spear-leaf trees and chokecherry thickets. There were no outbuildings that Fools Crow could see, nor could he see or hear any of the Napikwan animals that usually grazed near these dwellings in the cold moons of winter. As he sat on his horse and studied the house, he realized that although he didn't know who was inside, he was not afraid. He watched the smoke rise from a long black tube and knew there would be one of the Napikwan woodburners inside. He looked at a small square opening covered with the white man's ice-shield. He had seen them at the trader's house on the Bear River. When he had touched one, he had been surprised to feel that it was hard but not cold. Now he watched the yellow light behind the opening and knew that would be the white man's light-maker. So Nitsokan wishes me to enter this enemy's lodge, he thought. Then, it is necessary. He had his bow strung and an arrow notched. As he tested the pull of the twisted sinew, he remembered that Nitsokan had told him to come as a beggar. A beggar does not come with his weapons drawn but as a suppli- cant, so Fools Crow reluctantly slung the bow and quiver from the saddle horn.

He walked down into the hollow, his moccasins squeaking in the dry snow, and he felt naked and vulnerable. He imagined

Napikwans hiding in the chokecherry thickets and behind the spear-leaf trees, and he expected, with each step, a flash of fire and a greased shooter ripping into his heart. But he assured himself that Nitsokan had not brought him this far to be killed senselessly —and, too, Nitsokan had promised to return him to his people in seven sleeps.

Fools Crow stood for a long time before the door to the small lodge. Just as he began to think of calling out, the door opened. The yellow light framed a figure, and Fools Crow could see that it was a woman or a boy. Although the figure was bundled in a blanket, it was slender and did not take up much of the opening.

"Ok-yi," said the figure. "You have come."

"It has been a long journey," said Fools Crow.

"You have traveled far from your people."

"The way was difficult." Fools Crow felt suddenly that he was dissolving, that he was going to melt into the ground. His arms and legs felt like the bones and muscles had left them and his body felt as heavy as a winter sack of pemmican. Just before his mind wandered away, he thought, I have not eaten or slept for three days—and he saw the figure beckon to him.

Fools Crow lay on a sleeping platform under a strange puffy blanket. He raised his head and saw that there were many designs on the cloth. The only design he could make out was a blue tipi beside a river. Some kind of small animal lay beside the tipi. The whole was bathed in yellow light. He knew he must not go to sleep in this strange place but his eyes were heavy. From somewhere nearby he heard a soft song. It was a sleeping song and the voice reminded him of his own mother, but when he opened his eyes again he saw no one and the singing stopped. He propped himself up and looked around the room. Not far from him he saw an eating platform with a long sitting board beside it. On top of the platform he saw the light-maker with its small flame and the yellow liquid beneath it. Near it was another see-through container, this one filled with a red liquid. Then Fools Crow spied the sliced meat. It was on one of the smooth shiny rounds that

Napikwans used to hold their food. He threw back the puffy blanket and lifted himself from the sleeping platform and felt his knees go. They struck the hard earth floor and he pitched forward. He got to his knees, feeling foolish, but as he looked around, he could see no sign of the figure that had greeted him.

Fools Crow ate several slices of the meat. It was tough and stringy. It was the meat of the white bighead and Fools Crow wolfed it down. He lifted the vessel of red juice and smelled at the opening. Then he tasted it, and it was sweet and tart at the same time. He drank the chokecherry juice and the freshness made him gasp. There was something different about it, a warmth in his stomach, that made him feel heavy. He sat on the edge of the sleeping platform and rubbed his eyes. When he opened them, when the tangles went out of them, he found himself looking at a dog lying in front of the Napikwan heat-maker. He frowned. The dog raised his head, and Fools Crow could see freckles on his muzzle. The dog was black and white and young but the eyes were calm and deep.

"Sa-sak-si," said Fools Crow. "Freckle-face. Come here."

But the dog didn't move and Fools Crow was too tired to go to him.

"Sa-sak-si," he said again and then he lay down on the sleeping platform. This time the sleeping song came from farther away. He tried to open his eyes but he couldn't. Nitsokan, his dream helper, held his eyelids shut, and although he struggled, he felt himself drifting to a place closer to the sleeping song. And then he heard the chatter and laughter of children and let himself go.

The meadow was full of long grasses and thickets of willow and chokecherry beside a blue stream. The sun was warm on the backs of the many animals that grazed there. Although the larger animals remained in their own bands, they did not seem to be wary or hostile. The blackhorns grazed alongside the long-legs and prairie-runners and wags-his-tails. The bighorns and white bigheads ate mosses and grasses beneath a ledge on which a real-lion sunned himself. On the other side of the meadow, three real-bears, with cubs, sat in a huckleberry patch, oblivious to the rabbits and prairie chickens which scurried through the brush.

Fools Crow walked among these animals without giving or taking offense. The peaks and flat-irons that surrounded the meadow were cold gray, and the trees at the lower levels were dark and covered with thin snow. The thick grasses matted beneath Fools Crow's step and he found himself at the far end of the meadow, where the canyon walls loomed and the air grew chilly and damp. A thin crust of ice broke under his steps; beneath, the snow was grainy and when he pushed off with the balls of his feet he heard the snow squeak. But he did not hesitate. He entered the narrow canyon and was enveloped in thick white air. The canyon was filled with large round boulders that were not of the kind to be found in that country. But Fools Crow no longer knew what country he was in.

Three times he had to wade the stream to get around the boulders. Often he picked his way along a steep ledge that jutted twice the height of a man above the stream. Then he came to a boulder that blocked the whole of the narrow canyon. He tried the stream side and found that the ice had built up in the space beneath the upward curve of the stone. He hurried back toward the ledge and found that the boulder had crushed itself deep into the flaky shale. There was no way around the boulder, and the walls of the canyon were too steep to climb.

Fools Crow's eyes grew round with sudden alarm. Surely there was a way. But as he looked around, he knew there wasn't and he felt his heart fall down. He was cold and pulled the short-robe tight around his shoulders. The white air hung thickly in the canyon, and it seemed that the long, hard journey was over. His dream had failed. He slumped down on a stone by the creek and ran his fingers through his long hair. He felt tired and almost relieved. He knew he didn't have the power to make the dream work. Now he could return to Red Paint and take her north to the land of the Siksikas. Perhaps they would stay up there, not even return in the spring. They could learn to live in the mountains. At least they would be away from the threat of the seizers. What made him think he possessed the power to help his people?

He sat up straight and listened. Had he heard something? Then he heard it again, a yelp, followed by another. He stood and looked through the white air, trying to see down the canyon, but all he could make out were boulders and canyon wall. Then he saw movement beside a boulder; it was an animal, running toward him, yelping. He reached for his knife but the animal veered to the far side of the canyon. He was moving so fast, Fools Crow thought he would run full speed into the boulder that blocked the canyon. At the very instant that Fools Crow recognized the animal, the black-and-white dog slid under a ground juniper branch at the base of the boulder and disappeared.

Fools Crow walked slowly toward the juniper, his eyes wide in astonishment. Then he heard another sound and looked back and saw a dark long-haired animal. It chuckled and grunted as it ran after the dog, and Fools Crow saw the fangs and sharp claws flashing in the white air. Then the animal was past him, diving beneath the juniper branch. But the animal was larger than the dog and had to squirm through the flat opening.

"Skunk Bear!" shouted Fools Crow. "It is me, your brother!"

But the wolverine, with a last effort, squeezed through and vanished.

Fools Crow ran to the ground juniper and dropped to his knees. He pushed aside the branch and saw a low narrow crevice barely large enough for a man. He gathered his courage and sang his power song that Wolverine had given him; he dropped to his stomach and began to wriggle through the crevice. In the darkness of the tunnel he got to his hands and knees and tried to see ahead, but it was black and narrow. Far ahead he heard the claws of Wolverine scraping the rocky floor as he ran. And he smelled Wolverine, and the sour damp odor made his eyes water.

The tunnel was cool and a draft came up into his face, but Fools Crow soon found himself sweating. His hands and knees ached and burned from sliding along the slick surface of rock. Once he called out to Wolverine to let him catch up, but all he heard was the steady clicking of the animal's claws. Three times he panicked and tried to turn around but the space was too narrow and he succeeded only enough to get himself stuck and even more panicked. But each time he managed to free himself, and finally he was too tired and sore to even think. He crawled on, and each movement became a chant from deep within him:

Wolverine is my brother,
From Wolverine I take my courage,
Wolverine is my brother,
From Wolverine I take my strength.

The air was golden and the sky was the bottomless blue of summer. All around him the trees and shrubs were leafed out and moving with the warm breeze. He lowered his eyes from the glare of the sun and saw that he was sitting in a thicket of long grasses. A summer stream passed beside him, and he saw that the stones beneath the surface were dark and sharp. He stood and his legs were stiff. He stretched, then looked himself over. He expected to see his leggings in tatters and his knees raw, but there was no sign of his struggle through the tunnel. His hands were unmarked. He looked behind him to where the stream entered the canyon. There were no boulders, no fog, no sign of winter. He felt a stab of fear in his heart as he realized he had left that season behind—and the Lone Eaters. Would he be able to go back? Would he see Red Paint again? What was this summer land? He looked around. Where was Skunk Bear? But as he asked himself these questions, the fear that had prompted them subsided in the warm sun and he felt only wonder. He knew that this place was part of his journey and surely the end of it.

Fools Crow began to walk farther into the immense valley. All around him he could see the distant hazy peaks of the mountains. The stiffness left his legs and his stride became light. He walked for a long time, through grassy meadows, through groves of spear-leaf trees, toward a knoll that rose above even the highest trees. He climbed the slope to the top, and the sweat running down his face made him feel good and strong. At the top he looked out over the valley and could see that it was more a huge bowl than valley. He could see no entrances or exits, and yet not too far distant he saw a sandy-bottomed river and, beyond it, more trees and meadows. Although all that he could see was beautiful and lush with growth, he sensed that something about this country was different, as though he were alone in it. But the thought did not disturb him, and he trotted down the slope toward the river.

After his swim, Fools Crow lay down on the warm sand of the beach. The beads of water glistened on his body, and as he slung his forearm over his eyes, he wondered that Sun Chief never seemed to move from his position directly overhead. And he wondered at the silence, the stillness of the air. He breathed a long sigh and then he slept.

The woman stood against a tree about fifty paces from the naked man. Beside her, the black-and-white dog sprawled on the grassy dune, his head down between his paws. His eyes were less on the man than on the clothes, which were a few paces nearer. He considered the distance and the amount of time it would take to get to the clothes. He could feel the muscles tense in his hind legs, and his front paws curled slightly to gain purchase in the sandy soil. But just as he lifted his head, carefully, deliberately, he felt the woman's kick on his left thigh. He looked up and she waved her finger from side to side. He put his head down between his paws and closed his eyes, but he didn't sleep.

The woman wore a white doeskin dress which reached almost to the tops of her moccasins. A black leather belt, studded with brass tacks, encircled her waist, the two ends hanging down in front. There were no elk teeth, no shells, no fringes on the dress. Her moccasins were plain and she wore no necklace, no earrings, no feather or beaded medallions in her hair. Her graying hair was cut short and close to her head. She stroked it absently as she watched the sleeping man.

Fools Crow awoke and the sun was still high and warm. He stood and brushed the sand from his back and legs. He looked at the blue river and could see all the way down to its sandy bottom.

It puzzled him that he could see nothing but sand—no rocks, no water plants, no froth or debris, just sand. Then he listened. Although the day was at its midpoint, he should have heard some birds—a yellow-breast or a long-tail, perhaps. Or a raven from one of the distant mountainsides. But he heard nothing. And it struck him that he had seen no animals from the knoll. That was what he had expected to see—blackhorns, wags-his-tails, long-legs. In such lushness he had expected to see large herds of animals.

As he drew on his leggings Fools Crow thought of his own country. It seemed far away now, not just in seasons or sleeps but in the way that Sun or Night Red Light was distant. From the tunnel, he had emerged into a world where even the animals did not exist. But what will I eat? he thought. I haven't even seen any berries. Then he realized that he was not hungry, that the thought of food was only a thought. He tightened the blue breechcloth around his middle, then sat to brush his feet. The winter moccasins seemed strange in such country.

He saw the black-and-white dog as it charged straight at him. He jumped to his feet and pulled his knife, but the dog stopped suddenly at ten paces and sat down, eyeing the moccasins. Fools Crow recognized the dog again, then lifted his eyes to the patch of white at the edge of the treeline downstream.

30

ONE OF THE DAY-RIDERS guarding the horse herd saw the travois first. He had been huddled down in his robe, half asleep, when he felt his horse tense up beneath him. Still, he did not open his eyes until he heard several horses whicker and snort.

The horse pulling the travois answered them and began to trot toward the herd. The young man, Good Grass Bull, stood in his stirrups to see over the herd. The horse was a red roan, and he held his head high as he crossed the snowy field. The travois poles made smooth stripes in the snow on either side of the horse tracks. Good Grass Bull followed with his eyes the stripes up the sloping incline to the ridge above the Two Medicine valley. There he saw a dark figure on a horse, but he could not make out anything distinct about the rider. Just as he was about to call out a warning to the others, the figure whirled the horse around and disappeared behind the ridge.

Good Grass Bull cut through the herd toward the travois. He saw Calf Looking coming from the other perimeter. He swatted a red-and-white yearling with his quirt and the horse squealed, causing the other horses to make way.

The travois was made of two freshly cut, unpeeled lodgepole pines lashed together with rawhide latticework. Strapped to the latticework was a long bundle wrapped in a yellow tanned-on-both-sides hide. Calf Looking swatted away some horses that had come too near, then dismounted. He was older than Good Grass Bull and prided himself on his fearlessness.

"I saw something up there," Good Grass Bull pointed with his lips to the top of the ridge. "It was a rider. It could be an enemy."

Calf Looking touched the yellow hide. It was frozen hard. "It's a human being," he said. He glanced up at the ridge. "Someone makes us a gift of a dead one."

Both young men grew silent, each thinking of the possibility that the enemy was just over the ridge. Although both were prepared to defend the herd, they were perplexed and unsure of themselves in dealing with this strange travois. Finally Calf Looking said, "You go get some men. I'll warn the other riders." He patted the travois horse on the neck. Then he swung up on his own horse. "And go with speed. If there are enemies about, it will go hard on us."

Fast Horse had watched the travois horse pick his way down the slope to the river valley. He knew the day-riders would be half asleep, for he had been one himself when he was younger. He had spent his time dozing and daydreaming, dreaming of the day when his own horses would be many, when his lodge would be filled with wives and children. He had dreamed of war honors and strong medicine, an exalted place among the Pikunis. But that was not to be. Now he was a solitary figure in the isolation of a vast land.

He had told himself many times that it was his failure to find the ice spring of Cold Maker that made everything go bad—and for a while he had come to believe it. Even when he betrayed Yellow Kidney in the Crow camp, he felt that it was Cold Maker's doing, his revenge on the party for continuing their raid after failing to find the ice spring. But now he knew that it was he, and he alone, who created the disaster that led to Yellow Kidney's fall. And it was he who brought Yellow Kidney's body back to his people.

As he watched the travois horse cross the snowy field toward the herds, he felt an impulse to ride into camp, to the lodge of his father. But he knew he could not ask for forgiveness. He didn't have it in him anymore. The suffering he and Owl Child and the others had caused had hardened him in a way that was irreversible. To ask for forgiveness would be to ask for entry back into the lives of his people, and he was not one of them now; nor was he with Owl Child and his gang. He had left them at Bad Horse Butte after making the travois and strapping Yellow Kidney's body to it. He would not see them again.

He lifted his eyes across the valley to the rolling plains beyond. There was safety up there, beyond the Medicine Line, and he had some of the yellow dust that the Napikwans valued. He was alone now, but he knew he would be welcome at the whiskey forts in the north. There were many men alone up there.

He heard a horse whicker, then another, and he looked down at the horse herds. He saw one of the day-riders stir, then look up at him. He whirled his horse and galloped out of sight. He had returned Yellow Kidney.

31

THE WOMAN in the white doeskin dress approached boldly, and Fools Crow did not know what to make of her. From a distance she had looked old, but as she drew nearer the years seemed to fall away. Her face, beneath the gray cut-off hair, was wrinkled, but the wrinkles were those of a person who laughs much, who grows old but remains young. And yet she wore the short hair of one who mourns.

"Ok-yi," she said. "Welcome."

Fools Crow recognized her voice. She was the figure who had greeted him in the doorway of the small cabin.

"Who are you?" he said.

"The one who left meat and drink for you back there—to give you strength to complete your journey." She smiled and the wrinkles both deepened and disappeared.

"Is my journey done?"

"Yes." She laughed. "You are here."

"Where is this place?"

She walked around him and stood, looking off across the river. She walked lightly, but she stood with a firmness that suggested this was her world.

"Am I in the Shadowland then?"

The woman whirled around and laughed and her laughter was low and throaty. "Do you think you are in the Shadowland? Do you think these are the Sand Hills?" She waved her arm around the bowl to the distant mountains.

Fools Crow was ashamed of himself and yet relieved. Then he

grew annoyed with the woman. "You laugh at my ignorance, but you say nothing that informs me. I have traveled many sleeps to reach this place, and I lose track of time. I have endured hardships. Now I find myself in a land that is always summer. I am far from my people and I wish to return to them."

The woman stepped closer and touched his arm. "I have upset you. For this I am ashamed." She turned her head aside. "I do not see many of your people and I forget myself," she said.

Fools Crow looked down at the hand on his arm. Women do not touch a man so easily, he thought. Not in his world. But her touch was light and warm and it did not offend him.

"I do not live much in your world," she said. "I do not fully understand the ways of the Pikunis anymore." The smile returned to her face. "Are you hungry?"

Fools Crow looked at the woman. Her skin was a shade lighter than his, yet she did not look like a Napikwan. He looked into her face, and she looked back, smiling. Pikuni women were not that open; nor were the women of the other tribes he knew. He looked away, down the river where he had first seen her. "I do not feel hunger," he said.

"No, there is no hunger here." Her voice sounded almost wistful. "I have tobacco in my lodge." She turned and began to walk downriver. The dog ran ahead of her.

Fools Crow stood for a moment, confused at her openness, her boldness, but it did not seem offensive. Her touch had startled him, but it made him feel warm. Her smile and laughter too seemed easy, and as he thought about it, he found that he had enjoyed that too. But why had she cut off her hair? Whom did she mourn? He pulled on his winter moccasins and trotted after the woman.

The lodge was set back thirty paces from the river, on a short rise of tufted grass. Behind the lodge, away from the river, stood a grove of alder trees, the gray skin of their trunks standing starkly against the greens and yellows of the summer valley. The lodge itself was made of skins as white as the woman's dress. It too was unadorned. Fools Crow leaned against a backrest and smoked the woman's tobacco. It was sweeter and more fragrant than the Napikwan tobacco that his people had come to smoke. As he smoked he looked around the lodge and was surprised to see that it contained almost nothing besides the backrest and two white bighead robes, one on either side of the fire pit. Against the wall opposite the entrance lay a bulging sack, old and worn, filled with what appeared to be round objects. Next to the sack he saw a digging stick, like the one Red Paint used to dig roots.

Although the lodge with its white skins was almost as bright as the outside, the air was cooler, and the sweet tobacco made Fools Crow content. He felt as comfortable here as he did in his own lodge. He laid the pipe on a stone beside him and looked across at the woman. She had her head down, and he saw that she was painting a design on a yellow skin. Then she began to sing, and it was the sleeping song that Fools Crow had heard back in the cabin. He closed his eyes and listened to the sweetness in the voice. He felt no sense of urgency now. He had lost track of time and knew that the woman would speak to him when she was ready. This waiting was part of the journey. And so he listened to the woman's song and he heard, beyond her voice, the noise like a distant waterfall of children laughing.

He awoke to the blue light of false dawn. The walls of the tipi were blue, and when he looked at his hands he saw that they too were blue. He sat up quickly and looked across the fire pit. The woman was gone. He looked down at the small orange glow of the fire pit and felt a quiet sorrow spread through his body, and he couldn't account for it. It seemed to enter him from outside, as though the lodge itself were filled with sorrow. He looked around the empty space and spotted the yellow skin that the woman had been painting. He reached it and held it before him, but there was no design, no picture on it. He turned it over and that side was empty of paint too. He held it closer, but there was no trace of pigment on it. How is this, he thought, that she paints, yet there is nothing there, not even a smudge? Did I not see the design with my own eyes? But he could not remember the design or the colors. In his confusion he thought he had dreamed the woman in her world, but as he looked around he saw the white bighead pelts, the embers in the fire pit. She was real, and suddenly he wanted to see her again, to feel her touch on his arm, to hear her strong, laughing voice.

Fools Crow put the skin aside and stood. He was wearing only his breechcloth, and his skin looked pale in the blue light. Then he heard a sound from far off that he recognized as the cries of winter geese. Once, as a child in the big-wind moon, he had crouched on the brow of a hill and watched the geese coming and going, and he was blinded by their flashing wings in the gray sun. The large, shallow lake was covered with the flashing wings, and the commotion excited and frightened him. But it was the noise, the thousands of voices yelping shrilly in his ears, that caused him to fear for himself. For many sleeps after that he heard those voices, and they echoed and echoed deep within him until he thought he had become crazy and would die. Each night he dreamed of the winter geese, until Rides-at-the-door brought in a many-faces man to drive the voices from his body.

Fools Crow shivered now, as he listened to the distant yelping, and a thought crept into his mind: I have been tricked by Nitso-kan. He has brought me to this place to die. He has summoned the winter geese to kill me. And Wolverine helped him. Wolverine led me to this place. Ah, Skunk Bear, why do you betray me? Have I not helped you in your trouble? Twice I released you from the Napikwans' steel jaws, twice I have saved your life. Treacherous creature, your brothers are right not to trust you. You steal their kills. I have seen you steal the long-legs from the little bigmouths after they have brought it down. I have seen you steal even a mouse from Sinopa, the fox. You are evil, Skunk Bear, and that is why you roam these mountains alone, stealing kills and killing others for pleasure. And today you wish to steal my life too.

Now the winter geese were even closer, their cries entering Fools Crow's ears and plunging into his heart. He stood naked before the shrill onslaught. He did not even have a weapon with which to fight and die honorably. As his heart fell down, he thought of the woman and wondered why she had taken part in such a cruel trick. Had she not touched him, and had not that touch been warm and trusting?

Fools Crow quit the woman's lodge and began to walk toward the alder grove. The flashing wings and cries were all around him now and he knew that his power was gone, but he walked ahead as a man does who is dreaming. And like the dreaming man, he did not see the geese, for they were all within him and they consumed his power, and he walked among the gray trunks of the alders in the false dawn.

The woman knelt in a clearing beyond the alder grove. Her white dress was as bright as new snow in the blue light. She sat back on her heels and lifted her arms to the horizon on the eastern edge of the bowl. Beside her lay the bulging sack and before her, at her knees, lay the digging stick. She had fastened in her hair a yellow feather. In one hand she clutched a juniper bough. A spider's web was woven among the shiny fingers of the bough.

Fools Crow squatted at the edge of the clearing behind her, his back resting against an alder trunk. It was quiet in the bowl and he became aware, once again, of the absence of bird and animal. But as he thought this, he felt a presence behind him, a slow breathing. He turned his head quickly and saw the woman's dog, three paces behind and slightly to the side. The dog was sitting patiently, as though he had witnessed this scene in this clearing many times. Fools Crow looked into the dark eyes and the dog glanced at him, then returned his gaze to the woman.

"Sa-sak-si," whispered Fools Crow. "Come, Freckle-face."

The dog did not hesitate. He walked the few paces, then sat down beside Fools Crow.

"Tell me what your mistress is doing."

But the dog did not look at him.

Just then the woman began to sing. She sang softly, but her music filled the bowl; it was as though it were made to hold her song. The words echoed round and round, and Fools Crow was filled with awe.

> *"There is my son, and there is Morning Star,*
> *Together they ride forever, across the morning sky.*
> *Many have wanted to marry me,*
> *I love only Morning Star."*

Three times she sang this, then three times more, and when Fools Crow looked up at the horizon before her, he saw Morning Star and his son, Poia, against the deep blue of the false dawn. The woman began to wail, and her wailing filled the bowl with the voices of a thousand geese, and Fools Crow closed his eyes and clapped his hands over his ears, but the sound was once again in him and he was outside of himself, a child again, staring at the wintry lake and the flashing wings.

And then the wailing stopped. Fools Crow opened his eyes, and Early Riser and Poia were gone. The horizon was streaked with the pale yellow of dawn. There was the sound of a drum, and the sky turned lighter and lighter, and then Sun Chief himself entered the bowl, casting his brilliant light down to the small clearing, and the clean night smells gave way to the dusty odors of the moon of the burnt grass.

The woman sat with her back bent and her head down. Her arms were at her sides, and although she still held the juniper bough, it lay on the grass, dusty and limp. Fools Crow wanted to go away, to shrink back into the trees, but he could not bear to leave her this way. He walked quietly into the clearing, and when he reached her he touched her shoulder. He squatted beside her and looked into her face. The tears had dried, but something in the face told Fools Crow of a grief so deep it would always be there and no words from him could help. She opened her eyes and looked at him without seeing. Her eyes were the blue of the light in her lodge that Fools Crow had seen earlier, the light that created no shadows. Just then, Freckle-face, who had never left the edge of the clearing, barked and the woman blinked, and when she looked up the sun filled her eyes.

"Are you well?" said Fools Crow.

The woman slowly moved her head, taking in the clearing as though she were seeing it for the first time. "I was digging turnips," she said. "I must have lost my way." She heaved herself up from the ground, tired and heavy, like an old cow. She sighed and picked up her sack and digging stick. When she straightened up, she looked at Fools Crow and smiled and the youthful look returned. "Look, I have a whole bagful."

Fools Crow looked off to the eastern horizon. The mountain was a dusty green. Near the top, beneath the granite face, he could see a small pocket of yellow snow. On the other side of the peak, it would be winter, and his people would be there, waiting for a direction or a sign. Would they wait forever? Fools Crow turned back to the woman.

"Who do you mourn?" He was surprised by the anger in his voice. "Who are you?"

32

RIDES-AT-THE-DOOR sat facing the entrance to his lodge. It was his accustomed place, and usually he would be flanked on either side by family and friends. There would be the smell of meat roasting; there would be stories and laughter; there would be faces, the faces of those he loved. But not this night. This night he sat alone, smoking his short-pipe and thinking of the ways he had tried to be a good man, a man of wisdom and generosity whom the people respected and sought for counsel. He thought of the times he had helped Three Bears do the necessary thing for the Lone Eaters, the times he had helped the young men in their war and raiding pursuits. He had tried to be a good father—he had taught his sons to ride and to hunt, to drive an arrow deep in the right spot. He had given them strength and courage when facing the enemy. And he had made Fools Crow proud to be of the Lone Eaters and the Pikunis. But he had failed somehow in the case of Running Fisher. He had been caught up in Fools Crow's development as a man of many strengths; he hadn't noticed how Running Fisher had been twisting away from the good path. At first, Rides-at-the-door had taken the young man's haughty attitude as a sign of strength, of youthful pride, the way it is when a youth is full of himself. Sometimes that is a good quality in a young man, for he marks himself as one who will stand out in later life. Many times that quality brings honor to the man's family as well as himself.

Honor is all we have, thought Rides-at-the-door, that and the blackhorns. Take away one or the other and we have nothing.

One feeds us and the other nourishes us. And so I must do this thing for honor. It is not a good thing but it must be done.

The skin over the entrance rustled, and he watched Kills-close-to-the-lake enter and take a place far from him and the warmth of the fire. He looked at her without expression but he thought that she was indeed a lovely young woman, and he felt the sorrow he had felt when Striped Face told him of this thing. And the remorse—for he had deprived a young man of the chance to grow up with this young woman. He had taken her as a wife only as a favor to his pitiful friend, Mad Wolf. At the time it had seemed like an act of generosity, but now he wondered if he had taken her on as just another display. He had little patience with men who boasted of their wealth. Yet he questioned his own motives, for when she moved into his lodge, he had not only endured the teasing of his friends, he had enjoyed it.

Kills-close-to-the-lake sat with her head down, a woolen shawl covering her face. There were many troubles in her heart, but overriding all of them was a feeling of resignation. It had been present when she left her father's lodge in the camp of the Never Laughs. And it had been present when she moved into the lodge of Rides-at-the-door. She had endured his other wives' commands and scoldings with the same lack of emotion, for she was sure that she would never be happy again. Even when Fools Crow lived in the lodge, even when she fantasized a life with him, she knew that it could never be and so she held her feelings for him in check. There were only moments when he looked at her and she didn't avert her eyes that she felt something like hope come flooding into her heart. Only then would she allow herself to dream of a happy life with a man she could give herself to. And when he married Red Paint, she felt a pure and true emptiness and in a strange way welcomed it as though it completed her destiny.

But now a wave of despair came over her as she thought of Running Fisher, of his thin laughter and mocking eyes, and the way he entered her so roughly and spent himself so quickly. The thought of the way she clung to him even when he wished to be rid of her made her cheeks red with shame.

She heard the flap being pulled open and she felt the rush of cold air but she didn't look up. This night her shame would be known and she would be dealt with harshly, but she welcomed even that, even mutilation or death.

Rides-at-the-door motioned his son to sit. Then he opened his tobacco pouch and filled his short-pipe. He didn't know how to begin, and so he began in the middle of it.

"You have brought dishonor into my lodge," he said. He seemed to be addressing both of them but he looked only at Running Fisher. "My wife Striped Face tells me that you are copulating with each other. How she knows this I do not ask. For now I will take her at her word. I have never known her to lie about an important thing, and I do not think she is lying now."

A dog began to bark somewhere close; then another one, farther away, joined in.

"What do you say, Running Fisher?"

Rides-at-the-door listened to the dogs and watched his son's face. He wanted his son to deny this charge, to be indignant, outraged that his father could even think such a thing. He wanted his son to stand and fill the lodge with shouted invectives against him and Striped Face, the bringer of such vile lies. But as he watched his son's eyes focus themselves on the lodge wall behind him, he knew that the charges were true. He looked away when he heard his son's voice.

"It is as my near-mother says. Kills-close-to-the-lake has visited me in my lodge."

There were several dogs barking now. Their sounds were crisp, each voice distinct in the clear night air. On any other night Rides-at-the-door would have been interested in the cause of their commotion, but not this night. He felt the weight of his bones, his flesh, and he could not have moved them. Even the act of lighting his pipe required too much effort. Inside himself he felt the burdens of his people—the encroachment of the Napikwans, the demands of the seizers, the appearance once again of the white-scabs among the Pikunis. All seemed very black to him.

"My heart falls down to hear of your guilt, my son. If you had said otherwise, I would have gladly sacrificed my body to the

Medicine Pole, old as I am. I would have given away my belongings to hear you say otherwise. Already I share our people's sorrows—now I must suffer this affront too." The dogs had quit barking, and Rides-at-the-door's voice filled the lodge. "Perhaps this is my punishment for being greedy, for taking on a young wife when I knew in my heart that it was wrong. Your mother and your near-mother were not happy with me, but at the time I said I was doing it for my old friend, Mad Wolf." He turned to Kills-close-to-the-lake. Her face remained hidden in the shawl. "I have wronged you, my young wife, and I ask you to forgive me. I brought you into my lodge and then neglected you. I allowed my other wives to treat you badly. And now I caused you to commit this bad thing with my young son. I ask you to forgive me—but I do not forgive you. You bring dishonor into my lodge, and for that I cannot forgive you. But I can give you something. Look at me, wife!"

Kills-close-to-the-lake, startled by the sudden sharpness of his voice, jerked her head in his direction and the shawl fell around her shoulders. Her black hair glistened in the firelight.

"You have seen the cut-nose women of the other bands. There are three of them in the Hard Topknots alone. You have seen Throws-her-horse-away. She comes to visit her relatives here. She was once a beautiful young woman, like yourself. Now even her relatives do not like to look at her too closely. But these cut-noses are lucky in that they still cling to life. Many who betrayed their husbands are wandering in the Shadowland, killed by their husbands' warrior societies or relatives. To dishonor her husband this way is the worst thing a wife can do. Ten, fifteen winters ago, I would be tempted to have you mutilated, even killed. But I am older, older even than my years, and I see that I have wronged you. Just as badly, my son has wronged you. There is not much honor in him, I fear, and for that I also take the blame.

"I give you your freedom, young woman. You are no longer my wife. You will quit this camp in the morning before Sun Chief begins his journey. You may take your riding horse and three others from my herd. Tell your father they are a gift from his friend Rides-at-the-door. But he must never know the real reason for your return. You must vow to the Above Ones that you will tell no one of this."

Kills-close-to-the-lake had listened to these words—they had entered her ears but somehow had lost their way to her heart. She found herself sitting with the two men she had lived with, but they seemed like strangers to her. The very purpose of this confrontation seemed less important to her than the punishment she had expected, even desired. Her hands were folded in her lap and she looked at the stub of the little finger on her left hand, the finger she had sacrificed at the Sun Dance last summer. How far away that was! Although she only vaguely understood the reason for the sacrifice, she had felt good about it—she had felt virtuous. She had put Fools Crow away from her heart. She made a fist of the hand and the stub disappeared and she knew that she had not put him away. She would have gladly committed this offense with him and accepted the punishment. Now the thought of punishment faded from her mind and she felt only emptiness and she accepted that as her future.

Rides-at-the-door watched her slip out the entrance. Then he spoke to Running Fisher, his stare still focused on the skin flap.

"Your mother has relatives among the far north people, the Siksikas—you know them. Perhaps they will take you in. You must tell them that it had nothing to do with Double Strike Woman or Striped Face. Tell them you are pitiful and would live with them until the moon of the many drums. There is a Medicine Pipe man among them. You may tell him everything and beg him to remember you when he rolls out his bundle at the first thunder. Give him three horses if he consents to do this. You must walk among the Siksikas with your head down, for they are a proud people and will look upon you with kindness only if you humble yourself. It will be hard on you, my son, for you are young and prideful, but it must be done."

For the first time since entering the lodge, Running Fisher looked at his father. His eyes were clear and unwavering. "I have offended you," he said. "For this I deserve whatever punishment you wish. You are a man of great reputation and I am a nothing-one. It is true—I have been prideful, I have boasted to others of my accomplishments, but what are they? Twice I have taken scrawny horses from the Entrails People. I even captured a ball-and-powder gun, an old and poor weapon, hardly worth keeping. Many said then that I would become something, that I would capture the eyes of the Above Ones. I painted myself with designs I saw in a dream, and when I walked around camp I felt the eyes of the others on me. When I danced, I danced in my own way. I painted my arrows with a pigment I alone possessed. But through it all, I knew I was a nothing-one."

Running Fisher looked into his father's face and his eyes became dark and burning.

"I longed to be a man before I was one. I wished to sit in on the councils, to join an older society, to become a Crazy Dog or a Raven Carrier. I wanted my own lodge, my own band of horses. I wanted people to point at me and say, 'There goes Running Fisher, he is a wealthy man and a great warrior. His medicine is the most powerful of the Pikunis.' But two things occurred. I saw what happened to Fast Horse and I saw myself in him. As a child I watched him strut around the camp and I wanted to be just like him." Running Fisher tried to smile. "And now I am. I have dishonored those who trusted me and I am to be banished for it. It is right.

"But something else happened, something that causes me even greater shame. It happened the day Sun hid his face, when we were on the war trail to the Crow country to revenge—" Running Fisher stopped in mid-sentence, and the flame went out of his eyes. He slumped back, and his voice was low and discouraged. "I—I lost my courage that day. I trembled like the quaking-leaf tree. I prayed to Sun Chief to give me back my courage, to make me fierce against the Crows, to make my people proud of me. It didn't happen. When we charged down on the Crow village, I shot my gun in the air, I shouted threats and I rode hard. But I didn't enter the village. I was afraid, and so I stayed on the outside and shot into lodges. Then I retreated with the first wave of Pikunis. Even then I was afraid that a Crow would ride me down and kill me. I covered myself with shame that day, and now I must live with a coward's heart."

Both men shared the weight of those words in the quiet night. The fire flickered silently on the walls and all the camp dogs were silent. But Running Fisher was not finished.

"I see my brother, Fools Crow, acquire wealth and respect. He learns the ways of the many-faces. He sits at the council fire with the men. And he has a woman who gladly lies with him and carries his child. It is only with great effort that I can keep from hating my own brother. Before, I told myself, these things will come to me too, but I was not patient. I tried to act like a man, but I am worse than a child—I am nothing. The Above Ones do not even see Running Fisher. He is an insect, and now he commits a great offense against his father. And he dishonors Kills-close-to-the-lake." He looked down at his hands, which had been twisted into interlocking fists, the knuckles white and large. "For this I gladly accept your punishment."

Rides-at-the-door, for the first time that night, felt something other than sadness. His eyes were wet and bright in the firelight. He felt regret that he hadn't seen earlier what was happening to Running Fisher, that he hadn't been able to help him through this period. Then this bad thing would not have happened. But somewhere further inside, he felt a quickening of his spirit that his son should accept and understand the shame of his actions—and the consequences. Rides-at-the-door earlier had thought simply to banish his son, to cast him out into the cold, to allow him to attempt to survive the elements and the censure of his people. That would have been the proper thing. But he knew too many young men who had ended up full of bitterness and hatred and they never recovered—like Fast Horse. Rides-at-the-door wanted his son to have a chance to cleanse himself, to regain his dignity: possibly to return to the Lone Eaters, possibly to begin a new life elsewhere. He was young enough.

"If you are successful in your stay with the Siksikas, if you learn from them and purify yourself with their Medicine Pipe keeper, perhaps sometime you would return to the Lone Eaters. It is getting time for you to dance before the Medicine Pole. Perhaps I would assist you."

Running Fisher looked up at his father; he looked at him for a long time. His eyes, too, were shiny.

"I will do as you say, my father. I will leave tonight and I will pray to Cold Maker to allow me safe journey. I ask that you too pray for this nothing-one. If I return I will have the strength to ask your forgiveness in the proper way." He turned his head so that his father would not see the wetness on his cheeks. "If I do not return, I ask that you and my mother think of me as I once was, a loving and obedient son."

Double Strike Woman lay facing away from the fire. Only her loose hair was visible above the sleeping robes. Rides-at-the-door felt great pity for her. Her younger son was gone, banished by her husband. Her older son had been gone for six sleeps and she was sure he would not return, that he had been swallowed up by Cold Maker and would never be found. Her two sons were gone and neither would have a proper burial. They would not even be able to go to the Sand Hills to join their dear relatives. She had wept and wailed all night, and only by much talking and soothing could Rides-at-the-door convince her that it was not time to mourn, that both were still alive and both would return to her. At last she had looked into his eyes and seen the truth of it, or at least an earnestness that she could understand. Then she began to dig around among her belongings until she came up with her best elkskin robe and her small-bone breastplate. He had gone with her into the night, hurrying through the snow, until they came before two large spear-leaf trees. She placed the robe in one and the breastplate in the other. Together, they prayed to Sun Chief to accept their offerings and to look after their sons, to bring them safely home when the time came. Rides-at-the-door remembered looking up then and seeing the Star-that-stands-still and feeling that their prayer would be answered. The light from the star came straight down and the snow shone like the silver of the Many Bracelets People. They walked back to camp without speaking. He walked with his arm around her shoulders, but she felt small to him and far away in her thoughts.

Rides-at-the-door pushed a stick farther into the fire, and the lodge brightened. He looked over at the robes of Striped Face. She lay with one naked arm flung across her forehead. He could barely make out the hump of her belly beneath the shaggy robe. She was with child and would deliver within two moons. Rides-at-the-door marveled at how Mother Earth always took care of her children. Some die but there are others to take their place. Even as his sons were far from him, and in perilous circumstances, there was a new life in the lodge waiting to be born, to grow up and be strong. We will go on, he thought; as long as Mother Earth smiles on her children, we will continue to be a people. We will live and die and live on. It is the Pikuni way.

He lit his pipe and watched the belly of his second wife move up and down with her breathing. Although he had been angry with her earlier in the day, she had been right to tell him. If the two lovers had been allowed to continue, the whole camp, eventually all the Pikunis, would have known about it—if they don't already, he thought. He would have to tell his wives not to see White Grass Woman for a while. It would be difficult to keep the fat cow from learning about his disgrace and telling the whole camp, but they had to try, for honor's sake. Then he thought that his pitiful honor was as a hopping-biter on the blackhorn that was dying of the watery eye. The Pikunis were dying, and all he could think about was himself and his honor. Oh, hateful one! Your heart tonight is as small and hard as the seed of the stinking-weed. He buried his face in his hands and sat motionless, listening to the dry crackle of the fire. It seemed that every day brought news to cause him to feel more tired than the last. He wished he could have made himself feel better about Fools Crow's return, but he didn't even know where his son had gone. Red Paint would only say that he had had a dream and left the next morning.

He almost smiled as he thought of the talk in camp that day. Many people were now anxious to cross the Medicine Line to escape the white-scabs and the seizers. Even Sits-in-the-middle, so vocal in his opposition, now talked as though it had been his idea in the first place. Three Bears would go, to lead his people from danger, but he would rather die in his own country. He too had been looking old and tired these days. Rides-at-the-door was certain that to go north would be the best course, at least for the winter. And he knew that he could swing the decision. If he talked to Three Bears this night, they would pack up in the morning.

Double Strike Woman rolled onto her back and heaved a shuddering sigh. Several strands of hair were stuck to her cheek. As he looked at his sits-beside-him wife, he thought of the suffering she had endured just that evening. No, he could not move his family while Fools Crow was gone. They would wait until the time for the sore-eyes moon and beyond. They would keep vigil with Red Paint and the infant growing inside her. They would take their chances with the white-scabs disease and with the seizers. When the snow melted and when they could move about freely, perhaps it would be like it always had been.

Rides-at-the-door lit his pipe. In the back of his mind he heard a voice, and it told him he was a foolish man. He rolled his shoulders beneath the blackhorn robe and didn't listen to that voice. Instead, he thought that he would sweat with Mik-api in the morning. He would purify himself with his son's friend. Perhaps Mik-api would know something.

33

"Who do you mourn?" he said.

They were sitting across the cold fire pit from each other. She had spent the day painting a design on the yellow skin. Fools Crow had watched her mix her paints and he had watched her dab the paint on the skin, but when he looked at the skin he could not see her design. The paints vanished and yet she painted on, as though she could see some image emerging. After a time, Fools Crow had given up and gone for a walk. Then he returned to the lodge and smoked and thought about the woman's strange mourning in the clearing, but he could make no sense of it. Afterward she had walked down to the river and stripped off her dress and moccasins and bathed. He had watched her as she submerged herself, then came up, sputtering, tossing her short hair, wiping her face with her hands. She splashed water on her breasts and arms. She looked at him and smiled, and he realized that she was the first woman, other than Red Paint, that he had seen naked since becoming a man. And he felt no shame.

Now, as he looked into the pale blue eyes, he noticed that something about her had changed. Her eyes had changed. He saw age in them, the watery flat eyes of an old one. He thought again of her splashing water on her breasts and how he had marveled at their firmness, and the flatness of her belly.

"It is finished," she said. She rolled up the yellow skin and laid it aside. She wiped her fingers with a strip of skin, then looked across at Fools Crow. "I am So-at-sa-ki."

At first Fools Crow didn't make the connection. He had become used to the waiting, and the way she said the name seemed as timeless as everything else in her world. Then he felt the small prickles of sweat sting his forehead, and when he opened his mouth the words came out harshly: "Feather Woman!"

She smiled faintly.

"But you died—you died in mourning!"

"It is true that I mourned the loss of my husband, and it is true that I died. There was much sorrow in me and I did not care to live. And so I left your world, a pitiful creature whom no one missed or mourned. But I did not go to the Sand Hills to join my beloved relatives. I came here—Sun brought me here—to live in mourning. Now he sends my husband and son here each dawn to remind me of my transgression."

"Morning Star and Star Boy," murmured Fools Crow.

"Yes, they come every morning, and every morning I beg them to take me back, but they do not listen to an old woman." Feather Woman's voice had lost the vigor that Fools Crow had come to enjoy. She spoke in a grave, flat rhythm. "You saw me in the clearing. You saw the yellow feather and the juniper bough with the spider's web. These things were given to me that long-ago night Morning Star took me to live with him in Sun's house. The web is the ladder I climbed. Spider Man built the ladder to the sky, and I entered my husband's dwelling place and was embraced by his father and mother, Sun Chief and Night Red Light. We were very happy, all of us, and even happier when I gave birth to Star Boy, the one your people now call Poia. Sun and Moon beamed with pleasure each time they looked upon their grandson. Morning Star walked with great pride, and I—I was the happiest of all, for I was indeed blessed in that sacred lodge."

Feather Woman closed her eyes and smiled, as though she were reliving those happy times when she had lived with the Above Ones. Fools Crow sat in silence, for he was still stunned by her revelation. And he was suddenly frightened to be in the presence of one who had been sacred to his people and who had fallen so low that no one mourned her when she died. Yet when he looked into her eyes he saw only kindness and warmth.

"One morning I went out to dig turnips. I had been warned

by my mother-in-law not to dig the large turnip in the middle of the field, for it was a sacred turnip. I thanked her and told her I had no intention of doing so. All morning I dug, all the time coming nearer to the sacred turnip. The closer I came the more fascinated I became. I seemed to be drawn to it and then I was upon it. It was large and it frightened me and I ran away. I dug more turnips and soon I was near it again. Oh, I was frightened, but I had no control over myself. I dropped to my knees and started to dig. I dug deeper and deeper but to no avail. Finally, with all my strength I thrust my stick deep into the earth. I thought I would push back on the stick and pop the turnip out, but neither stick nor turnip would move. I had wedged the stick too tightly. Oh, I pushed and pulled, and then I became frantic because I was afraid Moon would find me doing what she had warned me against. I worked with all my strength to free my stick, but soon I became exhausted and lay down to rest and weep. Then I spotted two cranes flying overhead. I called out to them to help me, and after several circles they landed. They began to sing sacred songs, one to each of the four directions, and after the fourth song Crane Chief took the stick in his bill and started to move it. Before long, the turnip popped out and left a hole in the sky. I thanked the cranes and they flew on. It was then that I looked down into the hole and saw my people. I saw my mother and father, my sister, our lodge. I saw my village, and the people were busy and happy. Women were working on hides, children were playing in the river, men were making arrows and racing their horses. It was so lovely and peaceful that I became homesick. I wanted to be with them. I wanted to tease my sister, to hug my mother and to braid my father's hair. But I was so far away I could never be with them again. I cried and cried and soon Star Boy, who was an infant on my back, began to cry. After a while I overcame my sorrow and gathered up my sack of turnips and digging stick and returned to Sun's lodge. Morning Star, my dear husband, looked into my eyes and knew what I had done. Moon exclaimed, 'You foolish girl, you have done the one thing you were not to do.' Soon Sun arrived home and Moon told him of my sin. He became very angry and told me I must leave his house, for I would never be happy there again. I would always miss my people. He gave me the sacred medicine bonnet and my digging stick. Then he wrapped Star Boy and me in an elkskin and sent us back to our people's world."

Fools Crow had been looking at Feather Woman's hands, the very hands that had dug the sacred turnip, but in the silence he stole a glance outside the entrance. Freckle-face sat alertly, looking in at the woman. He did not seem to be aware of Fools Crow's presence.

"Storytellers say that Spider Man let you down and you became a bright fire in the sky. The people thought it was a feeding star, and when they found the spot it landed, there were you and Star Boy. They say you were never happy again, that you rejected your people, that each dawn you would beg Morning Star to take you back."

"It is so even now. One dawn, in the long-ago, he spoke to me. He said, 'You have brought upon yourself your own misery—and misery to your people.' And it is true. Now you see sickness and hunger, Napikwans and war. It is no wonder the people didn't mourn me when I left their world." A small joyless smile crossed her lips.

Fools Crow looked out at Freckle-face. He remembered the wailing of a thousand geese in the bowl that morning. He saw the great water birds' flashing wings and he saw Feather Woman with her arms outstretched, beseeching Morning Star and her son to allow her to fly with them across the sky. He couldn't understand—all these winters, these summers, why did she continue? It was so hopeless. Then he heard her voice and he realized with shame that she had read his thoughts.

"One day I will rejoin my husband and son. I will return with them to their lodge and there we will be happy again—and your people will suffer no more." Now her eyes were bright again, the eyes of a young one.

The spell had been broken and Fools Crow was again aware of light and shadows, of warmth and the odor of dusty summer pines. Freckle-face had entered the lodge and now sat beside Feather Woman, a look of contentment and loyalty on his face.

He has been her only companion all these winters forever, thought Fools Crow, and he suddenly loved them both and was glad he had come to their world.

"You should be proud of giving birth to Poia," he said, "for he has given the Pikunis their sacred summer ceremony. Long ago he taught the Pikunis the ways of the Sun Dance, and they honor Sun Chief exactly as he instructed. In this way you make Sun Chief to smile on his children and to provide for them."

Fools Crow was puzzled by the look of alarm on Feather Woman's face. Had he not spoken truly? Had she misunderstood him? For a short time she seemed hesitant, even timid. She had not been this way before. Even her wailing and crying had been strong, her grief full of resolve.

She picked up the yellow skin and unrolled it. She laid it on the white bighead robe and smoothed it out with her long brown fingers. Then she stood and left the tipi. Freckle-face followed her. At the entrance she looked back briefly, then was gone.

Fools Crow sat for a moment and looked out at the blue river. Somehow he knew that the point of his journey had been finally reached. He was in no hurry as he crept around the fire pit and knelt and looked down at the yellow skin. It was a well-tanned skin, creaseless, without thin spots or cracks.

At first he didn't see the designs. He rubbed his eyes and blinked and leaned closer—and he saw the first one. The pigments were not strong and he had a hard time seeing it in its entirety. The yellow light within the tipi was strong and almost washed the colors away. Then he saw a circle and, within the circle, the familiar triangular shapes of painted lodges. There were many lodges. In the middle were the lodges of the bear, elk, beaver and otter. Outside the circle many horses, bridled and painted, stood in a white background. Fools Crow was confused by the proximity of the sacred lodges surrounded by whiteness. These lodges belonged to different bands and came together only during the Sun Dance ceremonies; yet, in the design, the white represented the snow of winter moons. As he looked at the representation he thought at first that it was only a poorly done winter count or war history. But then the horses began to move; almost imperceptibly, the horses came alive. One switched its tail, another took a step, another pawed at the snow. Then he noticed a wisp of smoke coming from one of the lodges, and he saw a dog sit up and scratch his ear with a hind leg.

Fools Crow shrank back from the skin with a small cry. He trembled and he wanted to run away, to leave that place and the strange woman, to return to Red Paint and his family. He was no longer eager to complete his journey, to learn the fate of his people. Nitsokan. Why had Nitsokan chosen him? Why did he have to see this thing? He tried to stand, to leave, but his legs wouldn't move. He was rooted to that spot and he couldn't stop looking into the yellow skin. He was powerless to keep from seeing, and so he saw inside the lodges and he saw the agony of the sick ones, the grief of the mothers and fathers, the children, the old ones. And he saw the bundled bodies of the dead, slung across the painted horses being led from camp. He saw inside the lodges of all the Pikunis and he saw suffering and crying and wailing. He saw mothers mutilate themselves, men rush from lodge to lodge, clutching their young ones, the elders sending up their futile prayers.

Through his tears, Fools Crow felt his eyes wander over the design. He recognized people from the Hard Topknots, the Never Laughs, the Grease Melters, the Many Chiefs, but it was only after he had searched all the lodges did he know what he was looking for—his own lodge and that of his mother and father. They were not in the village. Nor were the lodges of most of the Lone Eaters. He let out his breath in a sigh, but a lodge on the edge of the encampment caught his eye. It was the painted ermine lodge of Three Bears. Outside, Three Bears' sits-beside-him wife knelt in the snow with her head down. There were two other lodges from the Lone Eaters band.

The white-scabs disease has reached us, thought Fools Crow. We did not act quickly enough. We did not go north to the land of the Siksikas. It will be only a matter of time before all the Lone Eaters join this village of sickness.

Then the village was gone and Fools Crow saw only the yellow skin. He sighed deeply, and his heart was heavy in his chest. He closed his eyes, and in his weariness he could think of nothing, could feel nothing but a mild gratitude that Red Paint had not yet moved their lodge to that village of death.

Fools Crow had seen enough, but when he opened his eyes he saw a faint design, as indistinct as a shadow. He bent forward and the shadow became a red wash across the skin. Then the red wash became a column of horses. Stick figures rode the horses and their heads were colored yellow. Small black curly marks turned into buffalo coats and one of the yellow-heads moved, turned around and looked at the other yellow-heads. And then the red horses were moving through a snowy valley. Fools Crow heard the squeak of leather and the bark of a dog. He looked back to the sound of the bark and saw the seizers' fort on Pile-of-rocks River. A small knot of men and women were watching the seizers ride off.

It was bitter cold and the seizers rode with their collars up and wool scarves tied over their caps and ears. Their horses lifted their legs high and snorted white smoke in the cold air. As Fools Crow swept the column, from rear to front, the number of seizers grew until he could see hundreds of them, each with a long-gun in his scabbard. At the head rode a seizer chief that Fools Crow had never seen before. But beside him, his broad yellow face partially hidden in the collar of his buffalo coat, rode the scout, Joe Kipp.

When the seizers reached the edge of the valley they rode up a wide gully and up to the short-grass prairie. Fools Crow put his hand to his mouth to muffle the cry that had begun in his throat. He recognized that gully. It was the one he had just ridden down on his black buffalo-runner. The seizers were traveling north to the country of the Pikunis.

Then the design faded but its image lingered in Fools Crow's mind. He wanted to call it back, to learn of the hairy faces' destination. All of the bands were camped in that direction, along the Two Medicine and Bear rivers. The seizers' journey in such weather most certainly had an object, a mission. Were they after Mountain Chief? Who would they make cry?

Fools Crow looked at the skin again for a trace of the design. Instead, it had become all-over yellow with wandering dark lines and splotches of blackness like fresh blackhorn dung. Gradually he began to see the features of the design, and it was the Pikuni country with its creeks and rivers and small mountain ranges. He noticed the Two Medicine River, but the winter camp of the Lone Eaters was not there. He could see so far he thought he must be on a cloud high above. He recognized the Bear River, the Sweet Grass Hills, the Bear Paws and the Little Mountains. To the south he saw the Big River and, farther south, the Yellow Mountains. Off to the west, he saw the upsweep of the Backbone, its forested darkness giving way to gray spires that rent the yellow sky. His eyes were filled with wonder at the grand sweep of prairie, the ground-of-many-gifts that had favored his people. After the other designs, this one filled him with peace and humility and his spirits rose up. The moon of the yellow grass meant good hunting, abundance for all. Fools Crow began to look for those places which the blackhorn herds favored this time of the year. He searched around the Sweet Grass Hills, the Yellow River, the Shield-floated-away River, Snake Butte and Round Butte. But he did not find the blackhorns. He looked along the breaks north of the Big River, and he looked to the country of the Hard Gooseneck and the White Grass Butte, the Meat Strings. But there were no blackhorns. And there were no long-legs and no bighorns. There were no wags-his-tails or prairie-runners.

It was as if the earth had swallowed up the animals. Where once there were rivers of dark blackhorns, now there were none. To see such a vast, empty prairie made Fools Crow uneasy. Perhaps the magic of the yellow skin had chosen to hide the blackhorns from him. Perhaps they were there but he was not meant to see them. As he thought these things, his eyes were focusing on something that seemed not to fit in the landscape. He looked closer. It was a square dwelling place like the Four Horns agency on the Milk River. But this one was farther north, on Badger Creek, in the heart of the Pikuni country. Then he saw the lodges pitched around the square compound and there was snow on the ground. He saw people standing around the tipis and the buildings. They were huddled in worn blankets. Some had scarves tied around their heads. Many had scraps of cloth tied around their feet. They were a pitiful people, and Fools Crow did not recognize them.

Near the entrance to the compound he saw a large-wheeled wagon and a team of large gray horses. There were three long boxes in the back. The horses started and they pulled the wagon across the flat and up the incline to the south. At the top of the ridge the wagon stopped and the four men who had been riding in back unloaded the boxes near a pile of other long boxes. As Fools Crow watched the wagon return to the compound, he felt something dark pass through his heart and he knew that the boxes contained dead ones. But what did they die of? There were more boxes on the ridge than he could count. Was it the white-scabs? And why didn't the people bury their dead in the proper way?

Once again he searched the yellow skin for an answer. But the yellow land told him nothing. Then he saw a woman carrying something from the compound. It was a metal bucket and it was filled halfway with guts. As he watched her hurry along, he recognized something about her. The gaunt hollow-cheeked face, the eyes that stared at nothing as she walked—they hid somebody that Fools Crow had known.

Three women who had been sitting beside their lodges got to their feet and began to approach the woman. They had their hands out and their voices were weak and piteous. The woman tried to walk by them but they blocked her path. As two of the women distracted her with their weak pawing, the third reached into the bucket and came up with a handful of intestines. She began to run away, followed by the other two. Fools Crow looked again into the familiar woman's face; in its gaunt hardness, he saw the girl his mother had wanted him to marry in happier days. Little Bird Woman, daughter of Crow Foot, hugged the bucket to her breast and hurried on.

Fools Crow began to frantically search the drab village. He saw many other familiar faces, but he did not take the time to identify them. Many were marked by the pocks of the white-scabs; many were too hollow to be recognizable. He saw four men carrying a burden in a blanket. As it passed beneath his eyes he saw it was the body of a boy, not much older than ten or twelve winters. One of the men holding a corner of the blanket looked up and Fools Crow looked into the face of Eagle Ribs, the horse-taker, the brave who had scouted on Fools Crow's first raid against the Crows. He shouted to Eagle Ribs but the man did not look up again. It was all he could do to carry his share of the burden.

The scene began to fade into the design, and that too faded, until there was nothing but the yellow skin. This time Fools Crow did not attempt to call it back. He had seen the end of the blackhorns and the starvation of the Pikunis. He had been brought here, to the strange woman's lodge in this strange world, to see the fate of his people. And he was powerless to change it, for he knew the yellow skin spoke a truth far greater than his meager powers, than the power of all his people.

As he sat in his hopeless resignation, he heard the sound of children laughing and he recognized it as the sound he had heard since entering this world. The laughter and chatter mocked him, but he was weary deep in his bones and he had no spirit to despise it. It took him a long time to realize that he was looking at another design on the skin. In the middle of the design was a long white building with four of the Napikwan square ice-shields on each of the long sides. The building was not far from a grove of big-leaf trees that marked the course of the Milk River as it spilled out from the Backbone. Fools Crow could see Ear Mountain and Danger Butte with its war lodge. The lodge was caved in, its poles and logs scattered in the long grass. He looked back to the white building and saw faces through the ice-shields, and they were young and open with laughter. Outside, there were other children, running and playing, laughing. The girls wore long dresses and high-topped shoes. They held hands and danced around and around in a circle. The boys, in white shirts and short pants, chased each other. But a small group of children stood on the edge, near the white building. They were dark-skinned, and they watched the other children. The two dark boys wore clothing like the other boys and their hair was cut short. The three girls wore cloth dresses and they stood timidly a short distance from a large white woman who held a brass bell. Around the building and the ground the children played on stood a fence made of twisted wire and pointed barbs. Beyond the fence there was nothing but the rolling prairie.

"You have seen something," said Feather Woman.

They walked together down toward the river. Sun was still high above them. Morning Star and Star Boy were up there too but hidden by Sun's brilliance. It is difficult for her to know that they are up there—far away, but there where they can look down upon her any time they wish, he thought. And for the first time, he came to think of them, the Above Ones, as cruel spirits to allow Feather Woman to suffer so. And to allow what he had seen.

"Yes," he said. His voice was flat but edged.

"It makes you angry?"

Fools Crow stopped and looked at her. "No," he said. "I am not angry. Anger can sometimes do a man good, but now it is futile. I am not angry now, and I will not be angry then, when it all happens as I saw it on the yellow skin."

"There is much good you can do for your people," said Feather Woman.

Fools Crow looked toward the river. His black buffalo-runner stood patiently, saddled and bridled, his eyes studying something far downstream.

"You can prepare them for the times to come. If they make peace within themselves, they will live a good life in the Sand Hills. There they will go on to live as they always have. Things will not change."

"I do not fear for my people now. As you say, we will go to a happier place, far from these Napikwans, this disease and starvation. But I grieve for our children and their children, who will not know the life their people once lived. I see them on the yellow skin and they are dressed like the Napikwans, they watch the Napikwans and learn much from them, but they are not happy. They lose their own way."

"Much will be lost to them," said Feather Woman. "But they will know the way it was. The stories will be handed down, and they will see that their people were proud and lived in accordance with the Below Ones, the Underwater People—and the Above Ones."

Fools Crow stood for a moment, considering Feather Woman. He thought of her transgression in digging the sacred turnip. Morning Star had said she would bring misery not only on herself but on her people by that act. And the misery was only beginning. But she was a good woman; her only sin was one of loneliness, then and now and forever. She had been punished and the people were being punished for a reason that Fools Crow could not understand. The people had always lived in harmony with their sacred beings. Always they had performed the ceremonies to the best of their ability. They sacrificed often and without stinginess. And yet they were being punished.

He stepped forward and hugged the woman with the cut-off hair and blue eyes. Her elkskin dress was warm beneath his hands. Then he walked quickly to the black horse and swung up on his back. He glanced at her and she was smiling and her eyes were bright. He dug his heels into the horse's sides and the horse began that fast easy trot. He was glad to be returning to his people, but he could not help feeling that someday he would like to come back to Feather Woman and this green sanctuary between earth and sky.

PART
FIVE

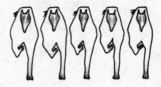

34

The infant had died during the early night, but still, in the gray light of dawn, the young woman hugged the body to her. Earlier she had bared a breast and put the small mouth to it, as though life would begin again with the simple act of suckling. But the mouth did not move and the body did not move, so the woman put away her breast and rocked back and forth, whispering soothing words into the tiny ear.

Her husband and his two other wives had tried to take the infant from her, but now they sat and watched and listened to the gentle murmur of the mother. They knew it would be for the best to get the infant away from camp, to bury it someplace far away. One of the other wives had prepared a winding cloth, a small dress and moccasins and some food to accompany the infant on the journey to the Sand Hills.

There was an air in the lodge of both expectation and resignation. This was the first death caused by the white-scabs in the winter camp of the Lone Eaters. It had not been a drawn-out death, full of agony and grief. Less than two sleeps ago, the mother had first noticed the red sores on the infant's scalp and chest. They were small and the women thought they were a rash, and like a rash they began to spread, first to the upper arms and then down to the belly. The women put a salve on the red areas that they had obtained from Mik-api. If they had been more observant, they would have noticed his silence as he made the paste. But these wives were young, the oldest not yet twenty winters, and so they chattered among themselves and did not remark on the old man's faraway face.

The end was very quick. No sooner had the women applied the salve than the infant, whose name was Long Tail because it had cried like a long-tail when it appeared in the world, convulsed and passed into the Shadowland.

Now the mother hugged the small body to herself, then handed it gently to one of the other young women, who placed the infant on the winding sheet. She and the other wife then dressed the infant and rolled it and a small sack of pemmican in the sheet.

The husband, who had already saddled and bridled his horse, took the bundle and left the lodge. The women inside heard the squeak of leather as the man put his weight in the stirrup. Then the horse danced a bit before it took off at a fast trot. The women listened to the muffled hoofbeats on the frozen earth. The mother began to sing to herself, a sleeping song that her mother had sung to her. The other two looked at each other. In spite of their youth and inexperience, they knew, had known for some time, that the infant had died of the white-scabs. One stood, as though in that silent communication she had been chosen, and hurried out of the lodge.

The sickness spread rapidly. There was no longer any talk of moving the camp to the land of the Siksikas. Three families who appeared to be still healthy did leave the winter camp but they traveled in the direction of the Four Horns agency. Some who watched them leave felt both envy and betrayal. Most of the others were too busy caring for the ill ones to notice the three circles of bare earth on the edge of the camp.

During the first three or four days, Mik-api and Boss Ribs went from lodge to lodge, performing their curing ceremonies. Fools Crow, who had returned to camp the night the infant died, stayed busy too, conducting purifying sessions in the sweat lodge, taking whole families who had not yet been touched by the sickness into the small skin-draped lodge. In between sessions he mixed medicines and took them to the two many-faces men. He built up the fires, heated stones, sweated, prayed and even tried his own healing on two members of Sits-in-the-middle's family. Soon after the long ceremony the two were dead. It was then that Fools Crow knew the ceremonies were futile—the healing and purifying were as meaningless as a raindrop in a spring river. Even if the healing worked, by the time the ceremony was over, twenty others would come down with the sickness.

Boss Ribs seemed to share this feeling of hopelessness. On the fifth day Fools Crow went to his lodge to deliver some fresh-ground medicine. Upon entering, he noticed that the many-faces man sat alone, hunched over a small fire. Beside him, the Beaver Medicine bundle lay open, its many skins and paraphernalia strewn about. At first, Fools Crow thought that Boss Ribs had been conducting the beaver ceremony and he felt his heart quicken with faint hope, but when he looked into the deep, sad eyes, he knew that whatever magic the keeper of the bundle had been searching for was not there.

"Are we lost then?" said Fools Crow as he squatted before the heap of objects. He was tired and his own words did not alarm him. The dying had begun and would continue. He had seen it on the yellow skin.

"The Above Ones will stop the suffering when they see fit. Our medicines are as powerless as grass before Wind Maker." Boss Ribs indicated the contents of the bundle. "I have been through the bundle three times since daybreak, searching for a ceremony, a song that might have some effect. . . ."

Fools Crow looked at the packet of herbs in his hand. "This white-scabs—it takes the strong as well as the weak, the young, the healthy ones, just as easily as the old and the sick. Whole families have perished!"

"How is it with your family, Fools Crow?"

"Nothing in my father's lodge, or in Yellow Kidney's. And Red Paint, she is healthy too. I have asked her to stay in the lodge, to open up to no one, but I saw her this morning going into her mother's lodge. I'm afraid for our soon-to-be son."

"You should take her away. Leave this camp. Go into the Backbone until this is over. There is plenty of meat there and no sickness. Sun Chief will watch over you."

Fools Crow thought of Feather Woman in the green bowl of the Backbone of the World. In the small pause that filled the lodge, the two men could hear the wailing of women in the next tipi. It was difficult to tell how many there were or who they mourned. Wailing no longer carried the urgency of grief; instead, it seemed more a ritual to be enacted because the Pikunis had always mourned their dead. Even the young had become inured to the deaths that surrounded them. Fools Crow placed the packet of herbs before Boss Ribs, then stood.

"And what of your family?" he said.

"A daughter died during the night—Bird Rattler. She was six winters." Boss Ribs pointed with puckered lips.

Fools Crow saw the small winding sheet. He touched the many-faces man on the shoulder and left, his thoughts far away and centered on the woman who mourned each new dawn with the wailing of a thousand geese.

He saw it in her eyes even as he entered his lodge. It was a look he had seen much of recently.

"One Spot and Good Young Man have the sickness!" The words came out in a breathless rush, but it took a space of time for them to register.

"Where?" he said dully.

"In my mother's lodge. She won't let me in!" And now Red Paint began to weep. Her small shoulders shook beneath the blackhorn robe and her sobs drove the yellow dog slinking out the entrance. Fools Crow crossed to her, his mind alert, and held her to his chest.

"She won't let me in," wailed Red Paint. "She won't let me help, she says I am not needed—and yet my two brothers are sick and dying of the dreadful spirit. I pray and pray to the Above Ones, but it is not enough. They know Red Paint is not significant and they laugh at her puny voice. Oh, she is a nothing-one and her own mother doesn't want her around!" She put her face into the folds of Fools Crow's shirt, but the muffled sobbing only increased.

As he held her, he felt her round belly jump each time her breath caught and he imagined the life within and he wanted to take her away, to the Backbone, to the land of the Siksikas, anywhere. But it was too late now. She would never leave her family. He caught her hands in his and pressed them flat against his chest. Her fingers were cold.

"Your mother is right to send you away. You must protect our child. He must be born strong, full of life. I am afraid for the Pikunis now, but we must think of the moons and winters to come. Our son must survive."

Fools Crow was gone all that day and far into the night. Three times Red Paint left the lodge, each time intent on going to her mother's. The second and third times she walked across camp and stood outside the lodge where her brothers lay sick. She heard the drumming and Fools Crow's husky chant. When darkness fell, she looked up at the stars and saw the Seven Persons and the Dusty Trail and the Star-that-stands-still. They were far away and bright and she noticed that Moon was not among them. She has chosen to hide her face from our troubles, thought Red Paint. She had always thought of Night Red Light as a protector, one who watched over the people while Sun Chief slept in his lodge. She was strong and her light betrayed many an enemy that sought to steal Lone Eater horses to take revenge on the sleeping village. Once, as a girl, Red Paint had become lost with two companions and had wandered across the monotonous prairies until Moon rose and showed them the way home. Now, not even Moon would help her people against this powerful sickness.

Red Paint returned to her lodge and lay down in her sleeping robes. There was a dull ache in her stomach and she knew she should eat something; instead, she closed her eyes and saw her father and brothers in happier times. She saw herself as a girl in that lodge with all of life before her. She shuddered as she thought of the day the men brought Yellow Kidney's body in on the makeshift travois. She had thought she would have to be strong for her mother's sake, to help her through the mourning period. But her mother surprised her by displaying very little emotion. The next day they had taken the body up into a grove of quaking-leaf trees in the upper Two Medicine River. There, they built a platform of branches and hoisted her father's body in place. When they rode back to the village, Red Paint noticed the look of peace on her mother's face.

A wave of guilt passed through her body and her cheeks burned. The thought confused her but the feeling was real enough. She would have remained that girl forever—she would have forsaken her life with Fools Crow—if it would have brought her father back healthy from the Crow raid and restored her mother's spirit, and if it would make her brothers well and happy again. If it had not been for her exhaustion, if she had not slipped away into a deep sleep, she might have made a vow that would have taken away what little comfort and happiness she knew, a vow as irretrievable as the leaves which fell each autumn.

As it was, when Fools Crow returned and lay down beside her, his arm flung over her shoulder, she became aware, for the first time since their marriage, that he was a person apart from her. She smelled his odor and she felt the weight of the arm, and she tried to remember his face, his smile of reassurance, but she couldn't. She lay there and thought of her family and of the new life within her, and she trembled beneath the dead weight of his arm.

35

On the morning of the thirteenth sleep of sickness in the Lone Eater camp, Fools Crow and his father, Rides-at-the-door, walked through the village. They went from lodge to lodge and called to the people within. There were still many sick and dying, but the number of new victims had gone down. The rage of the white-scabs was subsiding. It seemed impossible that it would last such a short time and leave so many dead or scarred for life by the draining sores. Others were out walking listlessly in the warm sun or just sitting outside their lodges. There was none of the bustle that usually occurred on a morning of winter camp. The people did not greet each other. If they met on the path to the river, they would move off the path and circle warily until they were well beyond. If a child was caught playing with the children from a family hard hit by the bad spirit, he would be called inside and scolded. But it was one old woman, the only survivor of her lodge, who sat and wailed and dug at the frozen ground until her fingers were raw and bloody—it was this old woman who made the people realize the extent of their loss. Gradually they emerged from the deep void of sickness and death and saw that they had become a different people.

As Fools Crow and Rides-at-the-door continued their count, they passed the painted ermine lodge of Three Bears. Prairie Runner Woman knelt outside the entrance, her eyes closed, her face raised to the sun. Neither man spoke out in greeting, for she was still numb with the death of the old chief. Rides-at-the-door had been present when Three Bears died. During one of his last lucid moments, the old man had given Rides-at-the-door his red-stone pipe. In that way he chose the younger man as his successor. Young Bird Chief had died, so there would be no opposition.

"There are thirty-seven dead ones," said Fools Crow.

"There will be more." They were walking in the shadows of a grove of big-leaf trees. They stopped to watch a man leading two packhorses from camp. There were two robe-draped bundles across the horses' backs. Rides-at-the-door pulled his capote tight around his neck. "The time before, the disease hit three different times. Just when it would appear to be over, a new wave of sickness would visit the people. I pray to the Above Ones that such a thing not occur again, but we must not allow ourselves to think we are out of it."

"There are only five newly stricken."

Rides-at-the-door grunted. After a time he said, "We must organize a hunt while some are still healthy. I'm afraid Cold Maker will visit any day and then it will go hard on us."

"The blackhorns will be south of the Big River, maybe along the Yellow River, maybe farther south." Fools Crow, even as he spoke, remembered the vision on the yellow skin, the vast plains empty of blackhorns. He had told his father and Three Bears—just before the old man got sick—of this vision, and of the others as well. After much deliberation, the two men had decided that the people should be kept ignorant of these designs until they grew stronger and were capable of deciding what should be done. But a feeling had been growing inside Fools Crow that there would be little deciding, that any decisions would be puny in the face of such powerful designs. He did not mention this feeling to his father.

"Go see the camp crier," Rides-at-the-door was saying. "Tell him to announce a meeting of all the men's societies for tonight. Our hunting parties will have a long way to go, and the sooner they start the better."

As Fools Crow hurried off, he realized that he was passing the lodge of Heavy Shield Woman. The only sign of activity was two dogs playing tug-of-war with a strip of deerskin. They were flattened almost to the ground and their low growling made a buffalo-runner, tethered in front of the next lodge, dance warily, his ears forward and eyes trained on the dogs.

Good Young Man had died the day after Fools Crow had performed his healing ritual. The convulsions had lasted a long time, and both Fools Crow and Heavy Shield Woman had breathed exhausted sighs when the end finally came. Fools Crow got directions from his mother-in-law and took the young body out to the quaking-leaf grove where Yellow Kidney rested. Heavy Shield Woman stayed behind to care for One Spot. And the boy survived. He came up out of his delirium and asked for soup. Because of his youth, he recovered rapidly. For the second time in three moons, he pulled back from the shadow of the Sand Hills. But he was changed, like all the Lone Eaters.

For two days Wind Maker howled from the north and kept the hunters in camp. The snow drifted into Two Medicine valley, until in some places it was as high as a man's waist. It covered the debris of the camp and filled in the prints of man, dog and horse as soon as they were made. Soon, nothing moved and only the smoke from the tops of the lodges gave away the existence of life in the village.

Each day at midmorning Fools Crow made his round of the camp, taking count of the sickness. Two of the five newly afflicted had died, and there were three new cases, including one of Boss Ribs' wives. She had been very active during the height of the plague, going from lodge to lodge, bathing the sick ones, feeding the others, caring for the children. Now she lay in her own robes, the disease sucking the life from her breast in spite of Boss Ribs' desolate songs.

Fools Crow reported his findings to Rides-at-the-door, then returned to his lodge. He drank a cup of broth and watched Red Paint, who had been quiet for the last couple of sleeps. He thought it was because of the death of her brother, and he thought she would get over her sadness in time, maybe when the weather broke, when she could safely visit her mother's lodge. But something about her made him think of Feather Woman and the way she looked that morning in the clearing, shoulders slumped, chin on her breast, oblivious to everything but her failed plea to Morning Star. Fools Crow picked up his many-shots gun and ran a greasy rag over the action. He had not shot it in a long time.

The third day dawned clear and cold. The sun was pale and high and the air was gray. The snow had ended and the hunters stood ready at the edge of camp. There were to be three groups of seven each. One group would go south, another southeast, and the third, of which Fools Crow was a member, would go directly east, following the course of the Two Medicine and Bear rivers until they reached the country between the Sweet Grass Hills and the Bear Paws. Although there would be hunters from other camps, maybe even from the Entrails People and the Cutthroats, the herd that often wintered there was large. The thought of encountering an enemy was almost welcome to the hunters after the ordeal within their own camp. They were mostly young and restless and, in spite of the intense cold, ready to risk anything out on the ground-of-many-gifts.

Fools Crow and the others made good time down the valley of the Two Medicine River. They kept to the open ground where the wind had scoured the snow away, and the packhorses drove easily before them. Sits-in-the-middle, who had a reputation as a good meat provider, led the party, and the others had great faith in his power to lead them to the blackhorns. By the time Sun was behind them, they had reached the confluence of the Two Medicine and Bear. They saw a winter camp and recognized it as that of the Hard Topknots. They drove the horses around the southern edge of the camp and Sits-in-the-middle and Fools Crow galloped over to the lodge of Crow Foot. Fools Crow rode apprehensively, several paces behind Sits-in-the-middle, for he remembered the design on the yellow skin. Again, he saw Little Bird Woman, Crow Foot's daughter, lugging the bucket of guts from the agency compound. He shuddered as he thought that at one time she had been chosen to become his wife.

Crow Foot welcomed them but he did not offer them a smoke. Although he had not been affected by the white-scabs, the hunters were almost frightened to see how thin he had become. Then he began to talk of the empty lodges in his camp—over half of the Hard Topknots had been carried away. He spoke the names of the dead as though he had memorized them. He told of the suffering and the desertions and the falling apart of the band. He spoke rapidly and he signed as he talked, as he would to strangers. And then he stopped talking and stared out at the camp, as if in a trance. Fools Crow looked around and he didn't see any of the Hard Topknots. This was unusual, for visitors brought the curious from their lodges to look, to laugh and point, to come join in the conversation. Now there was none of that. Not even dogs. The two hunters wished Crow Foot well and promised him meat on their return, but he didn't seem to hear them. They left him there, still staring in disbelief at the quiet camp.

That night they made camp in a thicket of willows on the north side of the Bear River. They had seen no game all day and so they ate handfuls of pemmican before sleeping. Fools Crow awoke twice during the night to the howling of the little-wolves, and each time he felt the cold sense of dread that had accompanied him since the party left their camp. When he finally slept, he dreamed of enemies.

The hunting party was up and on the move long before daylight. If they pushed hard this day, they would be in the blackhorn country within two more sleeps. Fools Crow rode beside Sits-in-the-middle at the head of the small group. Behind them, the others drove the pack animals. After a long period of silence in which the only sound was the rubbing of cold leather and the steady clopping of the horses' hooves, Fools Crow told the hunt leader of his dream of enemies. He had not seen them clearly in his dream, and in the darkness before dawn, the vision seemed less significant.

But Sits-in-the-middle listened and then he said, "This dream of yours does not make me happy. I am responsible for these young men and I must return them to their families. But the Lone Eaters need meat, that is our first concern, and so we must chance an encounter with our enemies."

Fools Crow glanced at Sits-in-the-middle. The light had increased enough so that he could see the dark frown on the hunt leader's face. It was a round, almost puffy face. Many in the camp secretly ridiculed Sits-in-the-middle, for his mother was a Snake woman who had been captured by the Lone Eaters many winters ago. She had been a slave until the Pikuni Hears-in-the-wind took her as a wife. Sits-in-the-middle was her only offspring. Fools Crow felt pity for him, for he was barely listened to in councils and was deemed capable only of leading a small party of young hunters.

"Perhaps our enemies are also down with the white-scabs," said Fools Crow. "My dream was less than clear. I do not attach much importance to it."

By midmorning the sun was high to the southeast and the hunters stopped to stretch their bodies and to slap the circulation back into their calves and thighs and arms. Again they had seen no sign of game, but they hadn't expected to. Because of the winter camps in the valley, the animals were scarce and moved only at night. After eating a handful of pemmican, Fools Crow mounted his black buffalo-runner. He felt the animal's warmth beneath his thighs and was grateful for it. Although there was no wind, the air was as cold as it had been that winter. He pulled his robe up over his capote and sat, waiting for the others to finish their cold meal. He gazed absently down the valley.

At first he didn't believe what he was seeing. He jumped up and stood on his horse's back and he could see more clearly the patches of color beneath a cutbank far in the distance. It took a while to see their movement, but soon he saw that the patches were people, on foot, and they were coming toward the hunters.

"What is it you look at?" said Sits-in-the-middle. He began to hurry to a piece of higher ground. The others followed, suddenly alert and expectant.

"Human beings. On foot. They are coming our way." He jumped down to the ground. He could only think of enemies. Only horse stealers traveled on foot in the winter.

After a quick look, Sits-in-the-middle ran down the small rise. The others followed, breathing hard, their excitement causing the horses to move restlessly. One of the pack animals began to whinny until a hunter reached him and clamped his hand over the muzzle.

"We must be ready," said Sits-in-the-middle. "They are coming straight down the river beneath the cutbank." There was no cover near, but the swale they were in hid them from view. The hunt leader instructed one of the young men to drive the pack animals back upstream and into a gully that opened out onto the river bottom.

Then the hunters waited, Fools Crow and Sits-in-the-middle lying below the lip of the rise. Both had repeating rifles, but the others had only bows. None of them had encountered an enemy before. Fools Crow looked back at them and they looked like prairie birds, crouched together, facing up at him. They are too young, he thought. If the raiders are experienced warriors it will go hard on us. He almost expressed his fear to Sits-in-the-middle, but as he looked down the valley at the approaching party, he felt his apprehension leave him.

"There are children among them," he whispered. "Little ones. And some of them move slowly, like old people." He lifted himself from the ground and knelt. "They carry nothing with them—no weapons."

Soon the people were close enough for Fools Crow to count. There were three old people, two young women, a youth of twelve or thirteen winters and two children. One of the young women was limping badly. The other was helping her. They were Pikunis. Fools Crow recognized the wounded one—White Crane Woman, a member of Heavy Runner's band. He looked downstream, in the direction the group had come from, but there were no others.

"Something has happened, something bad!" Fools Crow ran down the rise and threw himself on his horse. The others still crouched motionless, their mouths open like birds.

As he galloped the black buffalo-runner down the valley, he knew this scene had something to do with the yellow skin and the designs. It was the same weather, the same kind of day that the seizers rode north. He felt the fear and guilt rise and spread throughout his limbs and he was almost too weak to stay up. He had seen the design. "Why didn't I warn them?" he cried. "Why didn't I tell them?" The wind was in his eyes and the hoofbeats filled his ears and he pushed the horse even faster.

As he reined in, the horse skidded almost to his rump, and the people began to scramble back against the cutbank. Only the children, a boy and a girl, stood and watched him.

"It is Fools Crow—of the Lone Eaters! I have come to help you!"

White Crane Woman had fallen when her companion deserted her, but now she stood, her eyes dark and hard.

"White Crane Woman! You know me. Our families visit during the Sun Dance encampment." Fools Crow slid from his horse and ran to her. He caught her just as her energy faded and gently lowered her to the frozen ground. The old ones and the other woman slowly approached. The youth still clung to the side of the cutbank.

"What has happened to you?"

No one spoke. They stood and Fools Crow saw the fear return to their eyes. Then he heard the harsh thumping of the horses as the other hunters rode up. "They are also Lone Eaters. They too come to help." Fools Crow knelt beside White Crane Woman. The hem of her dress was bloody. He raised it and saw the bullet wound through the fleshy part of her calf. The skin was red and shredded where it had exited. Fools Crow had no medicine but he did have a piece of soft-tanned skin in his war bag. As he wrapped the wound, one of the old ones, a woman, knelt beside him and spoke. "It was the seizers. They sneaked up on us while we were still asleep. There was only a little light, just enough to see by, and they shot us in our lodges. Pretty soon, our people were running in all directions and still they shot us. Many of us are killed. We managed to slip away, down to the river, and run away below the cutbank. But one of the greased shooters found this one's leg. We ran away and now you have found us."

"The others—are they all dead?"

"I do not know this. We had to run and keep on going. But the shooters were still buzzing until finally we were beyond hearing."

The young woman who had been helping White Crane Woman came forward and squatted beside the old woman. Her eyes were flat with shock.

"They killed Heavy Runner," she said. She pointed with her lips to the youth who was now leaning back against the cutbank. "That boy there saw him fall."

Fools Crow tied off the bandage, then looked up at the two women. He was surprised at the calmness with which they related their news. They could have been telling him about a relative's visit or a berrying party. But as he looked into their eyes, he saw that the immensity of what had happened had left them numb.

"Where is your camp?" he said.

"In the big bend below the Medicine Rock. It is not long by horseback."

Fools Crow stood and turned to Sits-in-the-middle. "I will go there and see for myself."

A look of hesitancy came into Sits-in-the-middle's eyes, as though he too might be expected to go to the massacred camp.

"These people can find shelter in Crow Foot's camp," said Fools Crow. "They will need you to lead them."

"Yes, that is true. We will take them on the packhorses and wait for you there."

First there was the smoke, only slightly darker than the gray air. It rose from behind a bluff where the river curved to the south. The sun was behind it, and it looked orange and sharp-edged.

Then the black horse smelled it and stiffened beneath his rider. It was a smell not of smoke but of burnt things, and the smell was heavy in the air. Even though the bluff stood between the horse and the smell, he stopped, his shoulders and forelegs trembling. Fools Crow kicked the horse in the ribs, but still he did not move.

"You know what we are about to see. You have known for a long time, Heavy-charging-in-the-brush." Fools Crow let the horse settle down. "We will see it now. We will take heart from Wolverine, who always faces into the wind."

The horse moved forward and soon they were around the bluff and they saw the remains of the camp. There were no fires visible but the smoke was darker and thicker. It rose from many places until it became a cloud above the south bank of the river. As they moved up to higher ground, Fools Crow began to pick out the blackened lumps that emitted the smoke. Between the lumps, the snow was still white. Then a small wind blew the smoke toward him and the snow became yellow and dirty and the smell hit his nostrils, the smell of burnt skin. Fools Crow could almost taste it, and it was smoky and pleasant in his mouth. He began to weep and still the horse moved forward.

Then they were at the edge of the camp and the black lumps were lodges that had been burned. A dog lay in the snow a few paces away. Most of his hair had been burned off and his tongue was black against the white teeth. Then Fools Crow saw something else lying in a patch of blackened, melted snow. He kicked the horse in the ribs and moved toward it. The sight made his stomach come up against his ribs. It was an infant and its head was black and hairless. Specks of black ash lay in its wide eyes. Fools Crow fell from his horse and vomited up the handful of pemmican he had eaten earlier that morning. He was on his hands and knees and the convulsions wracked his body until only a thin yellow strand of saliva hung from his lips. He stayed in that position and gulped hard until the wracking stopped. He wiped his mouth and eyes, then stood. And he began to pick out the other bodies. Most of them had been thrown onto the burning lodges but they were not all black like the infant. There were scraps of clothes that hadn't burned. There was skin and hair and eyes. There were teeth and bone and arms and legs. One old woman lay on top on one of the smoking lumps, only the underside of her skin dress burned. Her feet were bare. Fools Crow, through his tears, saw the purple welts on her legs where she had slashed herself a long time ago in mourning a lost one.

As he wandered from smoking ruin to ruin, he didn't really know that his eyes had quit seeing, that his nose no longer burned with the smell of death. He didn't even notice that his feet had gotten wet from walking through the trampled melted snow. On the far side of camp, he kept moving until he came to a downed big-leaf. He sat slowly, carefully down on the smooth trunk and buried his face in his hands. He rubbed his eyes and there were no more tears, not from the smoke, not from his heart. He sat for a long time, tired and numb, until his mind came back and he remembered where he was, what he had seen. Still he was in no hurry to open his eyes.

Then he felt something on his knee. He opened his eyes and saw a red puppy standing before him, one paw on his knee, the other swiping the air as though he wanted to play. He reached out and touched the head and ran his hand all the way down to the tail. The puppy yipped and bit the air. Fools Crow smiled and the puppy sat back and scratched himself behind the ear.

Through the smoke, on the other side of the camp, Fools Crow saw a figure standing motionless, looking at him. It was a man and Fools Crow's heart quickened. He had only his knife in his belt. But the man was dressed in the way of the Pikunis. The knees of his leggings were black. Fools Crow stood quickly and the puppy tumbled away, yipping in fear. Then another figure emerged from the brush behind the man. It was an old woman, bent with age. Two more figures came forward, and they too were old.

When he reached them, Fools Crow saw that the first man was hardly more than a youth. He was tall but his shoulders slumped. Fools Crow looked at the others and he recognized Black Prairie Runner, once a man who had led many war parties against the enemies. His eyes were cloudy now and his long fingers, clutching a blanket over his shoulders, were bent and stiff.

"They drove off our horses," he said. His words were mild and flimsy in the cold air.

"Are there others? Others who survived?"

"Our horses are all gone. You see"—he waved his free arm around them—"there are no horses."

Fools Crow looked questioningly at the others.

The young man stepped forward. "I am called Bear Head. My father was also called Bear Head, and he was killed by Owl Child some winters ago."

"Yes," said Fools Crow. "They argued over who had killed a Cutthroat in battle. It is said that Owl Child made a false claim."

"All there knew that the Cutthroat was my father's kill. But

Owl Child was crazy and he killed my father rather than admit his falsehood." Bear Head stood straighter. "I will have my revenge."

Fools Crow was moved by this small introduction, for he knew Bear Head would have no satisfactory revenge. Even revenge had been slaughtered.

"I met some of your band, escaping up the river. The other hunters I was with have taken them to Crow Foot's camp. They told of the seizers."

"It was the seizers. I left camp before first light to get my horses. I had planned to do some hunting this day and I needed pack animals. The herds were down near the foot of Three Persons. I picked out four animals and was leading them back when I saw some movement on that low ridge over there. It was still dark down here but there was a faint light in the sky behind the ridge. At first I thought it was a pack of little-wolves up there, thinking to look for scraps around the camp. But then one of the shapes stood and I knew it for a man. I became frightened and began to run toward camp, leaving my horses where they stood. But just before entering that stand of spear-leafs, I saw the dark shapes before me. There was a man behind each tree. Then all at once came the thunder and fire of the big guns. I froze against a tree. All I could do was listen and pray that the thunder would end, but it went on and on until it was light enough to see the cloud of blue smoke from the guns. It hung in the trees and drifted toward me. I could taste it in my mouth. When I looked up at the ridge I could see hundreds of fire flashes through the smoke. But I still could not see my village so I began to run around the seizers in the trees. They were so intent on their work that they did not look around. Finally I was on the lower side, near the river and I saw my people—" Bear Head stopped, and Fools Crow could see his eyes wander beyond him to the remains of the camp. He seemed to focus on one of the smoking lumps. Fools Crow turned and saw that it had burned nearly to the ground.

"Besides my mother, I had three near-mothers and four sisters and a brother. Now they are gone from me. I do not know where they have gone—they did not have time to prepare themselves."

As Fools Crow stared out at the smoking ruins, he began to notice what was missing. The mention of Bear Head's mothers and sisters made him realize that he had seen only the bodies of old men and young boys among the women.

"Where are the men?" he said. He turned back to Bear Head. "Where are the warriors?"

One of the old women lifted her head. She had been watching the red puppy, who had followed Fools Crow and now lay with his head between his paws.

"Off hunting," she said. "There was no meat in camp, and a Pikuni does not live without meat." She said this fiercely.

"Those who weren't dead or sick with the white-scabs," said Bear Head. He looked uncomfortable. "I myself was leaving for the hunt this morning."

"A Pikuni does not live without meat," muttered the old woman.

Bear Head looked down at her. "Curlew Woman's two sons were to go with me. Now they are burned up."

Fools Crow could envision the hunters' return. Whether laden with meat or empty-handed, they would see something they would mourn for the rest of their lives.

"Where are the seizers now?" Fools Crow's voice was sharp. Anger welled up within him, an anger that was directed at the futility of attempting to make the seizers pay. He had always thought that the Pikunis could fight these hairy-faces. He had prepared himself for this fight, he was ready to die a good death to defend this country. Now he knew that his father had been right all along—the Pikunis were no match for the seizers and their weapons. That the camps were laid low with the white-scabs disease did not even matter. The disease, this massacre—Sun Chief favored the Napikwans. The Pikunis would never possess the power to make them cry.

He listened to Bear Head's weary voice recount the details of the massacre. "Curlew Woman says Heavy Runner was among the first to fall. He had a piece of paper that was signed by a seizer chief. It said that he and his people were friends to the Napikwans. But they shot him many times. By the time I could see the camp, there were only a few running, trying to escape. They were all cut down by the greased shooters. There were several lodges already on fire. Some of the seizers were aiming at the lodge bindings. Many of the lodge covers fell into the fires within and started burning. Then there was no more movement and I heard a seizer chief shout and the shooting stopped. By that time there was too much smoke in the air, dark smoke from the burning lodges, blue smoke from the shooting. The seizers waited awhile, then they came down from the ridge and out of the trees. I felt naked and exposed beside the river, so I crawled into some brush here behind us. The seizers walked among the lodges, at first quietly; then they became bolder and began to talk and laugh. Whenever they saw a movement from under one of the lodge covers they shot at it until it moved no more. They rounded up the bodies and threw them onto the fires. Those lodges that stood untouched by fire were ragged with bullet holes. The seizers cut the bindings and set these lodges on fire. They took what they valued and threw all the rest onto the fires. They drove off all our horses."

"Did any others get away?"

"I saw three women and their children. The seizers did not shoot them even though they stood beside these trees and watched the burning. I searched for them after the seizers left but I did not find them. Perhaps they left for Mountain Chief's camp. The Many Chiefs are camped just downriver."

Fools Crow suddenly remembered the rumor he had heard in his own camp. Owl Child had supposedly returned to Mountain Chief's village and was down with the white-scabs. He wondered if Fast Horse was there too, if he was sick—or dead. He knew that the Many Chiefs would be gone as soon as they learned of this disaster.

"Which way did the seizers go?"

Curlew Woman looked up again. She pointed to the hills behind the ridge from which the seizers slaughtered the camp. "Up there. Black Prairie Runner and Good Kill here"—she indicated the other old woman—"we ran up a draw over there. The seizers rode right by us—they saw us but they didn't shoot. Oh, how I wish they had! I cursed them, I stole their honor, but they only laughed."

"They will probably make camp at Dry Fork. Perhaps we could recover the horses if the hunters return." Fools Crow felt his spirit rise slightly. He turned to Curlew Woman. "It is good that you are alive. You will have much to teach the young ones about the Napikwans. Many of them will come into this world and grow up thinking that the Napikwans are their friends because they will be given a blanket or a tin of the white man's water. But here, you see, this is the Napikwan's real gift."

Black Prairie Runner, as though he had just come out of a trance, started, then spoke. "What you say is true, young man. But these women and I are old. We have seen much, we have seen the winter counts add up—some years were good, some were bad, but each design on the skin was something we could understand. Now they are all bad and we do not understand why. This world has changed and we do not belong to it. We would be better off to join our before-people in the Sand Hills. It is as Curlew Woman says. We would rather be killed by the Napikwans than live in their world."

"I listen to you with a good heart and I hear the truth in your voice. Many of our people feel this way. As we stand here, I see this tragedy that Sun Chief permits. I am tempted to wish that all the Pikuni people could go to that other world where there are no Napikwans. There the hunting is good and the people live according to the old ways. But this is the land of the Pikunis. This is where the long-ago people were born and lived and died. They would be angry with us if we just gave it up. They would say the Pikunis had become puny, that we would not fight for this land that they left us."

"But how can we fight?" Bear Head's voice was tense, as though a fire had begun to burn within him. "You see what they do to us. There are too many of them and their weapons are more powerful than ours. More Pikunis died this one day than in all the days since I have been alive. They kill our women and children. They kill our old ones!" Then, just as suddenly as it began, the fire went out. "They kill my mother, my sisters, my near-mothers. They kill us all. I, who have no family left, welcome it."

"This is bad talk," said Fools Crow, but he felt young and powerless, as though he talked into a strong wind. Listening to Curlew Woman and Black Prairie Runner, and now Bear Head, he felt his small hope fading and he wished for the presence of his father. Rides-at-the-door would say some words that would make them all see a reason to go on. He could talk with the wind's strength. Even Black Prairie Runner and Curlew Woman, who had lived so long and now wished to die, would feel that strength and they would know it was important to think of the children.

Fools Crow thought of the final design on the yellow skin in Feather Woman's lodge. He saw the Napikwan children playing and laughing in a world that they possessed. And he saw the Pikuni children, quiet and huddled together, alone and foreign in their own country.

"We must think of our children," he said. He lowered his eyes to the red puppy and it was quiet all around. The few survivors stared at the red puppy, who had rolled onto his back, his front legs tucked against his chest. They had no children.

36

It was the moon of the first thunder and Mik-api sat in his lodge alone and prayed. He wore only a breechcloth and a pair of winter moccasins. He sat cross-legged, his back hunched and narrow. His hair was gathered in a lump just above his forehead. He prayed out loud, but his words were scarcely a whisper in the gray light of the lodge. As he prayed his mind wandered and he remembered the day he had acquired the Thunder Pipe bundle. Forty winters had passed since that day; yet Mik-api remembered it well, for it was the day before his Black Paint wife had died of the white-scabs. The man who transferred the bundle had taught Mik-api the many songs and prayers and dances that went with the bundle. After seven days of such ceremony, Mik-api, who had paid with all his possessions, was the owner of the sacred bundle. He had vowed to acquire it because his wife was sick and he had thought the power of the ceremony would restore her health. She died the next day, but Mik-api did not doubt the power of the bundle. He doubted only his own.

In the years since then, he had become a heavy-singer-for-the-sick and his medicine was strong enough to instill faith and respect and even awe in his people. Those times his medicine didn't work, the people said the bad spirits had already claimed the body of the sick one. When the medicine succeeded, they said Mik-api had the greatest power of all the many-faces. For many winters he did possess a great healing power. He could cure anything from a broken leg to a broken spirit. Rare was the affliction that Mik-api couldn't ease. But now he felt the weight of his years and knew that he would not see the snow of the next winter. His dreams brought him closer and closer to the Sand Hills. He had been ready for some time and he welcomed each dream, for it was his Black Paint wife who appeared most often and filled him with a shyness that he had not felt for some time. They had spent only two years as man and wife before she died. Although he had grown old and had experienced many things, he did not find a woman to take her place. And so he dreamed of this reunion, dreamed with the shy pleasure of a young man who had much to look forward to.

He felt it more than he heard it when it happened. His prayers and thoughts had taken him from his lodge, but now he felt the long slow rumble of the many drums enter his body and his heart beat faster. The camp crier stuck his head into the entrance and said, "It is time."

Mik-api murmured his assent and the camp crier left to get the others. Mik-api said a prayer of thanks to Thunder Chief for coming once more to the country of the Pikunis. Then he untied the bundle. It was wrapped in the skin of the real-bear and decorated with eagle feathers and ermine skins.

When his assistants were seated, Mik-api unwrapped the Thunder Pipe stem and held it aloft. He said the prayers to the Above Ones, the Below Ones, the Underwater People. Then he fitted the sandstone bowl to the stem and filled it with tobacco. He smoked to the four directions, then placed new tobacco in the bundle. Perhaps Fools Crow will smoke this tobacco next thunder moon, he thought. The drumming and singing began. Mik-api stood and acted out the part of Real-bear, growling, thrusting his head this way and that, sniffing, making clawing gestures in the air. The assistants sang horse songs, owl songs and blackhorn songs, each time acting out the gestures of the animals. When they were finished with the long ceremony, Mik-api lit the pipe and offered the smoke again to the sacred beings, as well as the four directions. After his offering to Thunder Chief, the people smoked and prayed for good health, abundance and the ability to fulfill vows. They prayed for long summer grass, bushes thick with berries, all the things that grow in the ground-of-many-gifts. They prayed that the blackhorns would be thick all around them and nourish them as they had nourished the before-people.

The procession began, Mik-api in the lead, holding up the Thunder Pipe for all to see. As they paraded through the camp, others joined them, singing and drumming. There were fewer of them than in previous years, but the drumming and singing seemed louder, as though they sought to make up in enthusiasm what they lacked in numbers.

Fools Crow and Red Paint stood outside their lodge, waiting. He had painted his face and he carried a feathered shield and a bow. His braids were wrapped with ermine skins and tied with red yarn. Red Paint wore a dress of elkskin trimmed with several rows of elk teeth. Her cheeks were rouged and she stood shyly. The cradleboard was on her back. Not too many winters ago it had held Red Paint, then Good Young Man and One Spot. The blue, white and red quillwork designs were slightly faded, but the skin was as soft as ever. Butterfly had been sleeping, but as the procession approached and the drumming and singing got louder, he opened his eyes and looked at the pegs holding the front of the lodge skins together. His eyes were large and dark as he watched the butterfly fan his wings on a peg. Fools Crow stepped back and made a face at him, and Butterfly looked back with calm curiosity.

Then the procession was passing the lodge and Mik-api gave them a quick look. In his glance, Fools Crow saw a glint of almost youthful energy, a bright flame of pride that made the younger man smile. Mik-api's assistants danced behind him, now reserved and tall, no longer the men and women who had acted the animal roles in the lodge. Next came the elders, Rides-at-the-door and Double Strike Woman among them. Several small children danced behind them, the quick steps of a scalp dance. One Spot, his face painted and an owl feather in his hair, danced with the fury of a strutting grouse. Fools Crow and Red Paint fell in with the younger people. A clown, dressed in the fur and headdress of a little-wolf, danced behind Red Paint, making faces and yipping at Butterfly.

The procession managed a grave dignity as it wound its way through the camp. Only the few old people whose frail bodies would not allow them to join watched without getting up. But they too sang, and they remembered many hopeful springs when they had danced through camp, and they prayed that, after the sad winter they had lived through, there would be hope and joy this spring.

Fools Crow listened to the faraway rumble of Thunder Chief and felt his step become lighter. He felt in his heart, in the rhythm of the drum, a peculiar kind of happiness—a happiness that sleeps with sadness. And the feeling made his head light and he was removed from the others, dancing alone, singing a song that had to do with his life in this world, and in that other world he had visited in his vision. And then he saw the white lodge and the pale blue light and the woman sitting across from him. He knew that she was here, someplace, watching him, watching the procession, and he saw her smile in the blue light and he smiled. For even though he was, like Feather Woman, burdened with the knowledge of his people, their lives and the lives of their children, he knew they would survive, for they were the chosen ones.

A drop of water stung his head and he saw the hard drops falling all around him. He heard the drops bounce off the taut skins of the lodges, and he saw the drops gathered on the bare earth that countless feet had trampled smooth over the winter. He felt Red Paint's hand slip into his and he raised his face.

That night there was much feasting in all the Pikuni camps. Winter was over and the men talked of hunting, of moving the camps out of the valleys, of moving on. The women prepared their meager feast and fed their men, their children, their relatives and friends. They knew that soon the meat pots would be full and the hides would be drying in the sun. Outside, the children played in the rain, chasing each other, slipping and skidding in the mud. They were Pikunis and they played hard.

Far from the fires of the camps, out on the rain-dark prairies, in the swales and washes, on the rolling hills, the rivers of great animals moved. Their backs were dark with rain and the rain gathered and trickled down their shaggy heads. Some grazed, some slept. Some had begun to molt. Their dark horns glistened in the rain as they stood guard over the sleeping calves. The blackhorns had returned and, all around, it was as it should be.

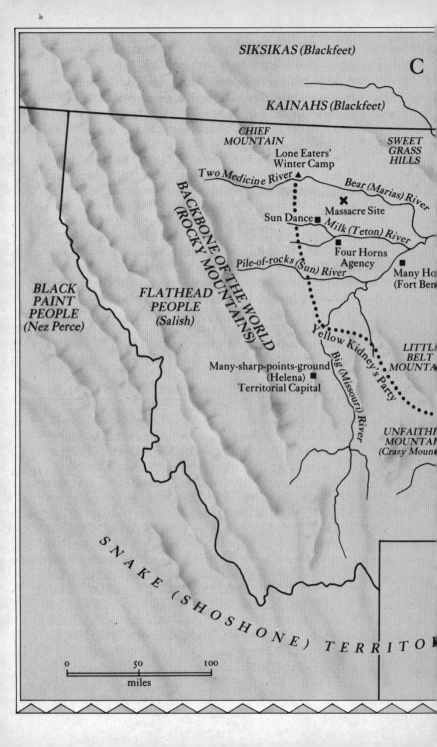